SEARING VEIL

A STORY BY

OLIVER LYNN HAYNES IV

The Searing Veil is a work of fiction. Names, characters, places, and incidents are either the product of the author's imagination, or are used fictitiously. Any resemblance to actual persons, living or dead, or actual events is purely coincidental.

Font is Garamond

Signature Edition

My Parents; Bonnie; The Lewis Family; Julie; Mr. Richburg; Dr. Stewart

Thank you

CONTENTS

Let us never lack
the perseverance to inspire

PROLOGUE

"People are a lot like plants, Roberto," my father said.

He stepped carefully around a large clump of stinging nettles.

"Come closer, I want you to see," he said, stooping over them. At his summons, my brother trudged into view, several freshly cut vines dragging along with his feet. I watched carefully from behind a tangled row of vines. He moved clumsily, like a puppy. My father stopped him short of the nettles. As often as my brother and I played in our father's vineyards, I had never noticed the burgundy-stemmed weed before.

"You see the little white hairs there on the stem?" my father asked. "Those are its defenses."

He brushed the back of his hand against the stem and winced, drawing air sharply through his teeth. It made me cringe. He held his hand out for my brother to see; I peaked my head further through the vines. I could narrowly make out the dollops of red rising against the farmer's hue of his rough skin. The inflammation spread wider and turned white. My father pressed it lightly with the tip of his finger.

"You see," he said, "defenses." He glanced up at me. I caught his glare and fell back through the vines, pulling a fistful of grapes with me. I felt myself drawing uncontrolled breaths, as I lay embarrassed amidst the scattered vintage. The blue-gray of his eyes was cruel. Always so cruel.

Slowly, I picked myself up from the ground, sliding beneath the overgrowth of vines. The little hand-scythe I clutched became slick with sweat from my palm. I pricked the ground with its point, trying to ward off my father's eyes. It had just been a glance, but the feeling lingered.

"People put up defenses too," he continued.

Some birds whistled and played behind me. I just wished I could fly away. The midmorning sun was lifting the moisture from the grass. I felt the earth warming beneath me; the dirt between my toes had lost its comforting coolness.

"You need to pay attention to peoples defenses, Roberto, it tells you a lot about them."

"Like what?" my brother's innocent chirp swept lightly over the vineyard.

"Like who you can trust. Consider the vines!" My father exclaimed.

He could compare anything to his vineyard. It was the source of his every truth – a garden of insight into all of life's questions.

"My vines are hearty, tall, proud, defenseless. They bear fruit and have nothing to hide, nothing to be ashamed of. We take care of them, and they can be trusted to give back to us generously. The nettle though, he hides amongst the weeds, stands at the foot of my vines and tries to steal the life from them. He keeps himself guarded, won't let you close, keeps up his defenses. The nettle can't be trusted."

My brother's eyes roved to and fro between nettle and vine, considering my father's words. "That seems easy enough," he at last concluded.

"Well, when you can see the difference, yes. But some people put up clever defenses, Roberto, ones you may not be able to see."

"Then how can I know who to trust?" My brother's troubled voice scratched the air like a crow's call.

"That is not so easy a question, my son. Trust is a double-edged sword. Trust is a thorn on the vine. Trust requires sacrifice; in time you will come to know what I mean. In time you will learn what signs to look for. But one thing is for sure, the man with too many defenses," my father said as he flattened the nettles beneath his heavy boot, "he must be stamped out before he can sting."

CHAPTER I

A STRANGE MEETING

The morning smelled of death and wildflowers as red horizons lighted the dew-laden hilltop. Syringe in hand, a lone traveler unbuttoned the firm fabric of the soldier's buff coat. *Fresh*, he thought as he loosened the coat, *not dead a day*. Looking greedily at the exposed flesh, the traveler marked a place on the soldier's neck. He stretched the skin tight between his fingers and inserted the hollowed needle. Suddenly, he felt the soldier tense, the lines of his jaw etched with fear, poised for death.

The unexpected jolt coursed up the traveler's arm like a contagion spreading itself until both men had succumbed to its paralysis. The soldier convulsed; the traveler smiled, a blithe shine reflected in his eye.

"Hold still, I'm dressing a wound to your neck," the traveler said, reaching into his shoulder bag for a cloth with which to bandage the small incision.

At the sound of a seemingly friendly voice, the soldier opened his eyes to the sight of a half-masked man eclipsing the rising sun.

"Stay prone," the masked traveler commanded as he finished wrapping the soldier's neck. "Rest a bit and try not to rise too quickly; take these as well," he said, producing a small loaf of bread and a jar of water; "you'll need them more than I do."

The traveler stood, turning to survey the field – an interposing collage of birth and death as flowers struggled to lift their drooping gaze toward the dawn and away from the myriad of lifeless bodies around them. Allowing his eye to meander over the hilltop, the traveler picked out the most pristine dead. Moving for the nearest body, his eclipsing presence abandoned the awakened soldier. The stark sunlight burning into his retinas, the soldier writhed like a worm scorched beneath its nauseating glare. He turned on his side, gasping and blinking away the silver-sparking fireflies of his dazed eyes. When his vision returned, there beside him he saw one of his comrades, his face blackened with bruises. Picking himself from the ground, the soldier knelt over his comrade, the smell of death presiding over all his senses. He began to cough and sputter.

Hearing the commotion, the traveler watched the soldier stumble back, rise to his feet and turn in place, heavy-breathed as he drank in the horror of death.

"†Nephilim," the traveler said, pointing, "you can tell by the bludgeoning, and the way some men form little foot-shaped depressions in the ground. You're lucky to be alive."

The soldier vomited.

"Lovely," the traveler said; distaste twisted on his lips. "Let your stomach settle before you try to eat my bread."

The soldier collapsed onto his knees and braced himself in the grass, *How did this happen?* The question tormented him. Hundreds of bodies littered the scene. The traveler continued to browse through them. He was nearing a fresh corpse when he heard a weak voice call from behind him, "Thank you."

"Excuse me?"

"For bandaging my neck, and for the food."

The traveler snorted and shook his head. "I need no thanks," he replied as he drew another syringe full of blood.

Fascinated by the eccentricity of this masked man, the soldier could do nothing but sit and watch as the traveler moved from body to body. Inserting his syringe into their necks, he would draw out a sample of blood and deposit it into a clear, glass vial. Filling the vial, he would move to the next body and repeat the process.

At length the soldier felt himself regain some composure. He finished his bread and water and did his best to ignore the ubiquity of death around him, blocking the consequence of reality from his mind. He stood and walked toward the traveler still bent in his methodical work. "What is your name?" the soldier asked as his shadow overtook the masked, syringe-wielding wayfarer.

The traveler stood, his back to the soldier, his mouth twisted in indecision. "Lucien," he replied with a callous glance over his shoulder. "My name is Lucien, but do not take my gesture of good will as one of friendship."

The soldier nodded contemplatively at the back of Lucien's head, watching as he walked purposefully to a nearby body. An airy feeling breezed through the soldier as he tried to focus on Lucien, and his head swirled as if it were the ocean itself. "Where are you from, Lucien?" the soldier called, hoping that words would set some foundation for his mind to steady itself.

"Now that's a dangerous question," Lucien said. He clicked his tongue and turned to face the soldier. "Perhaps I'm from †Aureus."

"Then I imagine I would be dead," the soldier solemnly replied as his eyes wandered from corpse to corpse.

Noting the soldier's lamenting eyes, Lucien replied, "Do not suffer the dead for they are gone and you are here; they shall see no other dawn but you have many yet to fear." A wry smile spread Lucien's lips apart at the disdain staining the soldier's face. "Perhaps that was callous of me," he continued. "I should be cognizant that not everyone shares my understanding of death. Apologies." He extended his regards to the soldier who made no motion to accept the offered hand.

"But, you're right," Lucien encouraged him with an uncanny buoyancy, "you *would* be dead unless there was some service that Aureus requested of you. Are you going to take my hand?"

The soldier responded with a cautious, steady stare.

Loosing an exasperated sigh Lucien rolled his eye, "I have not been sent by Aureus. As I may have said, I am a doctor of sorts; I simply happened upon this field."

His gaze darted pleadingly between the soldier's eyes. Lucien measured him, he was an average height and firmly crafted, his eyes commanding but indistinct; yet in the tension of their stare, he saw one thing: greatness. "What is your name, soldier?" Lucien asked, having leveled eyes with the man.

After a cautious assessment, the soldier responded, "My name is Alaric Folck. You have my gratitude for the service you have provided to me though I know you do not wish it." He grasped Lucien's still outstretched hand. In Alaric's eyes, Lucien cast a subtle aura. He was shrouded in a sort of eccentric mystery, blanketing what Alaric decided to be blatant madness.

"It was nothing. As I said, you needed the food more than I did. And I suppose I should apologize for my abruptness before; I expected you to be dead and, as you can imagine, I was a bit startled when you began to seizure."

"Death may have been my fate had you not come along. I am indebted to you."

"Well, either the sun or the stench of the bodies would have woken you eventually and you would have found your way home; so there is no debt to be paid – specifically in that I am not one who cares much for the company of others. It's like baggage: no matter how little you carry, it always seems to be too much; so, you may keep the jar."

Lucien gestured to the empty container in Alaric's hand and curtly nodded his head.

"Be on your way now, Alaric Folck. The sun rose in line with the mountain peak just over my left shoulder. That is east. Hopefully, you can find your way from there. Now please, leave me to my work."

Reticently, Alaric consented. He stepped slowly back from Lucien and called out as he turned away, "The †Shaddai guide your steps," as was customary.

Lucien's stance turned rigid. He felt the words crawling over his flesh and up into his ears. *It is all he could expect*, Lucien thought, biting his lower lip. The presence of the words resonated around him in an unpleasant atmosphere as he watched the soldier's departure over the hill and into the West. Turning abruptly on his heels, Lucien knelt down to resume his work.

* * *

Out of sight, Alaric stopped. There had been something strange about this Lucien; the obscurity of his appearance at the hill was unnerving. That he had claimed to be a doctor testified to extracting the blood, *but to serve what purpose?* Alaric thought. He allowed the peculiarity of it all to clutter his mind until he realized he was wandering aimlessly westward and resolved then to forget Lucien and press for home.

By midday, the landscape began to transform around Alaric from a flat terrain of scattered trees and scrambling bushes to a denser forest that funneled up from the southern mountains like a belt across the continent. The high canopies of ancient trees engulfed Alaric with a near cavernous effect, and the foliage, which had peppered the ground before, was overrun by a thick spongy moss blanketing the forest It absorbed the sound of Alaric's footsteps as he moved along, causing him to blend with the eerie silence of the wood. Though the air was damp and stale, it was a welcome relief from the pervasive scent of death.

After he had wandered far enough into the forest to be hidden in its density, Alaric let himself collapse into the thick carpet of moss at the base of a tree. His eyelids heavy, he relented his better judgment to his body's demand for sleep. Nestled against the tree, he felt protected but, unknowingly, he had been stalked for some time. Vulnerable as he now was, a wolf closed in upon him. It circled at a distance, keeping its leery eyes on Alaric. With every passing minute the wolf stalked towards its slumbering prey until, with a howl, it broke cover. In a bound, the wolf was on Alaric, its jaws latched to his neck. Alaric's eyes bulged with an overflow of tears and his cries swept through the trees like a great ripple before being swallowed in the depths of the forest.

The wolf jumped back, gauging Alaric as he reacted to the bite. Its mouth foamed red with the taint of blood. The taste was not enough and with another howl it leapt forward. Still on his back, Alaric grabbed the wolf's jaws as it pounced upon him. Madly, the wolf shook its head to escape as Alaric began to slowly stretch the wolf's jaws apart. Frantic, the wolf began to rip its fore claws into its prey's chest, shredding Alaric's buff coat and tearing into the first layer of his skin. The blood aroma ignited an insatiable lust in the very core of the beast.

Wrenching still at the wolf's jaws, Alaric slung the creature aside. Catching the glint of his dagger in the moss, he made a desperate grab for its hilt, exposing his chest. The wolf bounded back and sank its teeth into his right breast. Alaric twisted his body and planted his elbow into the side of the animal's head, and in the same motion he rolled himself over, grabbed his dagger and sliced at its throat.

The wolf's fur became matted with the garnet liquid gushing from the wound. It reared back, giving Alaric time to readjust his stance. Howling, it attacked again, leaping at its prey as its cry echoed through the trees. Again, Alaric grabbed hold of its jaws. Pulling with all of his might, he felt the jaw muscles begin to tear; he heard bone begin to crack under the pressure of his hands; he felt the wolf try to escape his vice.

Alaric's face hardened into a scowl. In anger and agony, he loosed a final surge of wrath. The wolf whimpered; the jaw split, and the moss beneath Alaric became red and marshy. The creature slumped and the light behind Alaric's eyes faded into blackness. He was alive and awake, but conscious of nothing. After some time, a dull warmth began to spill over him. Alaric felt himself lifted from the ground. His head nodded back and he could hear distant voices calling his name. A soft breeze carried beneath him, and he was succumb to a yawning darkness of unconsciousness.

CHAPTER II

HOME

Alaric awoke three days later to the sight of a white-jacketed attendant hovering over him. "Good morning Captain Folck, and welcome home," he said. "My name is Brancott."

He checked Alaric's wounds, refreshed his bandages, and apathetically asked him questions about his condition.

"Get some rest, Captain," Brancott said finishing his duties. "You'll be in recovery for at least a week." This said, he left Alaric to his thoughts of deepest consternation. It had been a week ago that he had marched from this network of caverns. The air had been fervent with enthusiasm. Scouts had reported sighting a dozen Nephilim headed from Aureus in search of a rumored refuge, their refuge – †Adullam. All believed the battle would be an easy victory – two hundred men against twelve Nephilim – and even now, Alaric could not reason how so many men could be so wrong.

He searched the cavern's ceiling for answers, but its jagged surface knew only shadow. In a deluge of blackened despair, he began to shake violently. As Alaric's bed rattled against the stone floor, Brancott turned from his work at the other end of the medical bay. He cried out to the other nurses and they rushed to Alaric's side to sedate him. He awoke the next day to the sound of angry shouts.

"A spy, I say he is!"

"And I agree! Why else would he be sneakn' 'round?"

"Gentlemen," the accused coerced, "do not be so hasty, I..."

"Do not speak," an accuser retorted. Angry, indiscernible shouts echoed in consent.

Hearing the commotion, Alaric rolled off his cot and stumbled toward the noise. Dressed in nothing more than a white robe, he limped from the Infirmary, both his eyes nearly blackened shut and his body aching in protest to movement. He placed his hand upon the rough walls of the corridor to guide himself down the passage.

The shouts continued to resonate through the halls, growing louder as a crowd began to form. Alaric rounded the corner to find an east-wing common room brimming with people.

"He must be taken to Stilguard for a trial!" one yelled out. There was a murmur of agreement at this remark, but a shout of compliance to the next, "No! There needn't be a trial; this man is obviously a spy! What other reason would he have for being here? And look at him – look at his mask!"

Instantly Alaric was reminded of his strange meeting several days prior. Lucien had donned a strange white mask. Alaric could see it now, covering the right side of Lucien's face, engraved with three black lines curving from the tear duct around the eye and to the cheek. Alaric burst out in a near battle cry for silence, pushing his way through the crowd to find the masked man. As the rabble opened for him, Lucien came into sight.

"My, you seem to be in considerably worse condition than when you left me," he said. "Should you be out of bed?"

"Alaric, you know this man?" Lucien's bewildered accuser asked.

"Yes," Alaric's voice unfolded over the mob like a blanket, "he saved my life and no one will touch him until Stilguard has passed jurisdiction."

"And you are sure it was *this* man?" the accuser posed, his tone edged with skepticism.

"Does this look like a man I could mistake, Barrius?" Alaric asked with an incredulous wave of his hands.

Barrius examined Lucien, studying his every facet. Beginning with his half-moon mask, to the turn of his collar, to the white pleated vest beneath his forest-green jacket with its silver peacock-feather and floral embroideries, and down to his fitted, silver-gray pants buttoned just below

18

the knee along with the black boots which swallowed everything else. Barrius memorized him. Lucien seemed to be from some forgotten century, a royal lost on his way to the masquerade.

"You presume," Alaric continued, "that you are entitled to subjugate your judgment upon this man?"

"Don't talk down to me, Alaric, about my presumptions," Barrius countered. "What am I to think when I find a masked man slinkin' through the corridor like I found him, aye? I think there is *subjugation* to be done!"

"Regardless, his fate is not your decision. He should have been taken to Stilguard immediately."

"He's a brigand, Alaric. I can smell it."

Ignoring Barrius, Alaric turned to address the restless crowd, "Trust your Steward to judge this man's fate; you will do well not to interfere further." Then, to Lucien, he said, "I apologize for the premature actions of my people. I will take you to Stilguard, and I am sure he will greet you warmly. Come, he should be in the North Wing." The crowd separated in whispering discontent as Alaric and Lucien waded out from them and proceeded to the Great Hall.

The two wound their way through shadowed corridors as sparse torchlight splashed the walls with a faint orange hue to guide them. As Lucien and Alaric entered into one of the older wings of the refuge, the halls became suddenly smooth. A soft murmur wafted through the corridor from ahead. Sensing possible apprehension in Lucien, Alaric paused, slumping against the corridor wall to rest himself. "We're coming up on the central cavern," he explained, "a sort of Market District – though there's no real economy. All necessities we share equally; luxury items and weapons, though, are bartered for. Anyway, I didn't want you to worry."

After a minute more, their corridor opened into the Market. Crowded with people and illuminated by torchlight, it was a near breathtaking transformation from what Lucien had seen through his furtive night wanderings when the torches where doused and the cavern was empty. Its vaulting halls boasted a seamless blend of artificial structures and natural formations. The Market melted into the cavern as if part of its nature, present and pervasive, yet unimposing. As Alaric and Lucien exited the small corridor, their shadows ballooned up toward the ceiling to mingle with the others of the people who bustled about in the Market. They made their way slowly through the crowd as Alaric struggled to keep himself steady. Apart from a barrage of puzzled glances at Lucien's eccentric attire, no one interfered with the two as they navigated through the tumult.

"Apart from trade, the Market also has its social functions," Alaric said pointing across the district. "The miners make up most of the scene; they come here after a day of mining ore, or expanding tunnels, or whatever they do. People like to dissolve in the crowd," he sighed, "where everyone's so distracted with themselves they don't have time for anyone or anything else."

Lucien followed Alaric's finger to the back of the Market where there seemed to be a sort of café. As Alaric said, there were the miners, distinguishable by their extra layer of earthen skin; among them, too, were soldiers who drank and carried on with the miners, generating most of the noise echoing round the cavern walls. From the café, Lucien's eye caught the sportive antics of children playing among the vendors' stands, hiding from their scolding mothers or chasing around with their friends.

"Let me help you," Lucien pleaded as Alaric strafed to the side in a painful stagger. "You really shouldn't be out of bed."

"No," Alaric waved him off, "no, I can handle myself."

As Alaric corrected his balance, a drop of water splashed against his cheek. He dragged his forefinger up the droplet's glistening trail and examined it on the tip of his finger. He turned to begin limping sideways through the crowd as he held his forefinger out for Lucien to see.

"Our water supply," Alaric said as he began to side step his way to the North Wing corridor, "comes from a small river that runs right along the western side of Adullam, accessible from the Southern Wing. We have redirected its flow a bit so it runs into a small alcove we dug out of the rock. It's just big enough to catch the running water that we can then draw as it cycles through and leaves the cave. Also, there is a large reservoir near the Barracks, which we use as our backup supply in case something happens to the river. We think the river used to run above ground, and the water that seeped down deep into the earth was filtered through a limestone ceiling and caught in the reservoir.

"Anyway, there is a rather clever irrigation system set up to deliver water all across Adullam. You'll notice this iron piping overhead most everywhere you go," Alaric said, pointing to the ceiling and then turning from Lucien to navigate through the corridor. "These are to transport running water. There are two small waterwheels in different parts of the river attached to some complicated piping. I'm not sure how it all works, just that it does, but I think you might find it interesting. It's all closely monitored, of course. We have to keep up with the sanitation and the total amount of water we have in the reservoir so we don't run out, but it's quite fascinating. I'll show you some time."

"That is assuming I am not executed," Lucien grinned back.

"You won't be. Stilguard is a good man; he would not sentence your death."

They entered another corridor and walked about fifty feet or so before making an abrupt right turn. The hall funneled out and up to provide space for a massive wooden door, one so large that Lucien had trouble imagining how it was fit through such tight corridors to stand where it presently did. Alaric walked to the door, placed a hand against it and turned to Lucien, "You will meet Stilguard through this door. But first, I have a report to give on our campaign, so wait for me to introduce you before you speak. We aren't much for formalities, but it helps to be courteous."

Lucien noticed that Alaric had developed a more personal tone. It was not friendly per say, but it meant that Alaric would not readily abandon him to the wanton will of his people's mob mentality.

Alaric shifted his weight, bending his knees to exert sufficient strength to heave open the chamber door. Its iron hinges groaned in protest as it swung slowly open. They entered into a large, half-spherical room, modestly furnished with a barren dining table and another shorter table, haloed by patterned cushions and carrying an assortment of small, curious leaves in glass containers. To the far side of the chamber an imposing chair stood sturdily on a slate platform. Its majesty did not constitute the title of a throne, but it did add a symbol of authority to the room.

The room was simple, and Lucien liked the practicality of it all. Two men stood in the center of the room, deep in discussion; upon hearing the groan of the heavy door they turned to the unsightly appearance of Alaric whose staggered approach made their jaws drop. One of the men stepped from the fire, head cocked in a dumbfounded stare and arms cradling the air as to receive Alaric. "Stilguard," Alaric said, raising his hand to wave off the man.

"Did the Infirmary grant you leave?" Stilguard sputtered out in disbelief.

"No, I was not granted leave," he said, and cringed with his last step to the fire. Nodding to the still silent man, he braced his hands on his hips and continued. "There was an incident. It needed to be addressed, but that can wait." His words spilled out between sharp, pain-filled breaths. "Before I go further, there is another matter we must discuss regarding the campaign."

"The report can wait, Alaric." Stilguard protested.

Alaric shook his sunken head and swallowed, looking up again at both men. "The Nephilim proved to be more formidable than we imagined, and bigger – much bigger." He sighed and let his breath steady to overcome the syncopated breadth of his sentences. "Their skin is like leather. Layers on layers on layers. It was hopeless. I was knocked unconscious within the first few minutes. Unless more have returned since my arrival..." His voice trailed, leaving the hollow words hanging in air.

Alaric brought his eyes to the still silent man. Slightly taller than Alaric, he had a head of short, scrambling gray hair, pursed lips, crossed arms and a face shadowed with gray stubble that accentuated his foreboding glare. His face was aged with lines and wrinkles, but even so, he was a stout man. From between the "V" of his dark green tunic sprouted thick curling hairs from the still pronounced bulge of his chest. "General Nestor," Alaric began, "our precision was faultless. Strategically, we didn't deviate from the battle plan, but we misjudged the strength of our opponent."

"Mmmm," Lucien hummed from the shadows behind Alaric. "It seems to me you misjudged something else. Not the strength of your enemy perhaps, but that of your tactics." He circled into the light of the fire, a complacent tilt in his head. "And who, may I ask, was your brilliant tactician?"

"I was!" Nestor barked, dropping his arms and rearing his shoulders. "Do you..."

"Do you presume," Stilguard interjected, flattening his hand on Nestor's chest, "to enter my halls and badger my general about matters which hardly concern you? I dare say I've never seen you before; you don't seem like the type I could overlook."

Stilguard narrowed an eye at Lucien's mask. "That you hide your face makes your presence ever less reputable. You speak out of turn."

"I speak out of experience."

"Lucien," Alaric interjected, "this is the Steward."

22

Lucien gauged Stilguard, assessing his demeanor, the shift of his weight, and the stature of his shoulders, the narrowing of his eyes as his mind turned ceaselessly in quiet reasoning. He was stout and hardened, though not as well built as Nestor. He had a heavy brow and penetrating gray eyes. A silvery scar marred his face as it stretched over his left eye from his long, flat forehead. He had short, unkempt black hair, aged by narrow streaks of gray. Clothed in a sturdy derision of Lucien's outspokenness, he looked at Alaric. "Who is this man?"

"I am the light in the darkness of your cave," Lucien responded. A chuckle bubbled up from this throat, echoing eerily around the room. "I am Lucien."

"And hiding behind your mask you feel you have the right to exert your opinion here? Where have you come from, †Bristing? I hope you can account for our wasted shipments?"

"No, no, no, not from Bristing."

"Then from where, and what is your business?" Stilguard asked steadily, but his tone betrayed a tremor of impatience, rocking his otherwise stoic demeanor.

"I've come from nowhere," Lucien answered cryptically. "More precisely no *one* – as I am sure that was the truer nature of your question. I have not been sent here for some purpose and I am not here to rob or to spy. I am here, because of Captain Folck. When I found him, his spirit was," he groped for the word, "inspiring to me. I decided that his place was better than no place and, if the people he resided with showed as much fortitude and courage as he, then I would do well to follow him. I must admit," Lucien held out his arms and turned around once to get a full view of the room, "I hardly expected something of this grandeur." As he finished speaking he stopped turning, looked straight at Stilguard, gave a polite smile and let his arms hang down at his side.

For a long while the room was silent. Alaric's anxious eyes searched Lucien for some grain of normality. "Captain Folck?" he heard the Steward's question reel him back to attention. "What can you say for this man?"

"Lucien saved my life, sir. He found me and fed me and sent me in the right direction."

With a short, sharp sigh Stilguard again addressed Lucien saying, "There remains, for me, one problem: the mask. Remove it, I won't trust a man whose face I cannot see."

Lucien shrugged, "The mask is nothing, it cradles a bandage to my face."

"Then remove it for us," Stilguard persisted.

"If it were merely linen on my face would you ask me to remove it?" Lucien objected as he caressed the edges of his mask. "This is no different. The linens become soaked with blood and fluid from the draining infection; as you can image that becomes unsightly – thus the mask."

As Lucien finished speaking, Alaric noticed a subtle tension relax in his form. A shift in his stance, a roll of his shoulder – that was all – but it betrayed to Alaric that somewhere beneath the blanket of Lucien's mysterious eccentricity, the mask held some sacred purpose.

"It seems to me," Stilguard continued, indulgent to Lucien's objection, "that you are not a dishonest man, but nor are you entirely honest. Do I speak rightly?"

Lucien returned an almost leery grin before answering, "I use my wits for more than speaking, and I pride myself on the subtlety of my movements. So if you still wish to keep the location of your refuge a secret from the Nephilim, and if your general can bear it," he glanced toward Nestor whose humor had not much improved, "I suggest you make use of my talents."

"You are in a fine spot to be dealing out threats." Stilguard responded.

"Just a suggestion." A smile danced playfully across Lucien's lips.

Stilguard mused over his proposal for a moment. He glanced toward the rigid figure of his general before returning his attention to Alaric. His eyes wandered over his captain, assessing his physical condition and the toll his exhaustion would have on his present rationale.

"I think now is not the appropriate time to discuss such matters," he finally concluded. "Lucien, I am sure you understand that I cannot, at this time, trust your advice. Moreover I think we all need time to recover. Alaric needs to be in a healthier condition; his exhaustion will no doubt have a toll on his mind and his input is necessary to our discussion. Lucien, I want you to escort Alaric back to the Medical Wing. Stay with him until he makes a full recovery. Tend to his needs and in this way I might see that you are deserving of our trust."

A sly glimmer sparked Lucien's eye, and a smile lingered on his face.

CHAPTER III

PHILOSOPHER KING

"You've been coughing incessantly."

The words stabbed sharp as a knife into Alaric's skull as he rolled over in his cot. Lucien stood above him with a book and a glass of water.

"Afternoon," he caroled handing the glass to Alaric, "how are you feeling?"

Alaric lay back and gazed at the ceiling, wiping the condensation of the glass across his forehead.

"Yes, I thought so," Lucien continued. "I have something that might help." He left Alaric to sulk in silence and crossed the room to a small assistant's table to begin mashing different herbs together into a type of paste. Collecting his concoction, he returned to Alaric's side and stirred it into his water. "Have you ever heard of the Visigoths?"

Accepting the concoction, Alaric darted disinterested eyes at his companion.

"They were a Germanic people, barbarians," Lucien mused, "led by a man named Alaric, two thousand and some odd years ago. Alaric marched his armies straight into the heart of Rome – arguably the greatest empire ever to exist – and overthrew its capital city." He nodded to himself and let his eyes fall slowly to the book in his hand.

Finishing the last bitter gulp of his drink, Alaric opened his mouth to speak, but a sudden bout of shouts ran through the atrium and caught his tongue. Two doctors rushed in carrying a young boy between them. Hearing the commotion, a third doctor appeared through the doorway of one of the back rooms. His bald head shone in the torchlight as he bustled towards the new patient.

The first two medics placed the child on a bed next to Alaric's. "He's broken a leg," one said.

The bald doctor decisively responded by grabbing a wooden splint and some bandages off the wall. He placed the splint against the boy's leg and began to tightly wind the bandage around it.

As Alaric looked on, a blur of green suddenly swept the scene as Lucien practically leapt over the bed into the doctor's midst.

"I'm sorry," Lucien interjected, "are you mad?"

"Oh irony," Alaric whimpered as he placed the pillow over his head to hide from the commotion.

Lucien clicked his tongue.

The bald doctor's expression could have blended with a blank wall.

"The boy's leg is broken?" Lucien asked. "When were you planning on setting the bone? After the infection had consumed his leg and you'd amputated it? That's usually the way I like to do things too, you know, but I've recently been exposed to this new methodology; it's called competency."

By now, the boy had passed out from the pain and Lucien parted the three doctors aside with his roving, cynical eye. He probed the boy's leg and, finding the break, snapped the bone back into place. "Give it some time to swell, then bind it with the splint." Shaking his head, he turned his attention to Alaric, "Feeling any better?"

* * *

Several hours later the boy began to stir. Lucien was quietly reading as Alaric slept. The boy tried to roll over onto his side but at the pain in his leg, decided a simple turn of his head would suffice. He watched Lucien read for a moment, studying his mask and strange, forest-green suit. "You dress funny," the thought fell from his mouth. Oval eyed, he quickly reached to cover his mouth, "sir," the boy added – to be respectful.

Snapping his book shut, Lucien straightened his shoulders and cast a glance of ill repute over to the boy. "How old are you?" he asked.

"Seven. Why do you wear a mask?"

Lucien thought for a moment and said, "The mask conceals a scar that covers the whole right side of my face. It's an unsightly wound so, rather than bear it on my face, I wear the mask."

Irritated with the boy's presence, Lucien turned back to his book and trailed his finger down the page trying to reclaim his lost position.

"I have a scar as well," the boy responded, attempting to mimic Lucien's elocution, "It is here upon my belly. It is an unsightly wound, though I bear it with great estem."

Lucien smiled over the top of his book. "The word you're looking for is 'esteem,'" he said, now slightly amused with room's new addition.

"Esteem," the boy whispered, his face sewn tight with concentration.

"Some scars can be worn so," Lucien continued; "others, however, are not so reputable."

"What do you mean? Where did your scar come from?"

Lucien shook his head, "A mistake, 'tis nothing for you to be concerned with; how is your leg?"

"Fine," the boy smiled.

"And where are your parents?"

The boy's face turned somber. He looked intently at Lucien and sighed, "I haven't seen my mother since I was very little, and my father," he scrunched his nose thoughtfully, "told me to be strong; that I was smart and would grow to be wise; that I should always be joyful because happiness will come and go, and that he-e-e," the boy strained the vowel as he counted on his fingers, "would be home in three days. My father is a solider, and he'll be home in three days."

"And when did your father tell you this?"

The boy counted again, "Seven days ago."

It was not hard for Lucien to figure out the situation. The boy's father had gone to fight the Nephilim just over a week ago, expecting to have returned by three days' time. Lucien found Alaric amidst his dead comrades a day or so after the army's departure from the refuge. It was four days after this that Alaric awoke and Lucien himself was found. Then another day in the Medical Wing with Alaric made seven days – give or take several hours – to compare with the departure of this boy's father. And here the boy sat, oblivious, smiling, self-assured that his father would be home soon. Though the caverns were perpetually cool, an unsettling warmth flushed through Lucien. "What is your name, child?" he asked.

"Mark is my name." The boy's head shrank into his shoulders. "Mark Legion."

"Well, Mark, my name is Lucien, and I am going to look after you until your father returns. Would that be all right?"

"Yes," the boy nodded.

Lucien stood from his chair and called for a doctor.

"Inform your superior that I will remain in the Medical Wing on a provisional basis to oversee the recovery of my friends. Once they've healed up I would like to be granted a more permanent status on your staff. I feel to make use of my medical experience is the best way to serve your people."

* * *

After another day or two, Alaric was in stable enough condition to counsel Stilguard. He and Lucien departed promptly from the Medical Wing, leaving Mark and his broken leg to mend. The two wound their way back through the dimly lit halls of Adullam to the Steward's Hall. As they approached the great wooden doors, Alaric turned to Lucien. "It may be best for you to wait outside for now; I will give a campaign report and intercede on your behalf. This should not take long, though I think it appropriate for me to converse with Stilguard alone at first."

Lucien nodded and Alaric went alone into the room. Several minutes after the door shut behind Alaric, it was reopened by General Nestor, glaring as he passed.

Alaric peered out and beckoned Lucien in. Stilguard was waiting in the center of the room and made no motion to acknowledge Lucien as he entered. When both had reached Stilguard, the Steward finally appeared to notice Lucien, addressing him stiffly. "We briefly went over the details of the campaign with the General though the results are rather self explanatory. I dismissed Nestor when the topic of conversation turned toward you. Alaric again affirms your integrity with shining recommendation. He also tells me of this boy, Mark Legion, whom you intend to safeguard. This, I say, is noble of you and, on such grounds as you have promised to keep watch over the boy, I give you asylum in our home.

"Alaric also tells me of your knowledge of medicine and that you have volunteered your services to our Infirmary. Perhaps your true sentiment is shown? Even if you choose to hide it behind a mask. You are closer to earning my trust and, for now, I welcome you to Adullam."

"I thank you, Steward, for extending your grace," Lucien replied, "though I dare say I deserve the flattery of being 'noble.' I merely know where I am needed and, having said so, I am needed at your side as well. You struggle to fight the Nephilim, but I know these creatures – know their weakness. Subversion and diversion: these are the tactics you need to employ."

"Yes, you spoke of these tactics last we met as I recall," Stilguard said, "much to the vexation of my General. Albeit, Nestor's methods seem to have failed us. I see no reason why I should not at least hear you out. Subversion you say?"

"Subversion," a thin smile spread across Lucien's face, shadowy and devious. "Sheer force will be matched with a far greater force, so upfront tactics are useless. Alaric, you have seen these beasts first hand. Recount for us, how large are they, both in height and stature?"

Alaric sighed and shook his head, "Massive," he began, "it's all almost a blur now. We knew they would be big, but never thought, *this*. They are shaped like men, but have an evil tint – a gray skin, tougher than leather. Twelve, maybe fifteen feet tall, they're sheer muscle and skin. It's like trying to fell a tree with a dagger."

Entranced by the memory of the battle, Alaric gazed steadily into the fire at the center of the room. Lucien nodded, entranced too by the fire. "But what's the point now?" Alaric continued, his tone listless and his eyes glassed. "What can we do – realistically – in the wake of our loss? Men are dead; resources are scarce. And where is Bristing?"

"Alaric," Stilguard growled. "You are a Captain of Adullam…"

"You mentioned Bristing before," Lucien said, an inquisitive eye trained on Stilguard.

The Steward reverted his attention. "A surface community to the West in the grasslands of the †Briswold; our partners in trade."

The room was silent save for the violent crackle of fire parroting the heated tension in the room.

"And how is it that your people ended up here in the dark?" Lucien sought to loosen the atmosphere.

"We've inhabited these halls for near a hundred and fifty years," Stilguard quietly explained. "Our ancestors lived along the southern coast near the mountains until the ocean's water became red as blood. It caused a plague to run though the community, killing thousands. Most of the survivors left for Bristing, hoping to forge a new life for themselves among the people there. Others moved into the Beltwood, woodlands to the Northeast on the other side of the mountains. Others still, due to the tragedy, fled to Aureus. Back then, The Golden City kept to itself, feigning the repute of righteousness. But eventually that changed and the Nephilim drove the woodland inhabitants back into Adullam. My family, the Stilguards, became Stewards of the people. Until recently, Aureus extended its reach no further than the Beltwood, but as of late its fingers have inched forward. Nestor and I, as well as many others in Adullam, feared that if we waited too long to meet this impending threat it would be too late and the whole refuge would be discovered to our doom. Nestor devised a plan to lash out against the Nephilim that had begun to patrol past the Beltwood but, as apparent, our attack was ill conceived.

"I'm just tired," the Steward continued through a sigh. "We're all tired of this waning existence. We thought we were ready to step from the darkness, ready to step out and face Aureus. I want there to be more than this for my people." Stilguard's eyes narrowed with their signature calculated reasoning. "We had a reason to be here once as bastion of freedom from Aureus. But all of that has withered with time and unless we can find some hope, some renewed purpose…" his voice trailed. "I thought if we could just scratch Aureus, then maybe that could spark a fire – could set some foundation for rebirth."

Silence as Lucien studied the lines of Stilguard's pensive expression.

"You did not truly believe you could so easily contend with the will of Aureus?" Lucien asked with a faint chortle of disbelief. "Or did you not know? Not even your Shaddai can bend his will. He seeks out all who would deny him lordship of the earth. By stepping out with such force you draw his focus. Soon you will have much more terrible things than the Nephilim slithering towards you."

Stilguard's calculating eyes wandered uneasily over Lucien's mask.

"No," Lucien asserted, a sly grin unfolding across his face, "the Nephilim are simple. The tendon running from heel and up the back of the leg, cut it at their ankle and they fall."

"So what do you propose?" asked Stilguard.

The firelight flickered off Lucien's mask, shadowing the rest of his face. "I know that I have not been here long – that my presence here has been... controversial. My proposition may sound bold, but I need for you to trust me. I will work in ways that your General Nestor cannot or will not understand. All I require is a handful of newly recruited soldiers, ones who share no real allegiance to Nestor; ones whom I can condition to fight the Nephilim."

Lucien could see the consent in Stilguard's eyes. Though a stoic barrier of reason shielded the Steward from impetuous action, Lucien could sense a yearning that despair had carved into his chest, a shadow of madness that crept along the recesses of his mind waiting to whisper to an impulse of faith. But the barrier was not worn so thin.

"I cannot yet give you an answer," the Steward replied decidedly. "I will consider your proposal and discuss it with Nestor, though he is not likely to release soldiers to any separate cause. I will keep you informed of my decision. For now," he added reassuringly, "know that you at least have my trust, and I am sure Alaric's."

Lucien nodded understandingly, feigning delight with the Steward's closing words. He was, in truth, relieved to have earned Stilguard's trust, but disappointment marred the success; he would have to remain patient for a little while longer. As their conversation trailed, both men noticed the absence of Alaric's presence. He still stood with them but his mind was elsewhere, his gaze captured in the fire. Shortly, he blinked, looking up at the pause in their conversation. Time had stopped and a haze began to swirl in his mind. His eyes watered, sensitive to the firelight and he pressed his fingers against the temples of his forehead. His knees weakened; his head swam. The pressure behind his eyes began to build up. His mouth fell agape as his head pounded with the hastened beating of his heart.

"What!" Alaric cried out, but could not hear himself speak – his mind was screaming; all he could hear was screaming – the voices of his comrades shouting, their blood splattering across his field of view. Their eyes were upon him now, the eyes of the dead. He was in a field among them, terror stricken and trembling. Then all was black.

Alaric's left knee gave way and he began to fall backwards. Lucien rushed to brace him but Alaric wouldn't have it. He tried to strike Lucien but missed. Swinging around, he stumbled and collapsed on the floor.

Alaric awoke several hours later back in the Infirmary to see Stilguard standing over his bed. Mark lay in the cot next to him in a deep, peaceful slumber, his paced breath caressing the air with its gentle throb. Alaric could still smell the sharp scent of burnt wood stuck to his clothes. Stilguard reached over to the nightstand and handed Alaric a small vial filled with the same yellowish-green liquid Lucien had prepared before.

"Lucien said once you had awakened to give you this, and that you must drink all of it."

Alaric took the glass from him.

Stilguard watched as Alaric began to drink and continued speaking, "I've sent him down to the Archive. He said he had some research he needed to do – asked if we had any maps. I told him if we did they would be in the Archive so I had him escorted there."

Alaric nodded as he swallowed the last of his remedy.

Stilguard began again, slightly hesitant, "Though I fear he will not have much to work with. There haven't been many cartographers since the rise of Aureus. Our few maps either chart the old world or are incomplete or inconsistent."

Alaric was about to speak when Lucien bustled through the atrium and proclaimed, "Ah! You've awoken. I thought you would be back with us by now. Have I missed anything important?" He looked from Alaric to Stilguard and back again expectantly, but he did not wait for them to answer. Lucien's breath was short and his complexion pallid, "I must go check on the other patients; I see that you are stable for now so, if you will kindly excuse me, I shall return as abruptly as possible." Flustered, Lucien scurried past them and disappeared into the next room.

Stilguard watched his exit and looked back at Alaric's crooked expression.

"What's that face for?"

"I've only ever seen him stride," Alaric whispered with a scowl. "Something's wrong."

"Yes," Stilguard mused in reply. "Lucien is in our graces for now, but I want you to keep watch over him. I don't think we know all we should about him." Saying this, the Steward turned and left Alaric alone with Mark who was just beginning to stir.

Lucien returned several minutes later with a renewed enthusiasm to see Mark awake and hobbling around on his splint. "I'm glad to see you are both well," he said to Alaric and the boy. "Forgive my haste but I must return to the Archive. I have much to do and the resources I have found thus far are scarce. Unfortunately, it seems there has been so little use of your Archive that no real catalog of books exists. Though I suppose I should be grateful that there are records at all," Lucien said in leaving. "If anything, Aureus has been quite successful in its attempt to erase old world knowledge." With this, he rounded the corner and was gone. His footsteps echoed along the corridor, growing ever fainter.

*　*　*

It's tragedy, Lucien thought as he scoured through shelves of frail books and tattered scrolls, *the state of this place*. He held a small candle up to the crumbling volumes and squinted at their titles sunk beneath an age-old dust. So intent on his search, he failed to hear the shuffling of feet entering the Archive behind him and was startled by a sudden, wizened voice asking, "What is it that you're looking for?"

Lucien's shoulders tensed instinctively and he turned quickly to meet the voice. "Maps," he said. "The two I've found are over on that table but they're inconsistent. The southeastern quadrants are not the same and one of the maps is missing the lands east of the Beltwood. I was hoping I could find another and perhaps translate all three into one. But there may not be another map. I'm afraid this place is rather derelict in its upkeep."

The old man pursed his lips as he took a few more steps closer. "I am in charge of its upkeep," he replied.

"Ah," mumbled Lucien. "Well, perhaps you would know if there is indeed another map."

Despite the insult, the old man gave several concise nods of his head and allowed a smile spread over his lips. "It has been a long time since I've shared any company in the Archive," he said. "Come, just around this way. I believe there is one other map of the area and a couple of the old world. Why do you need them?"

Lucien followed the old man around a shelf to see the maps hanging in plain sight upon the wall.

"I wanted to know exactly where I was. I needed another map because the other two were incongruent. I was going to compare them to a third, but this one looks complete."

"Aye," the old man said with another smile, "that is why it's on the wall."

Ignoring the man's dry humor, Lucien continued to study the map. He brushed away some of the dust with the back of his hand to see the lines better and then swept his finger across the central area looking for Adullam. "Am I not looking in the correct spot? I cannot find the place."

"No, you're correct. Adullam is not identified here as in the others. It was one of our early cartographers that made this map. The man would not have known of Adullam's location. But if you look here," the man stepped right up next to Lucien and placed his finger on the map, "you see the Beltwood spanning the center of the map. Just to the East, you see here, is our territory, †Drögerde. Where the wood begins to fan out in the North, just left of that is where we are, someplace in this general area. That has always been enough for me."

"I see," Lucien said, slightly disappointed.

But the old man was no longer paying attention to Lucien. He had taken to studying the old world maps. "I used to come and look at these maps often," he said and he blew some of the dust away from them. "I would like to have been to Spain, here, by the sea. There is a book somewhere in the Archive that talks about the beauty of the Spanish coastal regions." The old man sighed, "Oh, I would have liked to live in that world."

"Italy, I think, is more beautiful. And not nearly as corrupt in the last days," Lucien said.

"You speak as if you have been before," the old man chuckled.

Lucien by now had circled back around the shelf to look at the other maps. He smiled back at the old man, "That was three hundred years ago at least."

"Yet you speak with confidence," the man protested.

"What I know," said Lucien, walking back with the first two maps in his arms, "is that the city you see there, on the dot that says Barcelona, is the reason we are here."

"I know the stories," the old man said, looking at Lucien with mild admiration. "The †Narxus and its religious perversion. The †Indivinate One."

"Yes."

"But these things do not detract from the physical beauty."

"The people are half the beauty."

"And the people were deceived; you cannot hold that against them. It was their leaders who were corrupt I think," the old man asserted.

"The government is representative of its people," Lucien said, "and the people get the government they deserve. You are a Son of The Shaddai?" he asked. The man nodded in a fixated response and Lucien continued, "His Word commands submission to governing authorities, for there is no authority except that which He has established. I see your disbelief but you will find these things written. The Narxus served a terrible purpose, but it was a thing ordained. It was the judgment the world deserved."

"I do not think that is so."

"Read the histories," Lucien replied, gesturing around the whole room.

"I have read them," the old man cut off in a stubborn reply.

"Then you should know what I am saying is true."

"What you are saying is grounded, that I know. But when I look at Stilguard, I cannot agree. The people here do not deserve him as leader. They are petty; they have lost purpose beyond their own survival." The old man dropped his head and sighed. Lucien looked on, trying to empathize with his distress. In the dim light of the room his candlelit face was full of shadowed lines cast by age. With head hung, his brow loomed over his eyes, contoured like the mouths of two caverns delving into the darkness. One hundred and fifty years was far too long a time for a people such as this to be stuck in a cave. Lucien saw in these shadowed eyes the weight of the whole society bearing down upon the old man; if he could take their woe and loss he would, for even now he tried.

"And yet," the old man said, lifting his head with a smile, "you are familiar with the works of Plato?"

Lucien nodded slowly.

"I see our Steward as Plato's philosopher king, or as close to that as can be." Then with boyish curiosity the old man asked, "Do you know of what I speak?"

Lucien returned the smile graciously, "Remind me."

"Come this way," said the old man as he shuffled past Lucien to another shelf next to an old wooden table in the center of the Archive. He pulled a book from the shelf and laid it on the table. He wiped away the dust so that Lucien could see the title clearly. Lucien bent down to look at the book; from the corner of his eye saw the old man staring at him, delighted. *Plato's Republic.* Lucien could not help but grin.

"How do you have this? I was once a student of philosophy," Lucien's voice trailed off.

"How is it that you were a student?" the old man asked, intrigued. "Where did you say you were from?"

Lucien's face became hot. He glanced up at the man, trying to read the intention of a threat in his words. There was none though; he casually thumbed through the *Republic*, hardly concerned with Lucien's answer. "I, well, I was a student at my leisure. My grandfather gave me a copy of this book when I was younger. I have read it."

The old man hummed a response but was now intently reading a passage from Plato's work. "Ah!" he finally exclaimed, "Here it is. 'Until philosophers are kings, or the kings and princes of this world have the spirit and power of philosophy, and,'" he cleared his throat and raised his voice for emphasis, "'and political greatness and wisdom meet in one…cities will never have rest from their evils, – nor the human race, as I believe, – and then only will this our State have a possibility of life and behold the light of day.'"

The old man closed the book firmly into one hand and with the other he rubbed his eyes as if to block the tears that would otherwise be flowing freely. "We will behold the light of day," he said.

"You skipped a part, right after political greatness and wisdom meeting," Lucien said in a smiling response.

"Yes, well," the man exclaimed, flustered from almost shedding tears, "it's redundant." He gave a little snort of a laugh and replaced the book on the shelf.

"And that," Lucien continued with the conversation, "is what you believe Stilguard is?"

"Near enough, yes."

"I fear you are right." Lucien said, tracing his finger along the grooves of the aged table. Lucien's use of the word fear made the old man's brow raise in question, but Lucien proceeded. "I know Stilguard is Steward; Nestor is General; but what else figures into the governing of your Adullam?"

"It's a simple enough system really," the old man replied and pulled two chairs closer together. "Here, sit. Assets are divided up evenly among families or workers, depending on how many people you provide for. That is a part of Stilguard's job as Steward, to see that all these things are distributed properly. There is a commodity market in the central cavern of Adullam; if you have not yet seen it, it is impressively large. Assets can be used there to buy what qualify as luxury items. Food must be rationed and divided evenly; some complain, but that is really the most effective way to do things.

"You see, there is no real economy to speak of which is why things must be done this way. Essentially the labor is divided between miners who expand Adullam and mine ore; artisans who produce the luxury items and sell them; and traders or as some call farmers who are in charge of supplying the community with food. Traders are presided over by a council of twelve Trade Lords in charge of regulating rations and assets – an unfortunate but necessary bureaucratic aspect of our society. They establish a sort of balance to Stilguard's authority. Then there are some other lesser official positions. They take care of various infrastructure matters and, of course, there is the military.

"But, on a different note, we've been mining iron in Adullam for some two-hundred and fifty years; only in the last one hundred and fifty have we called it home. At any rate, we trade the iron with Bristing, which is a farming community to the West, for food. That's another part of the Trade Lords' role. Mainly we smelt the iron ourselves, sending them raw metal, but sometimes they require our artisans to make farming equipment or weapons that they are not skilled enough to forge themselves.

"As for Stilguard, his first name is Roderick. His position as Steward has been passed down through the generations. There has always been a Stilguard ruling Adullam, but at present there is no heir. He serves the aforementioned purpose of distributing assets and the only other two jobs a man in his position should be entitled to."

"Which are?" Lucien asked.

"Which are," the old man responded with a smile, "the suppression of any injustice against an individual of Adullam, and the defense against external threats, be it from Aureus or mother earth herself."

"Plato again?"

"Very good," the old man acclaimed with a wide smile.

"If that is the case," Lucien asked, "then why does Nestor assume so much power?"

"Really he does not have all that much power; it is as you said, assumed."

Both of them laughed at this little play on words before the old man continued speaking. "Stilguard is a soldier, all young men must go through training. Some of them stay in the military, some continue on with their father's work; but it is required of every male that he at least knows how to wield a sword. Stilguard can fight, he can fight quite well but, as I said, he is more of the 'philosopher king.' The battle with the Nephilim was orchestrated entirely by Nestor, for example. I keep records of their meetings sometimes, just to transcribe official directives and the sort. Nestor was determined to take up this battle. Stilguard trusted him to it and let Nestor fight. Ultimately he leaves the battling up to Nestor, and I think he is the better for it. I have never trusted a military ruler – too bent by blood."

Lucien responded by rocking his head back and forth in a thoughtful daze. Both men were contemplatively quiet for a moment before the old man broke the silence.

"Well," he said, "I'm afraid my time grows short, but perhaps, before other duties call me away, I could entreat you to have tea?"

"Yes, of course," Lucien eagerly responded. *How long has it been since I've had tea?* "Can I help you?"

"No, that's all right, I shall be back shortly. I'll leave you to ponder over those maps. You are more than welcome to take that other one off the wall."

"And what was your name?" Lucien asked, "I'm sorry."

"Bryan Rutherford," the old man nodded and hobbled excitedly out of the room.

CHAPTER IV

CONSPIRATORS

Barrius marched straight through the center of the Market, oblivious to anyone around him. The miners had quitted their work for the day, and the soldiers also had finished their daily duties and training. It was one soldier in particular that Barrius was seeking. The Market was full of its usual bustle, slowing everyone down except for Barrius. Indignantly, he plowed through the crowd as if running through waist deep water. At last he reached the back of the Market and surveyed the large shelf on which the miners and soldiers usually congregated. Barrius scoured the area, looking for the man whom he at last spotted laughing boisterously with glass raised to toast.

"Titus!" Barrius called, but the soldier did not hear. Barrius mounted the few steps up the shelf and came from behind the man, placing a hand on his shoulder. "Titus," he said, "I've been looking for you. We've things to discuss regarding…"

"Ah, yes!" Titus interjected, "I know what it is you're going to say. I was just having a laugh here with Ferron. He was insinuating that, well, what was it?" he said gesturing to Ferron to explain his joke.

"Oh," Ferron's lips curled in nervous grin, "it was nothing really."

"Well," Titus followed, lifting his blue eyes mirthfully to Ferron, "the best jokes are on the inside." Again they burst into fits of laughter, raising their glasses. Barrius remained unmoved, his face green with the same pungent grimace. Caught in the contagion of his silence, Titus and Ferron quieted down like two dogs caught in mischievous play. Ferron cleared his throat and pushed a stone along the floor with his boot to avoid Barrius' glare.

"Is this a man who can be trusted with our work?" Barrius asked, gesturing to Ferron.

"He can be trusted," Titus solemnly returned.

Barrius nodded and pulled Ferron in closer by the shoulder so the three of them were huddled together. "I have heard rumor, from a reliable source who shares our concerns, that Stilguard will be allowing Lucien control of some of Nestor's soldiers."

"The hell he will," Titus scoffed. "Nestor would never have it, nor would the soldiers." He lowered his voice. "I owe more to Nestor than to Stilguard. Don't get me wrong; I honor Stilguard's position as Steward but if he tries to put me under that bastard brigand… It won't happen."

"When did you hear this?" Ferron asked.

"Just moments before I came to you. Do you think, Titus, that you should inform the General?"

"No," Titus replied thoughtfully, "if this thing is carried out, he'll be the first to know. There's no need to put him on guard if Stilguard decides to change his mind. If there's confrontation between the two of them, that will only push Nestor further away from Stil's side. And Stilguard needs Nestor – the man's got no backbone, no convictions. I don't know what hold Lucien has on him, but we can't let it get any tighter."

"The brigand bastard!" Barrius hissed. "I'll kill him!"

"Settle, Barrius. That's something that cannot be done. His service in the Medical Wing has afforded him some favor, even in just the very few days he's been here. For one, Lucien allegedly saved Alaric's life, and since then he's helped care for several others who are spreading good will towards him. If *you* kill him and are discovered, well that could end terribly, not only for you but myself and Ferron and others – even Nestor. I don't like him being here; he should be dealt with, but why such hostility?"

"It was me who found him sneakin' like a rat around in the Western Wing. I called him out with my sword; he wouldn't submit. We fought but he bested me by using some sort of smoke to disorient me. He had me from behind and was about to kill me but the commotion of our fight had drawn a crowd. He was surrounded so he released me and tried to talk his way out of things. That was when Alaric showed up and took him away."

Titus shook his head, spitting on the ground. "Honorless," he said.

"So what is this conspiracy?" Ferron asked, biting his bottom lip.

"It's no conspiracy!" exclaimed Barrius.

Titus quieted Barrius with a wave of his hand. "It's not a conspiracy. We are looking out for the future of our people. We believe that Stilguard is not as capable as he once was to lead Adullam. I've spoken extensively to Nestor concerning his leadership in these last several weeks. Just look around you. Notice how the traders mill about with so little work – we haven't had food shipments in close to a month. I've talked to a couple of the traders who are with us. They say the reserves are running dry, yet they don't have permission to continue routes to Bristing. Ferron, you should notice: the iron ore stores are filling up, are they not? We haven't traded in a month. Couple all of that with this most recent battle against the Nephilim. Nestor said that Stilguard demanded it be carried out. The General urged Stil not to go on with it, that the strategy was flawed; the operation was a mistake. Now, look in the wake; we've hundreds of dead soldiers and fatherless children. The people are losing hope. They wander around this place like the walking dead. No one knows what to do any more. There is nothing *to* do."

"So it was Stilguard's plan to attack, not Nestor's?" Ferron interjected.

"Yes."

"That doesn't at all seem like Stilguard."

"Exactly," persisted Titus, "and if he continues to let Lucien take more control, then something must be done and perhaps more drastic than we had planned." He looked up to Barrius as he said this; his gaze was returned with a crooked smile.

"And you have people in support of this?"

"Of course. We have many. If we play this all wrong though, we can still lose the people's support but if orchestrated properly we can correct Adullam's problems. Hopefully, that won't mean removing Stilguard," he spoke reassuringly to Ferron whose face betrayed a scowl of concern at what he was hearing. "If it came to that, then be assured the proper avenues would be taken to ensure a right transition of Stewardship."

"Not to worry Ferron," Barrius said, smiling.

"Barrius," said Titus, "we meet with Nestor in a couple of hours, don't forget."

"I haven't, though as you know, I have some small business to take care of beforehand. I'll be done in plenty of time for our meeting, I'm sure."

* * *

Lucien was comparing the three maps he was able to uncover when he heard a soft thumping noise approaching from behind. As the noise grew closer, Lucien swung his head around to find Mark creeping towards him. Mark's head was bent low in concentration, focused on his feet as he tried to soften the *click clack* of his splint against the stone floor. Despite his concerted effort to surreptitiously enter the room, the boy was hopelessly clumsy.

"Mark," Lucien called in a hushed voice.

Mark froze, mid step, like a startled cat. Remaining motionless, he glanced up at Lucien and whispered an apology. Lucien shook his head. "What are you doing out of the Medical Wing? Is something the matter?" he asked.

"No," Mark replied, and loosened up. He hobbled over to the desk where Lucien was working and stood by him, looking down at the maps. "I'm fine, my leg feels loads better so I figured I better come help you. I heard you talking to Mr. Stilguard. You said you needed books and such," he looked up at Lucien very seriously, "and I said to myself, self, I've written a few books so I should come help Lucien." Unblinkingly, Mark held his stare with Lucien, expressing his earnest.

Lucien cleared his throat to force back a chuckle but smiled broadly. "Well, Master Legion, I humbly accept the offer of your services as a distinguished author. Are your books here in this Archive?"

"Yes," Mark replied nonchalantly, "But we don't need them right now, they're about rabbits and things." He turned and hobbled over to a bookshelf and, stroking his chin, thoughtfully scanned over the volumes, "I'll show you later."

"I would like that," Lucien said and smiled as he turned back to his maps.

Mark continued to look over the books on the shelf for no real reason other than to feel as if he were making a contribution to Lucien's efforts. Age had marred the once sturdy bookshelves with a contagious rot that crept up along the spines of books. Scrolls and loose paper lined the shelves and floor too, and a thick film of dust covered almost everything. The room was lit sparsely by the few candles Lucien had set around his desk, so even the book titles not corroded by rot, Mark could barely make out. After a few minutes of fruitless searching, he returned to Lucien's side to inspect the maps. He looked at them for a moment and asked, "So, what are we looking for?"

"Adullam," Lucien replied and continued to study the map. "I am trying to place it on this map." He leaned back in his chair and ran his hand through his hair. Reaching over to his right, Lucien lifted a book and set it on the table before him. Dust swirled out from beneath it. "We know its general location, here," he gestured to the map, "in Drögerde. This is an old record book that I found outlining Adullam's location relative to the surrounding land formations, but it's not really been any help. Unfortunately nothing is dated which makes it hard to determine anything – though that comes as little surprise. I'm not sure what sort of date would mean anything to anyone anymore. Nevertheless, it seems that none of the landmarks in this book are documented on any of the maps except this one that is incomplete and inconstant with these other two."

Mark blinked at the map, concentrating intently so as not to look confused. He scratched his nose, then looked over at Lucien and asked, "I see, so what's the problem?"

Lucien took a deep breath and exhaled, "Well, I think I am going to have to take these maps outside and figure it out myself." Lucien's attention passed from Mark to the approaching footsteps. It was Bryan reentering with the tea, and Lucien added, "though I am not sure I would be allowed to do that."

"Not allowed to wha…" Bryan began to say as he set the tea before Lucien. His question however, was cut off by Mark's exclamation,

"Oh, I've done that!" and with a broad smile Mark looked proudly back and forth between the two pair of skeptic eyes.

"What is it you have done?" Bryan was the first to ask.

"Taken the map outside to find Adullam."

"Ah yes," Bryan responded with a smile and turned to Lucien "Master Legion is quite an astute lad. Several months ago he took the maps out with his fa..." he paused.

Mark did not seem to notice the near reference; he was already busy hovering over the maps, spreading them out across the table so he could find the one he and his father had taken. He examined all three maps for a moment and then picked one up with his little fingers and held it out before Lucien. "Here," he said."It's this one. You see the dot there in the middle, that's the one dad and me made."

"But this is the wrong map," Lucien gently protested.

"Nope!" Mark fervently replied, "You're just not looking at it right," and he again laid the map back on the table to compare it with the other two. "Look, my dad showed me, if you look at the map this way it fits just right, 'cause we took it outside. He showed me. Look, this one has the big rocks an' the mountains an' everything so you can even check it, but it fits right in with these maps. It just seems different 'cause it's not straight – or finished."

Bryan tried to conceal his laughter behind a sip of tea from his large clay mug. He chuckled into his cup for a moment before extending it as a toast to the boy, saying, "I believe the boy is correct; you are most welcome to go and check for yourself, though you shall have to persuade the guards to let you out; it can be quite dangerous as of late. But from what I see, I think he's right. Well done, Mark," and he crowned his toast by taking another sip of his tea and laughing quietly to himself.

After hearing this, a giddy Mark looked Lucien square in the eye. His face was shining so brightly Lucien could hardly bare to look back. He forced a smile and ruffled Mark's blonde hair pulling him tightly against his chest to disrupt the gaze. "Well done," he whispered, and feigned another smile.

He released his grip on Mark and darted his eye back to the maps. Mark followed his gaze to find one of the old world maps lying off to the side of the table. He slowly cocked his head to the side to better observe it. "What's that map?" he asked, pointing, "I've never seen that one before."

"Ah," Lucien started.

"Before you begin," Bryan broke in, "I have other matters I must tend to, I apologize. I myself would like to hear your explanation, if indeed you have one, but I fear I must go."

"Of course. We shall talk some other time, perhaps you know more than I. I would be delighted to speak of it again."

Bryan gave a short bow and backed out of the room.

Returning to Mark's question, Lucien spoke, "This bears no easy explanation. As best I can say, the Earth experienced a great shift – a massive reconstruction of the surface world as a result of cataclysmic war and disaster – both natural and non. There was a man," he stammered, choosing carefully his next words, "perhaps you have heard stories of the Indivinate One?"

Mark shook his head, "No."

"Roberto Rosario," Lucien said, sliding his tongue between his teeth. "That was his name. The stage of the world was set for his conquest. Humanity reached the height of its conceit when this cluster of countries here," Lucien traced his finger over the whole of Europe, "succeeded in implementing the largest peace initiative ever endeavored. It blanketed the world, resolving every major conflict, reinventing the fundamentals of a world economy. They called it The Awakening.

"Now, Rosario had no hand in the treaty's creation. He was a religious leader in Spain," Lucien said, lightly tapping the Iberian Peninsula, "but after it was in effect, and people had become beguiled by peace and enamored with the height of their own virtue, Roberto tore the system down. The picture is impossible for me to paint for you now; I'm not sure that I even understand how what happened, happened. But, Rosario's religious influence somehow enabled him to attain heights of power that no one man should ever be exposed to. This won't mean much to you but, under him, La Sagrada Família de Barcelona became the center of the earth. For ten years or so there was peace under Rosario, but then his grip became too tight. The world, which rested in his open palm, was yet too big for him to grasp and countries began to slip through his fingers. Wars: here in Africa; here in the Middle East; here in Eastern Europe. So Rosario envisioned a smaller world, one he *could* hold – tightly. Do you know what a pole is?"

"A metal bar," Mark solemnly replied, transfixed by Lucien's story.

Lucien smiled, "Yes, but a pole, p-o-l-e, also means either the northern or southern-most points on the earth. The very top and bottom." Mark gave a slow nod of understanding and his left eye twitched a bit. "Rosario destroyed the poles; set fire to the ice."

"O-o-oh," Mark shuddered with delight at this turn of events, "that sounds like magic."

Lucien smiled weakly; he had lost himself in the story. "Not quite magic, Mark, though Rosario called it the 'Divine Fire' – claimed that God wished to baptize the whole earth, cleanse again the lands succumbed to war."

"So it really wasn't *his* magic?!" Mark shouted a questioning proposal.

"No."

"But it *was* magic. It still sounds like magic; *I* can't turn ice into fire."

Lucien chuckled before continuing the story, supposing it might as well be magic to Mark. "As the ice melted, the flooding began. People were forced to flee, abandon their homes and crowd together. It was then that Rosario built Aureus to bring the remaining world back under his control. Aureus is now the only real city. Rosario – even after the tragedies of The Awakening's Divine Fire – was still seen as an author of peace. The people ran by the thousands to Aureus." Lucien's tone reflected a deep remorse. His skin grew pallid and his eyes were lost in a dismal gaze into the darkest corner of the Archives.

The boy remained silent for some time, thinking less about the tortured fate of the world and more about magic. All of this information, suffice to say, had profoundly stumped the young lad. The story had been thrilling, but knowledge had been thrust upon him in such great quantities that he no longer had the willpower to figure it out. Instead, he resolved that it would be best to take a nap.

"Mr. Lucien," Mark said at last, "all of this dust is making my brain hurt. I think I'm going to go back. But the story was great! You can tell me another one later." He could never let on that the situation was too complex for him to understand for fear that Lucien would not tell him any more stories. Besides, he had figured the map out, so he must keep Lucien believing he was smart enough to understand a simple story about magic; he felt like he could be good at magic – he could almost turn himself into a rock and was convinced he would get it right some day.

"Very well, Mark," Lucien replied softly, patting the boy's shoulder.

Mark turned abruptly and hobbled out of the Archive, taking the corridor back towards the Medical Wing and leaving Lucien to himself.

As Mark passed through the dark of a torch-less corridor, a hand reached from the void and pulled him further into the shadows. Covering his mouth, the hand stifled the sound of his distress. "What are you doin' with that brigand, boy?" a voice whispered in his ear, but Mark was smothered from response. "There is nothing good that'll come of him," the voice continued. "A man who don't show his face don't deserve to be trusted. You keep away from him boy," and with this last sentence, Mark was released. He dropped to the ground, his broken leg bearing the brunt of the fall. In the wrack of his waning consciousness was the sound of heavy steps receding further into the darkness towards the Archive.

Mark lay, a formless mass upon the ground for several minutes, until a woman passing by with a basket of food nearly tripped over him. Setting her basket down, the woman groped through the darkness for Mark. His cold flesh stole her breath at first touch, but she quickly leaned in to gather him from the ground. His leg was throbbing and beginning to swell again, and the woman wrestled to help Mark up without hurting him. Once the boy was firmly on one foot, she offered herself as a crutch and the two limped away from the scene.

They arrived several minutes later at the Infirmary to find the front room empty save for the sleeping figure of Alaric. The woman caught herself staring at him as she walked Mark to his adjacent bed and quickly darted her gaze away. She lay Mark on his cot and heralded a doctor for help. She then left Mark in the doctor's care and went back to collect her basket. The doctor unwound Mark's bandages and let his leg swell as he checked to see if the bone was still set.

The swelling in Mark's leg had intensified since his return to the Medical Wing, and the pain drove the boy to tears. Awakened by the sound of his sobbing, Alaric tried unsuccessfully to comfort Mark. With all the doctors tied up with other patients, Alaric could merely console Mark and either hope the boy's pain subsided quickly or – more cynically – that it drove him unconscious.

Alaric pulled a chair up to the side of Mark's cot and had been trying to console him for some minutes when he heard someone softly enter the Infirmary. Thinking it was a doctor, he collapsed into his chair and leaned his head back to beg the doctor to tend to Mark. The approaching person was not, however, a doctor but the woman who had dropped Mark off several minutes before. Alaric's face fell flush at the sight of her. He felt himself driven by compulsion, disregarding the burn of his injuries as he shot straight from his chair. His body seared from the exertion and he shuffled sideways to brace himself on his bed. He was entranced by the sight of her. Embarrassed, the woman's gaze fell to the ground as she glided toward Mark's cot.

Bathed in the torches' flickering luminosity, she stepped between light and shadow with ethereal grace. Her pale skin was framed by wine-dark hair that draped around her delicate shoulders; as she moved, it swayed gently with her hips and her whole form seemed shaped by the caress of air. She rounded Mark's bed and, placing a hand on the tearful boy's head, smiled down tenderly at him. A stirring in Alaric's chest caused him to mirror the woman's tender gaze until he found himself caught in the stare of her steel blue eyes and all warmth was rent from him. Alaric was frozen beneath the ice of her glare.

"How could you have allowed him out of bed like this to wander the caves?" she accused.

Startled by the cruel tone of such a delicate creature, Alaric could only stand with his mouth agape.

"You were sleeping in here earlier, completely inattentive of the boy's needs," she reprimanded. She sized him up as she waited for a response and, noticing his wounds, remarked reproachfully. "Like father, like son I suppose."

"He's not mine," Alaric cried, awakening from the spell of her graze. "I'm a patient."

"Oh dear," the woman's eyes darkened with humiliation and she glanced down at Mark, stroking his face; his sobbing had somewhat subsided. "I'm sorry, I didn't realize; I shouldn't have; it wasn't my place." Her voice trailed and her gaze fluttered shyly up to Alaric.

"No, please…I admire your passion," Alaric said with an arch smile.

The woman curled her tongue between her teeth and with a quiet, soft laugh said, "No, I'm terribly embarrassed. Do you even know the boy?"

"His name is Mark, Mark Legion, I believe. He's been here for a few days."

"Poor thing," she said, wiping his tears away with her thumbs and smiling down at him. She tried to set him at ease by humming a little tune as she swept her fingers through his thick hair. Her eyes darted coyly in Alaric's direction. She smiled pleasantly to herself and then mimicked the tearful frown on Mark's face, trying to draw out a smile. When none came, her eyes shone empathetically; she reached down to her basket on the side of the bed. Her mannerisms were so wonderfully expressive it made Alaric ache. From her basket she retrieved a loaf of sweetbread and gave it to Mark. They all sat in silence as he ate and the woman continued to brush Mark's hair with her fingers. His stomach full of sweetbread, the boy fell fast asleep with what was nearly a smile.

"Finally," Alaric said, shaking his head with relief.
The young woman covered Mark's ears and glared at Alaric; the ice was back in her eyes. "He's adorable."

"As much as I love crying children..." Alaric said through a light laugh.

The woman kissed Mark softly on the forehead and stood to readdress Alaric. "If he isn't yours," she asked, "whose is he?"

"His mother I'm not sure, I think she passed away some time ago. His father was under my battalion..."

"You're," the young woman ventured, "Captain Folck?"

"Yes. Alaric."

"I'm sorry Captain Folck, I wouldn't have..."

"Please, call me Alaric, I'm just a soldier," he said. She nodded, looking steadily into his eyes. "But as far as I know, he doesn't have anyone. You're the first to come see him these several days."

"Poor thing," she said, stroking Mark's arm, "I found him in a heap on the floor in a dark part of one of the corridors. Why would he have been there?"

Alaric grimaced at the floor, "I don't know."

"I think I'll be by later to check on him; it's no good for him to be all alone."

"I...He would like that. I'm sure." Alaric coughed into his shoulder, breaking from the gaze of her demure smile.

"Well, Captain," she said, straightening her shoulders, "perhaps we'll see each other again."

Alaric stood and bowed slightly, smiling as she passed. Just before her lovely figure disappeared down the dark corridor from the Infirmary,

Alaric, caught by impulse, called out after her, "Wait, I'm sorry, your name. I never made your acquaintance."

The young woman posed in the doorway with her basket propped on her waist; there was immeasurable beauty in her modesty. "Alyssa," she called back and melted slowly into the shadows. The melody of her name wafted towards Alaric; he spoke it softly and sank back onto his cot, her presence was an untold relief to his ever-present pain.

CHAPTER V

THE BARRACKS

Meanwhile, in the Archives, Mark's assailant was peering around the corner, watching Lucien intently for any sign of treachery. Lucien, however, remained seated, still toiling over maps. Frustrated by the lack of apparent dishonesty, this spectral observer decided to make his presence known. He stepped from behind the door and swaggered in to formally proclaim his quarrel with Lucien. "I'm astounded, brigand," he began, "that they see fit to leave you down here all alone." He stopped a few feet short of Lucien and dropped his head in a menacing stare.

It was a wasted gesture. Lucien did not even show the courtesy of turning to face his accuser, but instead propped his head in his hands and released a heaving sigh. "And I, Barrius, am astounded by your ignorance."

"I wanted to have you know," Barrius continued, ignoring Lucien's statement, "that you aren't trusted here. I speak for many in Adullam who share my," he paused thoughtfully, "*concern* for your presence in our sacred home."

Lucien turned in his chair to face his adversary, his one eye fixed in a stare with Barrius. For several seconds Lucien made no reply, and the two sat in silent tension as Lucien tested Barrius' resolve; gauged the weight of his warning. Barrius remained stone still, looking unblinkingly into Lucien's eye. They were two shadows in the dark room. Barrius was a large man with an overbearing presence; the type of man, Lucien could see, who feels that if he is not at all times living up to his size, he might as well not be living. He had a broad chin, hooked nose, and a heavy brow with eyes that sank back like caverns in the dim light of the room. Lucien could barely stare at them properly. The only obvious weakness in his feature was his balding head, which he tried to disguise by keeping his hair brushed to the side.

Barrius opened his mouth to conclude the long silence but Lucien sharply cut him off, "You're like stagnant water, Barrius – stale and bitter and teaming with disease to poison those around you. Why, I ask, when your Steward trusts me, can you not take me into consideration for even a moment as an ally to you and your people? Your words against me are blind, and the blind cannot lead – they but fall by the wayside. Take heed, for this group for whom you speak is being led down a treacherous path, one from which they might not return. Mind your words and your actions, and do not cross me again."

Gaze fixed on Barrius, Lucien reached behind him and picked up a candle off the desk. He closed his eye and held the candle between them, breaking the line of sight. Lucien snuffed the candle and vanished. Barrius, whose eyes were not given time to adjust to the sudden change of lighting, fumbled in the darkness for the exit. He groped his way out and left the dust to settle upon the Archive.

* * *

Lucien came hastily through the door back into the Medical Wing. Alaric was seated on the side of his bed examining his wounds. Mark, too, was there smiling at Lucien as he entered. "Hello Mr. Lucien," he chimed brightly.

Hearing Mark's greetings, Alaric turned around.

Lucien smiled at Mark and walked abruptly to Alaric. "You seem to be doing better," he said, stopping short of his cot. "Are you well enough to show me to the Barracks?"

"I believe Stilguard wanted to. He was just here inquiring of your whereabouts. I sent him down to the Archive. Did you not pass him?"

Lucien glanced precariously behind him and lowered his voice, "No, I did not pass him. I had to take a roundabout way back to the Infirmary. I had another confrontation with Barrius, I wanted to make sure he was not going to follow me back here."

"I saw Mr. Barrius," chimed in Mark, but his tone grew darker as he proceeded, "or I heard him. He dropped me on my leg." Mark scowled down at the ground and Lucien looked at him, mouth agape. Mark continued, "It was right after I left the Archive. I was coming back here and he grabbed me from behind. He told me to stay away from you, Lucien, and then dropped me on my broken leg, but then a nice lady gave me sweetbread."

"Well, we need to do something about this," resolved Alaric.

"No," Lucien cut him off, "that will only give Barrius and those like him more reason to resent me. We should pay him no mind for the time being; our attention to his threats only gives him power. Alaric, if you can, I would like you to accompany me to the Barracks. I don't know where it is for one, and I would like to know a bit more about the soldiers' training."

Alaric conceded to Lucien's request and the two men started toward the door, Alaric bracing himself on Lucien's shoulder. From behind, Lucien heard the signature thumping of Mark's crutch as he hobbled after them. He turned on his heels and knelt down eye level with Mark. "I think it is best you stay here for now," he said, "to let your leg heal. I will be back along soon to check on you."

Mark scowled and Lucien laughed, twisting upright to return to Alaric's side and offer his shoulder. Alaric braced himself against Lucien and the two men then left the lonesome Mark in hopes of finding Stilguard before continuing to the Barracks.

As fortune favored, the two met Stilguard as he retraced his steps from the Archive to the Infirmary. They greeted him and Lucien apologized for being so elusive, but disclosed nothing about his encounter with Barrius. Together then, they continued to the Barracks for Lucien to be introduced to the soldiers.

"General Nestor and I have assessed the toll that our Nephilim offensive has taken upon our military force," Stilguard explained as they walked. "Thirty-three trained soldiers now remain in Adullam, and twenty-five or so have been recruited in the two weeks since the battle. A few men are changing professions to help fill the vacancies, but most are young still, and fresh; haven't even begun their compulsory training."

"Good," Lucien said quietly, nodding. "It's what we need."

They passed through a labyrinth of corridors and a host of passersby, each with their own sentiment towards Lucien. In some faces he read indifference, in some, questioning, some contentment, but overwhelmingly there was concern. Whether Stilguard was aware, Lucien could not tell, but every concerned glance that fell against Lucien would for an instant dart to the Steward. Narrowing eyes, heavy breaths, rigid faces, somber steps – all the traitors of each man's secret suspicions. Lucien straightened his coat.

Just at the end of the corridor, the Barracks came into view. Footsteps echoed towards them from inside. Out of the doorway stepped a man whom Lucien at first mistook as Barrius. The man took an undecided step, frozen for the blink of an eye in the face of their approach. He ducked his head, eyes trained on the Steward's feet. He was fitter than Barrius, younger, handsomer; his eyes blue and his head a mane of silver and white. As he neared, he picked his gaze from the ground, slowly raising it to Stilguard's face.

"Titus," the Steward said to him, "is Nestor there?"

"No sir, he is not," Titus replied, coming to attention. "I'm not sure where he is, in fact. Is there something I can help you with, sir?"

"No. Thank you, Titus, you may be on your way but if you see Nestor, tell him I wish to speak with him and that he can find me either here or in the Steward's Hall."

"I can do that, sir," Titus replied, giving a polite bow. "Anything I should explain to him about your presence down here, or is it of no concern?"

"Of no concern to him at the moment, but we will talk."

"Yes sir," he gave another bow and, glancing back at Lucien, walked past them to go and prepare for his meeting with Nestor and Barrius.

After Titus was gone, the three men walked on into the Barracks. Stilguard stopped just past the entrance and let Lucien wander out onto the training floor. The usual ground covering was pushed up against the wall and Lucien could see dark spots on the floor where men's blood had soaked through the covering and into the earth, staining Adullam.

"It's larger than I thought it would be. And it seems you do some proper training here," Lucien said, drawing his foot over the bloodstained floor and smiling over at Alaric. "This your blood?"

Alaric wheezed out a laugh as he stood bracing himself against a wall, "Not mine, I've lost too much in the last several days to waste it on the training floor."

Lucien smiled, looking down at the blood, and continued to wipe his foot across it.

"I do not yet know if I can entrust you with my soldiers," Stilguard finally said, "nor do I know if Nestor will allow it. I will speak with him this afternoon, and have a decision for you tomorrow – midmorning. That is what I can offer you at this time. How many soldiers would you want?"

"No more than twelve. I would take the younger, less experienced ones, as well as the new enlistments. Your trained force would suffer no loss, and the men I take would be solely yours rather than Nestor's."

"I will think hard on this. You have been helpful to us, Lucien. Know that if I cannot concede it is because I think it best for Adullam and that it is not because I hold anything against you."

"I understand, sire," Lucien said with a short bow.

"I'm not royalty, Lucien. Be at your leisure to continue looking around. I must go make ready to meet with Nestor."

CHAPTER VI

WITHOUT MADNESS…

Stilguard walked, focused on each step, yet his path was the furthest thing from his mind. He appeared to move with great purpose but, so often as movement betrays (if not to others, to ourselves) he had no direction. He wandered aimlessly through the stone corridors. He liked the sound of his footsteps reverberating along an empty tunnel. The rhythm of his step and the solitude it embodied through its echo cleared his mind – set him thinking straight. Shortly, he would have to confront Nestor.

His aimlessness at length led him to the Archive. From within, a faint light glimmered against the empty corridor wall. Stilguard smiled softly at the sound of rustling papers as Bryan sifted through the age-eaten records. Stilguard stepped softly through the door, observing Bryan's bustling in contented silence.

The old man gathered a stack of scrolls and stray sheets from beneath the desk. He bundled them in his arms and tiptoed around the maze of clutter on the ground.

"Bryan," Stilguard called as he strolled further into the Archive.

The old man poked his head out between the twin mountains of paper in his arms.

"Ah, Roderick!" came his delighted response, "what brings you to my world?"

"Philosophize with me, Bryan," Stilguard said, reaching out to save some of the scrolls falling over Bryan's shoulders.

"And what shall it be today, my Steward?" Bryan said, a youthful gaiety springing off his tongue. He took a large sidestep behind one of the shelves and dropped his load on the ground. Wiping the dust off his vest, he came inching back around to the shelf, pulling up an extra chair for Stilguard. He sneezed and let the feeling wriggle down his body before wiping away the last bit of dust from beneath his nose. "So," he said, motioning for Stilguard to sit.

"Madness versus reason," Stilguard said, sliding gently into his seat.

With an exasperated sigh, Bryan collapsed against the rickety backboard of his chair, cracking a splinter from the frame and shooting it across the Archive.

"Maybe it's time for a new one." Stilguard said, straying his eyes along the crack in the chair.

"No, no. This chair's been here as long as I have. First you replace the chair, next thing you know you're replacing me." He swished his jaw around as if he were tasting something sour. "Antique is a mark of quality."

Stilguard gave Bryan a guarded smile, shying his eyes away to the floor.

"What is it you've got on your mind, exactly?" Bryan asked, his tone turned serious.

"You've met Lucien?" Stilguard asked, looking up.

Bryan nodded thoughtfully, sitting himself straighter in his chair.

"And?"

"Mad."

Stilguard laughed.

"But with a brilliant eccentricity," Bryan said leaning purposefully forward. "It's almost intangible."

"Would you trust him?"

Bryan shrugged, leaning back again. "I'm not the Steward."

Stilguard smiled out of the corner of his mouth, nodding his head consentingly. "See that's just it," he began. "It's that eccentric spark that boasts something different, something I think can either destroy or redeem Adullam." He laughed. Bryan waited thoughtfully. "Our people are wasting away, the change in them is subtle, but once they realize their own end as I've seen it, there'll be no saving them.

"And the uncertainty that swirls around Lucien makes trusting him sound ridiculous," Stilguard continued. "Why trust someone who could bring ruin to Adullam? But there's the madness of it: if the course of things isn't altered, the people here will die – slowly, but eventually – of that I'm certain. And with Lucien, well, there's the likely chance we'll die a lot sooner, but at least it's only chance, not certainty."

Bryan crossed his arms, watching Stilguard search the ether for answers. "What's given him so much power in your eyes, Roderick?"

"I think he knows, Bryan. Lucien knows he can become the fulcrum on which the fate of Adullam is balanced. It's what allows him to be as bold as he is. But how can a man step into an unknown place and at once knows that he holds its future?"

"Perhaps," Bryan breathed, lifting his eyes contemplatively to the frame of the Archive's doorway, "a spark of the divine?"

"The Shaddai?" Stilguard asked hesitantly.

Bryan nodded his head carefully, bringing his eyes level again with the Steward's.

"I won't let mysticism cloud my better reason."

"Mysticism or faith – two ways to see it," Bryan said, a grandfatherly arch in his head.

"You think he's a prophet?" Stilguard asked, almost unwilling to accept the words coming from his mouth.

"I think he'll do what prophets have always done: challenge the way of things. Hasn't he already?"

"Is that enough?" Stilguard cried, his stoic temper fraying. "There's no reason in it, no rationale."

"Trust requires sacrifice," Bryan calmly replied.

"It's maddening," Stilguard sighed.

"Madness versus reason. Here we are philosophizing," Bryan said, coaxing a faint smile from Stilguard. "And while we're here, I'll posit you this: without madness is no progression."

Stilguard's eyes darkened in question.

Bryan sat abruptly up from the back of his chair, lifting his hands in demonstration. "Just as darkness is a term given to the absence of light, we can say madness is what defines action absent of reason."

Stilguard nodded slightly.

"By being absent of rational understanding," Bryan continued, "madness opens up another world of possibilities to us. Reason is but a sustainer. Without madness, there is no progression."

"I don't see it."

"Think about it in terms of good and evil then," Bryan said, the pitch of his voice wizened with exclamation. "What is goodness without evil? They're counterparts; when you take one out, the other has no meaning. It takes some evil in the world to lead us to what's good."

"And it takes some madness to lead us to what's rational," Stilguard said, his eyes lost in their ethereal search again.

Bryan smiled beneath the crook of his nose. "Without madness to some degree, we're stagnate; not all things can be accounted for by the principles of reason."

"Then by reason alone, life averages out through its ups and downs; yet, all I can think about is indifference – a gradual decline into indifference," Stilguard said, closing his eyes and shaking his head. "But madness. Madness creates, madness propels... What is – what is madness?!" he cried, pushing off his knees.

"Madness is trust," Bryan pleasantly returned. "Madness is faith. Madness is believing in the impossible, Roderick – madness is saving Adullam. You already know what you need to do," he said, his voice a paradigm of reassurance. "You'd decided it before you walked into my Archives."

"Trust Lucien." Stilguard said bluntly.

"If that is the Steward's decision."

A quick grin parted Stilguard's lips before he spoke. "As always you have been a most obliging mentor, Bryan."

"I do what I can to serve my Steward, sir."

Stilguard stood, clasping Bryan's right hand between his two. With a slight bow of his shoulders, he released his grip and walked purposefully out of the Archive. Making an abrupt left, Stilguard disappeared into the darkened corridor. He navigated the narrow passages expertly, sliding his hands along the damp walls as he tread forward, feeling Adullam, binding with the elemental course that had brought about its creation, and preparing for the uncertain course that would ensure its progression.

As he entered the Market District, Stilguard glimpsed the bald of Nestor's head wading through the crowds towards the Steward's Hall.

Stilguard livened his pace to catch up with the General, gaining him in the wide tunnel that led to the Steward's Hall. Hearing the approach of determined steps, Nestor glanced over his shoulder. Seeing Stilguard, he paused, eyes a-gloom, to wait for his Steward.

The air between them filled with a bitter dissonance. "Titus found you then, did he?" Stilguard asked.

"He did."

"Good, we shall talk in private."

Nothing more was said until they had entered the Steward's Hall. Nestor walked first into the room, heaving open the heavy doors and leaving them ajar as he passed. Stilguard followed and sealed the room shut behind them. Arms crossed, Nestor stood firmly to the other side of the fire in the center of the hall as if to play Steward, awaiting a disloyal servant. Flames whipped round his chest and shoulders, tempering his unyielding resolve.

"It seems as if Titus relayed his expectations for our impending conversation," Stilguard said, stepping to the other side of the fire.

Nestor remained silent and the Steward stared steadily into the silence before speaking again.

"We've been friends for a long time Marcus, don't let the strain of the last two weeks come between us."

"Oh, it's less of that," Nestor said; his tongue flickered distastefully over his lips. "More to do with this harlequin character you've got parading around."

"Lucien?" Stilguard asked, folding his arms to mirror Nestor's stance.

Nestor rocked his head slowly, lips pursed with ill content.

"He's done no harm…"

"Who knows what he's capable of doing, Roderick!" Nestor flailed his arms above his head. "How can you trust him? How could you have sent me away? After the things at our first meeting…" The coarseness of Nestor's voice scratched the air like a tiger's growl.

"Adullam is on a path to ruin, Marcus. Don't let your wounded pride cloud your judgment."

"Then don't let your desperation cloud yours!" he replied, circling the fire to storm out of the Steward's Hall.

"Marcus!" Stilguard called after him, leveling his tone.

Nestor stopped short of the doors.

"I am going to allow Lucien to take no more than twelve of your soldiers."

The General remained silent; Stilguard could see his shoulder's rise with each breath.

"He will only be allowed to pull from the fresh recruits, the young soldiers who have only begun their training or the others who have just reenlisted with you; they have not yet been in training for two weeks. With such a small force I know I am taking a lot from you but these men will still be soldiers, only subject to a different command – ultimately my command, and not Lucien's. I am doing this for Adullam, not for Lucien. I do not want you to feel as though I am robbing you of your position as my counsel or my general. Your place is no less important now than before. In truth, everyone's position is about to be elevated, especially your own. The purpose of things is about to be altered. Have you anything to say?"

"I have nothing."

Stilguard opened his mouth to speak but turned back to the fire instead, blinking his eyes against the sting of its heat. Faint in his ears came the sound Nestor's footsteps fading towards the back of the room, the grind of the doors' opening and the groan of their close.

"Kalit," Stilguard called for his attendant. A boy came rushing to the Steward's side from an adjacent room. "I need for you to gather the Trade Lords; tell them to meet with me here in an hour from now."

The boy bowed low and scurried out of the room without a word.

An hour later, the twelve Traders had assembled before Stilguard in the Steward's Hall. They sat around a large oval table with Stilguard positioned at the head. A large pot of tea was the centerpiece and each man had a steaming cup set before him. Stilguard was quietly talking to Bryan Rutherford who had been commissioned with transcribing the decisions made at the meeting. Some of the Traders conversed with one another; others set out paper and ink with which to follow the discussion and record their thoughts.

Stilguard called for order once he had finished instructing Bryan. The room fell silent and all ears where attentive to their Steward.

"I do not need to tell you why I have called this meeting; it will be evident to all of you. Many of you may be wondering why I have delayed this for so long and unfortunately I have no good reason. My apology goes out to you as well as to all the people of Adullam. Action is now crucial. What are our store levels?"

A voice from the council called out, "We are at ten percent of storage capacity; at current ration rates food will run dry in one week's time."

"Our stores have never been so low," Stilguard continued. "Our people are on the brink of starvation and it is time we do something."

"The time to do something was weeks ago, we have not received shipment from Bristing in thirty-two days."

"We have lost contact with Bristing," Stilguard continued. "Our couriers stopped corresponding just before production stopped. Scouting operations to assess the issue have been carried out; the scouts, on all three operations, have not returned. As you all know it is not unusual to experience a two-week period with no shipments. Intensive investigation thereafter was thwarted by our military operation against the Nephilim front – the result of which we are all aware, but a result that halted any extensive investigation until now.

"So that is the reason we have made no iron shipments in the past month?"

"Yes, we wanted a military inspection before we jeopardized our trading assets or presented an observable route by which Aureus could trace you back to Adullam."

"Now we see the reason!"

"Stilguard, you should have brought this to our attention sooner; it would have done a lot to soothe our apprehension."

"I do apologize," Stilguard said, "these have been difficult weeks for me."

"Difficult weeks for us all," one of the Trade Lords remarked. "We thought you were losing your head, Steward."

A nervous laughter filtered the air; Stilguard smiled at the comment as he sipped his tea. "Well, I was sure I was losing it, too," he said.

The laughter picked up again, relieved of previous apprehensions. Once they had all settled back to attention, Stilguard continued with his proposal.

"Now that the timing is so crucial, we will send out military personnel to determine what must be done. I would like perhaps six of you to join the operation to help assess the situation. No need to volunteer quite yet, I will plan for this in two days' time.

"Bryan, draft an edict for Nestor directing him to plan a large scale scouting operation, notify him of the timing, tell him there will be six traders in escort, and allow him the liberty of deciding upon the best course of action."

"Yes sir, this is to be delivered as soon as possible?"

"Yes."

"And is there anything else you would require of me at this time, sir?"

"That is all, thank you, Bryan. Any questions or proposals?"

"Yes," a voice addressed Stilguard. "In what condition do you expect to find Bristing?"

"To be honest, I don't know."

"Considering our scouts have not returned from three separate occasions over a period of a month, it must be Aureus," spoke a concerned voice.

"Such is my fear," Stilguard replied, "though it is impossible to be sure until we have investigated, which is my reasoning to bring six of you. You all have frequented Bristing, you know the location and the people and can help draw up the proper course of action regardless of the situation we find."

"Obviously, there will be risk involved?"

"I don't want to lie to you," Stilguard shrugged, his exhaustion all too evident.

The room was quiet then for a moment as the Trade Lords processed all that had been said. Many of them looked back over their notes, others stared blankly into empty teacups. All of this was an attempt to avoid eye contact as if, once two pairs of eyes met, the inevitable truth would spill out and no one could pretend any longer that this was some common issue. The Steward's eyes, however, wandered across the table and to the faces of each man present. He watched then as Bryan left with the official edict to be delivered to Nestor.

As soon as the door closed behind him one of the Traders spoke, lifting his eyes from a dazed stare into his tea. "The fate of Adullam lies in this," he said, and all pretense was shattered as the weight fell upon them.

No man moved; no man breathed; but, in each of them, there was a transformation. They seemed to age, as their eyes grew heavy. This one sentence of fate had immobilized those from whom mobility was expected. It was their own humanity that set in upon them now. They were no longer the revered Trade Lords of Adullam, but human and fearful. It was there that each, in his own way, realized that it was not their identity that founded their humanity, but their humanity that founded their identity; that beyond all else, they were subject to human nature, and it was the triumph over that nature which would allow them to do what was necessary for a common good among their people. It was those who were able to accept this course of reasoning that could step beyond the reasoning that compelled them not to volunteer and accept the madness of knowing they could be facing Aureus, thus a fate worse than death. It was they who, without further consideration, submitted themselves to Stilguard's plan. One by one they accepted, until at last six men embraced the inevitable knowledge that in two days' time they would perhaps never see this place again.

Stilguard commended those who had responded to his need so quickly and dismissed the Traders to be alone with his thoughts. He sank his head to the table in exhaustion, not just out of physical weariness, but his mind and his spirit too were plagued by burden beyond his ability to bear. He lifted a prayer up to the heavens and was answered by sleep, wrapped in a blanket of blissful unawareness that melted his concerns like wax. How long he slept, he did not know, but when he at last awoke the fire had dwindled to glowing embers and he was enveloped in darkness.

* * *

By this time Alaric and Lucien had returned to the Medical Wing as Lucien had insisted upon redressing Alaric's wounds. He wanted to check for infection and lend some more instruction to the other medics in the Infirmary.

Mark was overjoyed by their return, exclaiming they had been away for far too long and left him with nothing to do and, in a very grave tone, informed them that none of the other doctors would play with him. Alaric laughed and Lucien apologized but told Mark he could watch as he treated Alaric's wounds and learn how to check for infections. Shortly after, Lucien began treating Alaric and explaining to an enthralled Mark how to properly bandage a wound. He inspected all of Alaric's wounds, found no infection, called for a doctor to bring fresh bandages and assured Alaric that everything was healing nicely; he was nearly fit to leave the Infirmary.

Lucien left Mark and Alaric for a time and went to go check on some of the other patients. Many who had been in beds earlier in the morning were now gone, and Lucien noticed a new patient, covered in dirt, lying in one of the rooms next to Mark's. One of the doctors informed Lucien that the man had been in a mining accident earlier that morning. Lucien went over to him and inspected the work the doctors had done. The patient had some large bruises and a few minor cuts, his right arm and collarbone were broken, but the bones had been set and tended to properly. The man was still unconscious; so Lucien began cleaning him up a bit, removing dirt from inside and around his lacerations. There was no bleeding and Lucien figured that with the dirt removed, the man's own immune system could fight off any infection well enough.

After making a round through the Medical Wing, checking on patients and doctors, Lucien went back toward his room to read until he fell asleep. As he walked into the next room, he was perturbed to see the back of a young woman standing over Mark's bed and Alaric, eyes filled with boyish adoration, gazing longingly at her. The young woman tickled Mark's side and the boy keeled over with delight, spotting Lucien through mirth-slitted eyes.

"Lucien!" he cried through his laughter, and the young woman turned to see whom the boy addressed. The cheerful color in her face drained at the sight of the approaching olive-skinned, masked figure.

Witnessing the stark change in her expression, Lucien looked darkly at Alaric.

"Lucien," Alaric wrenched himself from his daze and circled Mark's bed to greet his friend, "this is Alyssa. She's the one who brought Mark back from the tunnel the other day," he said, hoping to use Mark as a common interest between them.

"A pleasure," Lucien said and extended his hand.

Alyssa smiled curtly and reached slowly to grasp Mark's hand rather than accept Lucien's. Lucien drew his hand away and folded it behind his back.

"Thank you for bringing him back to me," he said. "It would have been terrible for the boy to have been lost in the darkness for too long.

Such trauma has a way of permanently molding young minds for the worse."

"Oh, I can think of a thing or two more traumatic," she said, allowing her eyes to wander expressively over Lucien.

"Well, I think it fair enough to say the boy has had a traumatic few days. He could use a good night's rest. The last thing he needs now is suffer from exhaustion; it wouldn't do to have a nightmare looming over him whilst he sleeps." A broad smile colored the unmasked side of Lucien's face as he spoke. "It was lovely to make your acquaintance, madam."

The ice of Alyssa's gaze melted beneath the warmth of Lucien's farewell. Exacting revenge on Lucien's feigned courtesy, she glided to Alaric's side.

"It was good to see you again, Captain," she said, kissing him lightly on the cheek. She watched the color drain from Lucien's face and with a sly grace moved from Alaric's hip around to Mark's bed. Softly stroking the boy's hair she said goodnight and tucked him under his blanket before taking leave of the Infirmary, her sensual form accented by the flickering torchlight as she departed.

Alaric's face was hot, fervent from the touch of her skin, and his mouth dry as a desert.

Lucien stared contemptuously at him, the pigment of his skin as deathly as his expression. "Soft lips hide sharp teeth," he said in a harsh whisper. His hands were shaking and dark lines formed beneath his eye. "I need to go take blood samples."

He promptly left the room and Alaric started to follow but was stopped by the sound of Mark's voice from beneath his blanket, "She's nice, isn't she?"

"What?" Alaric said, turning from his pursuit.

Mark, who had shifted himself entirely under his blanket popped up from beneath it to be properly heard. "Miss Alyssa. She's nice, isn't she?"

A shy smile spread across Alaric's face, and his eyes cast off their guilt-ridden glow. Before he could speak, Lucien strode back in, his color very much back to normal and the sour tint beneath his eye, gone.

"Finished already?" Alaric asked.

"The task can wait for the morning. It would be unprofessional of me to wake the patients for something as trivial as blood samples."

"Your lip is bleeding." Alaric said, stepping forward; Lucien retreated, quickly wiping up the trickle of blood from his chin, drawing a sharp breath as its aroma passed his nose.

"Thank you," Lucien said, dabbing his bottom lip with his forefinger. "You should both get some rest now; it will help you heal. I will see you in the morning."

Lucien retired to his quarters and was setting about petty matters before sitting to read himself to sleep. He had just sat down to begin his book when he heard a soft knock at his door. Shortly following the sound was Mark's head as he cracked the door open to see inside. "Are you reading?" he asked quietly, seeing a book in Lucien's hand.

Lucien responded with the obvious, "Yes."

"I was hoping maybe you could read to me then – Mr. Alaric is asleep and it's lonely." The boy made a very exaggeratedly sorrowful face, trying to incite pity into Lucien's heart.

Fighting back laughter at the boy's all too apparent misfortune, Lucien gripped Mark's shoulder and with a smile led him back to his bed. He lit a candle on the nightstand and began to read, and it was not long before Mark was sound asleep. Lucien decided to follow suit and retired to his own quarters. He undressed and lay down to sleep. *Blood on my lips*, he thought, cradled in the absolute darkness of his room. *I've been careless.*

* * *

It was midmorning when Stilguard and Alaric arrived to collect Lucien. He was tending to patients, assisted by Mark who hobbled after him carrying bandages and absorbing everything he said. Hearing Stilguard chuckle at the sight, Lucien turned from his work to greet the two approaching men.

"Good morning, how can I be of service?" Lucien asked, nudging Mark to attention.

"I have spoken with Nestor," Stilguard promptly responded. "He will give you twelve soldiers."

"And I will remain with you," Alaric spoke, "to aid in training and help legitimize your new position."

"We've come to take you to the Barracks so you can make your selection," Stilguard continued, "unless you are too busy to take leave."

"No, not at all," Lucien exclaimed, his face aglow. "I'm just fulfilling routine work; anyone else can take care of it. Brancott," he called, "I would like for you to continue with this. Mark has the bandages and can get anything else you need. Would you like to do that Mark?"

"Mhmm, I can help Mr. Brancott," Mark replied, happy to be doing anything – especially at Lucien's request.

"Thank you, Mark, you've been very helpful."

The boy bobbed his head in a very official nod and turned back to the patient to resume his duties. With this, Lucien was free to carry on and in a matter of moments, he, Alaric, and Stilguard were on their way to the Barracks.

Their arrival was heralded by the recruits' shouts echoing down the stone corridors. As the three men stepped onto the padded training ground, the shouting stopped and the recruits stood at attention. Overseeing them stood Nestor with his arms crossed and back turned to the entrance of the Barracks. The sudden repose of his soldiers alerted the General of Stilguard's encroaching presence. He nodded at his men to continue their training as if to ignore the Steward's arrival, but slowly deigned to face his guests. He looked sourly at Lucien before passing his attention to Stilguard.

"Nestor," the Steward said, "allow us some time with the soldiers; you may take thirty minutes leave and, when you return, designate one of these side rooms for Lucien and Alaric to work."

Nestor nodded and pushed his way between Stilguard and Lucien. From the back of the room, Titus followed Nestor with his eyes until he disappeared through the exit. A grave determination shadowed his face as his livid gaze fell then on the Steward. Soon, he knew, there would be weighty matters to discuss.

"They're young," Lucien whispered as soon as the General had left. "So young."

If Alaric or Stilguard heard him, they decided not to show it; Lucien stepped forward, surveying the soldiers with his arms crossed tightly behind his back and his brow bent sternly above his eye. He watched them for several minutes. Circling the floor, he stepped with languid exaggeration, assessing each soldier's individual qualities as Alaric and Stilguard quietly observed from a distance. Lucien took a final turn around the training floor and raised his arms to address the men. "Everyone –

soldiers, let me have your attention." He paused to allow the room to settle. "I am here by Stilguard's orders to select an elite few of you for a *distinctive* type of training, to fight Nephilim. Nestor has no part in this, so those of you whom I choose should not consult him on matters concerning tactics or allegiances. If you train with me, your allegiance is to Stilguard and he alone."

Having said this, Lucien moved in among their ranks and selected twelve of the seventy or so men present. He pulled them away from the rest of the soldiers and had them form a circle. Joining them, he whispered a question, "Are you all new recruits or are any of you Nestor's old men?"

"I have been under Nestor for five years," one of the men volunteered.

Lucien nodded and asked, "Anyone else? I must know." No one else said a word and Lucien addressed the man who had spoken, "I need for you to leave then please, join the others. I cannot trust you to serve two masters."

The soldier looked at Lucien confusedly but he simply shook his head.

"Please, leave," Lucien repeated.

The soldier backed away and the eleven remaining men tightened the circle to fill his gap. Lucien looked deep into their eyes as he spoke, "I have chosen you eleven for three simple reasons. First, you are the most agile and nimble fighters of the lot. Second, none of you are highly skilled. To you, that quality or rather lack of quality, may seem an unorthodox criteria, but I assure you it is well reasoned. Finally, you are all new soldiery owing nothing to Nestor. As I said before, you will no longer be serving under his rank."

"Wait!" a soldier cried from outside the circle, stepping up to confront Lucien. "How can you do this? How can you just take these men, clearly without General Nestor's approval?"

Lucien pushed through his circle to confront the soldier, but Stilguard spoke before Lucien had the chance to answer. "Nestor is not a part of this. This is my personal operation. The General may not approve but he has consented and it is not your place to question."

"Captain Folck," another of Nestor's men pleaded, "is this right?"

Alaric was frozen on the spot, his mouth agape in hopes an answer would spill out on its own.

"Are you with them?" the man asked again. A clear murmur of bewilderment echoed his question as Nestor's men began to talk amongst themselves. Titus pushed his way through their conversation and stepped to the front of the crowd.

"Captain Folck," he announced, quieting the room, "will be facilitating these men's training. Am I right, Alaric?"

Alaric's shoulders arched instinctively. "I will be ensuring that these men's training meets the proper standards," Alaric responded to the questioning glares. "Your *Steward* has requested this of me and, as a citizen of Adullam, it is my duty to comply." His livid eyes locked with the smug expression lighting Titus' face.

"Captain," Stilguard addressed Titus from behind Alaric, "continue with your men's training. We'll move to the Steward's Hall for now."

Titus nodded, whistling to the soldiers to get back to work and, as he turned to oversee them, Lucien caught the glimpse of a crooked smile creasing his lips. Burying the hint of insurrection within himself, Lucien stepped backwards from the training room and beckoned his recruits to follow. He and his eleven, along with Alaric and Stilguard, left the Barracks, making their way for the Steward's Hall. None spoke until they all were locked safely behind its heavy doors.

"Gentlemen," Lucien began, "welcome to your first day as Adullam's *Elite Guard*. This meeting will serve primarily as an orientation. Over the next few weeks I will break you in order that you can be built back as new men, able to think beyond the grasps of a common warrior. I will teach you the fundamentals of deception and illusion; above fighters, you will be thinkers, able to manipulate your environment to your advantage and to *act* – with forethought – rather than simply *re*act.

"Let me be clear, you are no longer Nestor's men. You belong to your Steward and to him alone. You are not to discuss your training with anyone outside of this circle, especially the other soldiers. Remind them, whenever they confront you, that you are working for what is best for Adullam, just as they ought to be as well."

This said, their training commenced, stretching late into the night. After an exhaustive initiating session, the men at last took leave of the Steward's Hall. As the last man left, Stilguard remained behind, frowning into the embers of a dying fire, contemplating the rapid unfolding of events that had given Lucien so much influence over his people. He had all but dismissed Nestor from his council. The commoners grew restless in the shadow of defeat, and food was in as short supply as ever. An immense weight descended upon Stilguard, wrapping around him like a small child clinging to a father's neck, trying not to fall. The father is stifled by the child's grip but dares not break free for fear of losing what he loves, for fear of losing his invested dreams. So, like a father, Stilguard bore the burden silently, though the life of him was being choked out.

As the fire finally died out, so too did the Steward's silent resolve. He let the weight of his worry crush him as he collapsed to his knees, leaning in close to the fire's ashes to draw the last of their warmth. At length, he picked himself up from the ground and groped through the darkness to find his way to his private quarters. When at last he stumbled into his room, he could hear his wife's peaceful breathing. He made no effort to keep from waking her. Following the sound of her sleep, he found the bed and lay down in the folds of his quilt. Unrest, though, plagued his mind and kept his eyes from closing; he could do naught but stare into the blank ceiling, contemplating his people's future. For as far as he could see, only darkness and uncertainty lay ahead. Doubt plagued him, and fear fed off his own iniquity – his condemnation of Nestor.

He rolled onto his side and looked at his wife through the darkness in envy of her peace. The thought he had to burden her with his troubles faltered as he gently brushed the hair out of her face. He wanted desperately to smile. Stilguard rested his hand on his wife's shoulder and shook her gently, whispered her name. Joanna's lip curled into a scowl as she tried to turn away, but Stilguard's grip hardened on her shoulder. She groaned softly and at length blinked open reticent eyes.

"Hello," her tired voice uttered through the darkness, "what is it, what's the matter?" She could feel the insistence in her husband's presence.

Stilguard lay on his back and gazed into the blackness above. "I'm sorry, I didn't want to wake you but I'm," he sighed, begrudging his own weakness, "overwhelmed." Joanna's eyes grew wide, adjusting to the darkness and bearing the tenderness in her heart for her husband's confession.

Stilguard held his absent gaze upwards and continued to speak. "I dismissed Nestor today for the counsel of a complete stranger. My General, for a stranger. We've not hosted him in Adullam for two weeks yet and already I've allowed this man to serve as a top physician in the Medical

Wing and sought his counsel above my people's." Stilguard stuttered and recalculated his words, "And, I've let him begin training soldiers – supposedly answerable to me, but I don't know how I've let this happen; I don't know what to do anymore.

"I feel," he swallowed, "distant from my people. They've begun to resent me, I can feel it. The realization of our defeat two weeks ago is sinking in. Food is short – supply lines severed. We haven't heard a word from our scouts to Bristing in over a month. Adullam has stood for a hundred and fifty years; the people have been resilient, but I know their spirit is waning. They grow discontent with this place – with my leadership. Will it be in my generation that we fail? Am I not fit for the challenge as my father and his father before him were? Can I not lead as they led?" The Steward's words were filled with a manic unrest. "I fear this mantle is beyond me to bear." He released a long sigh and tried to blink the enveloping exhaustion out of his eyes.

Joanna smiled, her lips stretched soft with contentment and yet concern – with warmth and compassion and understanding. For the sake of her husband and Steward, she sat for a long time in quiet contemplation.

"My father used to say," Stilguard continued after a bout of silence, "'the art of desperation is manifold in the lives of the weak.' I never paid attention to what that meant. I thought he was just trying to seem wise, calling desperation an art. But now I see it. Art is merely the image of inspiration, and a desperate mind will draw from any inspiration. Thus, the end of such acts of desperation are," he paused, drowning in palpable sickness, "manifold; innumerable. And my actions are my art, the image of my inspiration, which have come – without consideration, without consultation – from anything with potential. But of course I cannot help but see potential in everything. Things here have just been so," he laughed at the irony, "desperate. And thus my father's statement is made true. I... I don't know."

Stilguard half expected not to receive an answer; he had awakened Joanna just to have his concerns heard. The silence following his words did not fill him with apprehension; he was lost in his thoughts. Nevertheless, after some time, Joanna responded. She moved in close to Stilguard, laying her head on his shoulder and moving her hand to his chest. She looked off into the darkness with him first and then slowly tilted her head back to stretch her eyes up to his face.

She spoke softly, "Don't be discouraged. You are as great a man as your father, and even his father. Your people love you, Roderick. The Stilguards have long been a blessing on this place. You are wiser than anyone I have ever known, so, as for this stranger – trust yourself. Your own counsel is better than anyone can give you. I spoke with Bryan today; he said you performed marvelously yesterday during your meeting with the Trade Lords; tomorrow you can further organize them. Hearing from you will give them all the encouragement they need to get the job done. Tonight, rest easy, don't worry about Nestor, he is still loyal to you. He is still a pivotal part of all that is done in Adullam; perhaps remind him. He hasn't lost any of his authority. He can suffer an aid to your leadership.

"I love you," she said to conclude her comforting, and pulled his grizzled face close to her own, kissing him on the cheek. She turned back and lay on her side, facing away from him. She smiled again to herself as she closed her eyes and her smile widened upon feeling her husband's breath in her ear and the reach of his arm around her waist. The two fell fast asleep together and did not stir until morning.

CHAPTER VII

SLEEPLESS

Mark did not sleep so soundly that night. At some early hour of the morning his leg began to throb with the rhythm of his heart and he awoke with tears already streaking his fleshy cheeks. Rolling out of bed, he hobbled through the dark Infirmary in search of Lucien. Shadows cast by a lone torch pranced along the walls, and Mark could almost hear the shadows' wicked laughter as they chased around him, mocking his tears.

At last, after following the walls of the Medical Wing round and round, he found the right corridor leading to Lucien's quarters. His room was at the end of a short hall, divided from the Medical Wing by a thin wooden door.

Leaning softly against the door, Mark began to let it creak open against his weight. He poked his head into the room to make sure Lucien was still sleeping soundly before he pushed the door a little further with his fingertips. Squeezing the rest of his body between the door and the frame, Mark took a large, unbalanced step into the room to crown the success of his discreet entrance. As he slid the last toe of his broken leg through the entrance, however, the door slammed shut behind him with a loud crash. Mark squealed and Lucien bolted upright in his bed, a scepter held aloft in his right hand. Patterned veins of gold wove along its grip and up to a massive ruby clasped in place by a golden talon at the peak of the armament. Crouching, petrified in the doorway, Mark imagined himself as a rock, hoping he would be convincing enough not to be spotted.

Unfortunately, the embarrassed child was the first thing to catch Lucien's eye. Relief sank him back into the folds of his blankets, and he rested his scepter on the bed, massaging his head between his forefinger and thumb. Looking back at Mark's stone form he said, "I fear there is no hope for you, my boy. Mark, if I were dead you could still have woken me. Is there something wrong?"

Mark made no reply; humiliation riveted him in place.

Lucien smiled and continued, "With a little more faith you may turn yourself into a rock."

How did he know! Mark's head cried, astonished.

"Come now, what's the matter; is your leg hurting?"

With a sobbing gasp the boy's statued pose crumbled to the floor, his eyes spouting out tears like a fountain. "Oh," Lucien exclaimed; his bemusement carried him from the bed to Mark's side. He bent down and gathered Mark up in his arms and his nightshirt fell loose around his neck. Mark grasped the collar with his little hand and nestled in close to Lucien's chest as he was carried back to his cot.

Entering the Infirmary bay, Lucien's gaze fixed itself on the tangle of Alaric's abandoned blankets. He laid Mark next to the Captain's empty cot as his eye scoured the room for any sign of Alaric. None to be found, Lucien returned his attention to Mark. He placed a hand on the boy's forehead to feel his temperature and then, going to the medicine table at the foot of the bed, fixed a draught to ease the pain in his leg and relieve his fever. Lucien crushed some small herbs and mixed them in a water solution. Returning to Mark's side, he gently lifted the boy's head and let him sip at the drink between sobs until he had taken all of it. The two sat in a silence, interrupted only by Mark's periodic, tearful hiccupping. After a minute or so, these subsided and for a short time neither of them made a sound. Mark broke the stillness by turning to Lucien and whispering, "Thank you."

Lucien responded with a smile. Another moment passed and then Lucien asked, "How is your leg?"

"Better," Mark replied weakly. Then he gave Lucien a curious look, "What happened to your face?"

Lucien felt the bandages covering the right side of his face. "I take my mask off when I sleep and just leave the bandages on. I sleep more comfortably that way."

"Oh. I wish I could sleep comfert'bly but my leg hurts too bad. When's it gonna get better, Lucien?"

Lucien pursed his lips to the side and responded, "I should imagine you will be better in a week or so."

Mark frowned down at his lap and groaned. "That's so long," he said, emphasizing his utter dissatisfaction with the healing process.

Lucien smiled and rubbed the sleep from his eye, forcing back a yawn.

"Well, could you tell me a story then?" Mark asked.

"I don't know that I have a story to tell you."

"Sure you do, you're an old man; my dad tells me the best stories and he doesn't even wear a mask!"

Lucien raised his eyebrow in contemplation of the absurd idea that because he wore a mask he must surely be a more qualified storyteller. This however made perfect sense to the mind of seven year old Mark who could find no better reason to wear a mask than to display the status of a first-rate raconteur.

Lucien fumbled for words.

"Oh! You aren't wearing your mask right now," Mark exclaimed in a sudden revelation. "Of course you can't tell me a good story. It's okay, do you want me to tell you my favorite story and then, when you have your mask on again, you can tell me one of yours?"

Lucien forced down a chuckle, trying not to offend the sympathy that Mark had extended to him and his current lack of storytelling prowess. "I would be honored to hear your favorite story," Lucien replied.

Mark beamed and sat up straighter to begin. He told a perfectly memorized narration about a young boy who lived on a farm with his father and mother and a little dog named Phillip. "On the farm," Mark recited, "the family grew all sorts of things to eat whenever they wanted and all they had to do was pull it off of trees or find it sitting on the ground. The little boy had friends too, a lot of them, and he would play with his friends and share food with them. They ran through huge fields of cool grass and climbed in great big trees and any time they fell from a tree, the branches would swoop down and catch them before they hit the ground. The sky was always blue and sunny, and there were never giants or shadows. That's my favorite," Mark concluded the story and let out a long yawn, laying his head back in bed smiling to himself.

Lucien, looking down at his feet asked, "Mark, do you know what grass is?"

Mark rolled his head to the side and gave Lucien a quick, puzzled look, but he was too tired now to be really concerned with the question; he gave Lucien a short, "No," and closed his eyes again. Lucien watched Mark breathe peacefully, tucked away from the neck down in want of sleep. His eye lingered with his thoughts; there were no other boys running round Adullam; there were no trees to climb, no sun to play in, and no fruit to pick. These were things Mark had never known, yet he described them so vibrantly that he must have clung to every one of his father's words, drinking them in with a relentless thirst and hope.

He had spoken as if this farm were from a distant and foreign world, a fantasy. Lucien remembered the vineyards of his childhood, before the Awakening; a world of ubiquitous vibrancy and color. But despite such disaster, there remained some color on the ever resilient earth, enough of it that Lucien would have expected Mark – at the very least – to have seen grass. But realizing grass and sunlight must be otherworldly to some people here; Mark's story began to bring new questions to the forefront of Lucien's mind. Before he could formulate them, however, he heard Mark's faint voice penetrate the silence of his contemplation, "Thanks for listening to my story, Uncle Lucien, don't forget it's your turn next."

"Uncle?" Lucien whispered; suddenly his breath was short.

Mark hummed back affirmatively

"Why did you call me Uncle?"

Mark rolled onto his stomach so the side of his face was smashed into the pillow and his response slightly muffled, "'Cause I never had an uncle, and I think you're a good one."

Lucien's voice shook as he replied, "Well, thank you Mark, I would like that." He felt faint, loathsome. He pulled the blanket a bit higher over Mark's shoulders, his hands trembling. His breath was short-paced and his body ached as he stood to return to his bedroom. He groped for anything tangible in the darkness, completely lost. *I'm blind*, he thought.

Finally returning to his room, he found the table under which he kept his satchel. He struggled to open it, not for the darkness, but for the shaking of his hands. His skin was cold and deathly, hued green with illness. His body felt feverish, frigid; sweat moistened the nape of his neck. After several desperate seconds, Lucien opened his bag and reached in. Slowly he drew out a vial, curled tightly in his fist. He uncorked it, drinking as if enslaved. With the last gulp, he dropped the vial and slumped to the floor, staying there throughout a sleepless night, unwilling to move.

Several hours passed until the pleasant, early morning rustle of the Infirmary aroused Lucien from his doleful respite. He emerged from beneath the table and lit a torch for himself to make ready for his morning duties. Several minutes later, refreshed and eager for distraction from the lonesome prison of his mind, he stepped from his room and into the atrium of the Infirmary precisely as Alaric was returning from his night out. He walked side-by-side with Alyssa, their heads bowed, smiling and whispering jovially of the night's event, neither wanting it to reach its inevitable end. Lucien strode silently across the atrium floor, disregarding the two in their entanglement of affection; though he meant not to intrude, his sudden appearance startled them from their tender moment.

Alyssa tensed and clutched her breast, gasping under her breath. Alaric teased her playfully for her nerves; she smiled but Alaric could see the concern reticent beneath her eyes. "What is it?" he asked, his tone mirroring her disquiet.

"Nothing," she whispered, her gaze distanced to the doorway through which Lucien had disappeared. She felt Alaric's eyes searching her enigmatic front and returned a wide smile, her gaze tempered with endearment. "Thank you for taking me out, Captain, it was lovely."

Warmed by her effervescent glow, Alaric's concern melted away with a puerile grin. "Will you ever use my name?" he asked.

Alyssa's smile twisted into a more thoughtful simper. She shrugged and disengaged her eyes, letting her hand brush against Alaric's as she passed him on her way from the Infirmary. Laughing softly, Alaric shook his head at the ground and waited for the sound of Alyssa's steps to fade from his ears before turning to watch her empty wake.

"My father," Lucien's voice resounded from behind Alaric, disparaging his morning's mirth, "was a vintner and a husband to three wives – each having gotten their comeuppance for chasing after his money; after the death of his third wife, my father decided not to remarry. By then, he knew women as well as he knew his wine. I was twelve when my second stepmother passed. My father sat my brother and me down among the vines of our plantation shortly after that day and said to us, 'You know boys, women are a lot like wine.' And so I will say to you – women are a lot like wine."

Alaric studied Lucien as he leaned, smugly poised, against the doorframe to the sickbay. "How so?"

"They are intoxicating," he aptly returned.

"You don't know her."

"I need not. I know you."

"You've known me for three weeks."

"And you've known her for three days, to which point I would imagine you've noticed the rift between Dearest and myself. Now, this need not be a point of discontent between us – have your little dalliance – but consider my position. Adullam is not a home to me as it is to you, to Mark, to Alyssa, or to anyone else. I am a stranger here and you are the rampart atop which I am safe. With enough wine any man may fancy himself divine, so don't get carried away and be poisoned with drunkenness – don't let her turn you against me."

Sobered by this confrontation, Alaric nodded slowly. "I think I'll take some breakfast. Can I bring you anything?" he asked in a way of apology.

"You can bring something for Mark; he'll be hungry when he wakes."

Lucien receded back into the sickbay. "Training in an hour," his disembodied voice called, and Alaric left for the Market Café hoping to drown his troubled conscious in a crowd of noise.

Alaric arrived at the Market, thankful to find it full of its usual bustle. He waded up to the café through the mess of people clogging the veins between market stands. The café was raised on a slate platform several feet above the rest of the Market. Upon mounting it, Alaric absently surveyed the people below, wistfully hoping to glimpse Alyssa among them. Without such luck, he turned to his more pressing desire: hunger. Most of the intricate, iron wrought tables spread throughout the platform were occupied with dismal faces beset by the murk of helpless angst. In the Infirmary he had been distant from the pains of Adullam – determined to overcome his own; but now, among the people for the first time in weeks,

Alaric could see in lightless eyes that unrest and disillusionment had set in with pervasive effect.

Determined to rise above the wraith hand of fear that would drag him among the rest, with feigned courage, Alaric wove through the maze of iron tables and stone faces to the back the café to buy breakfast. He had just sat down at the bar and was counting out credits, when from the corner of his eye he noticed two familiar figures rise from their table. Alaric looked up into the volatile eyes of General Nestor, behind whom stood his fellow captain, Titus, with every virtue of a loyal dog. Alaric began to stand at attention but the General bade him keep his seat with the wave of his hand.

"Don't bother," he said as he advanced with a certain swagger that carried into the tone of his tongue, "wouldn't want you to exert yourself more than necessary. I know better'n most how physical pain demands mental labor; you must be in a lot'a pain as lately it seems your mentality is all askew."

Alaric tried to speak but was stopped again by a wave of the General's hand.

"Captain, what you did last night was reckless. What you been doin' these past weeks is reckless. Now, I wan'a be certain you aren't forgetting who bred the boy out-a-ya' and raised the man that's inside."

"I'm not sure I know what you mean, General," Alaric said.

"I mean to say that you and I go way back. Hell, I still remember the first day you came to train in my Barracks all those years ago. An' look at ya' now, a Captain of Adullam. My Captain."

Alaric bent his shoulders over the countertop to keep his stomach from rising into his chest. His face was lathered white with a paste of humiliation.

"Taking that girl outside Adullam last night was dangerous..." Nestor said.

Alaric's pale countenance was overcome by a flush of blood to his cheeks. "Excuse me?"

"My cousin," came Titus' voice, "Alyssa." A constrained annoyance whined beneath his breath. Nestor clapped him twice on the back.

"...It's almost as dangerous as your friendship with Lucien."

"Is this some sort of a threat?" Alaric countered. "He is held in the Steward's trust."

"It's not meant to be a threat, it's a reminder. You need to remember who you are, and you need to remember *whose* you are."

"I belong to Stilguard," Alaric whispered, his voice tempered with defiance, "as do you, and as do you, Titus."

"For now. But, before long you'll be back. You'll know where you were meant to be, Captain. I eagerly anticipate that day. Enjoy your breakfast." With a quick twist of his heals, the General was gone, greeting heartily those whose tables he passed on his way from the café. Titus lingered behind and slid to Alaric's side, his elbow propped against the bar-top. His voice made sibilant behind clenched teeth, he whispered, "You watch yourself with my cousin, she has no one left but me."

"Debatable."

Titus grabbed Alaric's arm and wrenched him close. "And watch your mouth," he hissed.

"You watch your hand," Alaric nodded to the vice around his bicep, "and your master – you wouldn't want to lose him; I'm beginning to think you wouldn't know what to do."

"You've no idea what I can do."

"So show me! Show me what you can do. Gnaw off that leash of yours to Nestor before he drags you over the edge."

Titus grimaced and released Alaric's arm. "It's like the General said, 'you need to remember *whose* you are.'"

"That sounds renegade, Titus, you're being reckless."

"Who is the worse, the leader who betrays his people or the man who betrays that leader?"

"Are you seriously asking me? That sounded more like a statement than a question. I hope you're not insinuating that Stilguard has betrayed us."

Titus pushed away from the bar. He stood tall, lifting his shoulders determinedly, though his eyes darkened with dissension. He stepped slowly away from Alaric, "Do not mistake me for a fool, I know my place," he said, "and I know my play," he whispered. Promptly, he turned to pursue Nestor, his every muscle taut. Before returning to his breakfast, Alaric watched Titus sink slowly into the waves of the Market's crowd and disappear.

* * *

"You're nearly late," Lucien said, as Alaric walked briskly back into the Infirmary, Mark's breakfast boxed in his hands.

"Nearly's not."

"Brusque. I imagine Nestor is to be blamed."

"How did you know I spoke with Nestor?"

"Stilguard came to inform me that we had been granted a training room in the Barracks and that he would not be available today. He said that he had spotted you as he was passing through the Market District, taking breakfast with Nestor and another man, Titus."

"I wasn't taking breakfast with them," Alaric corrected with such exasperation he nearly spilled Mark's breakfast across the bed. Mark yelped and grabbed the box from Alaric before he lost the chance to fill his stomach.

Lucien crossed his arms behind his back and cocked his head to the side, looking at Alaric with an inquisitive eye. Mark cocked his head too, mirroring Lucien's inquisition.

"I'm sorry for being short," Alaric cried, looking between them both. His tone grew grave. "Titus was hinting at something. It sounded like Nestor meant to move against Stilguard."

"What's stirred your suspicion?" Lucien asked.

Alaric darted his eyes towards Mark, "Let's walk, we'll be late for training," he said. Lucien nodded and unwound his arms from behind his back, clapping Mark on the leg as he passed towards the door. When the two men had departed to the dark of a corridor, Alaric began again, "Titus asked me who was worse, the leader who betrays his people or the man who betrays that leader. It sounded too personal to have been hypothetical."

"It would be unwise to jump to conclusions at this point; wander not from where the path lay, lest in your wandering, you lose your way."

"I don't know what you mean."

"I mean for you not to follow this conjecture down some tangent that leads you from proper judgment."

"You can't expect me to ignore this."

"Don't ignore it, but don't act on it. Your action could be what justifies a reaction. Nestor is a child who has lost his toys in the dark and is looking for any excuse to steal Stilguard's – assuming there was any weight behind Titus' words."

"So their hope is that we give them a reasonable cause to move against Stilguard?"

"Possibly. They can nearly claim that I'm creating a private army. One misstep from you, Stilguard, or myself and that claim can be complete; they can seize control of Adullam, either masquerading as vanguards of the ideals of Stewardship, or asserting that Stilguard is no longer fit for the position, or both – depends on how smart they are."

Their conversation had led Alaric and Lucien to Adullam's Military Wing. Down the way, the Barracks was visible, men's shadows sparred along its walls and the sound of their crossed swords sang along the adjacent corridor. One shadow stood out among the rest – poised motionless, his stance wide and sturdy – Nestor.

Lucien wondered if all they knew of the General was an image, beset by fire, and passing silently along a wall; if the shadow of the man would ever yield to its full form; if his true nature could be known whilst crowded in the dark of a cave, or if it would take the day to expose him, to call him forth from this Adullam, this eternal night. As they reached the end of the corridor and entered the training room, combat's song fell silent and Nestor's eyes glowed orange by the torches' flame. *No,* Lucien thought, *the daylight would blind their innocent eyes.*

CHAPTER VIII

TOWARDS DAWN

The exchange between Lucien, Alaric and Nestor went without much incident. Each harbored thoughts of betrayal, and none wished them revealed. The Elite Guardsmen took to their training well; Lucien trained them fast and efficiently. While he was able to hone his focus to the task, Alaric's mind wandered as he had been warned against. Titus and Nestor both stood in the next room; Alaric could hear them even through the heavy stone walls. He could not block their shouts from his innermost conscience. He worried; he schemed; he crawled through his every encounter with them, scouring the depths of his recollection on hands and knees, searching for any sign that could set him on a definitive course.

It was not until nearly the end of the day's training that, trying to brighten his mental exhaustion, Alaric's thoughts turned to Alyssa and, in Alyssa, he stumbled upon a possible solution. His mind revitalized by revelation, Alaric contemplated the proper approach to confronting her. At the end of their training session, he tried to make a quick exit, curtly excusing himself and disappearing onto the main Barracks' floor. Lucien followed quietly and stopped him before he was able to quit the Military Wing.

Grabbing his wrist from behind, Lucien twisted Alaric against the wall and spoke close to his face. "I needn't guess at what's got you distracted. I warned you not to wander with this."

"I've wandered," Alaric said, fighting the tension of Lucien's grip, "and it's led me to answers."

"No, you're lost in your passion. Your adoration of Stilguard is admirable, but do not be rash."

"Just listen to what I have to say. Alyssa. She's Titus' cousin."

"And what does she have to do with this?"

"Nothing yet, but she's the answer. We can use her to get information from Titus; we can find out what he's planning – they're close…"

"…which makes her dangerous," Lucien corrected. "I know people; if they were books, I could recite them; you can't trust her."

Alaric wrenched himself free of Lucien's grip, pushing him back with his shoulder. "We'll see," he said, and marched promptly for the Housing District, leaving Lucien alone with his concerns. Several minutes later, Alaric arrived in the Housing District and wove his way through the labyrinth of subdivisions towards Alyssa's quarters. A curtain was drawn across the doorway. Alaric drew a deep breath and slid his hand between the curtain and frame, calling Alyssa's name. He heard her voice call faintly from a second room and carefully he entered, saying her name again. An unlit hearth adorned her left wall, but a low glow from the back room shed enough light for Alaric to outline objects across the room. As he stepped past the curtain, Alyssa's head appeared, hemmed by candle light from the back room.

"Who's there?" the melody of her voice washed across the dark.

"It's Alaric."

"Oh," her voice brightened. "It's dreadfully dark, I'm sorry." Her slender form appeared from behind the wall as she glided toward Alaric. They embraced and Alyssa curled up against Alaric's chest. "I was just getting ready for bed," she said with a shiver; "it's cold outside my blankets."

"I'm sorry," Alaric said, "I didn't realize it was so late."

"It's not," she laughed. "Someone kept me out all night last night; I'm a little tired."

Alaric felt the weight of Alyssa's head against the rise and fall of his chest as he laughed, "Maybe I'll have to find someone who will appreciate it next time."

"No, it was perfect. I've never seen a sunrise; it makes me want to leave this place. You forget there's a world out there."

"I know. It's never for a happy occasion that I step outside but, when I do, I try to take it all in. We weren't meant for this life."

"Last night wasn't a happy occasion?"

Alaric squeezed Alyssa's sides and she jolted away from him in a fit of laughter. "That was the first," he said.

"Well, I'm glad I was there for it. I'd love for you to take me again sometime."

"If you're nice. We'll have to see."

Alyssa scoffed and tried to pull away, but Alaric drew her back to him slowly. Their eyes locked and their lips met and Alaric wanted desperately to forget why he had come to see her and be lost in this moment. He nuzzled her head to the side with his nose and kissed her lightly on the cheek, "I ran into your cousin today – Titus."

"Is it not common for two captains to be acquainted?" Alyssa said, lifting her chin to kiss him again.

Alaric stroked his hand through her hair and allowed only for their lips to brush. "Before today, I was unaware of your relation. He brought it up this morning."

"After I left you in the Infirmary," she began to explain, "I went for some breakfast and saw him there. He asked where I was coming from at such an early hour and I told him I had been with you, that we had been on the surface to watch the sunrise over the mountains."

"He told me I should be careful."

"You *should* be careful," Alyssa joked, pushing playfully against Alaric's chest, "I'm a tough girl."

"Clearly," he responded, pulling close again. They both laughed softly, searching one another's eyes. "I'm worried about him though." Alaric's tone became grave.

"Why?" Alyssa asked with earnest eyes.

"I'm afraid he's getting himself involved in something dangerous, he and General Nestor."

"What kind of danger?"

"A conspiracy of some sort, but I'm not sure."

"I don't understand."

"I'm not sure what I can say at this point; it's just," Alaric sighed, "something about the way he was talking this morning..."

"Is it about the man in the mask?"

"Lucien? What do you know about him?"

"Only that he's despicable."

"Have Nestor or Titus spoken of him to you?"

Alyssa shrugged softly beneath Alaric's arms. "They haven't said anything really. I know Titus doesn't trust him, and neither does Nestor, and neither should you."

"No one's given him a chance..."

"He doesn't deserve a chance, he's unnatural – just the look of him – the olive of his skin, the emptiness of his eye..."

"Well, naturally his complexion would be different; he lived in the open before he came here."

"Exactly!" Alyssa jumped on this observation. "He lived outside; we don't know where he came from; we don't know what he's doing here. He's closer to Stilguard's ear than anyone; has his own private army; Shaddai knows what he does to the patients in the Infirmary. He's a liar and a brigand and he can't be trusted."

The word *brigand* crossed Alaric's mind curiously, bringing back the memory of his confrontation with Barrius when Lucian had first arrived. 'He's a brigand, Alaric,' Barrius had yelled. 'I can smell it.'

"Is this you talking," Alaric asked, "or Titus or his friend Barrius?"

"We aren't the only ones who don't trust Lucien, Alaric. There are many in Adullam who question the Steward's unfounded trust in him."

"But, plot against him?"

"Not against him," Alyssa stroked Alaric's face pleadingly, searching his stern eyes for understanding, "but you should be careful."

"Obviously so," he responded coldly, stepping away from her affectionate touch. "Your relation to Titus is no coincidence. Lucien was right."

"Lucien has lied!" cried Alyssa, trying to fold herself again in Alaric's embrace, but he would not have it, "to all of us."

"No," Alaric stepped further towards the exit, "no you've lied, all of this, this is a lie!"

"It's not," she protested, "they just needed someone to keep watch on Lucien. When Barrius left Mark in the corridor from the Archive, I was meant to find him and bring him back to the Medical Wing; I was meant to meet you. They wanted me to get to Lucien through you and try to talk some sense into your head while I was at it."

Alaric shook his head slowly with disbelief.

"You're a captain of Adullam, Alaric; you don't want to be caught up in his defense."

"You don't know what you've gotten yourself into. They mean to use Lucien as leverage against Stilguard."

"No, Titus and Nestor, they just want what's best for Adullam; they just want Lucien out of the way. I wish I was wrong about Lucien for your sake, but I'm not."

"For my sake?" Alaric scoffed.

"It wasn't meant to be like this; I was told only to make your acquaintance…"

"… and now we are acquainted," Alaric riposted, "good evening."

Alaric flung the curtain to Alyssa's quarters aside and stormed from the Housing District, his head heated by betrayal. He heard his name called once down the long gallery that made up the district; he did not turn or respond. Instead, burdened steps carried him to the Infirmary. Lucien heard his breath – arrested with grief and heavy with grit – well before he burst through the Infirmary entrance. Alaric stopped abruptly, his face adorned with a sickened scowl, his eyes ablaze in an angst-ridden stare at Lucien. "You were right," he said, panting out his dismay.

Lucien's eye, critical as a shrewd father's, scoured Alaric up and down. "Are you surprised?"

Before Alaric had time to react to his cynicism, the patter of swift feet along the stone floor called close behind him. Stilguard's attendant boy, Kalit, came to a sliding stop in the entranceway next to Alaric. "Captain Folck," he said, "you have been summoned to council, and your presence is requested promptly."

"Just me?"

Looking wide-eyed at Lucien, Kalit gave one grandiose nod, his shoulders and head working in tandem, "and the other captains."

"Thank you, Kalit."

"And the Trade Lords and General Nestor."

"Th-thank you." Alaric's voice trailed and Kalit bobbed his head vehemently before darting back down the corridor. "We'll discuss everything when I get back," Alaric said to Lucien when the sound of Kalit's frantic steps had subsided.

"Should I be concerned for my safety?"

"Probably."

"I'll be sleeping then; we can talk in the morning."

Lucien's encounter with Mark from the other night had already set him on edge; he had come to realize his vulnerability in sleeping and tonight – especially after Alaric's warning – would not let it get the best of him. As such, when in the early hours of the morning, two men came to rouse Lucien, he was quite aware of their approach. Before they had rounded the final corridor to the Infirmary, Lucien was out of the bed and half dressed. As they reached for his door, he stood over a basin of water, washing his face. When they demanded he come with them, his hand was rested on a carefully concealed dagger as he kindly waited for them to approach. "Can I help you Gentlemen?" he asked.

"The Steward has requested your presence at the Entrance Hall immediately," one of the soldiers said.

"Requested?"

"Demanded," the other asserted.

"And why?"

The second soldier answered with a slight shrug of his shoulders before speaking. "We have been ordered to escort you."

"Where is Captain Folck?"

"Waiting impatiently."

Lucien laughed off the remark. "Very well," he said and finished dressing. "Why are you wearing packs?"

The soldier's exchanged sideways glances and stared steadily back at Lucien.

"I'll bring mine then?" he asked.

Still they said nothing so Lucien cautiously reached down to collect his scepter and satchel. The soldiers made no protest; instead they promptly turned and opened the door out of his room. Lucien followed his escorts from the Infirmary towards the Entrance Hall. His eye wandered warily along the walls as he wondered what, exactly, Stilguard required of him at such an early hour.

He was led first along a winding passage with a naturally high, vaulted ceiling. Small drops of condensation dripped from above and landed cold on Lucien's cheek. The sudden cold startled him, and he wiped the drops away with his finger, flinging them to the ground; with his hand extended, he grabbed a torch and held it aloft to dismiss the surrounding shadows. Lucien's escorts jumped, turning simultaneously toward the shifting light. But seeing no cause for alarm, they beckoned him to lead the way along the sparsely lit passage.

Their tunnel narrowed after a while, making an abrupt turn before widening out to a spiral staircase cut straight into the rock. Lucien examined the stonework as he climbed the spiraling steps, quickly becoming lost in his thoughts. When he had surmounted the stairwell, he began to walk aimlessly through the halls, unaware of himself or his escorts. All at once he returned to the present, quickly looking behind him to see if his two companions still followed. They marched steadily behind and Lucien took this as a sign he was still walking in the right direction.

The passage ahead curved to the left and then diverged in two different directions. Lucien stopped. He was completely lost. He turned back again to his escorts and one of them nodded to the right. Lucien nodded in return and followed the passage towards the Entrance Hall, his attention again turned to the masonry. The walls along most of the caves had been smoothed out and the floors had been leveled, but there was a clear distinction between the work of the first generation and the subsequent tunneling. Older passages, distinguished by the darkened tint of their walls, had been cultivated with great care, while fresh cut stone remained jagged and untended.

This final passageway widened out and emptied into the Entrance Hall from the left corner. Waiting for Lucien and his escorts were forty or more men, including the eleven Elite Guardsmen, all crowded in the center of the room holding torches and conversing. Most of the congregated men were soldiers, but there were others scattered amongst them that Lucien did not recognize. Separate from the group, in a dimmer light near the exit of the cave, stood Stilguard and Nestor, quietly debating. As Lucien approached the group, Alaric stepped out and greeted him with a handshake. He too was wearing a set of light armor, prompting Lucien to ask, "What's the occasion for such an early hour?"

Alaric gave a sidelong nod at Nestor and Stilguard, saying quietly, "If you'll just wait a moment, everything will be explained."

No sooner had he spoken than Stilguard called for silence among the men crowded in the Entrance Hall. He carried his torch forward, leaving Nestor shadowed in the dark of the cavern. Gazing over his men, Stilguard sensed a feeling of desperation. The people needed a cause; they needed a glory-driven purpose to propel them on from past failures.

"Gentlemen," he began, "I have summoned you all here for the journey to Bristing. The sun will be up in three hours time so I will speak briefly and then we must make all haste; if we hurry we can reach the town by midday tomorrow. I hope you are all well rested, the trek will not be an easy one, and I do not intend to come home empty handed. Our reserves have run out and Bristing's caravans have stopped; we have had no contact with our allies in the Briswold for near a month. It is for sanctity that we venture out – and so that the sacrifice of our fallen comrades and forebears is not wasted. I do not exaggerate the severity of our situation. This is more than food, this is more than family, this is salvation."

There was a gathering strength behind his words as Stilguard continued his speech. "Everyday we survive is victory over Aureus; even in the midst of our defeat, in the dwindling of our hopes – and even though it may seem our existence is wasted in solitude and confinement – we are the ones who will inherit the earth!"

His closing words were met with a resounding cheer that echoed through Adullam's halls, ringing sweet in the ears of slumbering children and anxious wives; it was for an instant, the heart of Adullam, pumping warm blood throughout the body and restoring movement to its deadened hands. "I will go with you to secure this hope," he continued. "Nestor will stay, ruling in my stead until we return."

"That is not wise," Lucien whispered, astounded.

"It's political," Alaric returned, "and the day that wisdom and politics coincide, well, then we'll know the world is ending."

"That was quite philosophical of you."

"An unfortunate effect of looking after you."

"How ungrateful of you," Lucien said, his brow pricked with cynicism. "Seeing that I've been a whet stone to your wit as well, I would hardly call it unfortunate. Is there nothing we can do?"

Alaric stroked his chin anxiously, "This is why I was called to council last night, to refine and rehearse this operation. It's Nestor's plan but Stilguard is accompanying it as a show of good faith in his General."

"We may be away for several days," Stilguard began again, "depending on the situation we find in Bristing, but, as I said, I have no intention of returning empty handed. Our primary objective is to rebuild the caravan and see that it is maintained. This may entail creating a new route if the current one has been compromised. I know nothing about Bristing's condition or that of the route so we must be cautious. General Nestor has recommended that we proceed assuming that Aureus has swept the town.

"Now we must move. Be swift; be discreet. The time has come." With this, Stilguard turned to Nestor and the two men clasped hands. Nestor's embrace reassured Stilguard with the promise of safekeeping; yet Alaric felt its masked intentions. Emboldened, Stilguard threw up his hood and stepped back into the shadows leading to the mouth of the cave. The men followed him through the darkness and shortly stepped out into the predawn air.

CHAPTER IX

THE BRISWOLD

From the outside, there was almost no evidence of Adullam's existence. The mouth of the cave was snuck away between two small hills. The earth was barren, dry and red, stressed with small crevasses like scars round giant stones, which sprouted from the hills. Somewhere in their midst was a hole, hidden deep in the maze of stones. As Stilguard stepped from it, he noticed the morning air curiously thick with moisture.

He leapt from the cave and melded among the stones. He climbed atop a group of rocks several yards away and scanned the area for any sign of movement but, through the present mist, he could see nothing. Making use of this extra cover, Stilguard summoned his men with a birdlike whistle and watched as forty wraith figures glided through the mist, their path marked by swirling trails of moisture. They gathered around the base of the rocks, and Stilguard dropped down among them. He crouched low and whispered for his men to follow before disappearing silently into the mist.

One by one his men filed behind. Midway through the line, Alaric stepped in. He ran with the main group for several minutes but, as the mist was beginning to disperse beneath the rising heat, he waved his hand, signaling to his soldiers to follow his break from the group. Shortly, Alaric's group left the mist completely behind and continued silently over a dark and barren landscape. The sky was still black and the moon still hung full and bright over their heads, but the eastern horizon was beginning to brighten. It felt to Lucien as if the group fled the rising sun as they moved westward to the echo of his thoughts, *'the daylight would blind their innocent eyes.'*

For several miles in all directions the terrain was flat and naked, leaving them vulnerable. The first two hours of the journey were undoubtedly, in Alaric's mind, the most crucial and the most dangerous. They could hope to escape the virtual dessert that surrounded them just before the sun peaked the mountains from behind. By then, they should reach the foothills of Bristing's outer territories, the Briswold.

The Briswold grasslands fanned out to encompass most of the western portion of the continent before dissolving into the rocky Borderlands to the far north. The land over the past century or so had lost much of its fertility and the fields hosted a browning-yellow tint from a lack of nourishing rain. Clusters of trees were scattered sparsely across the landscape, soon to become waypoints for the two scouting parties as they flattened trails through the high grass.

For now they were still in the heart of Drögerde, the wasteland in which Adullam was hidden. The barren nature of the terrain made life harsher but, all the same, safer. Conditions above ground were far from suitable to sustain any life for any length of time, so ravaging parties from Aureus spent little effort searching through the dust.

The frail ground on which they stepped padded the men's feet as they ran; their steps sounded like fingers rapping in succession along a pillow. The dust they kicked up hung in the air in a small trail, and clung to their boots still wet from the mist.

The heavens had brightened from black to a dark blue, and the stars were beginning to fade as the moon lost its luminous glow to the eastern sky's herald. Alaric was beginning to see the first signs of the Briswold. Small patches of greenery sprouted along the ground – tufts of dry grass growing out of isolation and trying to root in the spent soil. On the horizon, wizened trees beckoned Alaric forward, proffering the vestiges of renewal. The sight of the trees gave him a reassurance he could not place but, with each footfall, he knew he was progressing.

Just before dawn had peaked the eastern horizon, the company reached the first trees of the Briswold. The line in front of Lucien came to a halt and the men formed around Alaric at the center of the small cluster of trees. He motioned for them all to huddle in closer and sit. Alaric himself sat amongst them as men passed around canteens of water. They drank in silence and recovered their breath. The sun was nearly shining in full, but the dense atmosphere would keep its true intensity hidden behind a thick gray haze until the later morning.

"Gentlemen," Alaric said, "we've reached the bounds between Drögerde and the Briswold. We're in a safer territory now; the trees will offer us reasonable cover so we'll follow them as best we can, but they remain sparse in some areas. From here we'll begin to bear more to the southwest and, by my reckoning, we should be a little more than a day's journey. The pace is good thus far; I'll give us five minutes and then we're off again, so rest and recover." He paused for a moment and glanced around the men. "All right, at ease," he said and brushed himself off as he stood.

Most of the men remained seated and spoke softly to one another; a few of them stood and backed off from the group to relax in their own way. Lucien stood several feet from the main group and faced their westward destination, his arms crossed behind his back. He breathed in deeply, shut his eye and let the air slip softly back out of his lungs. Alaric took cautious steps towards him, quietly flattening a trail through the grass. As he came to Lucien's side, Alaric tilted his head to study the mask. Shining opaque beneath the open sun, it was grained with lines of timeless stories, and tempered by the aging of deep mysteries. Alaric straightened himself up. He cleared his throat and looked out over the †wold, away from Lucien.

"How are you?" Lucien asked, reading the tension in Alaric's stance.

Alaric bobbed his head thoughtfully, "I'm fine, and you?"

"The moment's peaceful, though I shouldn't think that will last," Lucien said. He blinked regretfully, and his eye followed the currents of rippling grass. "The way the grass undulates in the wind, like the sea, it's soothing."

There was silence between them as Alaric searched for the same solace in the browning grass. From the corner of his eye, Lucien could read the concern weighted on Alaric. From the tension in his shoulders to the twiddling of his thumb through his fingers, there was something from which he sought distraction.

"I was noticing the craftsmanship throughout the tunnels on my way to the Entrance Hall this morning," Lucien's voice filled the rustling wind. "It's interesting to see how the patterns change throughout generations."

"How can you tell the difference?" Alaric asked.

"How can you not?" Lucien chuckled. "Subtleties. Different things: the hue of the stone, it's texture, and so on. The early work is leveled out, the style is consistent – intricate, professional – but in newer corridors the technique degenerates."

"It's strange, the things that you notice."

"Just because I have one eye doesn't mean I can't see. Stone masons were a scarce find in the age before Aureus and I found it interesting that any would have ended up here."

"Why is that?"

"Well," Lucien continued, "Rosario would have sought them out – contrary to legend, Aureus did not spring out of a hole in the ground."

"Rosario?"

"You don't know the stories? Roberto Rosario, the Indivinate One, whose crozier subdued the earth."

"I don't know the stories."

Lucien blinked his eye incredulously at Alaric. "Well, where do I even begin? Roberto Rosario was a religious leader who became too consumed with his assent to power and ultimately fancied himself a god. There was a society he belonged to, its origins founded in an ancient book of prophetic poetry. This society, The Narxus as it was called, was bent on realizing Salvation and brought peace to the world through a unified religion. But when that peace fell apart, Rosario built Aureus as a sanctuary from the fires of war, and in The Awakening he destroyed nearly everything else. Small societies, clinging to the ashen remains of righteousness are all that remain outside of Aureus. And Adullam may be one of the last.

"Men," Lucien continued, talking more to himself now than to Alaric, "had been seduced by a great power and a great lie – peace. The irony is that those who had resisted Rosario – those who had rebelled against the peace he offered, those whom the world had held as evil – have become the standard of righteousness. But, it seems to me that today, most people in Adullam live only by heritage or principle. You're no longer answering the call of your Shaddai as your ancestors thought they were doing. So what is righteousness? 'The truth that once was gray, now is lucid – night and day,' as the old poem goes.

"In the floods of the Awakening, those enamored by Rosario's peace fled to him, fled to his Aureus and were trapped as its lie was revealed; now their children's children have no choice but to serve the evil they were born into. Most who fled to Aureus felt they were fleeing toward salvation. The lie ran so deep that it seated its deception among the most devout who, bent on the fulfillment of redemption and salvation, plunged the world into darkness. Humanity was washed away alongside the buildings of its great cities. Once civilization collapsed and Aureus, 'The Golden City' arose, people flocked to its gates for deliverance.

"But," Lucien laughed, "I'm sure I'm boring you – to bring this all back to Adullam's stonework, I suppose the true artist would have been among the least likely to run for the city; so it isn't too surprising that a few stone masons would have ended up amongst your band of outcasts."

"Hmm," Alaric sighed at Lucien's conclusion. His focus had been elsewhere – on the struggle to voice his concern for Stilguard. He needed his troubled thoughts to be manifest in words, but the draw of his breath felt heavy in his chest as if his body was challenging his will to question the unknown. To question his fear meant ultimately to realize it, to give it life and let it lead him astray. He opened his mouth. "Do you think," he stuttered as words wavering through his shallow breath, "How do you think Stilguard's coming along?"

Lucien did not speak immediately, "I feel sure he's doing fine. He took the more direct route, yes?"

"He's following the original caravan," Alaric said, "so yes, it's much more direct, which is why we need to keep a good pace – in order to reach Bristing around the same time."

Lucien's brow furrowed. "I was not aware that they followed the path directly. Why would they take the caravan route when it's likely been compromised? Whose idea was that, not Stilguard's?"

"The plan was Nestor's," Alaric replied. "I raised the issue in council last night but, as I said before, it's political."

"It's foolish. And Stilguard proceeded on with it undoubtedly to appease Nestor's wounded pride. I must say, I fail to see why the Steward is making the journey and the General is not."

"It's a matter of integrity," Alaric responded defensively. "It's to bolster the courage of the men, to give hope to Adullam – to show them that their lives are in good hands. He's going…"

"Because he needs to reclaim his people," Lucien concluded in Alaric's stutter.

Alaric shifted his weight nervously, leaning away and narrowing his eyes at Lucien.

"It's obvious isn't it," Lucien continued, "that Stilguard has been losing support, that people are questioning his leadership, that they're losing faith?"

"Well, the times are difficult, and it's all just political quarreling."

"I understand the politics of your community but, in difficult times, people will always call for blood," he laughed. "In a sense we're still heathens. I don't believe humanity has really changed much, we just found ways to disguise ourselves."

Alaric nodded, his eyes skirting across the wind-swept grass. "And what you're saying is?"

"This is their plan, Alaric; both Nestor and Titus are safe and in control of Adullam, and the Steward is marked for death. And there's no blood on their hands. Fate will be fate."

"No." Alaric said, shaking his head at the wind. "No," but it was too late, Lucien was already on a tangent.

"But there has to be a contingency," Lucien said. "If fate *is* fate and Stilguard returns unscathed, what then? They wouldn't deign to repent and fall in line. There must be another avenue – a direct avenue. Think about it, Alaric. It's like a painting of a lion poised for the kill, it's all been composed; we're just waiting for it to happen."

A sickening feeling deepened in Alaric's stomach, turning his flesh white and cold as stone. "What if you're the contingency," Alaric mused darkly.

"How?"

"You were right about Alyssa."

"You told me," Lucien said, his monotone urging Alaric to go on.

"Titus had asked her to find out everything she could about you, through me. The whole thing was a set up, even from the beginning with her bringing Mark to the Infirmary. She told me that Nestor and Titus were after you, but what if that was only half of it. It was something she said –

how people's faith in the Steward has been shaken because of his unfounded trust in you. I didn't think far enough through when she told me," Alaric's voice rasped the air like wind, "but I think Nestor means to use you, Lucien, as leverage against Stilguard – to replace his Stewardship."

"Soft lips hide sharp teeth."

"Do you really think this is possible?" Alaric questioned, smoothing the breastplate of his leather cuirass.

Lucien tilted his head and stared confidently back into Alaric's urgent gaze.

Alaric kicked his toes at the dry grass, sighing.

"You have to make a choice, Alaric. You can't prance along indecisively and wait to see what happens. By then it could be too late."

"And what do I do from here?!" he whispered harshly. "We have this course to Bristing, and we have no way of communicating with Stilguard."

Lucien looked back over the brown sea of windswept grass.

In turn, Alaric rolled his head back on his shoulders to empty the clutter of his scattered thoughts. "There seems no way of knowing how to find Stilguard in time and in the end, would it make any difference? We're still riding on speculation. The best thing to do is press on and hope the others can handle themselves long enough to rendezvous in Bristing."

"I agree."

"Carmine!" Alaric yelled, looking past Lucien.

A tall, narrow-faced, blonde-haired solider jumped to attention.

"Round up the men, we're moving now!" Alaric looked again at Lucien, "We'll make for Bristing as planned but liven our pace. If Stilguard has not already arrived, we can track the caravan route back until we find them, but there is no way of finding their trail from here, we've no adequate bearing."

Less then a minute later they were all back in formation hastening their way toward Bristing and, hopefully, Stilguard.

CHAPTER X

PHILLIP

There was something about the path down which he walked that he felt resembled his own identity. Yet at the same time he felt this ironic as he could not even remember his own name. The path was carved into the desolate landscape by the millions of footsteps of those who had made their exodus already. Why he was so late in following – why he was not leading – he did not know. What he did know was, the further along this path he walked, the closer he came to himself.

"Phillíp!" a voice from behind called him; quickly he turned. He was a boy again, playing amongst the rows of his father's grapevines. He felt his bare toes dig nervously into the hardened soil as the looming, gray-haired figure of a man approached. "Where is your brother?"

"I don't know, papá, why do you need him?"

"I need his help."

"I can help you."

"No, I don't need you, Phillíp, I need him – you are too young."

Eyes tearing, the boy turned from his father. *But I have endured!* Enraged thoughts flooded his mind, and he opened his eyes again to the path. He was surrounded once more by a red sea of ash and dirt, the tears he cried as a boy evaporated into the dry air – *it is I who remain.*

He felt himself being led by the currents of his subconscious. As he walked, awareness would sweep across him in intervals as a shallow ocean current sweeps across a bleached shoreline, leaving behind things brought up from below the surface and readjusting pieces already placed. At the same time he was aware of himself in the present, he was observing himself from the future. He watched himself follow this path, his body a black silhouette against a red sun falling into the horizon in front of him.

His silhouette dissolved into that of his father's, seated in his heavy leather chair, the sun framed on the horizon through the sitting room window. His father formed a circle with three other men, caught deep in the thralls of conversation.

"Phillip!" an excited whisper called to him from the dark. A boy again, Phillip tore his attention away from his father's conversation. Crouched at the base of the stairwell was his brother, beckoning him to come close; he was only two years older, but those years had afforded him a great advancement in stature and strength. Phillip shook his head vigorously, making signs with his hands that he did not want to cross his father's view through the open door and be caught eavesdropping on his private meeting. Phillip pressed in close against the wall as he listened, melting into it, becoming invisible. He saw his brother do the same on his side of the door; they smiled slyly at one another.

"The truth that once was gray now is lucid – night and day."
Their father recited
"A fire comes;
the flood will follow;
the ground on which you stand – forsaken – not hallowed.
Then, in gates of gold, autumn is nigh;
the fates sing to death as they fly.
Soon the gates will open – let the righteous come through,
they, the ones, whom to me stayed true."

"Roberto, I don't think this can be understood out of context," one of their father's guests spoke. *"The Writ of Narxus* must be understood in its totality; you are thinking too far ahead."

"But this is our fate; this is our promise. We lose everything if we lose sight of the end – of Salvation."

"We will not know that this foreshadows our salvation until we have come nearer to it. There is yet too much unfulfilled. *The Writ of Narxus* has lived a thousand years; it may not be our generation that sees its fulfillment."

"But whatever knowledge we can pass on, we must."

"On that we are agreed, but we needn't jump too many poems ahead. It's imperative that we focus on the next step."

"Only as long as we don't lose sight of ultimate purpose," their father froze mid-speech. "Did you hear that?"

Phillíp glared at his brother. The wall he leaned against had creaked loudly beneath his weight.

"What is it, Roberto?"

"Someone is here," their father replied, standing slowly from his chair. The silence was heavy as death. Phillíp watched his brother's face turn white; the wall creaked again as he tried to move away. Their father leapt through the open, double-leaf door, spotting his elder son as he fled around the stairwell. Roberto grabbed his unwieldy boy by the arm, allowing Phillíp the chance to dart stealthily into the shadows of the next room. Smiling as he climbed the laundry shoot, Phillíp was glad to see that for once his brother's size was his shortcoming.

He emerged again to the barren scape. Walking upon the ground, he could see himself from all directions. He noticed as he circled around to the side of himself that he hadn't shaved in several days, and the hair on his face was beginning to thicken. His jaw was gaunt, the skin drawn tight against the bone, but the fresh beard masked his sunken cheeks. At the thought of being masked, he shut his eyes. He wondered for the first time at the split in his consciousness, why he knew so little but could see so much; why awareness would sweep across him in waves, cluttering his mind with new debris to collect when he had old debris still to gather. He was frustrated by the fact he could not explain this phenomena to himself. *Phillíp*, he now knew himself as, yet he could not identify his crisis of consciousness. Perhaps, he mused, that was the very reason for walking. Perhaps the future would come into focus as he carried on, and let the pieces of himself collect and make their own picture, where he would find communion with his prescient self. *That's worth the walk.*

Phillíp at last opened his eyes.

"Look what papá showed me."

Phillíp's brother stood before him, no longer a child, but in the eve of adolescence.

"Come on, with me."

Phillíp followed, his curiosity sparked by mystery. They walked cautiously into the sitting room; memories of their father's meeting played out before him. In an armoire on the far side of the room, his brother unlocked a hidden drawer. Phillíp waited by the window, eyes leery for the approach of his father. His brother beckoned him over. In his hands was a book, *The Writ of Narxus*. "Look!" he exclaimed, his eyes lit with wonder. "You remember this, right? From that night when papá found us watching."

"Found you," Phillíp corrected; his brother laughed.

"Look at the seal on the cover page," his finger stroked the image. "Papá explained it to me."

A flame was the center, and stretching out from it were two wings. On the right wing was a rook; on the left wing was an eye. A sword cut through the flame, and ringed around its hilt was a crown with eight spikes.

"The flame is purity and refinement, and the wings coming out from it represent divine protection. It stands for a new world – purified by fire and guarded by heaven. The rook is for strategy and wisdom, and the eye is all seeing. They stand for our learned wisdom under God's oversight. The sword is vengeance, God's vengeance against the wicked who would stand against the Narxus."

"What is the Narxus?"

Phillíp's brother shrugged and continued, "but the crown, it represents our royal inheritance – yours and mine – and all who follow faithfully, *The Writ of Narxus*."

"Why did papá tell you and not me?"

Phillíp's brother gazed knowingly back into his eyes but said nothing. The world flared red with resentment and faded out into dust-swept barrens. *The Narxus*, he thought, *it was no longer a mystery – its promises fulfilled*. Phillíp had been stationary with frustration for some time but was now able to step with the confidence of a purpose to boast. He took steady steps forward, but soon doubt crept within his present consciousness; he saw that he tread upon emptiness and was swept by prescience.

'*The souls, borne by vice,*
Will not seek the shards of their redemption

But whither shall the troubled men go?

For they tread upon emptiness,'

His brother stood beside him at attention; they both were in uniform. A small crowd sat in rows before them. Phillíp spotted his father among them, waiting for his sons to be initiated into the ranks of the Fuerzas Armadas Españolas. "Do you see papá?" his brother asked from the side of his mouth.

"The question is, does he see me?" Phillíp responded, tight-jawed.

"I'm sure," he said sympathetically. "The Spanish Legion, that's good work."

"Doesn't have quite the ring as Royal Guardsman – he'll continue to worship his namesake, I'll just be Phillíp."

"Will you not *seek the shards of your redemption?*" his brother joked.

"Don't quote that shit to me, I don't care to redeem myself in father's eyes – you've always been the favorite. I'd prefer to *tread on emptiness."*

"Roberto Rosario!" the name was called and Phillíp's brother stepped forward, shorted from response. Phillíp watched his father's proud eyes as they gazed upon the newest member of the Royal Guard.

"Phillíp Rosario!" his name was called next. He stepped forward to receive the insignia of the Spanish Legion, unblinking eyes trained on his father, but their gazes never met; the old man never so much as glanced from his favored son. Phillíp remained hidden behind his brother's golden aura, always a shadow. He saluted his superior and stepped back onto the dusty path of his lonely consciousness.

These fragments of memory were like reading a book for the second time, having forgotten the tale. Periodically, something would trigger and he would remember broken fragments of the story, of his story – buried so deep that its awakening burned unsparingly. At the same time that Phillíp was aware of his story, he was aware of himself observing it. Fate was the marriage of these two entities of awareness. As his future remembered the past, his present saw the future and the two became one. Their communion was in the destiny of Phillíp's path. He saw that his footsteps were no longer just empty prints left behind in the dust, indistinguishable from the billions that lay before him, but that he was indeed seeking *'the shards of his redemption.'* There was purpose. Reconciliation for his mind and redemption for his spirit. It was not vice that carried him but redemption, *'but whither shall,'* that man go to fill the *'emptiness?'*

To Aureus.

He was swept again with an inner sight causing his eyes to roll back and his body quiver as he stumbled forward.

"Phillíp," a voice called, "seen the paper today?"

Phillíp leaned over the open hood of a Humvee, tuning its engine, as the day's newspaper was dropped on the back of his head. He reached for the paper before it slid off his back. "You've read it?" he asked, shaking his head at the headline.

"Mhmm, thought you might like to see it."

"*General Roberto Rosario*," Phillíp read aloud, "*hero of Crown and Country … quoted yesterday reciting the motto of the Royal Guard, 'For Spain, Everything for Spain,' in response to our questions concerning his heroic acts to protect …* I can't read this. How does this take precedence over the greater war?"

"He's a national icon."

Phillíp shook his head, "hero of Crown and Country…" he sighed and let his angst simmer out. "I should call and congratulate him. It's frustrating, you know, to come home after all these years – on the real front, securing real peace – to see our efforts undercut by this," he dropped the paper on the ground. "We should be the heroes."

"I know, but that's the life of the GOE. We knew Special Ops was dark when we signed on. You and me, we're meant to be in the shadows – people don't know what we do, they can't know," and feigning a voice of grandeur he said, "mere mortals would not understand."

"One day we'll bridge the gap," Phillíp laughed, "we'll be made immortal."

"The Immortals!" his comrade roared, "Cheers to that, we deserve a drink."

Smiling at the fortune of his good company, Phillíp happily conceded. "I'll buy," he said, clapping his fellow soldier on the back. He closed the hood of his Humvee and, turning from it, slipped on a maintenance dolly, falling to the garage floor.

He caught himself on the ground and quickly looked down the footpath. The dust that his fall stirred up filled his lungs as he drew heavy breaths. Nothing, he saw nothing but ash and emptiness. He turned himself over and reclined on his elbows, staring down the path from whence he had been coming. Again seeing nothing, he frantically reared himself off the ground and circled as a combatant circles his opponent.

106

He had seen an old man, with sight or foresight he could not say but with the old man was death. Yet, now there was nothing. Dust parched his tongue; ash filled his lungs, and beads of perspiration rolled into his eyes. The sweat burned. Involuntarily he blinked, his eyes closed and the tide of foresight rolled over him like cold water and he was submerged, his senses deafened to the surface world. The current began to recede and panic flashed through him momentarily, he would no longer be hidden under the waters of his subconscious. As he was being pulled back to the present, he saw the old man was still a great distance away and the warrant of death remained with him. There was nothing yet to fear. He willed himself forward, but in the distance a black figure seemed to appear out of the setting sun. With the sight of it came the sensation of death, its spite a pulse – an awakening.

Gasping for breath, Lucien rose from his dream.

CHAPTER XI

BEFORE THE STORM

Lucien's observant eye flashed over the top of the high grass as he awoke. The moon still shone brightly, blinking through darkened boughs above. He crouched low, rising from his place shadowed beneath the tree, searching for the movement he knew he had heard. The deep blue shades of the rising morning had begun to show, and the scent of moisture hung lightly in the air. Lucien crept silently backwards, fleeing the luminescent call of dawn. Keeping his eye transfixed upon the empty scene in front of him, he melded into the boughs of his tree, hanging in wait.

Again he heard movement, closer now, but his view was blocked by dew-drooped limbs; soon the movement was joined by a dispersion of fervent rustling through the grass. Finally a figure stepped into Lucien's view, scouring the place beneath the tree. It was a soldier. He moved in closer still, bending low, unaware of the danger lurking above. Dropping from the boughs, Lucien planted his heel onto the soldier's tailbone, using the momentum of his fall to force the crouching soldier into the tree. Then, extending his other leg, he caught himself as he pushed away from the soldier, landing on his toes and, propelled by the force of his kick, he rolled into the grass and carried himself up, turning with one fluid motion to face the soldier in time to see his face glance across the base of the tree. Before the soldier could stand, Lucien had grabbed the neck of his cuirass and wrenched him from the ground. Pinning the soldier against the tree, he reared his scepter back threateningly. Though half his face was covered in blood, Lucien recognized the soldier by his blonde hair.

"Carmine," he exclaimed in a hushed voice.

"I'm sorry Lucien," the boy pleaded, "we're about to move, Alaric sent me to wake you."

"Did he now?" Lucien asked; the words practically slithered from between his lips.

"I did," Lucien heard Alaric's voice from behind. He looked around to see the Captain staring at him, his face stern, his eyes pleading. "I did not foresee it being a problem," Alaric said.

Lucien released his grip and replaced his scepter. Carmine remained bracing his back against the tree as the blood on his face had begun to drip down his chin. "My apologies, next time just call for me," Lucien said as he extended a hand to help Carmine stand. Lifting him up, he held the boy's chin and examined his face before reaching into his side bag to produce a cloth with which to clean the wound. "The abrasion is shallow; the bleeding should stop shortly. There's no need for me to bandage it; just keep the rag to clean off the blood until it stops flowing. But, you can see, it's already begun to coagulate. Is there any pain in your neck or shoulder?"

"No, they're fine," the soldier flatly responded.

"Good."

Alaric stepped to Carmine's side to examine the injury and nodded at the boy to leave. Avoiding Lucien's eye, Carmine darted off to gather his equipment.

Lucien remained still, distracted by some distant thought. He stood illuminated in a beam of moonlight perforating the tree cover, and for a moment Alaric studied the somber draw of his face, gaunt and accented in a half light. In the hollow of his cheeks was a forlorn tale, voiced without a sound – a voice of anger, of fear, of sorrow, of confusion. And upon his olive complexion was a madness – a look of angels and of demons raging inside, and a man stretched thin by the fight. It set Alaric on edge; cautiously, he let his hand hang by the hilt of his sword.

"Are you scared of me?" Lucien asked, his voice hollow, his eye offset to the horizon.

"Old habits," Alaric returned, crossing his arm away from his hilt.

"You're not that old."

A warm breeze tossed the grass around their boots.

"Your face is pale," Alaric said, nearly in a whisper.

"It is only the moonlight," Lucien said, turning to hide behind his mask. "Can we reach Bristing before sunrise?"

"I think so," Alaric replied, still on edge. "We've made good time thus far."

Lucien nodded and turned to form up with the rest of the men. Alaric walked softly behind, musing on Lucien's mood. He had glimpsed it before when Lucien had spoken of his past. Usually fleeting, this time it enraptured his whole being – a look of deplorable hopelessness. "Lucien," the words snuck out, "are you all right?"

"Of course," he responded with feigned buoyancy, looking back with the masked side of his face. "Why would you think otherwise?"

Less than a minute later the whole party had regrouped and was ready to depart. The soldiers formed a semicircle around Alaric, but Lucien stood to the back. "We are now only a few hours away from Bristing," Alaric told them. "We will lose this tree cover very soon. Stay alert, the moon is out so don't think we aren't in danger of being spotted in the open plains. We will need to reach Bristing before dawn," he said, looking at Lucien. "The Almighty go before us!"

"The Shaddai guide our steps!" they all, save for Lucien, cheered in response. Clustering together, the men fell in line behind Alaric and resumed their westward trek towards Bristing.

CHAPTER XII

BRISTING

The dawn was pre-born by fire. In the distance, even before they could see Bristing, the company of soldiers could see smoke rising to the heavens, distorting the setting moon. The sun had yet to peak the mountains but the fires lit the sky like day. Bristing had been razed, but Alaric could only think of Adullam and the fires that one day could ravage his people. He and his company stood shoulder to shoulder, silhouetted by disaster.

"It's not been burning for a day," Lucien said. He still was possessed by the same forlorn look from earlier in the night. "Why burn it now?"

"I don't see the other company," one of the soldiers said.

"Do you think they made it?" came another worried voice.

"This place was burned for them," Lucien responded, holding his gaze straight forward.

Hastily, Alaric spat out orders, "The three of you from the Elite Guard, go with Lucien; you three," he pointed, "escort the Trade Lords to the tree-cover at the southernmost part of the town. The rest of you, come with me. Securing the Steward, or anyone from his company is our primary objective. Lucien, you head up around the north of the town and secure its perimeter. My group will take to the south."

The groups split, and began their reconnaissance work on the outskirts of Bristing. The palisade walls surrounding the town center were near ash but still well ablaze. Lucien's team kept low, running crouched through the tall grass to conceal themselves from any watchful eye. Coming ever closer to the town, Lucien's eye darted the length of the wall, trying to find a way past the barrier of flames. Spotting a narrow breach, Lucien stopped and lay prostrate in the high grass. His Elite Guard formed up beside him as he spoke. "We'll see soon if the Nephilim are responsible for this. I know it's cruel to force this upon you after such short training but remember what I taught you. Those hours must now count for something but trust me, you will remember more than you think you learned. If we encounter a Nephilim I will draw its attention; you two," he pointed, "sever the tendon at the heel; and you," he looked demandingly into the other Guardsman's eyes, "you know."

A shiver passed over the Guardsman's body, but his face remained resolute, "What if there is more than one?" he asked.

"Then we do not engage. With four of us we can only handle one at a time. I would say keep a sharp eye out, but they're hard to miss. Are we ready?"

All the soldiers nodded. Lightly on his toes, Lucien picked himself up and darted through the grass towards the town. He and his men broke cover onto an earthen defense perimeter littered with sharp stakes jutting from the ground. Nimbly, Lucien navigated through them; his Elite Guardsmen followed close behind. Lucien took a last step toward the collapsed wall and dove head first over its remaining embers, rolling behind a small structure to his right. Not so adept as their leader, Lucien's three men trailed behind, fumbling through the exterior defenses.

Silently, Lucien beckoned them follow around the corner of the structure to another several yards away. Keeping low, they followed him one at a time until they had moved a bit further into the town. For some time they navigated cautiously through a network of burning buildings. Once they had penetrated far enough into the town, Lucien had mapped its basic layout and was drawn toward the largest column of smoke rising from the town's center – what seemed to be a community forum.

Four granite columns rose high above the surrounding buildings, marking the forum's corners. Lucien and his men crept to the edge of a building parallel to the forum. Peering around, Lucien took a quick inventory of the scene and signaled his men to move forward as a group. Everything around them was illuminated in a dancing blaze. Their faces were black with ash, their eyes red with sweat and fire.

Suddenly, Lucien froze; his back arched like a startled cat. His ears pricked at a faint sound coming from the forum, a moan. His breath began to pulse in his ears, drowning the faint noise in fear. He nodded to his men to follow and sprinted out from behind cover towards the moaning voice. He ran ahead, signaling his men to cover as he flattened himself against one of the granite columns. Its surface was still cool from the night air, and Lucien wiped his tired brow against it. He drew a sharp breath and leaned cautiously out from around the column. At the heart of the forum was a man, seated on his knees before a massive fire. His armor was torn and his body was black with ash. Lucien whistled to his Elite Guard and ran out to the man. The Guardsmen lay in wait to counter any ambush, their courage bolstered by Lucien's apparent trust in their ability.

Panic-eyed, the wounded man nearly fainted as Lucien reached him, relenting himself to a death avowing seizure. His eyes rolled into the back of his head, and a frothy vomit leaked from his mouth. He choked, coughing it up as Lucien caught his failing body. The man was another of Lucien's Elite Guardsmen, one who had been sent with Stilguard. Unable to remember his name, Lucien shook the man from his stupor, "Soldier, where is your company?"

Terrified, the soldier wrenched himself free of Lucien's grip and pushed himself towards the fire. Lucien fought to draw him back, pressing the soldier's hands down to his sides. "Soldier," he repeated, "where is your company?"

The soldier's eyes twitched and his breath hissed sharply between his teeth. "I came," he sputtered between sobs, "just as it started burning." His whole body trembled uncontrollably. "They burned, I was trying to find someone, anyone – to help. I couldn't," his voice mumbled, "I couldn't save anyone. And they're here, they're all *right* here but," his voice trailed into incoherent babbling.

"Who's here, I don't understand." Lucien protested, trying to shake the soldier straight.

"All of them!" he yelled and tears burst from his eyes. "They're all here. I couldn't, they're here! Right – right here!" he howled, flinging his arm back towards the fire. Lucien released him and let the soldier curl helplessly to the ground.

Standing slowly, Lucien looked into the fire; looked into the melting faces of men, women, and children; bodies upon bodies heaped into a burning pyre. Suddenly the smell of burning flesh registered, overwhelming Lucien. He stumbled away from the fire, looking wildly around for any sign of movement but there were only flames.

Lucien looked again at the soldier, "Who was it? Who was it that did this?" he asked

"I don't know. The Nephilim. I don't know," the soldier responded between sobs.

"Did you see them?"

"No, it was just here. Like this," his hysteria mounted. "Before the flesh had melted off, I saw their faces. They're all here."

"Where is Stilguard, where is the rest of your company?"

"Dead," the soldier responded and then began gasping for breath.

"How?" terror raced through Lucien's mind. This was their worst fear; visions of disaster rampaged through Lucien's head. All things would fall apart now. He thought back to Nestor, to Titus, to Barrius, to Mark. "How?" Lucien yelled again.

The soldier shook his head vigorously, unwilling to speak. He looked up at Lucien and only continued to shake his head. Lucien reached down and grabbed the soldier by his cuirass, "Tell me how!" he said and picked the man off the floor.

"Let go of me, let go!" the man screamed and shook himself free of Lucien's grip. He stumbled backwards toward the fire and bent low. Vomit poured from his mouth and he fell to his knees, his eyes shut tight. "We came across a caravan. It was broken down. The trader was dead." He drew a sharp breath and continued. "We were looking at it, just hours away from here and mm-suddenly, ambush." He broke down into sobs again.

Lucien let him cry. Wiping an arm beneath his nose, the soldier coughed and continued.

"I don't know where it came from. I, I've never seen," he shook his head and scowled. "It was bigger than...bigger than a man. Red, blood red. Horns that curled," his voice began to whine with fear, "out of the top of his head. Hooves like a horse, but stood on two legs. I don't – we," he began to cry again, "fought it. Slashed and stabbed. I ran my sword straight through it." He looked right at Lucien, "Straight through it and when I pulled free there was no wound. No wound! Like I hadn't even touched it. It. It killed Stilguard. I ran, I ran for Bristing to meet you, to find anyone and they're here. Here behind me. They're burning. I escaped. I thought…I thought you were all burning too."

Lucien's reply was whispered and solemn. "You didn't escape," he said, "It let you go."

"What, what do you mean, it let me go! What does that mean, what – that it's here?"

"Has there been any sign of it or the Nephilim since you arrived?"

"No, no nothing! It can't be here, no. No! I can't."

Lucien summoned the other Guardsmen to break from their cover and join him. They rushed to the pyre; one of them knelt down and grabbed his crying friend, lifting him from the ground and letting him sob into his shoulder. "What's happened?" he asked Lucien.

"Your Steward is dead, and we've been watched," he replied darkly. "We are in the wake of Aureus. The Golden City must be all – comparable to none; now only Adullam remains to challenge its singularity. Find Alaric," he said, directing two of his Guardsmen northwards. He looked back at his two remaining Elite Guards, one cradled in another's arm as vomit dripped from his chin. None of them spoke and after a moment, a sick feeling gripped Lucien. He turned from the soldier's gaze and to pyre as its flames licked away the flesh and bone of its prisoners. His stare turned to daze and the world became deaf.

CHAPTER XIII

ASHES

In the distance a black figure seemed to appear out of the setting sun; Phillíp raised an arm above his brow to see its slow approach. His hands trembled and instinct told him to run, the figure bore death. Yet Phillíp remained frozen with indecision. He knew the future – knew what awaited his path; he knew what he would become because he knew what he had done. And he knew the truth, a dark truth, that one day would hold him accountable – for everything. He turned from his path to flee his fate but there stood his brother, blocking his way, robed in white. They stood close, beneath the candle light of the cathedral's altar. The air was cool, the walls of Barcelona's Sagrada Família dark, and its pews scattered with disciples of a reborn faith. They spoke in whispers, through prayers of intercession crying out for renewal.

"Phillíp, why have you come?"

"You know."

"Yes, but I had hoped you were not so foolish as to question me here," Roberto leaned in close to his brother's face, "at the very seat of the Narxus."

"Is this not the appropriate forum?" Phillíp demanded rhetorically. "Are we not apostles of the same creed? I have every right to question you."

"But do you have the right to question the will of the Narxus and, vicariously, the will of God?"

"The will of the Narxus?! So, this is The Council's decision?" Phillíp asked, his hiss ringing across the dark vaults of the cathedral's ceiling.

"I do not need The Council," the words came seething from Roberto's mouth. "I brought a truth to the world that lay dormant within *The Writ of Narxus* for a thousand years, a truth that has transformed *everything*. For ten years there has been peace because of my faith."

"Your faith? Listen to yourself!"

Roberto's face flashed red, "I am the revelation! Do you see them," he pointed to the congregation, "kneeling in their pews? Do you know why they pray? They pray for peace to be renewed. Through the Narxus I gave them peace, and they pray to me as much as they pray to God to bring that peace back to them."

"But, not like this."

"Look at me, Phillíp, we have brought light to this world, and I will do what is necessary to preserve that light from the darkness of war. God has flooded the earth to cleanse its impurities before."

"But, you are not God!" Phillíp said, grabbing his brother's shoulder in earnest.

"Do not tell me what I am and what I am not! I have become all things to all men. The flood must follow the fire, as *The Writ of Narxus* proclaims."

"Billions will die."

"As one who is initiated into the mysteries of the Narxus, you should understand that some evils are necessary for the greater good. Think of Judas Iscariot betraying Christ to the Romans – mankind's greatest traitor, mankind's greatest hero. It was his betrayal that led to Christ's crucifixion and thus our salvation. I am no different."

"Roberto, this is mad."

"Good! God is mad. 'For as the heavens are higher than the earth, so are my ways higher than your ways, and my thoughts than your thoughts.' God gave us faith, the Devil gave us reason; I have no use for reason and, if faith has made me mad, then let me pass through the fire to bring forth the flood and renew the earth."

Before Phillip's eyes, his brother's face began to dissolve with age as the cathedral's walls collapsed around them. The world was rendered to a barren flatland; a single footpath marred the dry ground. Where his brother had stood was now an old man, his eyes emerald green, his body frail and small. A long white beard hung from his chin, dirty with the dusty air. Suddenly, there was a shout from behind Phillip; the old man caught fire. His body became enveloped in flames, but his eyes stared unmoving into Phillip's until the fire had claimed them. Nauseous, Phillip averted his gaze and realized the man was not alone. All around him were bodies, heaped together and burning. He again heard shouting from behind and movement.

* * *

Lucien turned his transfixed gaze away from the burning pile, awaking from his dream. Alaric's voice called out to him. He, with the rest of his company, ran toward Lucien, beyond expression at the sight of the fire. "Stilguard?" Alaric asked frantically, his eyes wild with apprehension.

"Gone," came the solemn response.

Alaric bit his lip to fight back the tears. He took a few dizzy steps backward, shaking his head, refusing the fate of his Steward – the fate of his friend. There was nothing to be done and no time to dwell on the nothingness. A horn sounded from the South, its bellow rippling debris through the air as it swept over the soldiers now trapped in Bristing. The call rushed at them like a tidal wave, overwhelming them with its deafening intensity. The men's shouts were swallowed as the wave passed over them and for a moment the world was naught but a terrible thunder of the horn's engulfing voice. The great pyre swelled as if stoked by a smith's bellows, its sharp scent stinging their noses. The call passed and thunder drummed from the South in its absence – a harbinger of the black clouds now crawling from the horizon. The billowing darkness pushed closer, set against clear northern skies. But then came the call of a second horn from the North. And as quickly as the first clouds had set upon the soldiers, more formed at the summoning of the second horn, siphoning their mass from the ground to cover the North with darkness.

Faint at first, the roar's gathering grew in intensity, its approach accompanied by a wall of ash lifted in the wave of sound. The ebony cinders alighted in the air like the devil's eyes and swarmed over the men, scoring their skin and choking their lungs. Again they were submersed in sound and all else was mute to their ears. Tormented in the shrieking silence, the soldiers fell to their knees, gasping, but Lucien stood rigid, his statued gaze aimed on the enclosing elements. The hair on his neck prickled against the cold of clouded light and a fear of the world ordained, finite. "The Searing Veil," he whispered, and the horizons faded into the ominous black.

Alaric ducked but tried to remain standing, tried to fight the insurmountable fear that welled inside, tried to keep a facade of courage for his men. He looked toward Lucien who stood straight, gazing out over the North, his eye as firm and clear as glass, his face placid – and pale with a frailty that crept across his skin like a plague. Above, the hemispheres of darkness loomed closer, enclosing from north and south, narrowing the path of the sun. Alaric looked back from the sky to Lucien's frigidly pale face, watching the last of the light glint off it and vanish as the sun was sealed behind impenetrable doors. A burst of warm air accompanied the sealing of the sun; it ruffled Lucien's hair and brought him from his trance. He looked at the men crouching low on the ground. Purple lightning danced in the clouds, and a low rumbling of thunder played on the men's nerves like coarse laughter. Slowly though, as their captain picked himself off the ground, the men rose, standing with drawn swords. Lucien strode steadily to Alaric's side. Everything seemed to move in slow motion as the veil of present reality had begun to sear away.

"What do you think?" Alaric asked in a low voice.

Lucien calmly responded, "Nephilim."

"How many?"

Lucien shook his head. "Impossible to say, but they've at least given away their position. Divide the men and form them on the northern and southern pillars of the forum; it is likely any opposition will come from there. Distribute the Elite Guards between the two groups; they will have to be the ones to mount the Nephilim. We have maybe a minute, probably less – the trumpets sounded from a distance but the brutes will come fast. Prepare the men, I'll be back in thirty-seconds."

"Wait! What?" Alaric cried.

Lucien ignored his question, yelling instead for Carmine, "Where is the cloth I lent you this morning?!"

The blonde soldier ran to him, presenting the bloody cloth. Lucien nodded and turned back to Alaric. "Assemble them," he said and, as fast as he could, ran from the forum and disappeared behind a burning building. The soldiers yelled at Alaric, frightened that Lucien had abandoned them, but Alaric silenced them, "He is not your concern! The Nephilim are approaching from the North and the South. They have met and felled our comrades, but they have not met us! Form two groups – two Elite Guards on each side to mount the Nephilim. Left group form on the column to the South; stop the gap. Right group, to the North column – same formation. Quickly!"

The men scattered to their posts and, as best they could, barricaded themselves in Bristing's forum. There were ten men to each side. Alaric remained in front of the pyre with sword drawn, directing the two groups. He watched his men form up to the South. Two hugged the large stone column; another stood several feet back from it. Two others crouched against a building adjacent to the column while the rest situated themselves across the entrance, barricading its opening. The men had set and suddenly Lucien appeared in the entrance. He jogged toward Alaric with an uncanny relaxation. In his hand was a small clay jar, its mouth stuffed with Carmine's rag. He hummed as he approached, adjusting the cloth in the mouth of his jar. A crash came from the South as a Nephilim began to tear through the ruins of Bristing towards the men. Alaric set his stance; Lucien remained seemingly unconcerned, humming louder. The Nephilim's steps pounded closer. Lucien hummed the final note of his tune, smiling as he stepped next to Alaric. He looked at his friend and extended the jar towards the pyre just as a Nephilim's roar bellowed through the forum.

The giant burst into sight, using the momentum of his charge to bring down the southern pillar, smashing the three men nearest it. The beast's eyes were ablaze with frenzy and every muscle in its body was tensed with rage. Failing to see the men crouching to its rear, the giant stared straight toward Alaric and Lucien. Immobilized by fear, Alaric stared back. The Nephilim towered above him, three times his size, and Alaric found himself caught in the terrible memory of his first encounter. Lucien still faced away from the giant, blinking into fire, waiting for the tail-like cloth to catch its flame. As it did, Lucien slid his foot back, squaring his shoulders with the Nephilim; he arched his back and steadied his stance, narrowing his eye at his target. With one final breath he lunged forward, hurling the jar at the Nephilim's head. The giant began its charge but, as it came, the jar exploded into its eyes, wrapping orange flames around its face. The creature slid to a halt and roared, rearing its head back in a deep bellow. Suddenly, from the North, came the thundering of footsteps.

"Why do you hesitate?" Lucien yelled out to the soldiers, drawing his scepter from his coat. With Lucien's words the soldiers stood and ran at the stalled giant, swords drawn. Following the lead of the Elite Guards, they hacked and sliced at the giant's heels.

Another Nephilim came crashing in from the North. Alaric turned, running toward it to serve as distraction.

Lucien marched steadily toward the first Nephilim as the men around its feet finally penetrated its leathery skin and severed the tendon. The broken tissue curled up the back of the giant's leg, forcing the creature onto one knee. One of the Guardsmen cried victoriously, jumping onto the Nephilim's back with two daggers drawn. Driving the daggers deep into the Nephilim's back, the soldier climbed to its neck. Blinded by fire and insufferable pain, the Nephilim began to flail its arms about, howling at the sky. Desperately it grabbed at the ground. Its monstrous fists swept the earth, battering several of the soldiers, sending them sprawling through the air, across the forum and into the burning wreckage of Bristing.

One soldier sailed helplessly across to the second Nephilim and was crushed beneath its foot as he hit the ground. As the Nephilim's foot hammered into the earth, an Elite Guardsmen drove his sword between its tendon and anklebone. Gritting his teeth, he clutched onto the hilt of his sword, trying to tear through the tendon. The Nephilim kicked and turned, trying to shake the Guardsman off, but the soldier held fast. Unable to force the soldier to relent his grip, the giant reached down and grabbed him, pulling the Guardsman off its heel, but as the soldier was torn from the Nephilim's heel like a thorn, his sword slid across the tendon, slicing it in half. Howling in pain, the Nephilim stamped its foot on the ground, raising the soldier to its face. Terror-stricken, the soldier flung his sword into the giant's gaping mouth. It struck the Nephilim in back of the throat and, in its screams, came blood for sound. It dropped the Guardsman and began to stumble about the forum, clutching its throat, quickly drowning in rivers of its own blood.

Now one giant remained, rendered immobile by a dagger through the top of its spine. It watched with livid eyes as Lucien strode calmly forward. When he had come within a foot of the Nephilim's charred face, he smiled and lifted his scepter, twisting the base of its handle to extend a concealed blade. He twirled the blade before the Nephilim's eyes mockingly before stabbing through the side of its skull. With a final spasm the beast died, flinging the Guardsman from its back. Lucien wiped his blade clean on the Nephilim's arm and turned away from it. Towards him marched Alaric, covered in blood. He was shaken — they all were shaken — but they were victorious.

Alaric grabbed Lucien's shoulder, panting and nodding. Lucien smiled and gave a fatigued laugh. Overcome with relief, Alaric laughed and released his grip, turning from Lucien. Lifting his sword, he cheered. The surviving men cried out in victory and began to regroup with their captain by the pyre. But their cheers were silenced by a sudden, sharp cry – not of man or of Nephilim, but of something different – guttural and sinister.

The clouds overhead grew darker, and bolts of lightning shot sporadically through the sky. From a burning longhouse aligned to the eastern side of the forum burst forth another creature. Flames billowed out after it, as if the beast were borne by fire. Two grey hooves fell heavily to the ground and an unearthly cry scratched the air. A creature, its legs like a goat, its chest like a man, its face a meld of both, stood before them. Grey, bushy hair curled from around two massive horns atop its head. A bristling beard clung to the pointed chin of its elongated face, and its goat-like ears flicked at the ash swirling round its head. Its body, save for the grey of its hooves and hair, was blood red, and its eyes, unblinking black. It stamped a hoof on the ground, testing the earth, preparing its charge.

But suddenly its eyes met Lucien. Barking, the creature took an unsure step back. It smacked its teeth indecisively and loosed another horrible screech. Regaining its ground, it seemed to speak at Lucien. It gestured to the men and the dead Nephilim, speaking with a guttural hiss.

Lucien walked carefully toward the creature, sidestepping his way through the ashes.

Stepping back, the creature stopped its hissing and barked.

"Hold!" Lucien called, raising his scepter, "Hold."

The beast hissed back as if responding to the order. Lucien was now within striking distance of the creature. "Hold," he said again, raising his scepter higher. With a quick lunge, he lashed out, severing a clawed hand from the creature as it jumped backward into the longhouse and disappeared into the town. Its screams faded through Bristing as it fled. Petrified, Lucien stared at the empty wake of the beast's retreat. Unable to hinder its escape, he looked down at its hand lying on the ground and moved to pick it up. Every man that could ran toward him. The severed hand smoked, cauterized by Lucien's blade. As he picked up the hand, it withered to ash and filtered through his fingers to the ground. The Guardsman who had escaped from Stilguard's company spoke solemnly.

"That was it," he said, "that was what attacked us on the caravan trail – what we couldn't so much as bruise, and here you've severed its hand."

Lucien stood, facing them plainly. "That," he said, pausing to look into each man's face, "that was a Satyr."

He was answered by an expectant silence.

"It is a lesser demon," Lucien continued. "That we can see him means that the veil between this world and the next is searing. I was able to wound the beast whereas you were not because of this," he held aloft his scepter with the blade still protruding from its base. "The red stone crowning my scepter – I call a †felstone; these creatures are unaffected by things corporeal, our means must transcend." His voice trailed and again Alaric was conscious of the frailty in Lucien's form. "Tend to the wounded and the dead, we need to be away from this place quickly."

The men continued to watch Lucien; some of them looked back to Alaric, unsure of whether to obey the order or not. Alaric interceded, commanding his troops: "Tend to the dying," he called bluntly, his eyes remained fixed on Lucien.

The men obeyed their captain's orders, bringing the wounded together in a semi-circle around the pyre. Lucien followed behind them to begin triage of the wounded according to the shouted diagnoses of their able comrades. In return, Lucien shouted to the men to apply pressure to wounds until he could come by to treat them. Throwing off his jacket and rolling up his sleeves, he set to work. Within minutes, he was up to his elbows in the soldiers' blood. One by one, he knelt over them, framed between fire and the black sky, resetting bones and binding wounds.

An hour passed before Lucien reached the final casualty. As he knelt down one last time, the soldier's breath came shallow from his open mouth. Lucien fought through the slick of blood on his fingers to open the man's cuirass. Loosening the sides, he could already feel the bulge of broken ribs. He leaned back; the soldier followed him with his eyes. "There's nothing I can do," Lucien whispered.

The soldier tried to pick himself up, the fear palpable in his eyes. His throat gargled as he struggled to lift his head; blood splashed onto his lips. He collapsed back down, his breath shorter now. His eyes widened with the thirst for air, trained on Lucien until, at last, the life faded from them. Nine now remained of all that had left from Adullam.

All around Lucien were strewn the bodies of the dead and the sullen spirits of the living. With heavy steps, the living ushered the dead into the pyre until none remained save for the soldier at Lucien's knees. Lucien stared down into his folded hands. The blood had dried thick. It peeled apart as Lucien knotted his fingers into fists. He pinched it away from his knuckles, leaving it in shreds around his knees.

"Lucien!" Alaric called, noticing him still kneeling by the pyre.

Startled from his trance, Lucien looked up and over his shoulder. The nine remaining soldiers had formed around Alaric, seated and somberly eating the last of their rations. Lucien waved and leaned back over the soldier.

Alaric watched as he slipped a vial full of the soldier's blood into a side-bag. He sat to eat but kept a distressed eye on Lucien, watching as he proceeded to draw five more vials. Finishing his work, Lucien lifted the battered body over his shoulder and trudged towards the pyre. Gently, he lowered the body and looked into its eyes as the flames swept around them. A shiver passed down his spine as he saw himself reflected in their emptiness. He felt his frailty – felt sick as to death. He reached for his bag.

Alaric watched from a distance as Lucien sank his hand into the bag; watched as he concealed a vial in his palm; watched as he raised it to his mouth and drank, careful that no one should see – but not careful enough.

Alyssa lingered in his mind; her words stirring his suspicion – *Titus doesn't trust him, and neither does Nestor, and neither should you.*

Lucien looked back into the soldier's eyes, grimacing at the reflection of himself in the deep mystery of death. Turning from the pyre, his eye met Alaric's stare. Their gazes locked, Lucien's a challenge to accusation, and Alaric's, a shadowed dread. The wind swirled a wraith of ash between them, breaking their line of sight. Alaric returned to his meal and Lucien strode steadily towards the company. He sat amongst the men and reached for his share of food, eating quietly. After several minutes, the fragility of his face was restored to its natural olive.

"We should begin moving out soon," Lucien said as he swallowed a bite of bread.

"I know," Alaric said softly, "we will. We've already been too long. My company passed a storehouse on the way to the forum. It somehow managed to escape the fire; we should stop back by it and collect more rations. We'll need them for the road home."

"What of Adullam?" one of the soldiers asked.

"All of the Trade Lords are dead. I," Alaric choked on his words, "there is not enough in the storehouse to feed Adullam – nothing but salted meat, bread, and rotten fruit. We need to find water, too. As for Adullam, I honestly don't know what to do. This is not what any of us expected. With the attack, there are not enough of us to take back sufficient supplies and obviously no way to restart the caravan."

There was silence following Alaric's words. He finished his meal quickly and looked at the faces of his sullen soldiers. "It's time to move," he said, and the men jumped to their feet, glad to have something beyond their sorrowful thoughts to occupy them. "We'll go first to the storehouse," Alaric continued, "and then head north out of the town. It'll be late afternoon by then and we'll find a place to rest until midnight. From there we go straight to Adullam – nonstop – so make sure to recuperate this afternoon."

Having instructed the men, Alaric stood and beckoned them to follow. He, Lucien, and the nine remaining soldiers headed out of the forum's northern entrance towards the storehouse. Most of the buildings were, by now, smoldering remains of what they had been. They navigated around them quickly and quietly, and soon they came to the storehouse. Though badly damaged, the building had somehow escaped the town's firing. The soldiers did not have to be ordered; they set straight to filling their packs and pockets with provisions. Alaric sent a pair of them out to find water while the rest collected food, and when they had returned, the company set out.

The eleven exited through a breach in the palisade walls and had been walking through the low grass for several minutes when Lucien noticed a peculiar smell. He looked around to see if others had picked up on the scent, and at length they did.

"Does anyone else smell that?" a soldier called out.

"Yea, I smell it, what is that?" another asked.

"I don't know, but I smell it too."

Lucien pushed his way through the group to Alaric. "Stale ash," he said as he began to jog ahead of the group.

The others maintained their pace with Alaric, watching closely as Lucien stopped fifty meters or so in front of them to wait. As the group approached, Alaric noticed the tension in Lucien's rigid stance; there was a problem. The smell of ash had become heavy in the air, almost nauseating.

Alaric stepped up beside Lucien and looked out over the plains – once fertile land – burned, rendered to ash.

CHAPTER XIV

PHOENIX

"What is this?" Alaric asked, looking over the waste.

"This *was* farmland," said Lucien. "You see the three windmills dotting the horizon?" He knelt down and shifted through the ash with the tips of his fingers.

"The Nephilim?"

"Why would they need to do this?" asked one of the soldiers.

"They were starving the people out, breaking their will," Alaric said. "It was a siege."

Lucien shook his head. "Not siege, it was sport," he countered. "The fields were burned well before the town, more than a week ago, I would estimate. There was a darker mind behind this. The Nephilim break bones, not will."

"The Satyr?"

Lucien nodded.

"However unlikely," Alaric began, "there may be survivors in those mills. We'll divide into three parties, each to a mill. Report back on the northern end of the fields after your inspections. I want to get as far away from Bristing as we can. Carmine, Michael, Barron, you three come with me. Leon, Orleans, Fields – go to the furthest mill, we'll rendezvous just beyond it so take Ranger with you. Hold him up as best as you can. Ranger," Alaric addressed the soldier, gripping his arm. His skin was cold to

Alaric's touch, his body shivered, but his eyes were filled with steady determination, "keep it up, you can rest once you're at the mill. Brace yourself between Orleans and Fields; go on ahead." Alaric waited as Ranger's group was a good ways off before turning to Lucien. "Is there nothing more you can do for him?" he whispered.

"He's bleeding internally. I can't stop it."

Crestfallen, Alaric nodded and gave out final orders, "Gaverick and Marion, go with Lucien. My group is going right; Lucien's, left."

The remaining two teams parted into the field. The ash-laden ground crunched forebodingly beneath their feet, and trails of black powder were left hanging in their path.

As Alaric's team made their approach, the windmill took proper shape, its detail growing ever clearer. It was in a more dilapidated shape than Alaric had suspected. Wrought of stone, only the framework remained, along with a skeleton of its fire-scarred, wooden vanes. The roofing had collapsed in, blocking the doorway, but a large hole was present in the side of the mill, *kicked out by a Nephilim*, Alaric assumed. The four soldiers approached the hole quietly, forming up alongside the wall just beneath its opening. Alaric knelt down toward Barron. He pounded his fist twice on his thigh and Barron smiled. Looking up at the hole, he stepped quickly away from the wall. He walked back a few steps, placed a dagger between his teeth and ran forward again; stepping high, he leapt off Alaric's bent knee, ran up the wall, grabbed the ledge at the base of the opening, and pulled himself up onto his feet. His head swiveled across the room and he jumped down to the floor.

Alaric watched him disappear and whispered sharply after him, "Barron?"

"It's alright, sir!" Barron called back, "The room's clear. The door is blocked in pretty good; there's enough rubble piled up on the ground for me to jump back out the opening. The gear shaft and the grinding wheel are shot – buried under the roof. No sign that anyone was ever in here – just the Nephilim and their sport."

"Understood," Alaric called in reply. He and the other two men had stepped back from the wall, expecting Barron's return. "Anything salvageable?"

"No sir," he called back, "not unless you have any use for a cracked shingle," and out of the hole came a roofing shingle, spinning past

Carmine's head. Barron leapt back into view, steadying himself against the wall and laughing at Carmine as he dodged the flying debris. Reaching to the ground, Carmine retrieved the shingle and sent it hurtling back toward Barron. It smashed against the wall several feet from its target and Barron gave another little chuckle. He jumped down from the hole and rolled to soften his landing, popping up in Carmine's face. "That was terrible," he said smiling.

"Enough," Alaric interjected as he stared out over the burnt fields trying to spot the other teams. "We don't have time for games. You're soldiers," he said, turning back to them, "and your Steward has died today."

"I don't see what that has to do with a shingle," Carmine whispered to Barron behind Alaric's back.

Alaric, whose ears were far more acute than Carmine gave them credit for being, swung around and hit the young soldier in the face with the back of his hand. The unexpected blow knocked Carmine onto the ground and left him with a bloodied lip. "Your friends have died today," Alaric retorted with placid fury. His face was sterner than the windmill's stone, "And if it were not for their deaths, *you* would have died. Fate has favored you today; show some respect. This is no time for games. We're not through this yet." He turned his scowl to the north, "Follow my lead to the rendezvous point, we need to form up with everyone else; see if they found anything."

The four had not been walking long when they heard a voice crying out for them. A man came running towards them, his breathless voice carrying hoarsely across the field; it was Leon. Alaric ran towards him and, as they neared one another, Leon stopped, putting his hands on his hips. He grimaced at the cramping pain in his side. "What is it? What's happened, Leon?" Alaric asked, placing a hand on Leon's shoulders.

Leon shook his head and stretched his tongue, trying to draw saliva from his dry mouth. Finally, he cleared his throat and spoke, "It's fine, we're fine. We found something."

"What is it? What did you find?" Alaric beseeched him.

Leon smiled and panted, "It's just to the left of the rendezvous point." He looked up at Alaric and laughed, "It's big. Go, I'll join you, I just need a moment's rest."

Alaric nodded and signaled to Carmine, "Stay with him and regroup with us quickly." Turning back to Leon he asked, "Are the others there still?"

"Yes, I believe so, they'll call out to you when you're closer."

"Very well, but don't stay too long; the night is closing in and we need to be positioned safely."

"Yes, sir," Leon respectfully replied; Alaric, Barron, and Michael sprinted off towards their other comrades. As they left, Alaric heard Carmine ask, "What is it that's up there? You have to tell me if I have to wait here with you."

Alaric heard Leon laugh and say, "All right, fair enough, I'll tell you…" – and as the distance grew between them, Leon's voice was phased out.

Alaric was fifty meters or so from the windmill when he heard a loud whistle from inside. Orleans stepped through the doorway of the mill with two fingers in his mouth and whistled to him again, waving his other hand in the air. Behind Orleans, Alaric could see Ranger propped up against the wall.

"Gentlemen," Orleans said in a gruff but tenor voice as Alaric and his men approached, "I've been beset here by Lucien to watch out for Ranger – keep 'im safe and comfortable."

"Thank you," Alaric said, looking past Orleans and down at Ranger as he slept.

"Most welcome, sir," he returned, "Fields is off with Lucien and the rest. They're a bit further north and to your left, you should have no trouble spottin' 'em."

"What is it they have found? Leon would not say."

"Well, sir, I'd love to tell ya' but ya' see, Ranger requested that we surprise you. Man's got it rough, sir; it's the least we can do 'im."

"Noble, Orleans," Alaric said, his tone slightly perturbed.

"Why thank you, sir."

Alaric left then without another word, and Michael followed. Barron tarried behind to shake his head disappointedly at Orleans.

"What ya' want me to say, lad?" Orleans said, trying to conceal a smile.

Glaring, Barron said nothing, but turned to catch up with Alaric and Michael, his feet drumming to the music of Orleans' laughter.

As Alaric stepped from the ashen fields, a strong, warm wind picked up from the West and spilled over the grassland, tossing its blades like a sea poured in the silver glint of the sun. Alaric looked into the wind to catch glimpse of Lucien running through the wold, wrapped in the orange of the setting sun. Stopping suddenly, he seemed to climb up on top of the grass as if floating on the wind.

As Alaric marched on, he could see that Lucien was perched on the crossbeam of a short, wooden fence. He stood stoutly; his feet spread the width of his shoulders and his palms rested atop the crowning stone of his scepter, its blade stuck securely in the fencepost to brace him. Elegantly posed, he stood awaiting Alaric's astonishment upon the realization that behind him were trapped a dozen horses and at least a thousand cattle.

Alaric stumbled forward, bracing himself on the fence to keep from sinking to his knees. A warm breeze danced across his face, opening his eyes to behold the myriad of creatures grazing in silver-green fields, beset by rays of golden hue and heavenly providence. The dying sun washed the world in a haze of brilliant light. Aghast, Alaric looked up at Lucien who remained poised on the fence, wrapped in the surreal. Alaric became detached from himself, hearing his voice speak to Lucien, "How many?"

Smiling, Lucien shrugged and said, "By estimation alone, there must be a thousand cattle, at least, and several horses are mixed in amongst them."

Alaric looked back over the herd. He stood dazed on the lower rung of the fence, trying to gain a higher vantage. He gazed at them all – trying to count – but became lost in the multitudes. Lucien spoke again, his voice drifted in Alaric's ears like the faint babble of water. "The fence is made from Bristing's palisade. I noticed when we first arrived that some of the fortifications had been uprooted. I was then unsure why and, focused on more pressing matters, dismissed the observation. Thinking back on it though, in the same spirit that the Nephilim burned Bristing's crops, they quarantined their cattle, uprooting the palisade."

"Why would they not have killed these alongside the people?" Alaric asked, snapping back from a type of waking dream.

"And waste them? Aureus must be fed," Lucien responded to the air. "Most likely, their intention was to herd them back to The Golden City." Lucien leaned into the wind and let himself fall a ways from the fence before he stretched out his legs to land softly in the grass. He looked back to Alaric and retracted his scepter, concealing it again in his coat. "We have an advantage now. With the horses we can make it back to Adullam in a fraction of the time it took us to get here." His eye darted out all across the East; he was lost to his thoughts. "We can begin the exodus; bring Adullam into the light; cross the Briswold to the Borderlands. Take the cattle – that can begin immediately – from there, your people stand a chance. Swiftly done though, Aureus will not tarry."

"Wait, what?" Alaric interjected Lucien's streaming conscious, "What are you saying? The Borderlands? Adullam is safer..."

"Alaric!" Orleans called from a distance with his unmistakable accent. Twice more he called until Alaric turned to see him, Leon, and Carmine carrying Ranger.

"He's all shivers," Orleans yelled, "coughin' out blood."

Alaric glanced back to Lucien and together they sprinted towards Ranger and the others. Orleans set Ranger softly in the grass as Alaric and Lucien knelt down on either side of him. Lucien set to work inspecting Ranger, while Alaric reached for his face. The dying soldier's eyes were closed, his breathing sporadic and shallow; his face was pale and spotted with blood from his coughing. Alaric shook him awake and pulled at the skin under Ranger's eyes with his thumbs. He coughed blood again and blinked his eyes open. With a whimpering laugh he whispered, "No, it's too late." He shook his head, "I'm just a hindrance anyway."

Lucien sat back slowly in the grass; Alaric continued to stare into Ranger's eyes, watching as the life faded from them. Gently, he laid the soldier's head on the ground, his death, again bringing forward the tragedy of the morning. Alaric stood; for a moment he remained staring quietly at Ranger. He then turned and walked alone into the fields of ash.

CHAPTER XV

WE WHO REMAIN

The night was full when the soldiers reconvened. They gathered round a fire lit in the ashen fields. From the darkness emerged a procession – of men and solemn marching, with Aaron Ranger borne above. The men lay their comrade gently onto the flames as Alaric came to the side of the fire, Aaron's sword lain across his open palms. All present closed in to form a circle around the fire as Alaric recited, "From the Holy Word of our Shaddai: 'Those who live by the sword, surely will die by it.' Ever true, The Almighty has called His children unto their fate. Today, we who remain behold that fate; from the dust, our comrades were formed, and to the dust do they now return." Alaric ceremoniously slid the blade across the palm of his left had, drawing his own blood. He passed the sword on, each man in the circle observing the same ritual. At last, opposite the fire from Alaric, the sword passed to Lucien.

Holding it aloft in both hands, Lucien hesitated. He looked from the blade in his hands, to the fire, and at last into Alaric's eyes. Slowly he drew the blade across his palm until he felt the warm trickle drop from his hand, giving back a taste of the blood he had stolen. Alaric's steady gaze passed to the next soldier and the sword was taken from Lucien's grasp. Finally, as the bloodstained blade came back to Alaric, he continued with the ceremony: "We shed our blood to remember that which was shed for us. For it was by blood we were purified and made whole, and it is by blood that we stand today. May this scar remain, lest we forget the sacrifices made for us." Stepping closer to the fire, Alaric laid the sword on Ranger's chest.

With the rite concluded, they silently processed away from the fire to let their comrade return to dust and join with the ash surrounding him. Once they reached the grass, the procession broke, but the men remained silent as they made their way to the far side of the cattle fence. As they gathered their equipment and congregated in a circle to build a small fire, Alaric stopped Lucien.

"We need to speak, come with me."

Lucien nodded and the two walked a little way into the solitude of the night.

Along the way he asked, "The service, for Aaron Ranger, is that a common rite?"

Alaric gave a concise reply, his thoughts elsewhere, "Yes, a soldier's rite. Usually the ceremony is a bit longer; each man present speaks briefly, commemorating the dead. We omitted that because, with our position to Bristing, I thought it wise to be brief."

"Wise indeed," Lucien responded.

"It is also wise," Alaric said, coming to a stop, "to know your enemies."

Lucien was glad the night hid the sudden flush of his face. "I'm not sure I understand what you mean," he lied.

"I saw you shudder during the ceremony when I was speaking about our purification through blood."

"Coincidence, I'm sure. It was nothing more than a cold shiver."

Ignoring the explanation Alaric continued, "I saw you drink the blood today, by the pyre in Bristing."

Lucien stood rigid.

"Is that why you've been working in the Infirmary? So you can always keep a fresh supply with no suspicion?"

"I'm a doctor," Lucien replied weakly.

"Exactly why no one would question your blood samples. When I first met you, out on the field, you were taking them; I thought for some experiment or testing – a medical reason, but you drink them. Why?"

Lucien remained silent, trapped.

"I've known you at least long enough to know you always have something to say," Alaric challenged, "so say it."

"I don't know what you think you saw today…"

"Oh, I think you know what I saw, Lucien. I saw *you* – the first real glimpse. So who are you, Lucien, what are you?"

"What am I?" Lucien asked, his tone incredulous.

"Yes, Lucien! What are you? Who are you? Give me something – anything! Something true for once. We'll start small, where are you from? That's easy enough."

But Lucien said nothing.

"Could you have saved him?"

"The Nephilim either crush you or they don't; there's not much in between."

Baring his teeth, Alaric charged forward and grabbed Lucien by the collar, driving his back against the trunk of a tree. He held Lucien's face close to his own, glaring into his one eye, its depths like eternity, a deathless void, an insurmountable darkness. Alaric sank into its placid emptiness, his breath beginning to tremble.

"You see it, don't you," Lucien whispered, "something deep and unsearchable. You see the end of all things, the lifeless mirror of my eye. You are not the first. My mother died giving birth to me; my father, as I've told you, was a vintner. We lived on a farm in the South. I'm not sure that he ever loved me – I know he didn't – all he ever saw was her death in my eyes. And I've been alone now far longer than I care to remember."

Shivering, Alaric released his grip, stepping slowly away to escape the black feeling.

"I couldn't save him, Alaric. He was dead before your men ever laid him at my feet."

"Then why the blood?" he asked.

"I don't know," Lucien's voice was weak and defeated, "it sustains me. I wish I could explain – even to myself."

"And the mask?"

Lucien drew a deep, unsure breath. "I've told you," he said, carefully removing the mask, "It's just a bandage." Tilting his head, he showed Alaric the stark linen beneath.

"So that's it then?" Alaric objected. "All the mystery; all the show, it's emptiness."

Afflicted souls... came a voice from the recess of Lucien's darkest memories ... *afflicted ... They tread upon emptiness ... upon emptiness... Forever they wander ... forever ... wander to prepare the night.* Slowly he nodded, biting his lips as they trembled, but his face remained firm, his eye hollow. For some time they stood together in silence; only the night was between them, Lucien revealed, defenseless. There was a questioning sensation in Alaric. There was yet a distance, of unspeakable things, of cavernous secrets, but there was shame overwhelming it all, and such a shame that Alaric could not blacken his resolve to pry on.

Just then, there came a rustling in the grass and Carmine stumbled from the shadows, a flask clutched against his chest. Alaric and Lucien exchanged sideways glances, offering respite from their solemn confrontation as Carmine stood between them trying to maintain his balance.

"That was remarkably fast," Lucien said, looking from the flask to Carmine's eyes, which, even in the dark, were observably bloodshot with drunkenness.

"We have questions," he stammered, swaying on his feet.

"Carmine," Alaric ordered, "stand down and return to the camp."

Carmine waved Alaric off and fixed his eyes on Lucien. "If you do not come with me, within a few seconds there will be several men with swords here who will no longer have time for questions. You surrender and come with me now to explain everything, or you die." He looked at Alaric, and stumbled to the side but caught himself before he fell to the ground. "We all need the truth, Alaric, and we are superseding any order you might give contrary to the contrary. Temporary mutiny you understand – just for the hour." Carmine hiccupped loudly and then continued, "Both of you, come with me."

"Soldier," Alaric ordered.

"Ten-seconds and he's dead," Carmine yelled, "don't – test it."

Alaric glared at the back of Carmine's head and begrudgingly followed him back to the camp alongside Lucien. The three of them crested a small hill and could see the small fire directly below. In no time, they had rejoined the soldiers and were met by cheers at Carmine's success.

"You were bluffing," Alaric fumed, observing the soldiers seated around the fire, "you were bluffing."

"'Course I am... was –" Carmine stammered again, turning directly toward Alaric to meet him nose to nose, "–I'm drunk." Saying this Carmine swiveled towards Lucien. "Your mouth," Carmine spoke to Lucien's wry expression, "is not for smiling – it is for talking." He concluded these words by falling backwards to sit amongst the soldiers.

"You commanded that Satyr," came a voice from the inquisitors. "We saw it, its confusion. It listened to you."

"Do you condemn me for striking against your adversary – the greatest one you have yet to meet? A creature that, according to Gaverick," Lucien said coolly, "killed your Steward."

Lucien looked into each man's face, forcing him to consider the question before he continued. "I have trained some of you, though briefly, to fight Nephilim. If we had had time for proper training not a man would have died today, yet we *were* able to overcome them. Are the bandages around your wounds not there by my hands? Did I not carefully tend to each of you? Here, you accuse me in spite of the things that I have done."

The muted light around the fire blurred their sight of Lucien's movement as he reached swiftly into his coat and drew his scepter, twisting its hilt to let the blade it concealed spring forth with a piercing ring. "This is why the Satyr feared me! This is what allowed me to sever its hand. It is time you understand what you are up against; it is time you choose loyalties."

To God and Truth locked behind its gate,
until the hour is darkest,
for their coming we wait.

Divided, the realms of sight and fate,
in this age of toil,
our questions never sate.

Nor until the reason of men is turned to faith,
beneath such a cloud,
the fears never abate.

We've come through the noise, the fury, the hate,
now the hour is darkest,
no longer we must wait.

It sears, it falls, it seals our fate
The Veil of Kingdoms
a new world, create.

Again to the earth, a mystery coronate
The Searing Veil
rend and reanimate.'

The soldiers sat in silent confusion.

"There is a veil," Lucien began to translate, "that divides the realms of this world, The Veil of Kingdoms, meant to separate our physical world from the transcendental. For thousands of years it has existed, but it has not always been, and will not always be. The old mythologies of the world were born through a more direct interaction with this transcendental realm. The first Nephilim were created by spiritual conception, these transcendental beings besetting women and conceiving giants – and just as before, they are again conceived in Aureus."

Lucien paused to gauge his audience's understanding and continued. "You have heard the teaching of The Shaddai, that our struggle is not against flesh and blood, but against the powers of the darkness of this age, and the spiritual forces of evil in the heavenly realms. This teaching marked a new age through the separation of Kingdoms behind The Veil, but a newer age is approaching – The Veil is searing – and as you previewed in Bristing, the powers of this dark world will take flesh, and they will take blood."

"Ridiculous!" Carmine yelled, his voice slurry. "That poem – terrible. *I* could have written a better poem than that."

"Stop taking the world so seriously," Lucien scoffed, "and believe in something bigger than you think you can imagine. That poem is from a collection of poems well over a thousand years old – *The Writ of Narxus* – mapping the culmination of existence, the salvation of man," he paused, "the end of the world."

Carmine fell down.

"It was written in the thirteenth century, by a mystic group of religious reformists calling themselves, *El Adviento del Sol* – The Advent of the Sun. They were destroyed, but some of their writings remained hidden

138

to be reanimated in a later century. Foremost among their writings was *The Writ of Narxus*, and from its pages, to protect and nurture its secrets, was born the society of the Narxus."

"What is Narxus? What does that mean?" a soldier asked.

Lucien shrugged, "Narxus, along with everything else – The Veil of Kingdoms, Searing Veil, all the names – all a revelation to some thirteenth century mystic. Narxus *is* what it means; there is nothing else. Like literature or music perhaps, its meaning doesn't carry in translation, if it's written or shown in any other way, it isn't what it was. Even Aureus," he suddenly emphasized, "was prophesied."

"Prophesied," Barron exclaimed, "by this *Writ of Narxus*?!"

"Of course," Lucien answered. "Do you think this is some sort of joke, that the man in the mask is here to entertain you with fairy stories round the campfire? What you saw today was real. When the Indivinate supplanted the nations, when the foundations of the earth where shaken and restructured, when Aureus took hold of the world and received his crown, we entered into a newer Age and The Veil of Kingdoms began to sear."

"How is it you know all of these things?" one of the soldiers protested.

"Because I know of the Narxus!" Lucien's breath was heavy and his eye wide as a zealot's. "The process was slow at the start, lesser beings came through the veil – the incubus, for example. They are kept within Aureus to ravish enslaved women and breed the Nephilim but, as The Veil sears further, greater beings will permeate through. The Satyr, though a lesser demon still, is a warning that the rift in The Veil has begun to open wide. Our fight is no longer within our spirits. The heavenly Kingdom is returning."

"What are you indoctrinating us with?" one man accused, cutting Lucien off from speaking further "He is…"

"…trying to explain," retorted Gaverick, jumping to his feet. "I fought the Satyr; I watched it kill Stilguard; I stabbed my sword into its chest. *None of us* could challenge it and, if this is just a lesser demon…" his voice trailed. "We've always known we live in the shadow of the end; we've always known things were destined to get worse – however much you care to deny it – we've known." Gaverick nodded that Lucien could continue and sat down.

"Once The Veil has torn wide enough – and this is *important* because it is man's faith that tears The Veil; when humanity is ripened to the point that it can be harvested, The Veil will be rent – and, once wide enough, a higher echelon of beings can permeate through: the benign, Angels, Archangels; Virtues, Dominations; Thrones, Seraphim; the world will open to them who sow the seeds of The Shaddai's redemption."

"There is no redemption," Carmine spoke, his mouth dry and dehydrated, and the words clung to the roof of his mouth. "The Shaddai is nothing more than the Creator – a clockmaker. Our time is set and once the clock stops ticking ... that's it; it's over. He sits and observes the sufferings of man and leaves us to our lonely demise, letting the earth run its course with no further regard. Why else would evils, such as we have endured our whole lives, befall us. If The Shaddai was more, He would stop our suffering."

"Is that so?" asked Lucien.

"It is. He makes no interaction with the course of nature He himself has set." The threatened feeling in Carmine was evident in the tremor of his voice. He seemed leery of Lucien's impending words.

"I ask you then, what clockmaker is not intimately familiar with his creation? What clockmaker does not fine-tune his clock or mend its gears when they jam? Why would he abandon his tedious work upon its completion and not enjoy the fruits of his labor or continue to ensure its proper functioning? And what clock ever understands its maker or can comprehend the complexity of its own design?"

"Humanity – the universe – is slightly more complicated than a clock," Carmine replied sarcastically. "I do not doubt His ability, only His motives. Perhaps we are dated, worn-out, obsolete, and He has moved on to better things. We are like an old, forgotten book on the shelf of an archive: once, we were fresh and interesting, but ages of existence and wear have made us less desirable. Three thousand, four thousand years ago," Carmine stuttered through the difficulty of his inebriated condition, "then He cared – but not today. Today we are abandoned and to say otherwise is deliberate ignorance."

All were silent. Lucien was poised to answer, but he let the tension of silence mount before he shattered it with elegant repose – inciting within himself an intoxicating passion befit to defend his conviction. "Ignorance," he paused thoughtfully, "or faith?" The question only thickened the atmosphere, dampening even the sounds of breathing. The firelight flickered off Carmine's fair skin, lighting his eyes with uncertainty. Lucien continued, "Can you not hear them? The harmonics of the universe – the balance and the symmetry in their tenor. The ebb and flow, the come and go, the resounding symphony of all souls borne upon the back of their creator, taken in His hands and caressed amidst the darkness of greatest despair. The whole universe cries out in a song of perfect precision within the purpose of its creation." Lucien tilted his head to the side as if listening to the heavens. He rocked his head softly to and fro, and a fragile smile spread across his face and a sadness filled the hollow of his eye. "The celestial bodies above glide upon their unmarked path through the oblivion of space, their grace of harmony not lost to a great void, but orchestrated by Him who transcends the workings of our frail minds."

The soldiers were still for a moment until Lucien removed his focus from the silent sounds of heaven and, gazing back upon Carmine, he said, "Simply because you do not understand life's circumstances does not mean you have been abandoned to face them until your undoing. It is not The Almighty that denies us, but we who deny The Almighty. You think that because you observe ritual, He owes you something. It is you who owes everything. If you are abandoned, it is because you have placed yourself in exile and have no true faith that He can bring you back." Lucien finished with a tongue of remorse, evoked by his own reconciliation of faith. Carmine sat down to be hidden amongst the shadows of his comrades.

It was then Alaric who spoke for the first time. Stepping from the darkness behind Lucien, he redirected the conversation, "The felstone you mentioned this morning, atop your scepter."

"Yes," Lucien said, blinking out of his contemplative stare to focus on his explanation, "the felstones – a name I coined myself this time. They were the stones adorning Aureus' crown before he was cast from on high. His crown was shattered as it landed upon the earth, and its stones lost. Upon his return to power, he commissioned his servants to gather them. But, corrupted by the stone's corrosive nature, these servants now hoard them away in secret."

"Their corrosive nature?" Gaverick asked.

"The power – which is not really the appropriate word – but the power they are imbued with does strange things to a purposeless mind.

"Since before the creation of The Veil," he continued, "the acquisition of relics – for example – has been a common religious practice as it was believed that certain items are afforded spiritual power which man can then harness for his own use. When The Veil of Kingdoms was set in place, the ancient relics of the world were believed to transcend its shielding as confluences of spiritual power. The felstones are similar, created for the heavens, their potency on earth will be felt by any demon. The acquisition of felstones will allow you to regain the authority you are so rapidly losing."

"How is it you have come by one of Aureus' stones?" Alaric cautiously asked.

Lucien turned to him and smiled. "I have found the ones tasked with the stones' excavation. From every corner of the earth the stones were collected, having been treasured and traded for countless centuries, but now they rest in the mountains of the Borderlands with those who found them."

CHAPTER XVI

THE LUCIEN

Before Phillíp stood a man, his eyes as emeralds; his body was frail and small, and his long white beard dirty with the dust hanging in the air along their sequestered path. Suddenly Phillíp felt very much alone in the face of this old man, accompanied only by the presence of fear circling above.

"I am," the elderly man spoke after a thoughtful investigation, "the Lucien."

At the sound of this name, Phillíp was lost in himself. The elderly man's beard began to retreat back into his face; the lines on his forehead and under his eyes stretched to more youthful years; stone walls burst forth from beneath the earth, showering the air with dust. When the filth had settled, Phillíp stared into the emerald green of his brother's zealot eyes. They stood together in the apse of the basilica beneath the cathedral of La Sagrada Família, the secret court of the Narxus. Roberto turned from Phillíp, seating himself in the center of a semi-circle formation of twelve thrones, the thrones of the Elders. He sat rigidly against the high backing of the throne and stared blankly down the dark hall of the basilica.

"The oceans have been rising for a week now," Phillíp spoke quietly, his voice easily penetrated the silence; retained within the basilica's heavy walls, it resonated round the domed apse. "Reports say there's no sign of it stopping. How do you know it won't consume us?"

"Our cause is just and our motives righteous," Roberto spoke to the emptiness before him; his voice was hollow and expressionless, "God will not allow us to be swept away. As he provided for Noah, he will provide for us."

"Our cause, Roberto, *our* motives? Where are the other Elders? Why have we not heard from them?"

"I speak for them!" Roberto's voice rang down the length of the basilica.

"I'm just concerned..."

"It is not your place to be concerned, Phillip, you are not an Elder; do not presume to be! You are a shadow! A nonentity! Your voice means nothing here!"

"I make no presumptions," Phillip bowed his eyes but his voice darkened, "but I know what you've done."

"Are you my accuser now?" Roberto asked, standing from his throne, his arms lifted in disbelief. "Is that why you have come? The rest of the world comes too! They come because I have called them. They come because I am their savior! But why dear brother have you come?"

"I have come for your confession."

"Ah! Not my accuser, my confessor. I stand corrected," he replied. "Very well, you've caught me, little brother, wouldn't father be proud." He smiled knowingly. "I see now why he never taught you of the Narxus; I see what he must have seen in you even from your childhood – you lack the courage and the understanding to do what is necessary for the salvation of man; you lack the will to follow through. I didn't see it then, so I taught you – taught you everything he taught me, and now we stand upon the threshold of salvation and you are blind to it.

"But very well, you want a confession? Well forgive me, father, for I have sinned," Roberto mocked. He laughed to himself and continued speaking, "There's enough of a nuclear arsenal on our continent alone to destroy the earth several times, you know, so it wasn't hard to gather enough to melt the Poles – not when the world beckons to my call. And it wasn't hard to convince the world that it was God who destroyed the Poles – not when I am their prophet. God's Divine Fire falls from the heavens at the axes of the earth to raise the oceans and flood the lands with sanctified

144

waters of purification – very biblical sounding; Sodom and Gomorrah without the pillars of salt and mix in Noah's Flood without the ark and you've got yourself an act of God. And in place of an ark, there is Aureus. People are coming already. I have called them and they have come, and people will continue to come as the waters continue to rise, and we can have peace again, Phillíp, peace! But you know all of this. You've not come to hear me rant about things you already know. You've come because I've killed them. I've killed the Elders and you want to know why. Is that it?"

Phillíp nodded slowly, sunken by the sound of the horrible truth.

"I killed them because, like you, they could not do what was necessary to restore peace and to bring salvation. They could only follow *The Writ of Narxus* so far and, at a point, it became beyond them to understand, just as it became beyond you to understand. I am its interpreter; *The Writ* has chosen me to fulfill its prophecies; the council of Elders had surpassed its purpose and would have only been an interference."

"It is not your place…" Phillíp said weakly.

"It *is* my place! And my place alone! Those who died deserved death; there is no one righteous! No one save for me! I stand alone to usher on man's end – to usher on man's salvation! The people will come! They will come to my Aureus and the heavens will open and the earth will be made new! For I am the Lucien – I am the light!"

Roberto had stepped close to Phillíp, his eyes glowing bright, glaring down with the pretense of a god; but he stood alone, stood in the solitude of the darkened basilica.

"And I am a shadow," Phillíp whispered, leaning to his brother's ear, "come to steal the light and make it his own."

Roberto gasped as the dagger slid silently into his gut; he collapsed to the floor as the blood flowed freely from around the blade's hilt.

"Oh light, oh light, who pierced the night, where has your flame gone now?" Phillíp chanted as his brother's lungs begged for air. As he looked down upon the dying figure, it began to transform. A white beard, a frail body, emerald eyes sunk deep beneath aged lines. "I am the Lucien," the old man said again, lying near death upon the dusted, barren path.

"You are an impostor," Phillíp replied, his voice callous and cold.

Drawing a last gasp of air the old man began to recite:

Prepare the night for day must break and fail

Afflicted souls borne across the sky
shall find no solace in the burdened air

Fight or fail as the sun
Its reflection willed to thee
As grace descends upon troubled hearts

The souls, borne by vice,
Will not seek the shards of their redemption

But whither shall the troubled men go
For they tread upon emptiness

Forever they wander to prepare night

Scour the globe oh troubled souls
Fill the air with your woe

Soon you say the sun must fail
But no it fights forever more

Blind are the souls borne by vice
For to them majesty is mockery

In pride, all fall far
Where hope can barely reach

Cower from the sun
Its rays pierce the essence of all

Reflected is the fate of man;
The face of their instability

'Tis pride that burns
For it is the marrow of men

Yet curse the sun for your burning passion
And seek the night forever more
But the sun shall never fail

They bear their weight and forge their way
Though grace is plain to see

Its rays descend to touch the troubled souls
But men are fools and ne'er shall know
So forever they prepare the night

"You would use *The Writ of Narxus* against me?" Phillíp asked, filled with a new vigor of rage. "You would corrupt its lines, its holy prominence, to deprive me my due reward? You have poisoned its prophecies!"

"You are blind to its prophecies," Lucien scoffed. "Even as I am before you, you cannot comprehend."

"I am justified," Phillíp spat bitterly.

Lucien shook his head and Phillíp knelt down beside him. Staring into his eyes, Phillíp smiled and said, "I will be welcomed as a Prince for this." He stood, lifting his foot high into the air, and dug his heel into the side of Lucien's face, breaking his neck. Lucien twitched as his nerves were severed, and lay dead upon the empty ground.

Lucien, the impostor, dead. Phillíp felt a new sensation permeating into him from the surrounding atmosphere. He had acted without understanding. Some prescient awareness emanated its anger upon him and he was surrounded by such humiliation that he began to drown. He felt its level rise. Helplessly he fell to his knees. Phillíp was aware of himself from all angles and watched in quiet as the humiliation rose up above his neck. Prescience justified this death – his own death – with placid irreverence. Phillíp could feel the pressure under his ears. He watched as he arched his head back and raked his fingers down his neck, straining his whole being to rise against the rushing tide. He had strayed from the shallows of his subconscious and into the deep places of his mind. The shore no longer visible, all the pieces of himself had been drawn into the sea.

As Phillíp was overtaken and completely submerged in the fatal hands of his future, the ground beneath his knees began to swell with deeds of his past, and from it grew an earthen figure in his likeness. It lifted him upon its shoulders so Phillip's head was above the drowning pool of humiliation. The earthen figure continued to grow as Phillip believed himself to be mastering his future. Soon he was towering above all condemnation, standing upon the justifications of his past until all that remained was the vain attempt to merit his own salvation; by that he was borne upon the shoulders of his past to Aureus. A fierce light shone then from above and, from the clouds emerged a shining figure, descending slowly from the heavens. As Phillip, borne upon the justification of his past, arrived at the golden gates of Aureus, the shining figure disappeared behind its walls.

As he reached the gates, Phillip's past began to dissolve back into the earth until finally it was no more and he was left alone, marveling at the seamless creation of Aureus' golden walls – the vibrancy of which shone greater than the sun. A great drum began to pound from behind the walls. Startled, Phillip stumbled backwards and a small crack appeared in the gate, a dark divide in the radiating glory. As the drums grew louder, the crack grew wider and soon, an even greater light shown forth from behind the doors. Phillip watched as two giants pushed the magnificent doors open in tune with the beating of the drum; caught in the radiant light, they seemed heavenly. They held the doors open for Phillip as he crossed the threshold of Aureus and, upon entering, he heard a voice, which radiated like the light – surrounding and engulfing him.

* * *

Lucien awoke in a cold sweat to the sound of Orleans' voice calling out for Alaric. He sat up in his place and blinked at the emerging light, still an opaque glow to the east but brighter than the blackness of his dream. He watched Alaric come out from amongst the cattle and step over the fence post to meet Orleans. Lucien picked himself up and took stiff steps towards them.

"Alaric," Orleans said, "I got ta' thinking 'bout this plan last night; and, I don't know, but it just don't sound like the wisest option."

"What's your concern?" Lucien heard Alaric respond, his voice slurred with an early morning blear. He was tired and restless. Lucien could see the toll that the past days had taken on him.

"I understand the exodus," Orleans continued, "makes sense ta' me, but here is my concern: what if – while I and everyone else are here with tha' cattle – if while we're here, tha' Nephilim come ta' collect their livestock?"

"You shouldn't worry yourself, Orleans," Lucien said, appearing beside them.

Orleans jumped at the sudden surprise of Lucien's voice, "Damn scary how ya' do that," he exclaimed back.

"They have twice as much ground to cover as we do," Lucien continued, "and, if Alaric and I can move swiftly, there'll be no problem."

"You've said that, but my thoughts are, if ya' goin' ta' bring all of Adullam out into tha' open, ya' gonna' be movin' a lot slower on tha' return."

"We send someone ahead," Alaric said, after a considerable moment of silence. "We have the horses."

"Well, if you goin' ta' do that then why can't we start ta' move tha' cattle now?" Orleans asked. "We have a general idea of where ta' go."

"The problem with that is we won't be able to coordinate where you are. We may not be able to find you."

"No," Lucien corrected, "I think Orleans is right. We can track their movements and catch up with them easily. I can even tell you directly where to go. You should be able to find the correct place on your own."

"If we can track them, so can the Nephilim though," Alaric said.

"Not likely, by the time the Nephilim reach this place the trail will be cold, there will not be any real sign of our movements."

"Sounds dodgy, Lucien," Orleans responded.

"That's all that can be done," he replied and yawned. "I thought we discussed all of this last night so as not to waste any more time. Quite simply, it's impossible, not to mention blindly ignorant to bring the cattle to Adullam. It would be the equivalent of personally inviting the Nephilim to your home and then opening your doors wide for the banquet."

"The banquet?" Orleans asked.

"Your children," Lucien said, and stepped back towards the corral.

"Our children?"

"Picture, if you will Orleans," Lucien called back, "little boys and girls, laying on a long banquet table, with apples stuffed in their mouths and a hall full of giants making toasts and complimenting the chef."

"There's nothin' clever about that in the least little bit, Lucien." Orleans' voice cried meekly, "Nothin't'all."

Alaric shrugged, shying away to shield his smile from Orleans' horror stricken eyes, and followed Lucien in amongst the livestock. As they pushed their way through the cattle to the nearest horses, Alaric stared contemplatively at the ground, guiding himself in Lucien's wake with his fingertips as they grazed across the sides of the cattle. He looked up from his thoughts just in time to stop himself from running into Lucien.

Lucien read the blush on Alaric's face and said, "I know what you're thinking. My friend, your countenance hasn't changed since yesterday. But, as simply as I told you last night, I can't explain."

"And I can't let you not explain, Lucien."

"This is about Alyssa," Lucien coaxed, "I warned you; remember whose side she is on."

"No, this is about you, Lucien. You drink blood, you drink *human* blood, and that fact cannot be left unanswered."

Lucien shrugged, "I've told you, Alaric; I don't know what more you want from me."

"I want the truth, Lucien."

"And the truth is," Lucien said flatly, "that *I* am not your enemy; *I* am not who you should be concerned about right now. Think about what we've been through, Alaric, *think* about it. Whom should you truly be concerned about right now?" Glaring at Alaric, Lucien took a few steps backwards and rested his hand on the mane of a horse. "The men. Out here, their loyalty lies with you – you are their commanding officer. In Adullam however, they are loyal to Nestor – Nestor is Steward now. And, with Stilguard gone, it's not a position he will give way to lightly, or possibly at all. As General, he has the right of succession, does he not?"

Alaric nodded, "Yes, but I don't understand what this has to do with drinking blood," he responded dryly.

The blue streak of a vein pulsed in and out of sight above Lucien's brow as he twirled his forefinger through the horse's mane. "All of this, listen, *all of this* is a question of loyalty. We are not simply going to waltz –"

"Waltz?"

Lucien shook his head, "Dance. We are not simply going to dance into Adullam and expect everyone's going to just follow us out to Borderlands without a fuss. We both know there is a proper course of action; we both want what is best for Adullam, despite your current concerns. I should say I have gone far beyond what most lifetime citizens of Adullam have done for their people."

Alaric opened his mouth.

"Have I not saved your life," Lucien cut across him, "and worked alongside Stilguard to save Adullam? Even Nestor's men will answer to me with some respect – and for weeks they've been inoculated with Nestor's crusade against me. And what we're embarking on now, to rescue Adullam, is it not *my* plan?

"But, for some unknown reason," Lucien continued, "I'm forced to drink blood and despite all else – despite all I've done for you and your people – *this* is held against me. If we are to succeed, if we are to survive, we must be loyal to one another. Trust me as I know I can trust in you – even with my life."

"You have a poetic way about you when you want," Alaric said with a click of his tongue. "Where did you learn to speak?"

Lucien laughed, "A light I stole from my brother."

"You have a brother?"

"Had," Lucien corrected grimly. "That was a long time ago but, to the question at hand, will you put these trivial concerns aside and concern yourself with what is best for Adullam?"

Alaric nodded wearily. "Go," he said, "the men should be well ready by now; explain to them where to go, and I'll ready the horses."

Lucien bowed his head and strode again toward the edge of the corral. From the corner of his eye, Alaric watched him leap onto the fence and call to the soldiers. Sighing, Alaric turned to a nearby mare.

"How do I ride you?" he asked softly, stroking her mane. Pulling at her reins, he navigated her to the gate, through seemingly endless ranks of stubborn cattle. Once on the outside, Alaric tied his mare to the fence with Lucien's makeshift, rope bridle and went back into the pen to bring out the other bridled horse. He waded through the cattle all the way towards the rear of the herd and brought out a dark brown stallion for Lucien. As he opened the makeshift gate to the cattle pen, he looked up at Lucien standing on the crossbeam of the fence, giving directions to the men.

"Why do I trust him, horse?" Alaric asked. He brought the stallion around the open gate and tethered him to the fencepost. "I think it's because he's stark, raving, mad. Would you trust a man who dressed like that?"

Alaric stroked the stallion's nose, letting his eyes follow his fingers up and down the length of it. "You wouldn't trust him, would you. That's because you're a smart horse. But, at the same time, it's that sword's edge of madness that makes me want to trust him – he's not afraid to challenge the accepted way of things, and that's exactly what we need."

"Are you talking to the horse?" Lucien appeared over Alaric's shoulder, crouching on a post.

"I was telling it not to bite the scary man with the mask."

"I'll bite him back," Lucien said, widening his eye at the stallion.

"Stark, raving, mad."

"Is that what you were telling him?"

"What?" Alaric asked the clouds, "We're all set?"

"The men have their instructions," Lucien said, smoothing his tongue over his teeth. "They'll be ready to depart shortly after us."

"Will we be able to track them on our return?"

"Hopefully we won't have to," Lucien said, looking over to make sure Orleans was keeping the men on task. "I've told them exactly how to reach the †Fomorii."

"The Fomorii?" Alaric asked.

"The creatures which inhabit the Borderland's caves; the ones who've claimed the felstones."

"I thought you said they were men."

"They were men, but the stones have corrupted them."

"Will they be dangerous?"

Lucien shrugged, "They're harmless really; too consumed with themselves. They'll give little notice to our men as long as they keep to the foothills. Once we all regroup we'll move up into the caves and you can witness firsthand the consequence of the Fomorii's greed."

As Lucien spoke, he untied the knot that tethered his horse to the fence. When he finished, he stood and pulled on the bridle to bring the horse closer to the fence. Once close enough, he swung his leg over the stallion to mount its bare back. Looping the reins over its head, he leaned down to check the bit and, with everything secure, looked expectantly at Alaric. "What's the matter? The sun's nearly risen. Mount up."

"Of course," Alaric said. He had been carefully observing Lucien's technique. "I was just…" his voice trailed as he shook his head and untied his mare from the fence. Reins in hand, Alaric climbed onto the fence and stretched his leg cautiously over his horse, sliding onto its back with a relieved shiver. He looked back at Lucien and tried to fix his awkward pose to match Lucien's.

Lucien looked back at Alaric to see if he was ready and kicked his horse into a trot, heading towards Orleans and the others as they gathered their equipment. He pulled his horse up to a stop near them and asked, "Is everyone clear on where to go and what to do?"

"Yes'sa," Orleans responded and the rest of the soldiers nodded in confirmation.

"Good luck, and don't waste any time in leaving this place, we want the trail to be cold for the Nephilim."

"What about your trail? If you follow us, will you not leave an even deeper imprint?" asked Carmine.

"We'll take a roundabout way on our return, so you shouldn't have trouble if you leave soon; our trail shouldn't be a problem. We'll send a scout out after you with a map to ensure you reach the proper destination.

"Are you set?" Lucien asked, readdressing Orleans. He answered with a smile and a nod, but quickly averted his eyes – his attention grabbed by something in the distance moving quickly through the fresh light. By the expression on Orleans' face, Lucien's heart stopped. Fearful of some imminent danger, Lucien pulled on the reins of his horse and followed Orleans' gaze with his own.

He peered into the dawn as it broke over the fields, searching for what had now stolen the attention of all men present. A few seconds of silence passed in watchful caution until Carmine began to laugh. He pointed into the distance and said, "See, there, by that mill to the left. It's Alaric. Don't think he's ever ridden a horse before." He smiled back at the rest of the soldiers who, in turn, belted out a chorus of laughter.

"The boy's prob'ly never even seen a horse," Orleans said, once the laughter had subsided. "Better go catch him, Lucien, we got things sorted here."

Lucien kicked his horse into full gallop to chase down his friend who, at present, was in a wild hurtle towards the ruin of Bristing. Lucien could already hear his desperate cries from two hundred yards out. The horse wound all about the fields, in full haste, trying to dismount its rider. Alaric groped desperately to the animal's neck, his head bouncing up and down with the horse's gait. Suddenly, in an attempt to throw him once and for all, the horse planted her front hooves in the ground and made a full turn towards the opposite direction, kicking her hind legs into the air. The force of the turn sent Alaric sliding headfirst off the back of the horse and over her neck.

With a flailing hand, he caught hold of the bridle just at the base of the horse's neck. The mare neighed loudly and began to run again, jostling her head to shake Alaric's hand from the bridle. He was now stuck between the horse's forelegs as they pounded mercilessly at the earth. Alaric's heels plowed the grass, kicking up against the belly of the horse with every bump and divot. He tried to stand and reposition himself so as not to be trampled by the frenzied animal, but the speed and sheer driving force of the horse sent him back to the ground.

They were now on a course directly towards Lucien. Alaric's horse, seeing Lucien charging for it, veered to the right, and Lucien jerked his reins left to come alongside her. Alaric reached out to Lucien and called his name but was pulled back under the thundering horse. His reins flailed down around the mare's neck, just out of Lucien's reach. Indignant, the stallion could not be swayed to move any closer to the mare's side. Three times Lucien pulled hard on the reins trying to bring his horse up against Alaric's. Finally, Lucien took his reins in one hand and whipped them from around the stallion's head. He leaned out to the right and, with his left hand pulled down on the bit, causing his horse's step to falter as its head dropped in pain. With Lucien's weight shifted to the right, his horse collided against Alaric's. Lucien's leg was caught between the weights of the two horses. He opened his mouth in protest of the pain and braced himself against Alaric's horse. He tried to lift himself free, pushing off the two horses with his left hand and knee to remove the pressure from his leg. As hard as he tried, he could not loosen the viselike grip.

He stopped bracing himself on Alaric's horse and reached for her reins, still waving uselessly about her neck. Lucien leaned in, stretching his fingers to their fullest. The reins danced around his fingertips, just beyond his reach, forcing him to lean further and further off the back of the horse.

Finally, the reins swung around and caught on one of Lucien's fingers. Wrenching them up, Lucien curled the reins around his fist and looked ahead. He felt a flash of heat course through his body as his heart stopped.

He pulled back on both reins. His stallion came to a sliding halt while the mare veered to the right. Lucien's fist, wrapped in the mare's reins, caught as she pulled away so that Lucien was stretched between the two horses. The reins of his stallion were wrenched from his hands as it stopped, but the momentum of Lucien's body carried his feet up the horse's neck. His foot snagged on the reins and his shoulder was nearly pulled out of socket by the mare as a small tree caught him just below the chest. The tree snapped at its base and collapsed under Lucien's weight. The mare lost traction on the dry earth; her legs slid out from underneath her body and she fell, disappearing with Alaric into a cloud of dust. Lucien's body folded around the small tree – his face, the first to meet the ground as it collapsed and his mind was forfeited to the yawning dark of unconsciousness.

* * *

"Welcome," the voice said, and Phillip imagined it the voice of a king. "Welcome good and faithful servant. I have seen your deeds and your faith has not gone unnoticed."

The doors closed behind him and the bright light faded away. It was then he realized the persistence of reality. The avenues of his consciousness had all converged upon this destination – from tributary to estuary, Phillip was now an ocean unto himself – all parts collected, deposited and brought under his control, all functioning as one system, in one purpose. The prescient reader was now subject to what was written – no longer beyond – and both were bound by the past in the unity of a man.

"I have always known you would do great things," the voice continued. "Where others saw nothing, I envisioned greatness in you and so you have overcome; you have endured where those around you have fallen short. Come and let me show you something."

Phillip felt himself caught up into the clouds; he was transported to the mountaintop of Montserrat. In the cool mountain air he stood looking over the distant city of Barcelona. He was caught up in an eternal moment, a collision of the past and the present, viewing two worlds at once. A chill wind brushed across his face, carrying with it the heavenly voice that pervaded the mountaintop air. "Before you is the splendor of my kingdom, a kingdom you have helped to forge. All that you see now is mine. All of this, I, in my benevolence, will give to you if you will but bow down and worship me. I know what lies within your heart, you desire to rise from the shadows; you desire power; you desire immortality; these can be yours."

In silence Phillip stood. The vast city with its golden walls unfolded before him as millions flooded through its gates to find salvation. The heavenly voice paralleled Phillip's thoughts, "a salvation you could champion by righting your brother's wrongs. He has destroyed the world, but you can renew it; I alone can give you that power if you will but bear my mark of fealty. Look at your feet."

Phillip obeyed. Looking down, he saw a scepter, a taloned arm wreathed in gold and clasping a red stone. "Its stone, I have taken from my own crown. Kneel and take it, the scepter is your right to power; the stone is your right to immortality." Carefully, Phillip knelt and placed his hands around the scepter. "You must yourself be renewed if you are to renew the world," the voice spoke again. "You must light the Golden City – my Aureus to which I descended from the heavens."

"I will light the city," Phillip called back to the winds, "for *I* am the light – *I* am the Lucien!"

"Then rise reborn," the voice radiated, "Lucien, Prince of Aureus!"

Triumphantly, Phillip stood – Lucien. The winds gathered around him and lifted him from his feet, throwing his rigid body against a stone. There he was held as the mountain became enshrouded in dark clouds. The darkness descended around him, freckled with golden spots of light like morning stars. The atmosphere swirled and the lights became concentrated into a single radiant column deep within the heart of the cloud. It approached through the wind, growing ever brighter until its full figure emerged – a man, beautiful and fierce. Suddenly he was upon Lucien, their faces nearly touching. "I am the Morning Star; I am the Son of Dawn; I am the Aureus, and you are my Lucien – my light. You have pledged to bear my mark," he said with a smile that shone like the sun.

He lifted a white-hot finger to Lucien's face. Slowly he pressed it into Lucien's forehead and began to carve, speaking through Lucien's screams.

"Though my crown-stone will maintain you, it will not sustain you. It will not perpetuate your youth, will not strengthen your vigor, will not embolden your mind. These virtues require sacrifice – they require toil and blood."

Lucien began to choke at the smell of his own burning flesh. His body began to shake. He fought to break away, to save himself, but all he could do was scream, scream and listen to Aureus' words slither down his ears.

"If you want to live an uncorrupted life – above the corrosion that my crown-stone will wreak on your body and mind – you will toil for me, leading my people as their Prince; every day you will drink their blood to remind them that they are subservient to you, and to remind you that you are subservient to me."

Screaming to life, Lucien clutched his burning face, opening his eye to see Alaric kneeling above him.

CHAPTER XVII

A GOOD MAN

Moments before, Alaric lay exhausted, hidden behind the faint body of his mare. He was dirty and bruised; his mouth was dry and filled with dust. He had not strayed from consciousness but strain and confusion left him dazed and numb. With his head propped up against the horse's stomach, Alaric gazed upwards, focusing on nothing other than his parched mouth. He rolled his tongue over his lips and teeth, trying to quench his wilted spirit. Slowly, he brought his breath under control to match the rise and fall of his mare's chest. With breathing in check, Alaric's senses began to return to him.

He needed water. He felt it flowing from his fingers and raised his hand to his lips but where the water flowed he tasted only blood. Suddenly, the smell of it filled his nostrils; the flesh on Alaric's fingers had been worn off in the chase and blood fitted his hand like a glove. Frantic, he stood. His fingers shook violently – his whole body shook violently. Desperately, Alaric searched for Lucien, holding his quivering, bloodied hand against his chest.

Neurotic eyes scanned the ground as he stumbled on his adrenaline-driven course around the mare. Beneath his foot he heard the peculiar sound of something other than the earth. Skittishly he jumped back, recoiling like a threatened snake. He had stepped on a fragment of some synthetic artifact. He knelt over it and reached down with his good hand. For a moment he examined the blood splatter, perplexed by it. Turning the fragment over, though, Alaric realized what he held; his mouth fell agape.

Alaric bolted upright. It was the top half of Lucien's mask, its inside covered in fresh blood. He took a faint step backwards, observing the world with rolling, dizzy eyes. Lucien's horse was grazing several meters away with a fallen tree caught in its reins. Alaric looked back at the bloodied inside of Lucien's mask and then tried to blink the rest of the world into focus.

A few paces away lay the other fragment of Lucien's mask, and a few more from that lay Lucien, bruised and unconscious. Alaric ran toward him, leaning down to pick up the rest of the mask on the way. He pieced the mask together between his hands as he reached his companion and kneeling, rolled Lucien onto his back to revive him. His face was bloodied nearly beyond recognition, and Alaric entertained the fear that he would not wake. He checked Lucien's pulse and felt nothing. Another surge of adrenaline hit him, and frantically he grabbed Lucien's face. Unsure of what to do, Alaric called his name and cradled his head against his chest, his heart beating fast enough for both of them.

I am a soldier. The flashing thought cut across Alaric's mind again and again as he sat helpless. With a heavy breath, Alaric composed himself, again checking Lucien's pulse. Again, he read nothing. He breathed into Lucien's mouth and compressed his chest. Again he breathed and pressed. Again, and again until, in vain he sat back on his knees, Lucien's blood covering his lips and chin. He checked Lucien's pulse, still there was nothing. Alaric gasped for breath, racking his mind for a solution.

He placed his ear on Lucien's chest to listen for a heart beat. He thought he heard a distant throb and elation flushed his cheeks. He pressed his ear harder against Lucien's heart to not miss another sounding. A second passed, and another, and Alaric began to believe he had heard nothing more than his own hope. He sat back up and yelled out, "Lucien!" He curled his hand into a fist and brought it down onto his friend's chest.

Lucien's eye bulged open; screaming to life, he awoke and clutched his burning face. Seeing Alaric sitting above him, reality collided with Lucien and he collapsed beneath it, moaning. His eye rolled back into his head and he fanned his arms across the dirt. His fingers brushed against the halves of his mask. His body tensed. He cocked his head quickly to the side and, seeing the broken mask beneath his fingers, jolted upright, drawing his hands across the bandage on his face, tracing the scars with his fingers – tracing the mark.

The bandage clung tight to Lucien's face, wet with blood and heavy with dirt. Alaric could make out some of the scars, but others were hidden behind thick clots. Lucien collected the two halves of his mask and looked listlessly at them. Dropping the bottom half to the ground, he replaced the top half to his face and stood. He gathered his scepter, which had fallen from his jacket and wiped the blood from under his chin.

Alaric continued to rest on his knees in a complicated blur of emotion – frightened, relieved, confused. Lucien concealed the scepter in his coat and stepped toward Alaric. He reached out a hand to lift his friend up. Alaric accepted the hand and once he was on his feet, Lucien turned from him, looking at the ground. He dug his toe under the bottom half of his mask and kicked it aside.

"Lucien," Alaric asked cautiously, "are you alright?"

Lucien nodded.

"My hand," Alaric stammered, holding up his injured hand. The blood had crept down around his elbow, enclosing his forearm in a scarlet glove.

Lucien watched the blood collect at Alaric's bent elbow and drip to the ground, pooling in the dust to be drunken by the dry ground. "I have bandages in my bag," he said as if speaking to himself. He was disconnected, part of himself broken off with the fragment of his mask. He trudged back to his stallion. It grazed a ways off, joined now by Alaric's mare. With both horses accounted for and in decent condition, Lucien reached into his saddlebag for the bandages. His hands trembled as he removed them. He fumbled with little coil of linen as he wound it around Alaric's hand and his eye kept darting at his saddlebag.

"Lucien," Alaric suddenly pleaded, "you're hurting my hand – it's too tight, I can't feel my fingers."

Lucien dropped the bandages and stepped away, ringing his hands, trying to rid himself of the blood that stained them. "I can't," he whispered, glancing back at his saddlebag, "I can't help you. I need it."

"What? Need what? Lucien, what is it, are you all right?"

"No," Lucien groaned, collapsing against his stallion. "Trust me please," he moaned, clutching desperately onto his bag.

"Lucien, what is it?" Alaric cried, grabbing Lucien beneath the shoulder and hoisting him above his own.

"I couldn't explain," he rambled. "I didn't know how – but the blood, the blood it sustains me; keeps me from becoming one of them."

"One of what? What are you talking about? Lucien rest, your head…"

"No," Lucien cried with a deep, wallowing voice, "it's not my head. I couldn't explain before," he repeated. "I didn't know how – but the blood, the blood it sustains me, otherwise I would be corrupted; I would become one of them, I would become a Fomorii."

Alaric stared hard into Lucien's eye, trying to reason what he was saying. "I don't understand," he said.

Lucien fought to keep himself steady; his voice was desperate and his words floundered from his mouth, "It's a covenant – it's a price. To wield the stone, the crown-stone, the felstone – and not become one of them – I must drink," his voice trailed from repeating the cursed solution. "It sustains me, keeps me whole, keeps me sound. I couldn't tell you, you wouldn't understand; but you see me now, you see the price, don't you? You see me?" His body quaked. "You see what I would become?"

Maddened, unable to control himself any longer, he delved into the bag. Bringing from it a vial of blood, he collapsed to the ground, shaking himself free of Alaric's support. He pushed himself from Alaric, sliding across the dirt, the vial clutched against his breast. Distancing himself, he uncorked the vial and drank greedily from it, draining it of every drop before he collapsed completely.

Alaric stared in horror, unable to react, unable to move at all. Lying on the ground, Lucien drew a deep, shivering breath, trying to keep his memory from involuntarily returning him to the clouded mountaintop, to all the fragments of a tortured and terrible past. His dream had been a culmination of his complete understanding of Aureus, of himself, of his choices, of his consequences. He caressed the rim of the vial with his thumb as he tried to lick any excess blood from his lip. "You see," he said quietly.

Alaric could say nothing

"But you can't understand," Lucien responded to his silence, "and you couldn't have before, and I couldn't expect you to – not yet, not until you've seen the Fomorii for yourself. That's why I didn't want to tell you, tell you why I drink blood. I thought if I could avoid the answer long enough for you to see, then you could understand."

"What are the Fomorii, tell me and maybe I can…"

"You won't," Lucien interjected, "not yet. I named them; I found them, many years after they had been sent out from Aureus. They had been tunneling in the Borderlands, hiding from the stones' master – from Aureus. The felstones corrupted them, misshaped them. I named them for the real Fomorii, violent and deformed creatures in ancient Irish mythology. It was the first thing that came to mind when I found them." Lucien shrugged and looked listlessly down at the vial in his open hand. Some of his natural color had begun to return.

He stood and dropped the vial back into his saddlebag and snorted out a little laugh, "I should have thought of this earlier. I suppose I forgot I had it." Lucien produced a vial of liquor he had taken from the flasks the night before. "This will sterilize the wound," he said, still unable to look at Alaric, "but it's going to hurt."

"I'm a soldier," Alaric said to try to lighten Lucien's mood.

"Well said," Lucien chuckled as he poured the vial, unsparingly, over Alaric's hand.

Alaric breathed heavily through his mouth, forcing air out through pursed lips. A single tear rolled down his cheek. He let it fall.

"How was that?" Lucien asked after Alaric seemed to have breathed away the pain.

"Nothing I can't handle."

"Obviously," Lucien said, flicking the tear from Alaric's fresh stubble.

Alaric lifted his hand to his face, stroking the bristle of his jaw. His beard was short but full. Curiously, he noticed, there was not so much as a shadow on Lucien's face. Alaric found himself thinking back over the past month and could not think of one instance when there had been. It was as if Lucien was preserved in some eternal moment.

A horse neighed and Alaric jumped, the flesh on his arms rising with little bumps. He let his concern at Lucien's polished face slide to a keener interest in properly mounting his mare. A few minutes later, and after much struggle, he was mounted. With Alaric on his horse, Lucien jumped upon his own, and the two began their way back to Adullam.

For the next hour, Alaric's mind was set on nothing save for staying mounted. He clung like a parasite to his horse's back and his eyes never strayed far from its reins. Lucien coached Alaric along as best he could, but at length he became absorbed in the ever-changing landscape, which blended and blurred past them, weaving patterns of dim green and faded gold. Once Alaric could sit on his mare without sliding off its bare back, his thoughts turned mechanically to Stilguard. The world passed him in a blur as he fell in place behind Lucien.

The stream of his scattered thoughts seemed to carry Alaric to three places at once. Trying to focus, he stared at the back of Lucien's head as his hair flourished to and fro in the air. Suddenly, it was the only thing that made sense any more – the principles that governed the wind-swept movements of Lucien's hair. The physics of the world, the order and the consistency that it sustained: the harmonics of the universe, as Lucien had said. The laws of the universe were constantly and rigorously maintained, from the minutest of details – like the motion of hair in the wind – to the rising and setting of the sun, to the rotation of the planets along their predetermined path. A predetermined path: it was what Alaric felt he was on now. Like Lucien's hair, only its whipping end was in focus; all that passed Alaric on the way was a furious blur, but no matter how fast or how hard he rode, the end forever seemed just beyond his grasp.

Alaric came to himself as a dull pain began to gnaw at his legs. He rode through the pain for some time, but as the sun crept lower through the sky, his legs went numb.

"Lucien!" Alaric cried, fighting to sit up straight.

Lucien glanced back. Reading the panic-stricken eyes of his companion, he slowed his gait to a trot and cut off Alaric's mare from galloping ahead.

"What's the matter?" Lucien asked, looking Alaric head to toe.

"My legs," Alaric said, sliding to the left, "I have to walk."

Before Lucien could raise a protest, Alaric was on the ground and stretching his bowed legs. Lucien shook his head and wiped the sweat from behind his stallion's ears. He gazed off as his horse carried him ahead, his eye caught by some distant thought. The sounds of Alaric's relieved sighs came faint to his ears, soon blending with the whispering wind. The red sun bled through a cloud behind them; Lucien rolled his shoulders to offset its shallow burn. A grasshopper clinging to his boot leapt high into the grass and vanished into the browning sea. He felt empty and alone.

"How desperate are we?" Alaric's voice intruded Lucien's solitude.

He stared further into the Briswold.

"We keep fighting for Adullam's salvation; we keep thinking that the next step is the last, that a plan will be in place – that we'll have some direction. But here we are, subject to unforeseeable events, always a step behind fate, set on some inescapable path."

"Life is a strange linking of contraries," Lucien mused, his rigid gaze unmoved.

"Does that settle it for you?"

"No matter how much control we may believe we exert, we are all the same subject to circumstance. There's no one to blame Alaric, least of all yourself."

Alaric's stare deadened at the ground beneath his steps. "I want to be beyond it. I don't want to feel like I'm falling through this life, with the purpose I should cling to forever at my fingertips but never in my grasp."

"Alaric."

"I could have stopped it in the council. I knew it was foolish, we all did. Why would we send the Steward straight down the caravan route – straight into harms way?"

"At the end of the day it was Stilguard's decision, Alaric – and Nestor's betrayal."

Alaric's countenance hardened. He flattened the grass firmly beneath his feet with each step.

"You're a good man, Alaric," Lucien said. "We all want to be triumphant, but rarely as people any more. Nestor, he has his mind on what he can justify, what he can get away with. You see what's right and what's wrong. You keep yourself accountable in a way most men don't – men who will stave off any sort of introspection. People have hidden from the mirror for so long they've forgotten what reality looks like and made it subjective.

"How often do we identify ourselves by things that are not ourselves," Lucien continued solemnly, running a finger down the rough edge of his mask. "Objects, conditions, affiliations – anything to keep us from evaluating who we are. We hide. And in trying to embody an existence beyond ourselves, we lose ourselves. We become tragic; we want to be tragic – even as I'm speaking now." Lucien laughed. "I don't know who I am anymore, Alaric. Don't become tragic."

Chapter XVIII

INTO THE DARK

By the time they had reached the watery entrance to Adullam, Alaric and Lucien had nearly exhausted the life from their horses. They had come several miles southwest of the main entrance to Adullam, at the point where the subterranean river that serves as Adullam's water source funnels out from under ground, an oasis of green among the brown of the Briswold's parched grass. The narrow river rolls out of the ground like the tongue of a gaping mouth, before being quickly consumed again into the greedy earth. Echoes of the running water babbled down the throat of the opening, and a curling nebulous of water vapor rushed into the sunlit air, tossing about the dangling roots of a tree that stood guard above the entrance. The horses surged with a new vigor to reach the clear, sand sifted water. Their hooves pounded firmly into the dry ground with the renewed rhythm of their gallop, kicking up tufts of earth and frail grass in the wake. Alaric clung dizzily onto the mane of his horse with his legs splayed across the length of it's back in helpless exhaustion.

Reaching the banks of the river, the horses leapt into its shallows without so much as hesitating for their riders to dismount. Lucien slid effortlessly from his stallion's back. Springing off its rear, the tips of his boots splashed gingerly into the edge of the river; the bit of mud clinging to them floated diffusely into the clear water. Lucien looked up from his boots to find Alaric trudging up from the riverbed, his countenance miserable and his whole body shivering like a wet rat. "I like your style," Lucien said with a wry smile.

Alaric responded with a dry snort and rolled onto the grass bank, gasping for air. "Five minutes and we move."

"No, we must go now. There can be no delay."

Alaric rolled his eyes up toward Lucien and curled his tongue between his teeth. "Five minutes."

He tried to sit up. Wincing, he collapsed back onto his elbows, immobilized by his cramping legs. Drawing sharp successive breaths he looked back at Lucien.

"Think of the horses," He concluded and closed his eyes.

Five minutes later, Alaric pulled himself from the ground, groaning and stiff-legged, to tend to his horse. Lucien sat in the grass above river's mouth, his olive skin radiating in a ray of sunlight seeping through the boughs of the tree. Alaric splashed water on his mare as he led her closer to the high bank of the river. He stopped the horse parallel to the embankment, clambered out of the river and leapt onto her back. Instinctively, the horse began to walk forward toward the mouth of the cave. Alaric made a grab at the reins, but they slipped down to hang at the horse's knees. Frantic, he tried to stretch out and grab the rope. His fingers flicked the frayed edges of rein, but they were just beyond his reach. He bolted upright, squeezing in on the mare's sides with his thighs, wriggling to and fro, pulling back on the horse's mane, but the stubborn animal sloshed ever forward.

Looking up at last, Alaric found himself only inches from the dangling roots overhanging the mouth of the cave. The mare dipped her head slightly to clear the low ceiling, and with a yelp, Alaric held up his hands to push against the rock. He felt the horse sliding out from under him. With a last, desperate attempt, he stretched his legs straight to cling on with his toes. "Lucien!" He cried as his body began to be swallowed beneath the earth.

Lucien blinked his eye open against the sunlight and leaned over the edge of the cave from his perch beneath the tree.

"Here," he said, leaning further down and extending a hand to Alaric.

Alaric grabbed for Lucien but lost his balance and, with the flick of the horses tail against his back, Alaric splashed into the river, sinking into its sandy shallows.

"And again…" Lucien said, as Alaric came sputtering out of the water.

Alaric shook his head   and slicked the hair out of his eyes.

"The cave is a bit too low then?" Lucien asked.

"A bit," he quietly responded.

"I tried," Lucien said, shrugging his shoulders.

"You didn't!" Alaric cried, pointing a finger at Lucien and marching into the cave. "You didn't," came the unamused echo of his voice as he trudged into the darkness.

Lucien bit the inside of his cheeks and smiled down at his muddled reflection in the churning water. *Even the small things we think we can control,* he thought, *are often beyond us.* He stretched his arms out in the sunlight and then pushed himself up off the ground, stepping over the high-arched roots, to lead himself down to the river to collect his horse.

The splash and slosh of Alaric's exerted efforts to reach his horse reverberated down the subterranean waterway as Lucien parted the dangling roots to let his horse pass. Lucien's ears rang with the sounds of Alaric's struggle as they echoed and merged into one harmony to encapsulate him in the darkness. Alaric left a small wake for him to follow, and faint light cast from the disappearing day behind them reflected silver against the turbulence of Alaric's movement. The patterns of light it created danced on the walls in tune with the rhythm of noise pervading the air to guide Lucien on his way. Further into the darkness Alaric's grumbling voice tethered his mare and the sound of his movements subsided as the water lay still before Lucien.

"Lucien!" Alaric called with a voice that made him wince as it bounded from wall to wall. He turned to see Lucien approaching him, an ethereal shadow against the dim light at his back.

The two companions, despite being together, walked in a type of solitude through the darkness. Occasionally, one would tell the other where to watch his step or how to lead his horse, but for a while they focused on the blankness before them and little else. The horses were stubborn, their legs were cold and they resented having to walk through the dark of a narrow passage in knee-deep water. "Does it scare you?" Alaric asked at length, "The absolute black?"

Lucien breathed deeply. "It soothes me. It's a moment's respite from the agonies of my life."

"Agonies?"

Lucien remained silent.

"I feel like I'm staring into oblivion," Alaric answered in his place, "like I don't exist any more."

"Does it scare *you*?"

"Yes," Alaric gulped. "But not just the darkness, it's that I'm moving through it and I don't know where it ends, or if it ends."

"Just because you can't see the light at the end of the tunnel doesn't mean it doesn't exist."

"I know. I just…"

"They'll be fine, Alaric – all of them."

Their conversation fell silent again for a moment until Lucien asked, "How much further do you think?"

Alaric loosed a muted laugh.

"I don't mean to be introspective, it's important," Lucien countered.

"Not much, the walk seems a lot further than it is. I've been through here before. I used to sneak out this way when I was a boy because the main entrance was always watched."

"You mean the way isn't guarded?"

"Hardly. There may be a patrol that comes a ways down the passage once, maybe twice a day, depending on how loyal he is to his rounds, but other than that there is no guard. No one uses it as an exit – why would they want to – and I doubt any intruder would think to crawl into a cave and follow an underground river expecting to find a race of people."

"Undoubtedly," Lucien answered reflectively. "So, in the brief moments we have until we reach the other side, what is your plan?" he asked.

"My plan?" Alaric looked at the empty space from which Lucien's voice had emanated.

"Obviously, you have thought about how to present the crisis to Adullam and deal with Nestor – he *is* acting Steward."

"Yes," Alaric sighed thoughtfully.

"And there is the chance Nestor intended for Stilguard to die."

Alaric ran his hand through his hair, digging his nails into his scalp. "I," he spoke cautiously, "am not decided on how to approach the situation. It's hard for me to know what things will be like once we reach Adullam."

"It's funny," Lucien scoffed. "The way you people don't see things – or maybe you do, but you just hide from them because that's what you're good at."

"What do you mean?" Alaric asked, his flesh flushed hot.

"How do you get to this place; how do you get to where we are now?"

"It's been complicated," Alaric stuttered back.

"Oh, I've no doubt it's been complicated; you've let your world come to this. You're in the shadow of a tidal wave and you're thanking it for blocking the sun."

"I understand the dangers," Alaric hissed back. "I understand the magnitude of what's going on! I understand the fear, and the calamity, and the disaster that's about to strike!"

"But are you prepared to navigate it?"

Alaric drew heavy breaths, shivering now from the cold of the water.

"The very thing your people need for strength is also their weakness," Lucien continued calmly, "their need for purpose. You've been trapped in the dark for so long that you've gotten used to seeing only five feet in front of you – you've forgotten there's a horizon. Your survival has no purpose; you need a purpose to drive Adullam, to reset its course, to give its people hope. But the danger is that the face of that purpose can be anything – can be righteous, can be corrupt – it's all a matter of who shouts louder. You need to be ready to shout, Alaric."

"We have Gaverick's testimony, of his encounter with the Satyr," a sudden feeling of resolution swept over Alaric. "The death of Stilguard is a tragedy but, if we give it a spirit of martyrdom instead of mourning, it could light a fire."

"Good!" Lucien said.

"The plan then, essentially, is to take Adullam to the food because we can no longer bring food to Adullam. We could claim a threat that our location is compromised, and that Aureus may know where Adullam is, having been able to trace the caravan route back to us."

"As logical as that sounds, will Nestor believe that, or even care? As soon as the people step foot outside these halls, Nestor loses an element of control."

"Then the decision should not rest with Nestor, it should be with the people," Alaric insisted. "The laws deem that no person can leave Adullam without proper clearance through a networking of authorities, or direct leave from the Steward. But..."

"And what are the authorities?" Lucien asked.

"Well, a request must be brought before the Trade Lords and ratified by a small council of three military officials, one of whom is myself but the other two will be under the thumb of Nestor and it must be a majority concession."

"That would pose a problem," Lucien spoke with a click of his tongue.

"What would you have me do?" Alaric asked, catching Lucien's undertone.

"Think, that's all."

"What are *your* ideas then?"

"I have professed none. These are your people, Captain, and you must be the one to lead them."

"Break the rules?"

"Everything is permissible..." Lucien smiled, knowing Alaric could not see.

"As we said, take the solution to the people, leave the decision with them as individuals. We present our plan to the remaining Trade Lords, too. I feel they'd be in favor of evacuating Adullam – all things considered."

"Especially if they thought they could consolidate power over the livestock headed for the Borderlands."

"Perhaps," Alaric responded thoughtfully.

"Their truer side is shown. Greed is a powerful thing – transformative; this you will see when we reach the Borderlands," Lucien foreshadowed.

"The six Trade Lords who died with us – they were heroes." Alaric shot a glaring eye toward the empty space Lucien's head most likely occupied.

"No one could convince me otherwise. Their commitment was valiant."

Satisfied, Alaric turned his head forward again. He tripped on a loose stone and cursed at the blackness through which he waded. Whereas Lucien took advantage of the total darkness – emoting every moment of their discussion with uncharacteristically expressive gestures – Alaric was becoming increasingly disillusioned with this solitude of sightlessness.

"My point," Lucien continued, "was only to say that our livestock will help legitimize our proposal and perhaps encourage the Trade Lords' cooperation. They would be assets in maintaining order and a power structure once the exodus begins."

"But if they don't cooperate," Alaric began.

"Then it makes no difference; we essentially supersede their authority and Nestor's, but I think the Trade Lords will be motivated by sheer desperation, and have no choice but to sanction an evacuation on our terms." Lucien finished.

"And what of Nestor after all of this? We will have no military support."

"He can rot in the lonely halls of Adullam, and there is hardly enough military left in these caves to support either him or ourselves."

Alaric nodded.

"Nestor," Lucien continued, "I imagine, will lead some sort of opposition in order to maintain power, especially with the death of Stilguard. Men like Nestor – only one thing registers as important, that is control. People like him cannot control themselves and so they try to control others, disguising their lack of willpower with a uniform and a fist so no one dare say otherwise."

"A leader should first be a servant," Alaric spoke softly, reminiscent of Stilguard.

"No truer words have been spoken."

"The Shaddai watch him in sleeping, that in waking he may be guided to new life," Alaric sighed. "I'm going to have to tell Joanna, she should be the first to know."

"Stilguard's wife?" Lucien asked.

"Yes." Alaric responded solemnly. "Is this whole thing just blatant madness?"

"This is reason with the face of madness. The only reasonable option is exodus. This is the bridle to the wild horse that brought us here," Lucien said, stroking his stallion's nose. "This is where we redirect its course.

"What is decided?" asked Lucien, after a moment's pause.

"First, I tell Joanna about her husband. Give her time."

"She cannot have time, it jeopardizes everything."

"She can have time," Alaric retorted, the stress was mounting in his voice. "Not much, but she deserves an hour or so before all of Adullam is in an uproar. We'll need to assemble the council of Trade Lords, and I'm sure we'll have to report to Nestor before we set anything in motion. As long as I can tell Joanna before then, she'll have the time she deserves.

"That aside," Alaric continued, "assembling the Trade Lords will be the first order of business. We'll explain the razing of Bristing, the death of Stilguard, the potential that Aureus knows Adullam's location."

"Make them fear for their own safety at the loss of their fellow Trade Lords," advised Lucien.

"Yes, good point, and turn their fear into action by providing a solution. Let them brood on the problems so they're well relieved when they learn of the livestock in the Borderlands. That said, we introduce the necessity for an evacuation – an exodus to the Borderlands to meet our comrades and our new found resources. We promise them authority over the stock in order that they maintain authority over the people of Adullam through this crisis.

"Nestor," Alaric continued, changing tones, "should play no part in this, and the Trade Lords must be aware we are supplanting his authority. Once we have the support of the Traders, we make an open announcement to the people – allow them to choose their fate; tell them there is nothing left to sustain Adullam; we're upon the fringe of exhaustion, and they must make the exodus."

"To escape the creeping tendrils of Aureus and its evils," Lucien garnished the plan with a poetic finish.

"It will take almost a day to mobilize everyone if we work through the night."

"I don't think we have the luxury of such time," cautioned Lucien.

"We're in no immediate threat, the food stores should last another day if they've been rationed properly. Unless you think there is a possibility the trade routes *were* tracked back to Adullam." Alaric's voice became wary in Lucien's uneasiness.

"No," Lucien replied with a bite like a dog. He cleared his throat, "The threat lies in the journey. We need to be far enough ahead of Aureus that we're not caught in transit. If we leave too late we run a greater risk of being overtaken. We'll obviously take a route to avoid any confrontation, but the longer we wait the higher the odds rise against us. If I know Aureus, it will come searching for us with a vengeance."

"I see your point. Then we'll tell them to be quick with the preparations. We should subdivide everyone, I think, into separate organizational parties to minimize confusion. That will also increase mobility options and smooth the transition from the inside of the cave to the outside, which should be done during the cover of night. Shaddai knows, we don't need two thousand people standing in the open in the middle of the day. Though," Alaric paused, "that will extend our time tables. We wouldn't be able to move until tomorrow night which could be a good thing, allowing us to deal with Nestor in a proper manner and plan further."

"Spoken like a Steward," Lucien proclaimed.

"What do you mean?" Alaric asked, but there was no reply. Lucien had stopped moving; Alaric could no longer hear the slosh of his boots through the thigh-deep water. He wanted to call for Lucien but in his state of confusion he mimicked the silence and melded to the cavern walls. In vain, Alaric searched the emptiness behind him.

Suddenly, he heard a splash come from up river. Alaric darted his head towards the sound and pressed his back harder against the wet walls of their subterranean passage. A dim, almost imperceptible light freckled the water. Slowly the orange glow grew brighter and Alaric could tell he was seeing torchlight reflected from around a bend in the river. The light continued to grow brighter and, though still some distance away, Alaric could only assume it was the river guard and the reason for Lucien's silence.

CHAPTER XIX

EMPTY HALLS

Alaric felt a warm breath against his ear and a cold hand over his mouth. A rope slid into his hands and the breath upon his ear whispered such subtle instructions that it might not have whispered at all. "Do not move; mind my horse," Alaric was almost certain he heard.

Moments later a dark mass stood against the orange reflections on the water, interrupting their lambent pattern. The mass was nearly formless, only a slender figure amidst the soft light surrounding it, but as the guard and his light came closer, the mass took the most basic shape of a man and slid silently down into the shadows of oblivion.

Alaric could hear the sloshing of the river guard from ahead. He was nearing a bend in the canal and soon would be upon Alaric. *He'll see the horses first*, Alaric thought. He contemplated slipping away behind the horses and quietly moving further down the passage, but Lucien's silent words played in his head like a recurrent dream – 'do not move' – and kept him riveted to the wall.

Alaric's heart pounded so hard he feared the guard would hear its beat like the sound of a drum. He would be turning the corner soon, the torch would expose him, or at least the gleam of his eyes in the light would betray his existence.

Suddenly, the sounds of movement's echoing stopped, and the water was still. Alaric heard the billowing crackle of the torch wave through the air. The torch billowed again, the crackle like a malice of laughter to Alaric's ears. He pressed himself harder against the damp walls and the cool sent shivers across his skin. The torch crackled; hissed; and all was silent.

Alaric began to feel faint. He had stopped breathing. He slit his eyelids open to peer into the pitch-dark of his unobservable fate. The light was out and the horses breathed steadily behind him. Alaric remembered to breathe and welcomed in a healthy burst of oxygen. He bent his knees and slid into a more comfortable waiting position.

He tried to be patient and wait for Lucien's call, but a frantic concern seized him. He began to shiver. His shaking legs whisked the water, stirring it with a slight but perceptible sound. Suddenly there was whispering, just as before: a noise half audible and half visceral. The whispering crept down the passage toward him like a distant echo. Alaric leaned into the darkness trying to decipher the sound when, inexplicably, it was upon him.

Alaric gasped and jumped back from the horses where the whispering had suddenly manifested. "Help me get him on the horse," came the voice. As if the voice had been his own thoughts, Alaric reached out blindly to feel the mass of a wet body. His thoughts caught up to him as instantly as they had left him, registering the whisper as external, and Alaric withdrew his hand.

"What are you doing?" Alaric whispered back with a trembling voice, fearful of both the voice and the instruction.

"The guard," returned the whisper, "he's unconscious. We need to drape him over the horse to get him out of the river."

"Right," Alaric said, recognizing the voice as Lucien's now. "He'll be all right when he comes around, won't he?"

"Yes," Lucien reassured him as he heaved the body upwards, "nothing to worry about; he was an easy take."

As he helped lift, Alaric brushed against Lucien. "How did you get so wet?" Alaric asked, thinking back to the shapeless figure sliding silently down into the darkness.

"I could not very well walk up to the man. He was an unnecessary complication," Lucien added, anticipating Alaric's next question, "and he needed to be removed for our own safety and that of Adullam."

Alaric had nothing to argue with. The man was already unconscious and their job was made easier by not having to answer to a guard in the confusion of the darkness.

"Your whisper," Alaric began to ask, "that voice; the way it carried, how did you do that?"

"It's written, the tongue is sharper than a double edged sword," Lucien let his voice trail off before he continued. "Everything that is, was spoken into existence; there is power in the word if one can learn to use it."

"How did you learn to use it?"

"It is nothing special," Lucien said bluntly. "How much further are we?"

"Once we turn this bend, fifty meters."

"Good," Lucien said, and they walked the rest of the way in silence.

Guided by a torch in the corridor leading away from the river, Alaric and Lucien took their final steps up to the dry threshold of Adullam. The light made Alaric's eyes dizzy and unfocused; he stumbled as he stepped onto the dry ground, nearly stepping off the small ledge channeling the river.

Lucien worked quickly to get Alaric's horse out of the water. Once Alaric had adjusted to the light, he helped hoist the guard off Lucien's horse and bring him onto the platform. He lay the guard down and they tethered the horses to him to keep them from wandering away.

They left the river's side and made their way through a small passageway, which lead to a bridge spanning back across the river. Adjacent to the bridge was a platform jutting out upriver. It encircling a contraption made of crude piping and twisting gears that made a persistent lapping sound in the water.

"There's one of the waterwheels I was telling you about when you first arrived," Alaric said with a nervous jolt, pointing to the machine. "You never really got a chance to see it, did you?"

"Yes, I saw it," Lucien lied, to keep from delay, "not this one but the other, while one of the engineers was working on it. He explained everything to me."

"Good," Alaric responded, "I trust you found it interesting. I was going to say it is a shame you won't get to see it now even while we're so close."

"Yes," Lucien said, laughing to himself. "It would have been a shame." He looked carefully at the machine as they passed, knowing this would perhaps be his only chance. A system of catch-flows drew the water straight from the river and funneled it into pipes to be distributed across Adullam, while the main waterwheel seemed to help maintain pressure in the pipes and prevent back flow – or at least that was Lucien's best guess.

They crossed the bridge into the southern-most-part of Adullam from where they would have to surreptitiously navigate to the Trade Lords' Council Chambers.

As they passed into the Housing District, Alaric reached his hand backwards to Lucien's chest, signaling him to stop. He listened intently, and waved his hand at Lucien not to follow. He took several steps forward to duck his head down the Western Apartment corridor. Seeing nothing, Alaric moved further on past it to the Eastern corridor of the district. On both sides, the halls fanned out like the skeleton of a leaf, consisting of main sectors and sub-corridors that wove like little veins through the leaf's flesh.

The district, usually bustling with life and sound, was empty. Alaric stood and walked cautiously into the center of the high-vaulted hall, turning in every direction as he walked. Eventually he came to a halt, wiping his hand slowly across his mouth. He looked back to signal Lucien who had carefully concealed himself in the shadows between torches.

"No one is here," Alaric said as Lucien stepped into the light. "Something isn't right, the Housing District is never empty like this."

"The river guard was in place, so the people must still be in Adullam somewhere," Lucien suggested.

"I was thinking the same thing, they're here; I just am not sure where they could all be. If they were in the Market, we'd have heard them by now, and I can't imagine there is anything left to barter."

"Maybe Nestor has them assembled somewhere."

"Perhaps, but the Market is the only place big enough to host them. We'll have to cross through it to get to the Council Chambers anyway; we'll see soon enough."

Alaric stepped forward with great unease, rocking back on his left heel as he stepped forward. Lucien remained in a cautiously crouched position as he followed after Alaric, making sure to survey every corner and shadow as they progressed towards the Market District. Several tedious minutes later, they arrived to find it as empty as the Housing District. Alaric took long steps to the center of the Market's stands and circling around and searching frantically for any signs of life.

"We wanted to reach the Council Room with as little contact as possible, but not like this," Alaric said, panicked with the evolving mystery. "Do you think they are hiding in the mines? Perhaps there has been some kind of trouble that the river guard was simply unaware of. They could even be held prisoner there; the mines are large enough to hold everyone twice over."

Alaric was losing his composure, his resolve deteriorating as he wound his gaze around the giant room. Lucien walked slowly to him, his eye lifted apathetically at Alaric's heat streaked face. Reaching out, he grabbed Alaric's shoulder and looked at him with a deadened stare. Alaric's eyes returned a plea for understanding. "Where are they?" His voice trembled.

Lucien shook his head. "Be silent."

Alaric opened his mouth to yell.

"Be silent!" Lucien's voice rang sharp, wrapping around Alaric's mind in a silvery hiss. In the split second before realization caught up with Alaric, Lucien was already behind him, covering his mouth and keeping him from struggling. Alaric's fear for Adullam sent him into a frenzy; he struggled against Lucien's grip and tried to yell out to anyone. *Someone must know what is happening*, he thought, *someone must be here*.

There was no one. No one to see his fear, no one to hear his cries; there was only Lucien.

"Do not make this any harder," Lucien said. "This does not have to be difficult. Stop fighting, your panic achieves nothing." Lucien pressed his arm against Alaric's throat, suffocating him. "Be calm, I know you are afraid, but you must stop and think."

Alaric tried to breathe but the pressure of Lucien's grip prohibited him. He kicked and tried to slip through Lucien's arms but slowly his vision began to blur. His body quivered and grew heavy. His mind began to grow dark, the panic subsided.

He grew calm – nearly lifeless. Alaric's body slumped against Lucien's and his thoughts grew calmer until he could sense nothing except the slow beat of his heart. He closed his eyes and saw a faceless figure before him, dawning in a brilliant red dress, standing against the blackness of the inside of his eyelids. *That's a peculiar thing to see,* Alaric thought, and then breathed in deeply.

CHAPTER XX

RIOTS

Alaric exhaled and drew in new air, suddenly aware he was breathing again. He opened his eyes. Someone grabbed his arm and wrenched him from the ground. Alaric turned to see Lucien looking at him, a cool firmness in his eye. "You need to be calm and think," he said, releasing Alaric's arm; "now listen."

Alaric listened. He took deep breaths, trying not to be seized again by the distress of uncertainty and fear. He closed his eyes and listened, calming himself with every breath. At first he only heard the sound of his own breathing but soon that faded into another sound: a murmur, from the North Wing. It was the sound Lucien wanted him to hear; it was the sound of voices in the distance

Relieved to the point of joy, Alaric sprang to his feet before the sobering thought of captivity crossed his mind. The voices could be those of assembled prisoners; perhaps the Satyr had traced the route back to Adullam. Alaric wished he could mimic Lucien's coolly objective attitude, but he was fevered with emotions and unable to hold himself still. He mustered all his available composure to steady himself in preparation to move closer to the commotion, which was, for now, little more than a low rumble.

Looking back at Lucien, who was patiently awaiting his next command, Alaric signaled him to move along the eastern wall of the Market while Alaric himself moved along the western.

The two crept along their respective walls, coming ever closer to the sound of voices down the adjacent corridor. The crowd sounded angry, and a low rhythmic pound reverberated several pitches below them. Wondering at the tone, Alaric carelessly hastened his pace, forgoing the wall to maintain a crouched charge towards the North Wing entrance.

He came to a sliding stop at the corner of the passage and looked across the empty Market at Lucien. Cautiously, he peered around the corner but because of a bend in the corridor Alaric could only see a few people facing away, yelling and shaking fists. All the torches had been robbed from their designated battens so that light flooded solely from the end of the hall. He rushed forward again in a crouched position across the corridor and to the first bend.

He pressed his chest against the wall and arched his head back to gaze over the crowd. Cries of justice and perseverance and preservation rose into the air like smoke from their torches. The crowd moved like a great ocean, receding back and then crashing hard against the great wooden doors of the Council Chamber. It seemed, every citizen – man, woman, child – was present and a part of this great tide whose waters would soon breach the doors. On the opposite side of the corridor, the Steward's Hall doors lay across the threshold, the hinges ripped from the stone. They carried the clap of thunder against the stone floor as a siege of people swelled atop them, jumping in unison and chanting their outrage with clenched fists.

Caught in the pervasive uproar, Alaric stepped out from his cover and proceeded to the rear of the crowd. The people's frenzied riot left little room in their minds to notice Alaric. He looked back into the Steward's Hall. Ranks of people filled its floor, yelling and chanting. They lined the walls, danced atop the tables, and hung from the throne, caught in a thunderstorm of revolt.

The doors of the Trade Lords' Council Chambers were beginning to give way under the pressure of the crowd. A large crack ran the length of the left door and with each push, the crevice widened. Terrified, Alaric turned and ran back toward Lucien. The moment he entered the shadows of the darkened corridor he felt a large weight collapse on him.

Lucien had been hanging, invisible, from the main water piping on the ceiling of the passage. All Alaric saw was the flash of his white mask cross the darkness and, in a vicious twirl of cloth and flesh, Alaric was off his feet, his senses in disarray.

As quickly as Lucien had descended on him, Alaric was thrown to the ground of the Marketplace. "Careless!" Lucien hissed and strode threateningly toward Alaric.

Alaric slid himself against the damp floor, away from Lucien. He backed himself up against a tapering column of calcium salt deposits and pushed against it to rise to his feet. Immediately, he drew his sword against the forcefully advancing Lucien.

Lucien paused and cocked his head to the side, smiling faintly.

"We do not have time for this," Alaric said as he circled around Lucien. "There's a hidden exit from the Council Chambers – I found it when I was a child. We need to get to it before the main doors are breached."

Lucien heard Alaric sheathe his sword and he turned his head so only his mask was exposed.

"There is no time." Alaric pleaded and began to walk away from Lucien.

"This place is not my home as it is yours," Lucien said with a steady voice. "If you are found then so too will I be found; and I will not be received as well as you."

"You're being paranoid; it's all just conjecture. Stilguard…"

"Is dead, Alaric. I have no protection here any longer. I may have done nothing wrong, I may be fighting for these people the same as you; there may be every reason to trust me, but do you think Nestor gives a damn about reason?"

Alaric was frozen. "The doors are coming down," he heard himself say. There was a blankness in his mind, like a white sheet cast over his head. "If something happens to Nestor or the Trade Lords, the whole system collapses, there'll be no way to rein in the mob rule of Adullam."

"Go," Lucien said, "bring them to the Medical Wing, I'll meet you there."

"The Medical Wing?" Alaric asked; he began to step away from Lucien.

"Yes, I'll prepare it." Lucien raised his voice as Alaric disappeared into the shadows of the Market. "Bring them all into the Medical Wing."

Alaric's footsteps crunched and slipped across the cavern floor until the sound was lost to the noise of the rioters. Lucien stood in solitude for a moment, gathering his bearings in the dark before taking off toward the Medical Wing.

The first thing to meet Lucien as he turned the corner into the Infirmary was the back of Mark's head and his elbows, which wove sporadically back and forth as he played with the medical equipment at one of the tables. He was making little chinking noises as he played, and the occasional pounding rumble would escape from his lips followed by little voices crying out in dismay.

Lucien slid to a halt at seeing Mark. He drew in a loud breath and, as if in a dream, Mark turned around toward him, his face lighting up with more joy than Lucien had ever seen in his life.

"Uncle Lucien!" he cried and rushed toward Lucien, his leg seeming to have healed nicely. "You were gone for a real long time," he said as he hugged Lucien's legs. "Why are you all wet?" Mark quickly stepped away, dancing to shake the water off himself.

"Sorry, Mark," Lucien said, crouching down level with the young boy. "I fell in a river."

"Well that was silly. How did you fall in a river?" Mark asked and then excitedly interjected his own question, "What happened to your mask? It's broken!"

"It is a long story," Lucien smiled, "I'll tell you another time; right now I have something very important for you to do."

Mark snapped to attention and looked squarely at Lucien, ready to oblige any order.

"Go and get Mr. Brancott," Lucien continued. "Tell him I need fresh beds in bay two. I need eight beds and, if we have time, I would like all the patients moved into bay one. Do you understand?"

"Yes sir!" Mark called out and gave Lucien a little salute as he ran off to find Brancott.

Lucien followed Mark with his eye for a moment, enjoying the ephemeral happiness while he could. He then stood from his kneeling position and went into his private quarters. He filled his washbasin with water, removed his mask and the blood-soaked bandage beneath. With his finger, he traced the lines of the scar his mask concealed before reaching into a nearby cabinet to retrieve a fresh bandage. He placed it on the table next to the basin and sank his hands into the water. He positioned his face just above the surface of the water and brought his hands up to cleanse himself of the blood the river had not washed away. He sat staring at his reflection in the basin of rippling water. His breath began to quiver and he looked quickly away, reaching for his mask. He sank it in the basin, now rose-tinted with blood, and filed away some of the splinters from its edge. He dipped it again and watched the rose beads of blood and water roll off as he withdrew it. Drying the mask with the caress of his thumbs, Lucien turned it over and over – enraptured by the sight of it.

He replaced the mask to his face and returned to the atrium of the Infirmary to see Brancott pushing a fresh bed into bay two. Mark held fast to the front of it like the figurehead at the prow of an old galleon, trying desperately not to fall and be run over, yet reveling in the excitement of the danger. Mark looked up to see Lucien and, waving a hand excitedly, nearly did fall. Catching himself, he gasped and called out, "I got him, Uncle Lucien!" He laughed as he disappeared with the bed into bay two.

Lucien's solemnity was immediately changed by Mark's contagious laughter. Remembering then that he had only a few minutes to prepare the Medical Wing, he dashed into bay two to gauge the situation. Two patients remained in the bay; both were sleeping so Lucien carefully rolled them into bay one as Brancott and Mark brought fresh beds to replace them. Once the room had been prepared, Lucien went rummaging behind a desk. He had just knelt down to begin his search when he heard the rustling of feet echoing down the hallway. He stood and strode to the center of the atrium to meet the enclosing party. A tall, dark-haired man hastened around the corner and stepped into the atrium. His eyes met Lucien and he stopped. Panting deeply, the man walked toward Lucien. Shortly after he had entered, another man appeared and then another and another until, finally, Nestor pushed his way through the small group to confront Lucien.

Scowling as he tried to decipher the situation, Nestor, glared into Lucien's eye. "This was a set up!" he proclaimed to the group striding further forward. With a yell, he swung a fist at Lucien.

Stepping lightly back, Lucien retorted, "I would expect as much. Do not make helping you any harder than it is, Nestor."

"Nestor!" one of the six remaining Trade Lords pleaded, "Hear him out." There was a murmur of agreement and Nestor dropped his attack but kept wary footing.

"Thank you, sir," Lucien said. "Now, I need all of you to go into bay two directly behind me, choose a bed, cover yourself under the sheets as if dead and wait for me to tell you to move. Do not make a sound, and if you can manage it, do not breathe."

From behind, Lucien heard Mark giggle and whisper something to Brancott.

The six Trade Lords were the first to obey, scurrying out from behind Nestor like insects caught in the light. Nestor moved slowly, keeping his glare steady on Lucien. For the first time, it crossed Lucien's mind how much the man before him resembled an animal. Looking at the General was like looking at a jackal – there was nothing regal about it, just animal.

From the corner of his eye, he noticed Barrius bickering quietly with Titus.

"There is room for you both," Lucien called to them. "I suggest you hurry before I change my mind."

Barrius scoffed and Titus' eyes flickered with polite disgust.

"Though," Lucien said, thoughtfully lifting his chin at Titus, "we have yet to be introduced."

Titus put his hands by his side, inflating his chest as he strode slowly towards Lucien. His expression of polite disgust remained unchanged as if Lucien were receiving an honor he did not deserve.

"Titus Valerius," he said coolly and pushed past Lucien.

Barrius kept to his heels, giving Lucien a cautioning prod as he passed. "Brigand," he spat beneath his breath.

Lucien stared straight ahead through their mockery. "'In pride, all fall far where hope can barely reach'," he murmured to himself and watched with a smile as Mark skipped up to him.

Mark stopped with a bounce and grabbed Lucien's sleeve. "Where is Mr. Alaric?"

* * *

The doors to the Council Chamber splintered. Triumphant voices shouted from the other side. Another heave or two and the masses would be through. Alaric cleared away the crude barricade made from the giant council table and the twelve chairs that had surrounded it, pushing the debris to either side and bringing one chair to the very center of the chamber. There he sat and listened as the door's bracing cracked. This would be it; the next blow would bring the door down and hundreds would come pouring through.

The sound of thunder and cheering; the rush of orange light through a haze of dust; the stampede of footsteps through the open door; and Alaric's voice above it all, "Hold!" he cried, drawing out the word like the blare of a trumpet.

"Be still and listen to my voice! All of you!" Alaric stood from his chair as his eyes met those of the first through the entrance.

The mass semi-circled itself around Alaric and voices from the crowd demanded, "Where have they gone?"

"All of you! Pay careful attention to my words."

Alaric's speech was cut off by people shouting out through the crowd, relaying the circumstances to those who were not at the front, "'Nestor is gone!' 'The Trade Lords aren't here!' 'They've escaped; search the caves!'"

"Be still!" Alaric's voice rose above them all but it was too late; some at the rear of the group had already disengaged to seek out Nestor and the others. "I know your anger!" He called to the remaining majority, "I feel it as well. If we continue like this we will tear ourselves apart and Adullam will fall forever. Our children will starve and there will be no hope for a future. I beg you, *listen*!"

The remaining crowd fell silent at these words and Alaric looked over the whole congregation, meeting what eyes he could. "I have just returned from Bristing," he continued. "We were met with great tragedy, but also triumph. You are angry. Good! And rightfully you should be. Harness your anger and do not waste its energy with rioting. There is food to save you, to save all of you!"

This announcement was met with cheers and, from some, tears of joy and laughter.

"But I tell you now," Alaric cut across them, "Nestor cannot provide it! The Trade Lords cannot provide it! Nonetheless, their position maintains the integrity of our people. Cut them off and everything is laid to ruin. I ask you now to forgive them; for a time, set aside your anger at their negligence. Circumstance is often beyond any of us to control. Nestor and the Trade Lords – they are only human. Soon we will be entering into a new era of existence, and survival hinges upon your cooperation."

"Where is Stilguard?" A shout came from the crowd.

"Stilguard," Alaric stammered. He blinked rapidly and his whole body became hot. He could not bring himself to utter the words. He thought of Joanna. Was she in the crowd? Would this be how she learned? Alaric desperately hoped not. "Stilguard is dead."

A low murmur rushed across the crowd. Those who had been filled with tears of joy only moments before now wept for the loss of their Steward.

"Now is not the time," Alaric wheezed, trying to put strength back into his voice. He gasped and swallowed hard, choking the emotion away. "There will be a time to mourn. Stilguard died for the sake of Adullam. He died a hero, but now we must focus on the future or the past will consume us to our ruin! The food we need is to the West in the Borderlands. We must go to it; it is too dangerous and the supply too large to bring here."

"What, we leave Adullam?" A man from the front of the crowd stepped out before Alaric.

"That is our only option."

"We can't leave!" The man cried out echoed by shouts of consent. "It's madness!"

But all at once, Alaric saw fate unfold before him. A torrent of words flooded into his consciousness until, in overflow, they spilled uncontrollably from his mouth. "It *is* madness!" he cried, "but even madness has its reasons. For too long Adullam has sat in a dark and forgotten existence, simply trying to maintain, to survive. Life, I tell you, is not survival. Survival is the nature of animals and desperate men!

"We have existed on rational decision after rational decision, leading inexorably down a path to our eventual demise – scared to take a chance, scared to test fate." Alaric's voice lifted courageously, "We have lost sight of purpose and foregone progression for darkness. We have slipped beyond madness and into insanity – rotting slowly away like plagued wood. Madness, my friends, is progression! You want to be reasonable? Then sit here in your dark, decrepit hole – continue to relinquish any purpose – and you will starve.

"But set your minds and hearts on eternity. Again I tell you: this madness is preceded by reason, and if you stand before me unable to see that reason, then you have already decided to abandon yourself. If you wish to live, to really live – not just survive – then embrace the madness to see the light of day, to feel its warmth, and to know why you were created; because you were not born to live beneath the earth! This place has been our haven, but it has also been our ruin! Come now into the light! Come now into freedom from this place! Come now into freedom from Aureus!"

The crowd erupted with roars of affirmation. The man who had stepped out to confront Alaric nodded his head submissively as he walked back to his place in the crowd.

Alaric smiled and let out a gracious sigh of relief, laughing and shaking his head. He raised his hands to silence the persistent cheers. The shouts quieted from the front and the silence simmered down through to the back. Once he had regained their attention, Alaric gave final instructions.

"We must be out of Adullam by tomorrow. Gather your families, collect your belongings; pack light; we will be three days on foot. The most important thing is to bring any food you have at your disposal. Now, my friends, is a time of perseverance. We will empty the stores and ration out the last of the food. Everyone please stay calm and orderly. Sleep well tonight so that you are rested for tomorrow's endeavor. Once the exodus is underway, there is no turning back so be sure you have everything you need. I expect tomorrow morning we will have more to announce."

CHAPTER XXI

OLD ENEMIES

Lucien's fingers flicked through the refuse of a desk drawer in the corner of the Infirmary's atrium. Tossing some old files aside, he finally found what he was looking for. Glancing across the length of the atrium, he circled the desk; the sound of hastened footsteps grew louder down the corridor. Stepping to the threshold of bay two's entrance, he fastened a sign reading 'MORGUE' to the lintel – and just in time.

Bursting into the atrium came the dozen or so irate citizens who had abandoned Alaric's speech for the pursuit of Nestor and the others. Lucien nudged the sign straight and turned to the mob, watching as they spread throughout bay one and into his private quarters. Finding nothing, they reconvened in the atrium, approaching Lucien as he stood blocking bay two. One of the men stepped forward. "Stand aside," he commanded.

Lucien glared back at the man as if horrified by his imposition. "Perhaps," he said, affecting great distaste, "you did not see the sign?" He waved a hand at the morgue notice.

The man glanced at it. With a disregarding snort, he tried to push around Lucien.

"I'm sorry sir," Lucien said, stepping back. "Protocol dictates that I cannot let you in for sanitary issues and out of simple respect for the dead."

He shriveled into himself, drawing his hands and neck in around his shoulders.

"Doctor," the man said, "you do good work here and I want to be respectful of that but if you do not move, I will move you."

"Sir," Lucien winced, "I am not supposed to let any unauthorized person into the morgue. If the head physician were here he may be able to make exceptions but I simply cannot, sir." Lucien's eye darted timidly across the angry faces of the mob. He twisted his lips in an apologetic smile. "If you must go in, please, tell the others to remain here."

The man swung his head over his shoulder, evincing his cooperation to the others with disgruntled nod. "Fine," he said.

Lucien smiled cautiously and drew the curtain back.

"If Nestor and the Trade Lords are here, be ready to block their escape," he said, taking a heavy breath to enter the morgue.

Lucien followed him, letting the curtain drop closed in their wake. Ten beds lay before them, each occupied by a body concealed under a white sheet. The room was lit sparsely by a single torch.

"The fire draws moisture from the bodies," Lucien explained as the man blinked his eyes to see through the dark. "It causes them to decay faster, thus there's only one torch. Normally it's not lit at all."

The man waved off Lucien's explanation and quietly surveyed the room. He walked up to the nearest bed and reached out his hand to felt for the edge of the sheet.

Lucien touched the man's shoulder but shied away at his glare. His face graven with determination, the man lifted the corner of the sheet. Lucien saw him draw back at the sight of a body's bloated face. He flipped the cover back over the face and shivered.

"There," Lucien said, a perfect tone of paranoia. "Are you satisfied?"

"No," the man responded. "I want to see them all."

"Sir, it is a matter of personal safety that you do not examine these bodies, some are quite foul." Lucien imagined Barrius' eyes narrowing angrily.

"It makes no difference."

"No sir," Lucien spoke more definitively this time. "I have cooperated this far against my own will and against direct protocol, but I will let this go no further."

Ignoring Lucien, the man moved to the second bed. He reached out to find the edge of the sheet but Lucien caught his hand. He twisted the man's arm around behind his back and slammed his head into the near wall. The man slumped and Lucien let him fall to the ground. Already his forehead had swollen into shades of black and blue. Lucien picked him back up by the nape of his neck and whispered sharply in his ear, "Like I told you, it's a matter of personal safety that you don't belong here."

The man groaned and Lucien set him to his feet.

"Can you find the exit," Lucien asked, "or must I show you the way out?"

The man shook his head and placed his hand over his forehead. "No," he whined and tried to stray from Lucien's grip.

"Good," Lucien growled, releasing him. "If anyone comes in here at your defense, tell them they will be leaving in a small cot under a white sheet."

The man stumbled through the curtain and Lucien stared after him, listening to the clutter of voices. Soon the sound of protest died away, and Lucien heard footsteps receding from the Atrium.

Shortly after, Mark burst through the door. "Uncle Lucien!" he exclaimed. "I saw that big ole' mean man come out of here! Did you do that to him?" Mark pointed to his own forehead.

"Yes," Lucien said.

Mark uttered something to the extent of a cruel laugh, finding the man's unfortunate condition deviously hilarious.

"My fine gentlemen," Lucien said, making a face at Mark as he ruffled the boy's hair, "it is safe for you all to come out."

The Trade Lords were the first to poke their heads from under the sheets, though all were wary to move. Once it seemed the Traders had safely revealed themselves, Barrius, Nestor, and Titus moved from their places beneath the sheets.

"What now?" Nestor asked, obviously sickened at having to be at the mercy of his nemesis.

"We wait for Alaric; everything depends on his success."

Nestor walked steadily towards Lucien, his sights unwavering. "Our fates depend on nothing but my leadership; it would be wise of you to remember that."

A sway in his step, Nestor walked past Lucien to look out the bay door. Mark stuck out his tongue and made a motion to kick the old General as he turned away. Lucien smiled and pulled Mark close, but Titus knelt down and grabbed the boy's chin, tilting it towards him.

"That is your Steward, boy," he said, and flung Mark's head to the side with his forefinger. Titus stood and looked passively at Lucien as if he was not even worth a rude gesture.

"Funny thing about pride," Lucien said, "the way it tears us apart while seeming to hold us together all at once."

Titus' face twisted like a snorting bull. He charged Lucien, stopping just short to breathe down his ear. "I'll see to your ruin," he hissed and rocked back on his heels. He stepped slowly away, his ardent eyes not straying from Lucien for several paces.

Lucien's eye danced impishly in the torchlight as he returned the gaze. For the next few minutes everyone remained mired in the tense silence between them. Lucien and Mark stood together in the middle, patiently awaiting Alaric's arrival. The Trade Lords made their place among the beds; all six stood huddled together, conversing in whispers. Nestor and his consort schemed in malicious tones, every so often glancing back at Lucien. Another minute passed and the sound of footsteps came dashing down the corridor towards them.

Nestor and Titus shied from immediate view, and Barrius threw back the sheet to the nearest cot, prepped to disappear beneath it. Lucien strode into the atrium, throwing back the curtain separating it from the morgue. The huddle of Trade Lords cringed in the fresh torchlight and Alaric stepped short-breathed into the Infirmary.

He wheezed for air and bent over his knees to evade the cramping pain in his side. He smiled at Lucien, bobbing his head before panting at the ground. "I saw," he said rearing straight, "a group leaving here all in a rage and carrying a man who looked fairly roughed up. You wouldn't know anything about that would you?"

Lucien returned Alaric's lingering smile with an innocent shake of his head.

"Well," Alaric continued, "they said they were just leaving the Medical Wing, having set out to find Nestor and the others. I stopped them and set everything straight; they will be headed to the Housing District to prepare with the others."

"Excellent," Lucien said, "it was a success then?"

"Absolutely, we have their full cooperation."

Mark ran out from the bay and extended a warm hand to Alaric. "Hello, Mr. Alaric," he said.

"Hello, Mark," Alaric returned, shaking the boy's hand.

Mark smiled and then turned back to Lucien, but his eyes widened and he pointed towards the bay's entrance. Titus, Barrius, Nestor, and the Trade Lords were carefully watching them. Alaric stepped past Lucien, saluting Nestor and bowing to the Trade Lords.

"The people are compliant," he said. "I have sent them back to the Housing District. My Lords," he addressed the Traders, "I suggest you return to the Council Chambers; it is the most appropriate place for you to be at this time. I assure you it is quite safe from danger, I have spoken to all the citizens; they are no longer a threat to you."

"Where is Stilguard?" Nestor cut across, questioning Alaric at this junction.

Alaric looked down and shook his head. "Our Steward is dead."

One of the Trade Lords stepped up to join the rough circle of confrontation. "Emergency delegations are in order," he said. "We must deliberate upon this as quickly as possible. The structure and integrity of our system must be maintained in such an unstable time. There can be no delay in our procedures." A murmur of agreement was uttered from the remaining five Trade Lords.

"We must also elect six new trade representatives – unless any of them have returned?"

"None, I am afraid," Alaric said.

"You must regale us immediately then upon the outcome of the scouting operation. Were the two of you the only to return? Did you reconnect the trade route with Bristing?"

Alaric exchanged sideways glances with Lucien. He twitched his nose and rubbed his palms together, feeling the sweat leak from between his fingers. "We found Bristing razed to the ground, its people dead, its buildings burning."

Shallow gasps passed through the Trade Lords.

"We engaged two Nephilim in the town's forum," Alaric continued. "Lucien and I, and nine others en route to the Borderlands are all that remain."

"En route to the Borderlands?" Nestor shouted. A clamor of voices rose behind him.

"Patience. Patience!" Lucien cried.

The room fell silent.

"All of this can be explained in due time," he continued, "I think for now, we should take leave of one another to compose ourselves. The days, no doubt, have been tempering."

"Silence, you," Nestor spat. "You have no say in this state's affairs."

Alaric leaned to Lucien's ear. "This was not supposed to take place for hours."

Lucien pressed Alaric's chest with the back of his hand.

"Regardless," one of the Trade Lords spoke. "I think Lucien is right. We should take leave of one another for maybe an hour or so."

"I agree," Alaric said. "We need some time to think about the future of our society and the possibility that our system may not function as it did before. We must be willing to adapt; I ask you all keep this in mind."

Alaric's last words stirred whispers. Nestor stepped from around Barrius, but Titus grabbed his arm. "For once," Titus said, "Alaric may have a point. We all need some time to collect ourselves. Why don't we reconvene in the Council Chamber in say, an hour and a half?"

Nestor pulled his arm free of Titus' grip. "We will meet in two hours," he snapped, rearing a poisonous glare at Titus. He stormed passed Alaric and from the Infirmary.

A snake's grin passed across Titus' face; Lucien could almost see his forked tongue flicking out from between his lips. Followed by Barrius, he strode after the General, gaining him just outside the Infirmary's corridor.

"Did you see the way Alaric carried himself?" Barrius muttered, rounding in front of Nestor. "Did you see how he spoke? He may well fancy himself Steward, and the brigand…"

"Yes, Barrius," Titus soothed, a storm brimming his eyes, "and we will deal with it when the time is right."

"We only have two hours."

Ignoring him, Titus and Nestor continued their brisk pace down the half-lighted passage.

Barrius shrugged off their disregard and fell in line behind them again.

"They have something planned," Titus said, after a moment. "That much is obvious. I would almost undoubtedly say they are conspiring against your authority, General Nestor. It seems that Alaric has the favor of the people as well; he may try to capitalize upon that."

"I must be alone," Nestor said, cutting Titus short. "Leave me, both of you, and meet in the Steward's Hall half an hour before the decided time. I will be in my private quarters."

"Very well," Titus said, easing his pace. He came to a halt with Barrius at his side. Titus watched through halls darkened by dissention as Nestor shrank down the corridor and disappeared towards the Military Ward.

* * *

"I think we need to speak with Bryan," Lucien said.

Alaric nodded in approval and Mark piped in as he scampered up to Lucien, "Ooh, I like Bryan, he's funny. Are we going now, Uncle Lucien?"

Lucien looked from Mark to Alaric and creased his lips. He then knelt down to Mark's level and cuffed him gently on the ear. "I'm sorry Mark," he said, "you're going to have to stay here for now."

"But I've been here for days and days and days-s-s-s," he whined.

Lucien laughed and said, "Just for a few more hours; then guess what?"

"What?" Mark asked through a flare of disappointment, sinking his neck into his hunched shoulders.

"Tomorrow I'll take you outside."

"No!" Mark exclaimed, his neck sprouting like a turtle from its shell.

Lucien reassured him with a resolute nod.

"You promise?"

"I promise," Lucien said. "You'll see grass and, if you're patient, I'll let you climb in a tree."

Mark threw back his head in a wild cackle and skipped around the room, stopping short of Brancott's overcoat. "Mr. Brancott," he announced, "tomorrow I will be going outside; as such, we have work to do. There are patients to be tended to and I have a pocket full of bandages." He produced a handful of bandages, knotted together in his fist.

Brancott smiled and looked at Lucien for further instruction.

"That sounds like a fine plan," Lucien reaffirmed. "I should be along later to check on things. There is nothing too serious that is the matter I trust?"

Brancott shook his head and retired to his work in bay one, leading Mark by the nape of his neck.

"Well," Lucien said at last, "I believe it is time to return to the Archives. Bryan should be of great assistance to the transition of power as our plans have been thrown rather askew."

The two conspirators then left the atrium of the Infirmary and set off in the direction of the Archives. Along the way they crossed paths with Ferron. He stopped and backed against the wall to let Alaric and Lucien through the narrow corridor.

"Captain," he said as Alaric passed.

Alaric nodded and continued on, but Lucien narrowed his eye at Ferron's half-shadowed face.

"Who is he?" Lucien whispered when Ferron faded from sight.

Alaric shrugged. "Miner probably, I've never seen him."

Lucien nodded contemplatively and glanced back over his shoulder. No one was in sight.

Ferron waited for their footsteps to empty down the corridor before he began to follow. When at last the pair disappeared into the Archives, Ferron crept steadily to the entrance and perched himself in the shadows just outside, listening.

CHAPTER XXII

THE STEWARDSHIP

"Bryan," Lucien said to the elderly man bent over the candle-lit top of the Archives' table, "it is good to see you again, my friend."

Bryan stood to meet his visitors, smiling at the sight of Lucien's return. "Dear Lucien, how are you? And, Captain, it is good to see you in such fine condition. I was halfway worried neither of you would return; though I dare say I should have expected your homecoming when the rioters were quelled. I could hardly concentrate on my reading they were making such a racket."

"You were here the whole time?" Alaric asked.

"Oh yes," Bryan laughed, "I am too old for rioting. So uncivil," he grumbled as he replaced his tattered book on its shelf. "Now," he said more cheerily, "can I make you two some tea?"

"No thank you, Bryan. I lament to say we don't have the time for pleasantries. We have two hours to act and Alaric and I are in need of your assistance."

"To act?" Bryan asked, looking at the two of them with an impish grin. "Well, this should be interesting."

Lucien cast a confident glance at Alaric.

"Bryan," Alaric said, "the first thing you should know is that Stilguard has been killed."

Bryan collapsed back in his chair. "How did this happen?" he asked, his whisper tapering.

"He and his men were ambushed along the trade route after we set out from Adullam. They came across an abandoned caravan and were attacked by a," he paused and looked at Lucien who filled in the word, "satyr."

Bryan looked contemplatively between Alaric and Lucien, exhibiting his disbelief a stern chin.

"No," Alaric said, "I wouldn't have believed it either if I hadn't seen it myself."

"A satyr?" Bryan's brow lifted incredulously. "One of those beasts from old mythology?"

"A manifestation of The Searing Veil," Lucien explained.

Bryan's expression remained unchanged.

"It's a term meant to represent the final approach of a new age where the veil that hides the transcendental from our eyes is torn away, 'it sears, if falls, it seals our fate.'"

"The coming of The Shaddai?" Bryan asked, sitting straighter in his chair.

"He approaches," Lucien replied warily, "but others will come first."

"Others like this satyr?"

"And worse, which is why we need to be quick."

"Well then, I won't waste your time trying to understand. My guess is you've come for advice in the wake of the Steward's death."

"Precisely," Lucien said.

"Well, explain to me the current situation and what plans you have established thus far."

"Very well," Alaric spoke up. "In returning, it's now obvious that Nestor and the Trade Lords hold little influence over the people. We had always planned action against Nestor, but we had hoped to come into agreement with the remaining Trade Lords," Alaric slowed his voice to offset his callous explanation, "the others having died in the fight at Bristing. As I said, we had hoped to garner the support of the Trade Lords; however, that no longer seems to be an issue. I feel we could do quite well without them."

"Their support might actually hinder our efforts at this point," considering the riots," Lucien said.

"Not likely," Bryan carefully mused. "If you could assure the people that their trust would be well founded in the Trade Lords, you would do a lot to legitimize your new establishment by not seeming too totalitarian. You want people to see that you're willing to cooperate with the old ways – it will allow you to modify more in the end."

"Essentially," Alaric continued, "from there we intended to rally support around an exodus to the Borderlands – every man, woman, and child. Our venture to Bristing was not a complete waste. We managed to –" Alaric paused for loss of words.

"requisition," Lucien interjected in Alaric's silence.

"– requisition a large herd of cattle and a dozen or so horses. They are, as we speak, en route to the Borderlands. Orleans, Gaverick, and some of the other soldiers are driving them there to await our arrival."

"We feared that bringing the cattle to Adullam," Lucien continued, "would compromise our security by bringing unnecessary attention to the surface. A herd of the size we have acquired would not go unnoticed in Drögerde, and it would not be long before Aureus was at our steps. The Borderlands is the furthest place away from Aureus that could sustain and conceal our population."

"There is truly no other option for Adullam at this point," Alaric said. "Our salvation is on its way to the Borderlands. There is simply no other food source, and no way to deliver it safely to Adullam."

"Furthermore," Lucien said, "the satyr had formed an ambush along our trade route. It is wise, I think, to infer that the route has been traced back to Adullam."

"I see," Bryan said. "You make a good point. You were right, I think – however large a gamble it is – to send the cattle away and rally an exodus. All of this has cataclysmic implications upon the very foundation of our society. I dare say we will never see this place again if we leave. There is sadness in that thought and some joy," Bryan laughed. "Fresh air would do these old bones some good – it's been years since I tasted it. But, back to business," he said firmly. "I assume your next question was going to be something like, 'how do we deal with Nestor and his position as interim Steward?' as I am perfectly sure you know he will not give that position away lightly."

Alaric nodded solemnly.

"Right," Bryan continued, "well, there are the proper avenues – or there were before six Trade Lords died. Now the dynamic has changed and in order to play by the rules, there must be elections. And when is this grand exodus meant to be taken?"

"Tomorrow," Lucien and Alaric said in unison.

"Well, elections are out of the question, aren't they? Especially with the rioting," Bryan said. "Let me think then. Without a full committee of Trade Lords, the Steward cannot be voted out of his position unless it is by unanimous concession of the General and his top three ranking officers. The General, however, is currently the Steward and his officers are fanatically loyal to him; that is except for you, Captain. The odds are against you, Alaric."

"There is," Lucien proposed, "another way."

By the tone of his voice, Bryan knew his intentions. "That is a dangerous road to tarry," he warned, "and may bring you ruin in the end. I would advise against it until every other option has been expunged."

"Everything is permissible," Lucien said, fingering the dust along the spine of a book.

" – but not everything is beneficial." Bryan finished. "An advantage you have is that the people do not trust Nestor. The only truly necessary step is to rally the support of the people. A government is nothing without a people to be governed. Government is the system of society; so it should be to society's benefit – not to the benefit of the few at the top. If the people refuse to be dictated to by Nestor, then he has no power. His army has been reduced to nearly nothing over these past months; he has no power to oppress Adullam under a leadership the people do not desire. However, someone must fill in the gap."

Both Lucien and Bryan looked at Alaric.

"I," he stammered, flustered by their directed gazes, "I only wanted to make a way for our people to escape, to find our freedom."

"And how are they to find freedom with no one to lead them to it?" Bryan asked.

"Well, by restoring power to the Trade Lords – legitimizing their position and speaking on their behalf, and by removing the mantle from Nestor."

"When a mantle is removed, it must be passed. There must be a Steward, lest the Trade Lords become tyrants. There must be a balance of power."

"Well, not me!" Alaric cried, "Why must it be me?"

"You ordered two-thousand angry souls to forget their outrage as they battered down the Council Chamber's doors; they're primed for your next order. The people respect you and revere you as a friend of Stilguard, and you're a natural leader yourself."

"You must have known this was the necessary step if we were to successfully overcome Nestor," Lucien asserted.

"But the end was never for me to take on the title of Steward. That is not a burden I could bear – not in such a time. I'm not fit," he stuttered.

"No one is fit." Lucien raised his voice.

"For now, the power should remain in the hands of the Trade Lords," Alaric fumbled for alternatives, "as long as their position can be legitimized, we can promote..."

"No," Lucien, struck across Alaric's feeble response, "there is nothing to promote! There is only you and the authority you don't see you possess. Fate has called upon *you* in this time, Alaric; now rise up and accept it. Step into your purpose."

* * *

These were the last words Ferron heard before he dashed off down the corridor to find Titus. He needed hear no more. The conspiracy was complete and his diligence would soon be rewarded for its efforts. There was enough time yet before the two-hour deadline to make use of all this information. Every moment Titus and Nestor remained unaware was a moment wasted, so Ferron made all haste, scurrying along the empty halls like a rat in a mad search for crumbles of cheese discarded on a dirty floor.

He passed the same corridors again and again, scouring the halls for Titus or anyone who might know his whereabouts. But there was no one; the halls were completely empty save for himself and the echoes his feet left scattering down the dark tunnels. At last, after agonizing minutes of searching, Ferron saw his prize – Titus walking down a corridor away from him. Summoning the last of his energy, Ferron sprinted down the hall after him.

Sliding to a halt at Titus' side, Ferron grabbed his arm, gasping for breath.

"What's gotten you in such a fix?" Titus asked, the shadow over his eyes darkening with the bend of his brow.

Ferron cleared his throat to speak, but struggled to catch his breath.

"I'm headed for the Steward's Hall; come tell me as we walk," Titus said, laughing, and picked up his friend by the elbow to drag him along.

As soon as Ferron had regained his breath, he unfolded the details of his previous hour: his coincidental run-in with Alaric and Lucien; how he had followed them to their meeting with Bryan; the conspiring nature of their conversation. He gave special attention to Lucien's allusion to forcefully remove Nestor from his position, and was careful to mention Alaric's decided purpose as the new Steward of Adullam, his plan for the exodus, as well as the location of the cattle.

Ferron finished his tale just as the two entered into the Steward's Hall. They found Barrius already waiting for them, balancing on an edge of the battered door. Titus froze on the threshold like a statue, his eyes darting left and right, as if set by the gears of a clock.

"What's the matter?" Barrius asked, to the echo of loose debris scattering behind him as he jumped down from the door. "What's gotten into him?" he whispered to Ferron.

"Quiet, the both of you," Titus silenced them. "Listen to what I'm about to say. Ferron, I want you to explain the situation to Barrius. I must go alert Nestor; he may be in danger. I will return with him here and we will wait for the council then to convene. Barrius, go to the Barracks, bring the remaining guards back to the Steward's Hall and have them ready to arrest Lucien and Alaric for conspiring against the Steward."

"What!?" Barrius cried out.

"Ferron will explain, now go and do as I said, but nothing else before I return; we do not want to alert Alaric or his counterpart to any threat or they may escape. Once you have returned with the guards, keep yourselves hidden in the Steward's Hall. I will take care of the General. Go now!"

CHAPTER XXIII

BETRAYAL

Titus came to the door just outside Nestor's private quarters. Lingering, he collected himself, allowing his arrested breath to settle. He knocked quietly, but pushed the door open without waiting for a response.

Nestor stood facing away, brooding over his desk with his knuckles planted firmly against the wooden frame; his belt and dagger rested too among scattered piles of paper. Nestor lifted his ear to the creaking noise of the door. Ducking his head, Titus shut the door softly behind him. "General," he said, giving a quick salute.

"That's Steward, Captain," Nestor said.

"Not yet," Titus said weakly as he came closer to Nestor, eyes trained to the floor.

Nestor cracked his neck to one side and pivoted to face Titus.

"I meant no disrespect," he said, "only that there may be complications."

"Go on."

Titus lifted his head; his eyes ticked like the pendulum of a clock as he dissected every visible facet of Nestor... Little droplets of water remained collected on his chin and jaw, caught in the stubble of his unshaven face – remnants from the washbasin on the adjacent table. The lines of Nestor's forehead were drawn tight above the heavy set of his greying brow. The breadth of his shoulders arched with the steady pace of his breath. The age-marked flesh on his arms, the sway of his stance, the shine of his boots in the candle light – every detail – Titus siphoned into account. "There is a plot against your title of Steward," he said.

"By whom?" Nestor asked as Titus circled slowly around behind him.

"Need you ask?"

"I haven't the time, Titus. What have you come to tell me?"

"Forgive me," Titus smiled, his eyes aglow. "It seems that Alaric, aided of course by dear Lucien, is vying for the Stewardship of Adullam. As you saw, they've already displayed their influence over the people, sir, and they may very well – I would say perhaps without a shadow of a doubt – be able to sway the Trade Lords' support to their own favor."

"Impossible," Nestor retorted.

"No sir. I believe they're far more formidable than we accounted for. All the same, it's not too late," he said as he continued circling.

Nestor stroked the hair on his chin with his thumbnail, making a soft grating sound. "Not too late?"

"No sir. Stopping their assent will come at a price, but I believe I have a solution," Titus said, now leaning comfortably against Nestor's desk, his hands folded behind his back.

"And what is that?" Nestor asked, his back now to the door.

Titus' eyes dilated, bringing everything again into sharp focus. His vision narrowed, and the room began to pulse, his head humming with a heightened consciousness; he stared back at Nestor.

"What is this solution?!" Nestor belted.

The humming stopped.

"Pay the price," Titus whispered. Blood spurted from Nestor's neck as Titus released the hilt of the dagger. Nestor's breath gargled as he fought to stand upright, his own blade sheathed in his throat. Titus stepped to the side and let him collapse on the floor, watching his life spill out red onto the floor. He prodded the body with his foot, and backed slowly away. He paused, trying to keep his legs from shaking. Pressing his face against the cool of the cavern wall, he breathed and shivered in the dark. Without looking back, he flung the door open, tearing out of the General's quarters. The door bashed against the adjacent wall with a *crack* that offset its hinges.

Titus fled as fast as he could, affecting fear and outrage. He called for help as he rounded the bend to the Council Chambers. Ferron, Barrius, and a handful of iron clad soldiers came rushing into the hallway to meet him.

Feet slipping as he ran, Titus cascaded himself across the chamber floor, gasping for breath. Barrius knelt and gave him his hand, setting Titus to his feet and dusting the dirt from his jacket. His expression was an engraving of horror. In the direst voice Titus could summon, he wailed, "It's already too late. They've gotten him." He moaned wildly. "They've gotten him."

"It's too late?" Barrius exclaimed. "Lucien already… Ferron told me…"

"Alaric, and that Lucien," Titus spat, turning to the guards. "They were conspiring against the Steward – I'm sure Ferron alerted you – I went to go and warn Nestor but it was too late. He lay on the ground with a dagger," he paused as if unable to call forth words, "his own dagger, buried into the side of his neck.

"I can only suppose," he continued, "it was the two, the conspirators, Lucien and Alaric. They'll be in Council Chambers any moment now. If we hurry, we can catch them off guard and have them arrested. Form up on either side of the entrance and we can surprise them."

The four guards split to either side of the Council Chamber's threshold and crouched in waiting for Alaric and Lucien's arrival. In the meantime, Titus, Barrius, Ferron, and the Trade Lords stood in the center of the room, trembling in wait of the supposed murderers.

Soon, slow footsteps approached down the hall. The circle around Titus opened to see Alaric and Lucien's entrance. The Trade Lords shifted into the background as the pair came into sight. Titus stepped forward, nodding to the hidden soldiers. Lucien was the first over the chamber's threshold. The Traders stood rigid, lined shoulder to shoulder. Warned by the tension in their gaze, Lucien feinted forward and the soldiers jumped from their cover. Missing Lucien, they knocked Alaric to the ground, holding him there with the sharp end of a short spear.

Three of the soldiers doubled back and charged Lucien. He drew his scepter from the inside of his jacket, and keeping the blade concealed, parried the soldier's advance until he had backed himself against a wall. With three spears at his neck Lucien relented, holding out his scepter by the clasp, securing the felstone. One of the guards reached to take it, but with a flick of his wrist Lucien sent the concealed blade shooting through the soldier's hand. The soldier yelped and Lucien twisted his hand behind his back, taking him hostage. He slid the blade from the soldier's hand and pushed him in the midst of the other two. They stumbled and Lucien leapt past them, sweeping his blade through the wooden handle of the spear at Alaric's neck.

The next thing Lucien knew, two men had grabbed him from behind. "For the exit!" he yelled at Alaric as he was forced to his knees. Alaric rolled back onto his feet and darted from the room, two soldiers in close pursuit.

Lucien felt the blunt end of a spear bludgeon the back of his head. He fell against the hard floor, his mask making a grating noise against the stone as he slid prostrate.

"It is as I told you!" Titus proclaimed. "He was expecting confrontation; he was prepared. Did you see?"

The words were faint and hollow in Lucien's head.

"He killed Nestor, and may have meant to kill us all."

No, Lucien thought, *kill Nestor?* His head throbbed and Titus voice swirled dizzily in his head. He laughed aloud, rolling on his back to stare at the ceiling. Titus raised his voice, but his words were less than echoes in Lucien's ears.

"Are you so petty?" Lucien called; his tongue curled around his teeth. His eye spiraled around the room. "Can you see nothing?" he mocked. "Your life here is a shadow of reality."

"Silence him," Titus ordered.

Lucien's laugh crackled and hissed like a billowing fire. "You must think yourself important, Titus Valerius, your head full of delusions of power, but the real power is coming – it may already be at your doorstep and it is cruel, and it is relentless, and you will not escape it."

The last thing Lucien saw was the shadow of a boot as it collided against his the side of his head.

The voices drifted away and Lucien found himself alone in the dark. Sometime later he awoke into a semiconscious state. His eye rendered still to the void, disembodied voices carried melodiously through his mind. "Captain Titus," he heard, "because of the conspiracy set against the Stewardship by your contemporary, the former Captain Alaric Folck, and because of your courageous actions to secure the solidarity of our state, as the next ranking officer below the late General Nestor, we hereby see it fit that you, Titus Valerius, be the new acting Steward until the present crisis is resolved." Lucien gasped quietly for air, forcing his eye open. Titus and the six Trade Lords spun around the room as nausea overwhelmed Lucien. He shut his eye again and woke up some hours later in the captivity of Adullam's prison.

* * *

Alaric was frantic and fleeing blindly through empty corridors as the guards from the Council Chamber continued their relentless pursuit. He had lost himself in the dark but he could not stop running. Though the guards had fallen from his sight, the sound of their chase still echoed all around Alaric. Coming to a split in the corridor, he slowed. His fingers traced the edge of the wall and he stole a glance behind. The flicker of their torchlight and the ring of iron on stone grew stronger. Alaric wrestled down the fear that battered his chest and tried to tame the wailing sound of his lungs. Closer still his pursuers came; their footfalls shattered Alaric's eardrums. He shook his head to clear the noise, and beneath their clatter flowed a fainter sound – the river. He dodged right, disappearing towards the Housing District.

He bounded through the narrow pools of torchlight, phasing in and out of the dark. The way widened before him and the ceiling vaulted beyond his sight, opening into the Market. Alaric was suddenly struck by remembrance of the guard that he and Lucien had left bound and incapacitated at the platform by the river's edge. Alaric stopped short his scramble into the Housing District, its halls full of commotion. His mind was a haze. He ran back several paces to the Market's center and soon could hear the sounds of the soldiers' approach, even over the bustle of people making ready for the exodus.

The soldiers grew louder until their echoes resounded aloft the Market's high halls. Alaric slid over a table and disappeared behind a row of stands.

The soldiers emerged and fanned out across the room.

Shuffling across the ground, Alaric wound through a labyrinth of stands towards the Barracks. The last stretch through the Market was exposed. With soldiers closing in from every side, overturning stands and scouring every crevice, Alaric sprang from cover. Shouts gained his ears, and the uniform clash of iron picked up a swift pace behind him. He darted over a few market stands and disappeared down the corridor to the Barracks in the West Wing of Adullam.

Alaric rolled each step on the outside of his foot, careful not to let the sound of his flight resound through the Barracks. Dashing around a small bend in the passage, he suddenly slid to a halt. Emerging from the Soldier's Quarters was Barrius, leading a new guard patrol. Breathless, Alaric ducked into the dark of a corner between the training grounds and the armory, praying the shadows would contain him.

Reflected in the torchlight, Barrius and his armored men shone like fire rolling from a dragon's throat. Alaric shut his eyes and held his breath, fighting back the tremor of his spine. The fire rolled ever closer to his hidden spot. He pressed himself harder against the wall, waiting for the men to pass. Their footfalls rang like a slow clap rising to its crescendo. Inches away from Alaric, they stopped. Alaric's breath hung in the air. Barrius cocked his head to the side and listened intently to the sound of the soldiers in pursuit of Alaric rounding the corner to the Barracks. They came charging down the passage, stopping short of Barrius.

"Sir," one of the soldiers spoke to Barrius as they met, "Captain Folck is in the Barracks."

"No," Barrius retaliated, "he isn't! You've lost him."

"Sir, we tailed Captain..."

"If the *former* Captain had come back this way, don't you think we would have seen him?"

The soldier lowered his gaze to the ground.

"He isn't in the Barracks! He must have hidden and doubled back around."

"Sir, I don't feel there is any way..." another soldier began to say, but was silenced by a whirlwind of Barrius' rage. "I don't care what you feel, soldier!" Barrius yelled. "He's doubled back around! Now as there are nine of you, I expect you to have him caught in the next few minutes. Steward Valerius will want to make an example of him."

Steward Valerius!?

Alaric held his breath and let his head shrink into his shoulders. The words cascaded into his stomach, knotting it in coils. He pressed against his chest to suppress the sound of his heart as it pounded out of his ears. His lungs begged for breath, deep, mind-opening breaths to take him out of this dark clutter of confusion. His eyes roved wildly between the soldiers standing over him, searching their countenance for understanding.

"Divide up into groups of two," Barrius barked another set of orders. "Alaric will have worked himself towards the prisons in the North Wing. Cover all the exits and move slowly to cut off his escape if he's somehow able to free Lucien. Is that understood?"

The soldiers chorused a "Yes sir," as they broke quickly into groups of two.

"And do not let him slip past you again," Barrius raised his voice for a final command. "Steward Valerius is about to address the people concerning the General's death. I will be with him in the Market where the announcement is to be made. I expect this traitor to be caught so that all of Adullam can see his shame."

The soldiers shot off a round of salutes and clamored down the hall out of sight.

Barrius straightened his shoulders as he stood alone in the dark, watching the soldiers carry out his orders. He cracked his neck, tucked his hand between the buttons of his vest and strode slowly forward, pursing his lips with the pride of a spoiled prince. Alaric crept out of his corner. *A knife in the dark would be nothing too grave.*

He followed Barrius at a distance, back into the Market. As he veered left towards the café, Alaric kept to the shadows of the southern wall. A crowd was forming at the base of the shelf. The Trade Lords stood atop it, and behind them, on one of the iron wrought tables, was the newly appointed Steward Valerius, his chin lifted to the crowd. By the time Alaric had reached the shadows edging the entrance of the Housing District, most of the citizens had filtered out, their heads wandering curiously across the Market for a hint of purpose in their gathering. Alaric heard his name in whispers diffusing across the crowd as the people took notice of Titus standing on high. He began to speak to the crowd, but Alaric paid no attention until he was caught by the phrase... "I lament to say, that I have attained this position through the greatest of tragedies."

A murmur of uncertainty wandered through the crowd.

"Captain Alaric Folck," Titus continued, "has aided in the assassination of the Interim-Steward and General, Marcus Nestor. Earlier this evening he proposed to you a plan to leave Adullam and begin a new life elsewhere. This, however, was nothing more than an attempt to leave his treachery and betrayal behind as he assumed an unjust power over all of us. His proposed exodus is nothing short of suicide! He would have led all of us to ruin for his own delusions of glory!"

Curses filled the vaulted cavern's ceiling like incense. The heavy scent of it sickened Alaric as he crept along the back wall towards the Housing District. Blue veins lifted against his pale skin as the poison of Titus' words worked their way through Alaric's system. His legs twitched to break from the shadows and charge against his accusation, but some other force kept him glued to wall toward his careful escape.

"Adullam is our home!" Titus yelled. "And we shall never abandon it."

Cheers set flame to the fuming incense pervading the cavern.

"It has borne us for a hundred and fifty years and it shall not be this generation that it forsakes! Nor shall it forsake our children or their children, or theirs! My brothers and sisters, my friends and comrades, you should not be brought to food, but food should be brought to you. You are not cattle or swine, but men and women of strength and valor and heritage, and this place – these caverns – belong to you!"

Alaric escaped the fervent roar, making his way to the back of the crowd and through the entrance of the empty Housing District.

"Your salvation is not out there! No, my good friends," Alaric heard Titus' voice echoing down the lonely halls, "your fate lies here!"

With this final exclamation, a thundering bellow deafened the halls. The whole of Adullam shook, breaking debris into the crowd. The force of it knocked Alaric to the ground as he ran along the corridor towards the river. He rolled over and shuffled several feet backwards across the floor. In the clamor's wake, everything fell silent and the crowd's attention turned towards Adullam's main entrance. A harsh light began to peak over the top of the crowd, silhouetting them like trees against a rising sun. Unearthly screeches resounded through the halls and, as the people turned to run, a large bolt of fire streaked across their escape into the Housing District.

The bolt burned into Alaric's eyes, turning his vision purple. As he fought to regain his vision he could see nothing but flames curling and licking their way across the entrance to the Housing District. Smaller flames dropped from the larger bolt, blazing furiously and bouncing up and down as if alive. The little flames surrounded the assembly in the Market, cutting off any escape. They thrashed and screeched as they bounded around, sending sparks and embers flaking off in all directions. As Alaric slid himself frantically away and into the deeper shadows of the Housing District, the sound of harsh laughter spilled after him.

Soon the laughing flames began to burn down, combusting in short bursts until the fires dissipated into a yellow and orange glow. Twig-like legs appeared at the base of the dying flames, and little arms flailed wildly though the air. With some, wings burst from the fires, waving vigorously to lift the emerging figures off the ground for a short time. One by one the little flames died down reveal the burnt, gray-green skin of imps. The creatures danced ferociously in place, gnashing their teeth and flashing their claws at their captive crowd, taking delight in the people's tormented screams. Hundreds of them surrounded the crowd.

"Aureus," Alaric whispered in a breathless shock and slid himself further down the dark of the corridor.

CHAPTER XXIV

SOLUS

Alaric thought he had been terrified before – hunched in a dark corner beneath the feet of Barrius and his soldiers – if he was terrified then, words could not describe the combination of horror and adrenaline that was presently rioting through him. Even as Alaric began to hear the river's bramble deep within the Southern Wing, the shrill echo of his people's tortured fates bombarded his senses. Illusions of fire sprang out of every shadow as he sprinted down the deserted hallway. A burning sensation ignited his heels, growing hotter with every step as Alaric imagined a wave of flame closing in on him. Sweat poured from his brow into his eyes, and the blood rushed from his arms. Dizzy and faint he crashed into the wall, splaying himself across the ground. He rolled over, vomit pouring out of his nose and mouth. Alaric dragged himself along the side of the passage and lay curled in a ball, breathing.

He spat the taste of vomit from his mouth and began trying to wipe away the sweat from his eyes as the trembling in his hands gradually subsided. The imps' screeches were fainter now, and a cool draft lifting from the river breezed over Alaric's hot skin. The darkness of his home had never before daunted him, but now in every shadow was born a demon. Nothing seemed to work together for good, and the only thing that kept

Alaric reaching ahead in uncertainty was the knowledge of what he was leaving behind.

Sluggishly, Alaric picked himself off the ground, bracing himself against the corridor wall as he rose. His palms rested against the coarse stone and his fingers crept along like a ten-legged spider, leading him toward the river. He sidestepped nervously, sliding his feet noiselessly across the floor. After several minutes of tedious progress, Alaric crept away from the wall, stirred on by the rush of the river. He shivered against the cold deep of Adullam and livened his pace to warm his senses. Before long, he could see the warm glow of the river post torch thrown faint across the corridor, and the rhythmic click of the waterwheel beckoned him across the bridge.

As the wooden planks rattled beneath his boots, Alaric saw the light cast on the body of the guard lying limp where Lucien had left him. The horses neighed as Alaric came into sight, a bit of the guard's tunic hanging from one's mouth as it lifted its head. As Alaric neared, he noticed a few bruises and cuts around the guard's shoulder blades where the horses' teeth had nicked his skin while grazing. Alaric rushed across the bridge and around the alcove to untether the guard. The horses stamped their hooves impatiently and pranced at Alaric, edging him back towards the bank of the river. The stallion snorted and clicked his hoof on the stone, bowing his head defensively. His wide eyes shown like huge black pearls, beautiful but daunting. Foam from the river brushed Alaric's heels as it swept by, and he struggled to maintain balance as the stallion's eyes bore down against him. With no other option, Alaric took a decisive step forward, glaring back into the stallion's pitiless eyes, and thwacked it across the nose. The stallion tensed and reared its head back with a wild neigh, and Alaric crumpled to the ground.

As his shoulder crashed against the cold floor, Alaric broke like an egg, his arms and legs spread out around him. His embarrassed grunt cracked into a squeak as he jolted to pick himself back up. "I hate horses," he exclaimed behind clenched teeth as he brushed the dirt from his rear.

The stallion stepped back in submission and stood with the mare; the two had taken to nuzzling one another in the corner of the alcove. Alaric wiped the hot streak of embarrassment from his face, glaring at the stallion. He straightened his back as he approached the river guard, and at last turned his attention away from the horses. Kneeling, he rolled the body over. There was no immediate response, and Alaric tried to shake him awake. The guard's head nodded lifelessly in Alaric's arms. He checked the pulse at his wrists. Feeling nothing, Alaric's fingers skirted to the guard's neck; his breath fluttered nervously out of his dry mouth as he pressed for the pulse. Panic pricked the back of Alaric's neck – there was still nothing.

Crouching, he dragged the guard to the edge of the river. He cupped some water in his palms and with a final prayer, splashed it on the guard's face. As if struck by lightning, his eyes bolted open. He rolled onto his stomach and tried to slide away into the river, but Alaric grabbed him by the ankle and tackled him into submission. The guard struggled to free himself, striking back with his elbows. Alaric took an elbow to the chin, reared back and flipped the guard onto his back. Quickly, he put his finger to his lips. Realizing who had pinned him, the guard sank his shoulders into the ground with a sigh. Alaric looked back toward the bridge to make sure nothing had heard their scuffle.

"Someone's come through the river entrance!" the guard whispered. "They came from behind me, dragged me under the water, left me for dead. I don't know how many, but it's not safe."

Alaric signaled for him to be quiet and kept his eyes steady on the bridge so nothing could surprise them.

"Are you hearing me, Captain?" the guard asked, his voice high-pitched with fear.

Alaric looked down and nodded, giving one more glance to the bridge before stepping back to help the guard up. "You're right," he said, "we have been compromised. There's been an invasion; almost everyone's held up in the Market."

The guard's face became white with a sickened feeling of failure. "What's happened?" he asked, barely able to form the words.

Alaric shook his head, "Aureus. There was an explosion from the main entrance. Huge walls of fire stretched out in all directions, engulfing the Marketplace and enclosing everyone in it. Then the fire began to die into smaller flames that shrank into," Alaric stammered, "imps."

"But," the guard stammered, "someone came through the river, who was that?"

"They've taken most of Adullam captive," he continued, disregarding the question, "including the Trade Lords. I escaped down here to follow the river back up to the North Wing. A few people are still there and may not have been caught. If we hurry, I think we can reach them before the imps do."

The guard swallowed hard, his eyes still in a slitted gaze of uncertainty. Suddenly he noticed his tunic sliding down his arm. "What in the hell?" he exclaimed, lifting his ragged tunic as it dangled on his forearm.

"I'm sorry about that," Alaric glowered, "I didn't know they would try to eat it."

"What?" the guard asked.

Alaric nodded to the shadowed corner of the alcove.

"What are they?" the guard's voice rang timid as he stepped behind Alaric.

"Horses," Alaric said, watching them with mild distaste.

"What a strange world," he whispered, peering over Alaric's shoulder. "And imps?"

"About a hundred of them."

"I guess I'll have to believe you now." His eyes wide still.

"It's best that you did," Alaric said. Emblazoned in his mind were the waves of fire tumbling through vast halls and the tumult of screams. "For now we'll leave the horses; we need to forge upriver and see who else we can rescue."

Alaric grabbed the torch from its batten, and stepped into the waist deep water. The guard took a timid step behind him, and slid slowly into the river. Alaric began to wade against the current, and the water folded up around his stomach, sending him shivers. The guard followed close in Alaric's wake, wading on the tip of his toes to avoid the rush of water against his bare stomach. As Alaric held the torch aloft for the guard to weave past the water wheel, its light cast an otherworldly glow against the agitated water. "What is your name?" Alaric asked, unable to stand the silence any longer.

"Nathan Blair," the soldier softly responded; Alaric could hear the fear in his voice and the chill on his teeth.

"Nathan Blair?" Alaric calmly asked.

"Yes sir, it is."

"Nice to be acquainted; my name is…"

"Captain Folck, yes sir, I know," Blair finished, "you helped train me three years back. And, well, it's important to know your superior officers."

"Ah, I remember you now. You cracked your head open on the training floor," Alaric cringed at the memory, but it made Blair laugh.

"Yes sir, that was me. I'm surprised you remembered."

"I don't think I'll ever forget that, Blair," he said and tried to laugh too, but found his mind still mired by imps and ill fate.

Alaric waved the torch back to share some extra light, and as he did, a cinder fell sizzling from the flame. It broke apart on Alaric's arm, causing him to drop the torch. The river engulfed their flame with a hiss reminiscent of the imps' shrill voices. Alaric's spine quaked cold; he cursed under his breath and felt for the wall, submersed again in total darkness. Behind him, Alaric could hear Blair's teeth chattering.

As they forged slowly up the river, Blair began to seize up his breath in shallow gasps to stop his chattering; at length, however, he could no longer control the sound. The burden of having been the orchestrator of Blair's misery began to weigh on Alaric's conscience. The young soldier tread steadfast through his discomfort until Alaric whistled at him to stop. A heavy fabric was pushed against Blair's chest. He jumped back at first and steadied himself on the wall.

"What is it?" his frantic whisper pierced the darkness.

"So you won't be so cold," Alaric replied, waving the fabric towards Blair's body, "my cuirass."

"But what will you…"

"I still have my tunic," Alaric said, dismissing the question. "You need to stay warm, I need you thinking straight."

Guided by the faint oaken smell of worn leather, Blair groped through the black for the garment. He gathered it in his arms and threw it over his shoulders, wriggling into it. It was rough against his chest with no undergarment, but the residual warmth from Alaric's body heat was a welcome relief. By now, the feel of icy water had turned to fire against the numbness in Blair's extremities. Each step felt like wading through a bed of coals as the burning sensation rose from the riverbed through his toes and up to his groin. The rhythm of his wincing breath set in on Alaric's pace, driving him to take longer strides against the onrushing water.

Beyond the cold numbing his limbs, distress had thoroughly numbed Alaric's mind. The lapping sound of the North Wing water wheel emerged and strengthened with each step, but Alaric pressed forward, oblivious. His face was just inches away from one of the beams supporting the North Wing bridge before he realized where he was. Coming to, Alaric reached back for Blair and felt the rough touch of leather compress against his palm. Alaric made a soft snap with his fingers and pointed at the bridge through the soft light now emanating from the connecting corridor.

Alaric grasped the railings of the bridge and slowly pulled himself up so not to disturb the water. A gnawing sensation seared against the strain of his muscles grown stiff in the cold. Gritting his teeth to stave off the pain, Alaric fought to lift himself free of the river's hold. With a final surge, he pulled his chin up over the balustrade and rest it there to keep from falling back. After a moment's shuffling he was able to find a hold for his feet, and at last picked himself up over the railing and onto the bridge. Exhausted, Alaric sat and nestled his back between the coarse frame of two heavy balusters. Beneath the heavy draws of his recovering breath, however, he began to hear the unnerving sound of Blair's urgent whispers.

Like a spider, his frail voice crawled across the balustrade and into Alaric's ears. He jumped to his feet, turning to face Blair's plea for help. He found Blair locked against the side of the bridge, his arms constricted by the cold and refusing to respond. He hung immobile, his feet dangling just above the water's surface and the tremor in his fingers was causing his grip to slide slowly away. Alaric dove against the railing and flung his chest over the balustrade, swinging his arms down to catch Blair just as one of his hands slipped.

Blair's foot splashed lightly on the surface of the water, burning his toes with cold. He could feel Alaric's grip tight around his wrist, and a sigh of relief leaked out of him as he watched the water curl around the tip of his boot. Blair felt himself being drawn up until at last he was able to find footing on the side of the bridge. In a dreamlike sensation, he felt Alaric pulling at his cuirass, floating him over the balustrade and onto the sturdy ground. He let himself collapse in a withering heap against the damp lumber. His skin was pale and shriveled, his hair curled across his face like a wet rat, and his body shook like a tree in the wind. His eyes were closed and his teeth chattered as his breath wavered in and out. Alaric picked Blair's limp body up and embraced him allowing him to feed off his body for warmth. Blair rested his chin against Alaric's shoulder and after several seconds began regaining a steady pace of breath. Alaric gave Blair a couple of claps on his back and released his embrace, taking Blair by the elbow to lift him off the ground.

Blair cracked his neck, braced himself against Alaric's shifted weight and steadily rose to his feet. He followed quietly behind Alaric as they snuck toward the lighted corridor. Just before stepping in range of the torch, Alaric paused. He turned to Blair and said softly, "We're making for the prison. There is someone who needs to be freed and there should be another soldier or two watching over him. From there we'll see who else can be rescued." Blair nodded and they continued on.

The halls leading back from the river were narrow and the shadows cast by each torch were long. Alaric stepped carefully between them to be sure that as he walked, his shadow did not precede him down the corridor. Blair followed his example and both crept along the passage back and forth between the adjacent walls. Eventually, the way joined with a wider corridor along the back wall of the Steward's Hall. Here they turned left and headed eastwardly. The prison was located between the Medical Wing and the Steward's Hall along one of the main passages that circled around the northern sectors of Adullam connecting the Medical Wing, the Mines, and the Barracks before looping back into the Marketplace.

Alaric began to move quickly, picking up his pace to a stifled jog. Suddenly, a screech shot through the silence from further along the corridor. Heart-stopped, Alaric slid to a halt. He stepped on something loose. He felt the ground giving way beneath him as he shifted his weight to catch himself, but it was too late. A loose rock went skipping from beneath his heel and down the corridor towards the screech. Alaric reached out for the wall, but his body was already parallel to the ground. His head slammed against the stone floor and the world went dark.

He opened his eyes to the sight of Blair's panicked face. Alaric felt himself sliding backwards across the ground as Blair tried to drag him around the bend of the corridor. The sound of screeches blared like a siren of impending doom down the passage, accompanied by the furious approach of scrambling claws against stone. Another wave of screeching drew Alaric from the depths of his daze and put him on his feet. He turned himself over and pushed Blair forward. They darted several feet past where Alaric had fallen and ducked into a darkened side passage, pressing themselves against the walls.

A band of three furious little creatures sprang into view. Alaric could feel the fear rising off Blair's chest in a palpable languor at his first sighting of the imps. One jolted along in a far-flung gallop like motion as another glided across the floor, flaring up sparks and scarring the stone with its claws. The final imp leapt into view and hurtled over the other two with a fan of its bat-like wings. Alaric worried for a moment the creatures would sense their presence, but as quickly as they had appeared, they disappeared from view down the hallway. He turned his head towards Blair whose close-eyed countenance stood rigid and pale. Alaric watched him and listened for the sound of the imps' chase to dampen down the hallway.

Blair opened his eyes and on cue Alaric bolted from the passage and ran toward the prison. Blair kept close at his heels and within a minute, they had reached the entrance to the prison. Alaric stopped just outside the doorway to catch his breath and Blair backed up against him, watching their rear for any sign of the imps' return. Slowly, Alaric crept towards the turn in the entrance, dreading the inevitable approach. As he came nearer and nearer the prison, he could feel a pulse rise in his neck. At last, when the time came for him to round the corner, he paused to listen one last time. His ears empty, Alaric stepped out from behind the wall and into the prison.

In the small room was a row of locked prison cells. Towards the end of the line, however, obscured by the faint light, one cell stood open. Lying next to the door was a set of iron keys with a trail of blood connecting it to the corpse of the prison guard. Alaric made a steady approach toward the cell. He knelt down to gather the keys and looked through the open door. Lucien was gone. Casting a forlorn gaze to the guard, Alaric choked. The man's chest a marsh of blood and shredded leather; Alaric fought back the urge to cough. With a repugnant swallow, he pressed his tunic against his nose and tried to close the guard's stricken eyes. He turned and let the keys fall loose from his fingers as he left the prison. "We have to find him," Alaric said as he met back with Blair at the threshold.

"Whoever it is, it's too late," Blair protested. "We have to leave."

"Stay here if you like," he said firmly, "but I'm going to find him."

"Who are we even going to find?" Blair asked, the ardent plea whining off his tongue. But Alaric was already gone, out the door and down the hallway. Blair hugged the prison doorframe, leaning out into the hallway to follow Alaric with his eyes. He glanced back over his shoulder and biting his lower lip, stepped out after his Captain.

It did not take Blair long to catch back up with Alaric's creeping pace alongside corridor wall. The two moved carefully, stopping at every sound to look for its source. Alaric kept his hand on the hilt of his sword while Blair kept a dagger drawn and ready. Before long they began to hear a faint but persistent noise. As they came closer, they realized it was the drone of wailing voices, above which came the shrill cry of imps. Alaric knew that with the next turn, the Market would be in sight. He moved to the inside wall and Blair pressed in close behind him. Alaric then lay prone and slid himself forward; he motioned to Blair to keep watch of their rear.

The sight was much the same as when he had escaped it. People remained huddled together in fright, surrounded by scores of imps. This time, however, Lucien was present. He stood on the outskirts of the group, surrounded by a personal entourage of imps, all jumping and screeching to their fellow demons. Suddenly, there was the sound of a drum, deep and foreboding through the reaches of the cavern. It approached from just beyond the Marketplace and sent the imps into an uproar. Leaping and dancing and cheering, they worked themselves into a frenzy. Some of them stood on their hands and flicked their barbed tails in the air while others bounded into the air as high as their bat-like wings would carry them. All the while, their shrill voices resounded in unison through the whole of Adullam.

The drumming rolled louder. Lucien sat, vanishing beneath the imps' frenzied acrobatics. Suddenly, Blair heard a screech from behind. He looked at Alaric and they both swung around to the sight of an imp skipping excitedly along the corridor. With its grasp on the wall opposite them, it tried to jump to the ceiling and hang upside down as it skipped.

Alaric was frozen, but something in the drumming ignited daring in Blair; he charged the imp before it could spot them, dashing across the corridor towards the devil as it jumped against the wall. With a lunge, he grabbed the imp by the throat and brought it crashing against the ground. Blair's grip stifled its screech but could do nothing to stop its claws from tearing deep into his forearm. Reeling back, Blair threw the creature down the corridor and Alaric joined the dash, kicking the imp as it hit the ground. It sailed back into the air, just high enough to catch the sweep of Alaric's sword. His blade cut clean through the imp, but when the creature hit the ground, it was whole, without so much as a scratch.

Disoriented from the blow, the imp released a long, rasping moan as it tried to stand. Before it could move though, Blair was on it again. He kicked the creature back against a wall. It skidded across the jagged stone and rolled onto the floor. Picking itself up, it tried to scamper around its pursuers to make it back to the Marketplace. Alaric cut off its escape and drove it further down the corridor. The imp tried to scream to its companions in the Market, but could only utter hoarse cries, which withered against the stone walls around it. Alaric hit the creature across the head with the flat of his sword, sending it reeling again against the wall. Blair charged again to cut off its escape, forcing it instead down the passage leading to the river. The men charged single file down the passage after the frightened demon. As the narrow way opened onto the bridge, they spotted it again, clawing at the balustrade in search of another route.

Its eyes bulged and the red hue of its irises tightened around the pit of its pupil. Another hoarse cry ushered from its throat as it bared its teeth. Hopping along the balustrade, it wriggled its neck with its claws coughing and sputtering, trying to coax the sound out. The demon wagged its tongue, hissing at Alaric and Blair. Both stood between the imp and its escape, their swords drawn. As they kept advancing, the imp crouched; setting its stance, it jumped from the balustrade and over the men's heads. Alaric swung, hitting the imp with the flat of his sword. It rolled off the tip of the blade, bounced back across the balustrade, and splashed into the river. For a moment it struggled on the surface, trying to flap its wings and lift itself from the river, but with a final gurgle the current carried it away, dragging it under the water.

Collapsing against the corner of the entryway, Alaric passed a relieved smile over to Blair. The young soldier stood grimacing at his arm. He held it tightly with his other hand and little pools of blood overflowed from between his fingers where the imp's claws had left their mark.

Picking himself up, Alaric ripped off the sleeve of his tunic and wrapped it tightly around Blair's wounds. "We need to go," he said as he tied off the tunic. "Some of the scouting party sent to Bristing is held up in the Borderlands; we can regroup."

Blair winced. He twiddled his fingers and made fist, feeling the flex of the bandage.

"How does it feel?" Alaric asked.

"I'll survive," Blair returned. "Thanks for that."

"There are some extra linens with the horses, I'll wrap it up a little more when we reach them."

"How did they get here?" Blair asked, suddenly remembering the horses and his half eaten shirt. "Did you try to drown me?"

"It was Lucien," Alaric asserted defensively. "I told him to be gentle."

CHAPTER XXV

MALIK

Silence struck the Marketplace as two gray satyrs entered with a final pounding of their drums. The beasts marched to either side of the Market's entrance and a number of the imps set their skin ablaze with excited anticipation for what was next to come. Into the Market strode a man. The satyrs straightened with respect and the imps fell deathly quiet. At first sight there was nothing distinguished about him, but as he strode into plainer view there was a low gasp of horror from the captives. The man stopped just short of the crowd and laughed a frightening, wispy laugh like the chuckle of a small boy. His face and body were bloated, his skin pasty and dry, and his eyes were a fierce red, rimmed with putrid yellow. Thin, white hair protruded from the top of his head like a clump of wild grass. His fingernails, thick and long, scratched the dead skin from his jaw as he came to a halt.

A wry delight spread across his wandering eyes. He took another half step forward, breathed in deeply and spoke in a gruesomely pleasant voice: "Well, I'm glad to see all of you here; I trust that no one is absent?" He looked around the large sea of heads as they looked down, away from him. "Today is particularly grand," he paced to the right, "for me. After one hundred and fifty years we are finally met. In fact, I have awaited this day since before we forced your fathers' fathers from their leafy homes in the

Beltwood. We offered them, as I will offer *you*, a simpler existence. Instead, it seems, they chose a hole. But I feel uncouth, barging in here with imps and drums and no introduction." He paced back to the left and then took another half step forward. "I am Malik of Aureus."

The imps received his introduction with fervent screeches. They jumped and danced and hopped across people's heads from one side of the crowd to the other. The people remained silent and cowering in an unwavering stillness beset upon them at the name of Aureus.

Displeased, Malik took a vengeful step forward to stand right at the edge of crowd. "You do not applaud my name like the imps. Did I not say that today was a grand day? Have I not come to simplify your existence and to take you away from this fetid hole? I would think you would receive me with tumultuous applause." Malik paused and his eyes dilated, the yellow rims widened and shone more profoundly. His round face became tight, its color changed from pale to pink. "You must think me mad?"

He laughed again in an airy tone. "You can always pick out madness. It's like greatness, you can just," he paused to grin malevolently, "feel it. Those who are mad have a presence about them, a density," he cocked his head back and rolled it left to right, "that weighs down on the minds of others." Malik then squatted and crept in close to one of the captives – a woman – who began to shiver and wince. Malik's left hand twitched and he began to massage his fingers with his thumb.

He leaned in slowly, the glare in his eyes growing ever more fierce. "Can you feel my weight?" he asked, staring at the woman. His head began to bob mechanically, almost as if to music. Malik's left hand twitched again; as if unhinged from his shoulder, it writhed like a snake against his body.

The woman began to shake more intensely. Tears streaked her face now; she whimpered and screamed through clenched teeth. Malik turned his ear toward her and smiled up at the ceiling, his mouth wide open. His lips cracked, spilling fresh blood down his chin. His writhing hand shot up to wipe away the blood before reaching out to caress the woman's face. He bolted upright, turned from his captives with arms outstretched, "You think the mind is a box unto itself?" he yelled.

The woman was now rocking back and forth on the ground – eyes shut tight.

"Ask your friend here what she thinks about that." Malik enunciated every word carefully, ticking his head mechanically to and fro.

After a moment he gave a soft laugh. His hand twitched and writhed back against his body. He again smiled with his eyes, letting them roll slowly towards the Market's vaulted ceiling. "Now. I feel that I've drawn far too much attention to myself," Malik said. "Where is the man of the hour? Where is Lucien?" He darted his smiling eyes around the crowd. "Lucien," he sang aloud.

When there was no response, Malik closed his eyes and cocked his head to the side. "Get up, get up, get up, get up, get up," he croaked until his words turned into a soft groan.

From the back of the room, Lucien stood, craning his back and panting, his eye shut tight. Malik looked at him and smiled, "Ah yes, I would like to introduce you all to my dear friend, Lucien."

A murmur of hushed gasps and angry musings rose above the crowd of captives. Like steam rising from a boiling pot, Lucien could feel their rage lifted in the hardened glares of a thousand eyes. He cast his gaze downwards. To his horror he saw Mark, curled upon the floor, tears streaming down his face. The boy would not look at Lucien, he merely rocked back and forth, seething and muttering to himself. Embracing him from the side was Alyssa; she rocked with him and whispered into his ear, her ice-ridden eyes fixed on Lucien. Mark's gargled breath worked to fight back his tears; Lucien drew his face into a scowl; his upper lip quivering as he struggled to keep his eye averted from Malik. He cleared his throat and folded his arms behind his back.

Mark's lip quivered and he curled himself up tighter, sinking his head into his knees.

Lucien shut down. He could not think, could not hear, could see nothing, could move nowhere. Trapped alone in a hole, his screams reverberated back inside him, never to be heard by anyone but himself.

"Oh Lucien," Malik's voice caroled inside Lucien's head. "Doff your mask for us, and show everyone your truer side." Lucien felt the voice deaden his will. His palm was planted flat against his mask. He felt it tremble against his cheek. Eye closed, he let the mask slide from his face and tap-dance across the stone floor. His exposed skin bore a seal, burned deep into his flesh. A flame was carved into his cheek and stretching out from it were two wings. On the right wing was a rook and on the left wing was Lucien's eye. A sword cut through the flame and, surmounting its hilt was spiked a crown – the seal of the Narxus; Aureus' mark.

Malik laughed deep from inside himself and removed the black glove from his writhing hand, rigid fingers uncurling to reveal the same mark that marred Lucien's face. The yellow-rimmed smile of Malik's red eyes beamed across his captive crowd. His hand twisted back against his chest, his thumb massaging his fingers. "Perhaps you should be reintroduced," Malik cried out, "to Lucien, The Prince of Aureus.

"You've had nobility amongst you and didn't even know it. You should all feel quite honored to have lived in the presence of such a faithful servant of Aureus for so long."

Lucien could hear Mark's crying distinct from all the others.

"Step forward, Lucien," Malik commanded. Lucien obeyed, walking around the captives to stand next to Malik. "Behold with pride the great culmination of your efforts."

He lifted his hands, presenting the people to Lucien, but Lucien stared unmoved over the tops of their heads. "What's the matter, my Prince? Why so *down*cast?" Malik asked.

"They are not all accounted for," Lucien returned, his eye darting to the fragment of his abandoned mask.

"And you were afraid I would be disappointed?" Malik asked, jeering at Lucien's mood.

"Your approval means little to me, Malik."

"Ah, you are worried about His Majesty's approval. Well, I assure you, dear Lucien, that he is well pleased."

"Even so, I would like to correct my mistake and go after the missing ones."

"That is not necessary, they are of no consequence and will die out soon enough. Aureus has commanded that you return home with me to celebrate this occasion."

"Very well." Lucien said; his gaze passed over the crowd to the figure of Titus huddled amidst the captives.

"Very well indeed," Malik echoed him, and turned to the imps, speaking in a strange, sharp language. The imps bellowed and shrieked and hopped closer to their captives, forcing them to stand. Malik rocked back slowly on his heels and turned himself around. He rolled his eyes at Lucien and smiled, cracking open the skin on his lips; blood filled the grooves of his teeth. He beckoned for Lucien to follow and together they walked out of the Market, leading the procession of imps and captives.

Malik turned to Lucien just before they reached the narrow tunnel leading to the surface. "Maelstrom is waiting for them," he said and chuckled with boyish gaiety before disappearing down the tunnel. Lucien followed close behind him and stepped out into an early morning of fading stars and purple horizons.

The predawn air almost choked Lucien as he clambered out from Adullam's underground. Even before he had fully emerged, he could see Maelstrom's giant head blotting out the moon. He stood with a battalion of Nephilim, the tallest only measuring up to the broad shoulders of his forest-green mantle.

Swinging from Maelstrom's hand was the end of a long chain wrapping its way behind him and curled in heaps across the folded arms of his battalion. Lucien braced himself against a boulder and stepped from view. When he had circled around, he climbed between another boulder until he was standing on top. Maelstrom laughed with a rumble like distant thunder. "Perhaps with a hundred more you will be as tall as I," he said.

Lucien looked indifferently at him and back down to the tunnel. Like ants, the people of Adullam began filing out of the hole. He heard the coil of Maelstrom's chain rattling behind him.

"You worm," Maelstrom bellowed. "How have you liked your hole? Did it start to suit you? Did you forget why you were there?"

"Silence, Maelstrom," Malik said, joining Lucien on his rock. "There is a long road ahead of us." He hunched over and shifted himself around gracelessly to face Lucien. His hand writhed back against his chest and his eyes smiled gleefully. "He will have ample time to explain himself."

Lucien continued to watch the prisoners file out from Adullam. Their eyes passed over him on the way down from Maelstrom's imposing figure. Lucien could feel their defeat.

Malik followed Lucien's glower into the crowd. "I don't know what you're looking for," he said, "but I'm not worried about the throngs on the inside. It's those on the outskirts of the group you should be looking out for Lucien. The outsiders are always shifty." Malik curled his lip and bending low, swept a fiery gaze across a row of prisoners. They fell back, covering their faces.

Malik threw back a shrill and distorted laugh. "Watch the outside," he said, looking back at Lucien with a pluck of his brow. "Make sure none of them try to run."

Malik leapt from the boulder and bounded to the ground to disappear in the dust. Lucien remained unmoved. None would run in the shadow of the Nephilim.

At length, the final prisoner was taken from Adullam. Twenty or Thirty imps spilled after him like spiders bursting from their egg, gnawing and screeching and laughing. The prisoners at the rear pressed in close against the heels of their companions. Lucien remained on his rock, watching as the Nephilim's massive chain was shackled to every last citizen. Nearly each link had its own manacle, leaving the prisoners packed so tight they could barely move.

Maelstrom drew a long black whip from beneath his cloak. It unfurled from his hand and curled across the ground like a giant black snake. Lucien could almost hear it hissing.

The oily sound of Malik's voice spilled over the crowd. "I would warn you, my children, not to step out of line, lest you want to feel the bite of Maelstrom's whip. Like a terrible black adder, it thirsts for any excuse to taste the sweet rapture of human flesh. Anyone who does not believe my warning, please attempt an escape. I would be delighted then to see anyone try a second time."

Another thunder rolled from Maelstrom's laughter and he cracked his whip through in a flash like lightning.

Malik mounted a dark horse and dragged another by the reins to Lucien. "Why don't you come on down, dear Prince, and ride with me."

Lucien jumped from his boulder and to the ground, seizing the reins from Malik's rotted hands. He looped the reins over the horse's head and jumped onto its back, kicking it into motion. Malik trotted behind him, eyes drowning in delight.

The Nephilim formed up on either side of the long line of prisoners; Malik and Lucien rode past them to the head. Malik whistled loudly and waved a bloated hand in the air. The imps swarmed around the Nephilim's feet, leaping up their backs and onto their shoulders. The giants bellowed a loud and disorderly song, carried by the beat of the prisoners' dragging chain as their long procession to Aureus began.

Along the journey, some of the imps made a game of trying to vault themselves over the heads of the prisoners. Seldom did they make it, more often crashing into the crowd, dancing from head to head, licking someone's ear and sending them out of line. The crack of Maelstrom's whip would sing through the air.

Malik and Lucien galloped to the head of the line, distancing themselves from the processions' clamor.

"Make yourself comfortable, my Prince," Malik said, "we won't be stopping until we've passed the Beltwood."

"The Beltwood?" Lucien repeated warily, "That is more than a day's journey from here."

"I know."

"Some of them won't make it without rest."

"Then they will have to drag their dead," Malik responded. "That does not suit you, my Prince?"

"For myself, I do not mind the journey. My concern is for His Majesty's property. Does he not want them fresh?"

"He wants them strong, dear Lucien, and he wants the weak cast aside from the harvest like weeds – they strangulate the crop; the sooner they're dead the better."

"Is that His Majesty's philosophy Malik, or yours?"

"You are in no position to ask such questions," Malik spat. "You've been with these wretches in their hole for too long. They've made you soft."

"You are the child of necromancy, Malik. I wouldn't expect you to understand suffering when the only thing human left about you is your flesh; but even that is rotting away. What was your name before? John-Paul. Father John-Paul, I remember calling you."

"Silence!" Malik hissed, his voice perverted with venomous anger. "You live only by blood and magic. How long do you think you could last if I took your little philosopher's stone away?"

"I would rather die than have some demon sustaining my soul, Father John-Paul."

"That is not my name." Malik breathed heavily through his teeth; his hand writhed and slithered across his shoulders.

"He must be in there somewhere," Lucien said. "You are of a passing age, Malik. What will be left of you when your body turns to dust? You endure by the will of a demon; what use are you to the future of Aureus?"

"I have been more use than you!" Malik screamed. He reared his horse up and drove its fore-hooves into the ground. "Where have you been, Prince, these past months? You were sent out to expose the last of lawless people, and last you were sighted, it was killing Nephilim. I must say I am surprised at Maelstrom for not wrapping his whip around your neck."

"There was a time I considered you a mentor. Do you remember nothing of humanity, John?"

"Do not speak that name again!" The words flew out between blood and spit. Malik's breath grained against his throat.

"Everything was set in motion," Lucien's voice smoothed the air. "If you had but waited one day longer, I would have delivered these people into your hands."

A guttural laugh spilled from Malik's mouth like bile. "Is that so, my dear?" he jeered.

"Shall I tell you the whole story as we ride? There's an entire day ahead of us."

"I think that would be wise of you, Prince. If it were up to me, you know," Malik laughed, "you would be in those shackles, too."

Lucien sat rigid on his mount, but let his shoulders sway with the quiet clod of the horse's gait. "I suppose His Majesty Aureus commanded you otherwise?"

Lucien's lips twisted into a wry smile towards Malik.

"Say it." Malik commanded.

Lucien shook his head, the corners of his mouth tightening.

"Say it!" Malik spat. "You prideful prick! You ruin!"

"Enough, Malik! I won't give you the pleasure."

Malik cackled. "Fine. Don't play my games then. But, my dear, you owe me that story."

Lucien drew a deep breath. "As you know, I was sent to follow the survivor whom the Nephilim had left alive after their fight on the far side of the Beltwood. His name was Alaric and, as luck would have it, he was a high-ranking officer and friend to the Steward of Adullam. I made it seem that I had saved Alaric from certain death and so I gained a tentative trust with the Steward. I spent the first week or so of my time in Adullam tending to Alaric's wounds – showing myself to be of superior medical savvy – and was thus allowed to stay on as the head physician. I had constant access to patients, which meant a fresh supply of blood to keep me stable – I could extract it from them at any time under the pretense of 'blood testing.'

"Eventually, I learned of an Archive not far from the Medical Wing. I frequented it and befriended the old scholar who took care of it. He explained the inner workings of their society to me, and most importantly, their leadership structure."

"Stop!" Malik growled. "I don't care to hear you weave some story together to distract me. If you have any defense for your negligence, then speak it."

"There was a reason *I* was sent, Malik: to break these peoples' will; to unravel their society; to create disunity; to destroy their spirit of perseverance. No one else, *no one*, could have accomplished what I have achieved. You were met with the entire populace assembled together; on whose account do you think they were meeting? Did you lift a finger to capture them, Malik, or did they submit? How do you think they became so hopeless? Now," Lucien said, resetting his tone, "let me continue."

Malik choked up a black mucus, and spat it in Lucien's path.

"Once I understood their society, I could better manipulate it. There were many, most importantly the laughably ignorant General, who did not trust my presence in their refuge. I made a point of exploiting this distrust to sow disunity amongst the people, putting me between the Steward and his General. I found a map in the Archive with the locations of Adullam and Bristing."

"We knew of Bristing; we have always kept it under watch," said Malik, impatient.

"Well, yes," Lucien countered curtly. "My point in telling you was that I could not simply walk out and hand you a map, Malik. I tried on occasions to leave and deliver the location, but no one is allowed to leave the cave without certain approval so the exits are well guarded. When my scholar friend, however, told me about the trade market between Bristing and Adullam, I tried to use my gaining influence to encourage traffic between the two. I hoped their interactions would draw attention to the hidden entrance of Adullam; that perhaps the surveillance watching Bristing would follow the scouting parties and the trade carts back to Adullam. Instead, the scouts and traders were killed. I trust it was not you who issued such enlightened orders," Lucien challenged Malik rhetorically. "All of this would have taken a much easier course had they not been killed, and in turn I would not have had to kill our own.

"But, despite this set back," Lucien continued, "Adullam still relied on Bristing for food. Such a delicate trading balance, I'm surprised they've survived as long as they have. When no food came and the stores began to run dry – the leadership became desperate. I had already used their past failure against the Nephilim to gain control of a significant portion of their army to make an Elite Guard, answerable to me alone. This caused further controversy throughout Adullam and, when a plan was set in motion to restore the trade routes with Bristing, my Elite Guard was the obvious catalyst for the operation. I brought with me six of their Trade Lords and their Steward, all of whom I sent along the trade route, expecting they would be killed as had the others."

"Ridiculous," Malik spat. His hand slithered across his concerned face, "Your silk tongue is twisting the tricks of fate. A people on the brink are not so trusting."

"'Whomever exalts himself will be humbled, and whomever humbles himself will be exalted,'" Lucien responded. "I was merely a servant: I pledged fealty to the Steward; I tended to many of the ailing and wounded; I kept a young, fatherless boy; I taught and I trained; I fought and I saved and I loved. I served and for that I was respected and trusted."

Malik hissed.

"I can stop. I have no obligation to you, Malik."

"No," Malik shot back, "finish."

"The rest of us," Lucien continued, "who followed a different path from Adullam, found Bristing razed; its people burning in the center of the town."

A ferocious glee filled Malik's eyes. "The satyr is such a sly creature," he croaked.

Lucien ignored him. "With the Steward and his Trade Lords dead, I knew the great spirit of desperation that would find Adullam. I began calculating the means for exodus. I wanted to bring the people back into the open, knowing – from your aggressive behavior – they would be captured. Fate found me well when we discovered the cattle penned by the Nephilim. It gave me the perfect reason to suggest an exodus from Adullam. We could not safely herd the stock back to the people; it would bring too much attention to the surface.

"The only thing that made sense then was to bring the people out of hiding, otherwise they would starve." Lucien adjusted his saddle. "Alaric and I left the other soldiers with the livestock and made our way back to Adullam. When we arrived, we proclaimed the unfortunate demise of the Steward and his Trade Lords. The political situation erupted. After I gifted their interim Steward with a knife in the dark, we harnessed the people in their disarray by introducing our plans for the exodus. There is hardly a person more malleable than a hungry one. Tomorrow, today actually – in the evening – you could have taken them above ground with just the Nephilim, and spared yourself the use of imps." Lucien finished with a grimace as one of the little demons began plucking hairs from his horse's tail.

"Well, Prince," Malik said, "I'm almost impressed. Some communication on your part, my dear, would have served us both well."

Lucien shook his head wearily. "I tried to communicate. Appreciate the delicate position I found myself in over the past several months."

"My final question. Where then are the others you spoke of, the ones you left with the cattle? Where have they gone?"

"That is not for your greedy ears," Lucien remarked. "You're taking credit for months of my work. The least I deserve is the right to bring in the last of them. I will not have you seize any more undeserved glory."

"Undeserved?" Malik screamed, and his hand coiled back like a snake ready to strike. "I worked from my own initiative when no word came from you on the inside! I razed Bristing and I have captured these peasants, and I will bring them in front of His Majesty for my due reward!"

"No," Lucien responded coolly, "you will not."

"Haven't we played this game already?" Lucien heard Malik's voice inside his head. A sharp hiss enraptured his whole conscious and Lucien keeled over in pain. He braced himself on his horse's neck to keep from falling over as Malik's voice penetrated his mind, "Your story is a sound one; it works together for your defense, but if you do not tell me – my dearest – where the others have gone, I will give no credence to your tale." Malik bore down on Lucien's mind, his eyes bulging to burst under the pressure of his gaze.

"Enough!" Lucien commanded through his clenched teeth.

Malik's gaze dropped blank at the ripple of Lucien's voice. He cracked his neck out of the phase, laughing as he sat back straight.

"Such a slight tone beneath your breath," Malik said as he scratched the loose skin from his face, "but sharp as a double-edged sword." Another fit of laughter curdled from his tongue.

"Do not flatter yourself," Lucien replied, "by expecting that I need you as an apologist. You are of a passing age; The Veil is almost torn, and your breed will be outworn. The remaining insurgents, they are far beyond your reach, *my dear.*"

Chapter XXVI

THE BORDERLANDS

Alaric and Blair rode hard into the Briswold through the morning and into the night. After a timid plunge back into Adullam's subterranean waterway, the two soldiers swam to the southern platform to collect the horses – trusting their imp had been swept away with the current. They followed the river until it met with open skies, and after several frustrated minutes, they were able to mount their steeds and begin their gallop Westward from Drögerde.

In the intervals of walking between their sprints through the grasslands, Alaric regaled Blair on the past week's events. He unfolded the whole tale: the razing of Bristing; the death of Stilguard; the stock of cattle and horses headed for the Borderlands; the plans for an exodus; and the murder of Nestor. Once these essential details had passed, the two soldiers kept to themselves until they were well into the Briswold.

The moon hung high in the sky, its aura illuminated over them in halos through a thin film of clouds. Made silver by its glow, the grass waved beneath the warm-winded evening. Alaric and Blair ran through the world like shadows fettered to the silver face of an ethereal plain, caught in a nightmare of perfect serenity.

After several hours, other shadows began to bloom on the horizon – clusters of trees spotting the grasslands. Alaric shifted their course towards a cluster where a rippled image of the moon reflected off a large puddle of water between trees. They slowed their horses to a walk, and the animals made straight for the water. Shakily, Blair and Alaric dismounted, moaning and groaning as they stretched their legs.

"How long are we going to stay?" Blair asked between sharp breaths.

"An hour maybe," Alaric said with a deep yawn, "I haven't slept in days and the horses deserve a little rest. I think we still have a day-and-a-half's ride to the Borderlands."

From beneath his tunic, Alaric pulled out a map of the countryside he had taken after meeting with Bryan. He laid it out on the grass and pointed.

"We started here," he said and walked his fingers across the map. "I imagine we're in this area now, still half a day's journey to Bristing. We'll go up to the Northwest, past Bristing, and then around this group of mountains. That should take us to the Borderlands and hopefully to our comrades."

"What are we going to do when we find them, sir?"

Alaric sighed and bit his bottom lip. His eyes wandered listless over the map. "I don't know, Blair."

A flush of fear spread across Blair's cheeks. "I think I might take some rest before we begin again," he said, standing.

"Very well," Alaric replied, his eyes still downcast, "tether the horses before you do."

"Yes sir," Blair said. He saluted and started to turn when the whisper of Alaric's voice came to his ears like the wind.

"What does it all mean?"

Blair turned, uncertain of whether he had imagined the voice. Alaric remained knelt over his map, his fingers pressed against its corners.

"Sir?" Blair asked.

"What does it all mean?" Alaric sat back in the grass, folding the map slowly back into his tunic. At last he looked up from the ground. "Ten. Ten free men remain in this world. You and I and the eight others held up in the mountains. What did it all mean, for us to have struggled so long? You grow up hearing stories about Aureus, and that we're the legacy of the free men who fought its lie. It makes you think there's a purpose to it all, to us, to our existence. And yet here we are, at the seat of ruin, in a night dark as the depths of hell and our best laid plans tortured at every step by circumstances beyond us to control. You go your whole life pretending there might be some good in the world, that we aren't alone in our struggle, that providence might one day shed some light." Alaric looked back down at his crossed legs, plucking the grass between them.

Blair stood silent, playing with the bandage wrapped around his forearm, his eyes searching Alaric. "I'll tie up the horses," he said at length and stepped quietly away.

Darkness thickened as the moon was lost beyond the horizon and the pale morning made ready to rise to the East.

"Captain."

The word swirled in Alaric's head like smoke twisting from a pipe.

"Captain," the voice came again. Alaric awoke with a start, clutching the grass beneath his fingers. He blinked and pushed himself from the ground.

"We've slept too long," Alaric groused, pressing his palms firmly against his eye sockets. "Where are the horses?"

"Just here," Blair said. He paced to them and untied their reins from the tree. Leading the horses back to Alaric, he placed a rein in his hand. "You're going to have to help me back on, I think."

"We'll help each other. Once I lift you up and you're set, give me a hand so I can lift myself up."

Once they were both set, Alaric made sure their map was secure inside his tunic and kicked his horse into a gallop.

Blair bounced up and down, whistling and calling for his horse to move. Stone still, the horse snorted and bent down to graze. "Come on!" Blair called, frantic not to fall behind. "Come on!" He bounced and shook and pulled back on the reins. With another snort the horse shot its head forward and wrenched the reins from Blair's hands. "Horse!" he yelled and kicked the mare's sides. With this, the four-legged beast reared up and jumped straight into a gallop, tossing Blair down her back. Blair lurched forward, grabbing the horse's mane as his legs dangled behind him. With Blair screaming all the way, the pair bolted onward into the night.

They rested again around noonday when the sun hit its peak. What water they had been able to carry from their last stop, they gave to the horses and collapsed beneath the boughs of a tree. "Best if we didn't both sleep again," Alaric said.

"Yes sir. Why don't you take some rest, Captain."

Alaric nodded and ran his tongue behind his parched lips. The silver scape of the Briswold had turned almost red as day overcame the night. Save for the blue mountains melting into the northern horizon, there was nothing but stillness and dried grass for miles around them. "When the sun touches the top of those mountains," Alaric said, "wake me."

Blair nodded and Alaric propped his back against the trunk of the tree. He looked out over the fields, a not so distant resemblance of where the cattle had been penned, the golden hue of limitless skies, the grass fluttering with the breeze like silver-green waves in the sea. But today, the skies held the weight to smother the earth and the grass stood still and wilted in the heat. No soft breeze to soothe burning skin and no hope filled the hearts of desperate men. "There must be hope," Alaric whispered, as the day began to fade between his slanting eyes. He fell asleep, hiding from the sun as best he could in the shadow of the tree.

When the westward course of the sun set a level horizon with mountains, Blair woke Alaric. "Feeling any better, sir?"

Alaric straightened his back and slowly smoothed his hands across his face and eyes. "It's more than just a lack of sleep," he sighed.

Blair reached down a hand to help him up. "How much further?"

"We should be to the Borderlands before the night's full," Alaric's voice drummed hollow.

"That sun will be a blister to ride straight into," Blair said, covering his eyes to look out towards the mountains. He turned around to find Alaric already mounting his horse.

"We'll ride to the Northwest, avoid the direct gaze. Just keep your head down until it sets behind the ridge."

Blair clamored onto the back of his horse and circled up with Alaric. They reset their course for the Borderlands, making their way towards its foothills further north. Once there, however, they were forced to ride directly west. The sun's rays spotted off the top of the mountains and blistered their eyes like embers stirred from a fire. They kept their heads down until the sun sank further beneath the mountains, leaving only a red hue behind their gray forms reaching into the heavens. Before the stars were out and the moon was full, Alaric and Blair had reached the edge of the range and the doorstep of the Borderlands.

From there, the mountains changed course from their westward stretch and veered north. The two stopped for a brief rest, just long enough for Alaric to examine the map. He scoured through the dark for Lucien's mark and after a moment's search, found it amidst the northerly turn in the mountains. He folded the map and replaced it inside his tunic. Mounting again, the two followed their new course along the mountains.

The terrain changed little at first, but as they carried on further into the Borderlands, the foothills began to fill with rocks and boulders jutting up at angles from the ground as if the mountain had been pulled apart and its pieces flung into the hills.

Hindered by their winding path among the boulders, Blair and Alaric changed course to distance themselves from the slopes. They moved to the grasses just below the foothills, caught now between the mountains and a ravine left by an empty riverbed scarring the countryside. Beyond the ravine grew a young forest, which disappeared into the distant mountains. Alaric suddenly felt unsafe, trapped along a one-way thoroughfare. He searched for a point to re-enter the foothills, but rocks and hollowed depressions strewn throughout made it too dangerous for the horses. He sat back on the hind legs of his horse and tested the weight of the sword at his hip. Looking back, he read the same disconcertedness on Blair's face. An unspoken sense of urgency passed between them and Alaric returned vigilant eyes to his surroundings.

"Things are wilder here," Alaric heard Blair's voice from behind. "Drögerde is empty; the Briswold is flat and tame. The Beltwood is ancient and slumbering. The forest here isn't like the Beltwood. It seems alive – feral."

A deep sense of foreboding crept into Alaric as his eyes wandered over the forests across the ravine. The trees were smaller, untamed, and packed together with every sort of shrub sprouting up to fill the gaps. There was movement, too, in the boughs; here and there a branch would break with a loud *snap*, the sound reverberating through the ravine.

"Do you see the shadows?" Blair suddenly cried. "Moving there through the foothills?"

Alaric's gaze swung from the forests to the foothills. He scanned its breadth for any sign of movement.

"There," Blair called, his voice a harrowing whisper.

"I don't see it." Alaric mimicked his tone.

"Through the moonlight, between the boulders. There again!" A cold wind slid down from mountain.

"I see it," Alaric said at last, his breath caught high in his chest. One shadow, two, three, bounding intermittently between the boulders and disappearing into the night.

"What are they?" Blair's harsh whisper came again.

Alaric shook his head, straining his eyes for another sight of them. Suddenly a cry pierced the silence of the night. The horses jolted and came to a halt, refusing to take another step. The gathering wind continued to blow down from the mountain, pushing clouds over the moon's light. Alaric and Blair were submersed in near total darkness. The cry ushered again from the black of the foothills, and then another followed from the depths of the forest. A rustling in the trees, the *snap* of a branch, something echoed as it fell into the ravine, and then silence. Alaric and Blair sat, breathing. Alaric could feel his horse shaking beneath him.

"Anything?" Blair's voice came.

"Nothing," Alaric replied. He could feel the wind whispering through his ears; the cold made his jaws tight. He urged his horse on. It swayed forward and eventually began to take timid steps. The night held no more surprises, but until the sun dawned for the new day, dread was ever their third companion.

When the sun finally peaked its first rays over the top of the mountains, it brought with it a brilliant light of relief. The threat of shadows and their strange noises evaporated with the morning dew. The boulders in the foothills had grown larger and more numerous while the ravine had planed out to a shallow cut in the ground. As the air had thinned with their rise in altitude, so too had the forests across the ravine become a less dominating feature of the landscape. They were high enough above the Briswold now to see its expanse for miles until it disappeared into a haze of heat and rising moisture.

Alaric began to see cattle strewn throughout the ravine as if they had transformed from the boulders.

"Is this the herd?" Blair asked. "Are these cattle?"

"Have you never seen cattle before?" Alaric asked, an air of excitement un-concealable in his tone.

"Why would I have? I never made the trip to Bristing."

"Well then yes," Alaric responded, "these are cattle – our cattle. We're close."

They slowed their horses into a trot and worked their way towards the shallow stream in which the cattle had settled.

Among the herd, Alaric spotted a few horses drinking from an inlet in the stream. He left Blair and forded up the stream. Stubborn and tired, his horse stammered its step and tried to reach its head down and drink. Too anxious to deal with the animal, Alaric dismounted, and with a small splash jogged on without it. A bed of brown and gray rocks carried the stream on its way into the ravine until it was absorbed into the ground of the old riverbed. Alaric splashed through the stream and felt the rocks shift and grind together under his boots; the flow of water captured the sounds, garbling the sharp tones of their protest.

It was a short walk along the cobbled stones before Alaric began to hear voices. Excitedly, he pushed himself through a group of cattle as they tried to drink and stepped up onto a mossy embankment. Just ahead under a tree, sat Gaverick, Fields, and Barron in the throes of a very serious discussion. Alaric hesitated to call out for them. Instead, he approached quietly from the side. The moss softened Alaric's step but as he waded closer through some low lying ferns, the three soldiers heard the crunch of foliage under his boots.

It was Gaverick who looked over first. He stared blankly at Alaric, unsure of how to register his sudden appearance to their mossy knoll. Barron was first to his feet, standing in salute. Fields was quick to mimic the salute but Gaverick remained on the ground, caught in a boisterous laugh of relief. He sat back on his hands and pushed himself from the moss. Still laughing, he gave a half-salute as he walked toward Alaric.

"Well aren't you a sight for sore eyes," he said, extending his hand. "We were beginning to get lonesome up here."

Alaric took his hand and smiled. The others began laughing and cheering at the return of their comrade and captain. Their commotion brought Blair running up from the stream.

"Nathan!" Barron cried as he saw Blair approach from a distance. He ran towards him and the two embraced. Barron cuffed Blair playfully on his ear and said, "It is good to see you, cousin. I didn't fancy you'd be the first to come. Which reminds me," He laughed and turned to Alaric, his expression growing grave. "There is someone here to see you – two someone's actually. I'm not sure how they found us but they only just arrived before you did. We've been trying to figure it," Barron finished, gesturing to Fields and Gaverick.

"Where are they?" Alaric asked concernedly.

"Up a ways towards the mountain," Blair responded, looking back north and pointing in the appropriate direction, "with Orleans and the others. I think they're friendly, but strange, Alaric. It's strange. We've got to stay and keep an eye on the herd, but you should go and speak with them – they were very eager to see you."

Alaric kept silent, passing questioning eyes between the men. "Have they said anything about their reasons for seeking us out? Where are they from?"

"You'll have to just go and meet them yourself. They wouldn't say much to us," Fields replied.

"Very well," Alaric nodded. The men returned a salute and let Alaric pass on his way up the hill. Blair started to follow but Barron caught him by the arm. "Hold a tick, cousin, I want to hear about your journey. How far off are the others?" he asked.

Alaric felt the blood drain from his face. Blair tried to stammer out a few words, but Alaric turned and called out over him, "It would be best if you all came with me. The cattle will tend to themselves."

CHAPTER XXVII

FROM BEYOND THE MOUNTAINS

Alaric had not noticed before, but now as he looked ahead expectantly, he saw smoke rising from behind a moss-covered boulder. The smoke carried with it the smell of freshly roasted meat infused with the delicate fragrance of the surrounding flora. He realized it had been several days since his last real meal. The aroma made his stomach quiver and his mouth water. As the smell set in, Alaric grew faint, bracing himself so not to fall. Coming closer to the boulder, he recomposed himself and leaned against the rock to wait for Blair and the others. When they had caught up, some of Alaric's feebleness had left him and he stepped out to present himself to the strangers.

As he rounded the moss-covered boulder, the scene came into full view. Laid against the boulder was Marion, still deeply wounded from the fight in Bristing. He appeared to be sleeping as one of the strangers knelt over him, examining his wound. Carmine sat just a ways from them, tending the fire and passing cautious glances at the white-cloaked stranger. Michael and Leon were nearby, stripping the rest of the meat from a carcass. They kept their heads bent low, speaking to one another in furtive voices. Orleans stood furthest back, talking quietly with another white-clad stranger.

When Alaric came into full view, everything stopped save for the crackle and hiss of the fire. The stranger tending to Marion turned to face Alaric, and the other stepped past Orleans to make himself seen. A voice came from one of them, submerging Alaric and his men in a sound spun from the ether, "Do not be afraid," it said, and like a spider's web, the melodious tones of the voice wove themselves together, capturing the men like flies. Traces of the words lingered amongst them like dust stirred up by a breath of air.

"We have come to your aid." A second breath of words resonated through the dust, reverberating in their ears.

Another voice seeped into the atmosphere like a trickle of water through the desert, "I am †Aletheia." The voice came from the veiled figure previously kneeling over Marion. It fluttered with an unmistakable feminine ambiance, drawing the men out from the spider's web of resonant sound. Aletheia's eyes were soft and brown, splintered with sparks of bright amber like rays of sunlight emanating from behind an eclipsed moon. As she locked eyes with Alaric, he felt himself caught up in the timeless mystery of their gaze, but the other ethereal voice hollowed out Alaric's enchantment, drawing him back into the present.

"And I am †Addeus," the second veiled figure said. Piercingly determined eyes of azure and gray peered like a colorless sky from behind his veil. Alaric sensed a foreboding in his gaze, a warning of things to come.

The strangers came to stand together before Alaric, tall and slender, with blonde hair so bright it shone like melted gold. The fold of their silk veils revealed in both of them, pronounced cheekbones, and gaunt facial frames with distinguished jaw lines. A white hood lay over their heads and their faces gleamed from the shadow of its covering with a radiant, bronze luminescence. Both wore a solid white tabard and mantle under which a set of silver-white, fish scale spaulders folded across their shoulders. A cuirass of the same silvery material glinted from beneath the tabards, which beset a blue undergarment mirroring Addeus' eyes. The silver-white cuff of their chain mail protruded from blue sleeves and hung loosely over gauntlets to match their spaulders. A white skirt draped down just above their knees concealing a tasset and below that fish scale greaves tucked into knee-high brown leather boots protected their legs.

Overwhelmed, Alaric could only stare in wondrous silence. As Aletheia and Addeus approached, the flow of time seemed to waiver, intermittently stopping Alaric's heart. The pair stopped several feet short of him. "What is your business with us?" Alaric asked, frightened to look too long into either pair of eyes.

"We have come from far beyond the mountains," Aletheia said.

Alaric was drawn into the amber of her eyes, melting beneath their glow. He felt himself flooded by a warmth of unspoken knowledge, inexpressible truths, fitted within the bowels of creation – *Do not linger* – a black sensation rushed over him.

"And *what* is your business here?" Alaric asked again.

"The drums of war from your land have been echoing through our halls for a very long time," returned Addeus.

"The drums of war?"

"Surely you have heard them; surely they too have been echoing through the halls of Adullam."

The sharp sound of iron pierced the air as Alaric and his company unsheathed their swords. "How do you know of such things?"

Aletheia spoke again, her amber eyes now glistening with a golden mirth, "Do not be afraid." The words swirled among them like leaves carried on a breeze.

Addeus filled the wake, playing his voice off Aletheia's resonate mood, "There is much you do not understand, much you cannot understand –"

"– and much you must render unto faith," Aletheia finished. The tension, heavy set upon them all, suddenly dissipated with her words. Together the men breathed in, their shoulders slumping and their legs shaking. Exhausted, Alaric lowered his sword, pressing its point softly in the grass to rest on.

Aletheia laughed quietly, and the notes of her merriment wove themselves among the soldiers, becoming almost visible, trembling in the air even after the sound had past. "Reason has been little benefit to you," said Aletheia, and laughter spilled from her mouth again like a stream eddying and swirling into a larger estuary.

"What?" Alaric whispered, his head struggling to breach the surface of swirling waters.

"Strike us down with your blades if you must, if that is what you *think* is best. But again I tell you the truth, there is much now you must give unto faith." Another fit of laughter followed.

Alaric hesitated before he spoke. "What is this game?" he stammered. "What reason…"

"Reason!" Addeus cut across the lingering of Aletheia's laugh with sharp distinction. "This is no game, there are no reasons," Addeus continued. "We can follow the rabbit trails of reason until the end of this eternity. Look only at the places your reasons have taken you and decide now whether it is better to be reasonable or faithful."

"Faithful in *what*?" Alaric cried, the fluttering of Aletheia's laughter and the weight of Addeus' voice had made him nauseous. He felt himself being tossed into roiling waters where the dead beckoned him drown with them. Fleshless fingers gripped his throat, a voice trapped in the depth of his soul screamed for freedom.

"Faithful in The Shaddai? Is that what you mean?" Alaric screamed.

The air quivered.

"Haven't I been?" The words seeped through Alaric's half-clenched teeth. He shifted his weight onto his sword, leaning against its hilt for support. It was more than the earth could bear and the point of the sword slid into the ground. Alaric lost his balance. The strength of his heart could no longer carry the weight on his knees and he sank to the grass, a scowl wrestling back relentless tears.

"I have read His words and those of His prophets'," Alaric spoke through sharp breaths. "I have lived faithfully. Who are you to come and challenge my devotion? And where is He!? – The Shaddai."

Slowly Alaric picked his head up from between his shoulders, scornful eyes strained into the valley beneath them. "This is not how it should be," he mused, his brow flattening. He lifted a dark gaze to the two strangers. "You ask me to be faithful?" Slowly he picked himself up, bracing against the hilt of his sword as he rose. "My faith died with my people."

Addeus summoned Alaric's focus, drawing him up into the sky blue of his eyes. Gliding like a falcon on the wind, Aletheia walked steadily forward. Alaric's men bent their knees, bracing themselves. All of the sudden, Alaric was in a free fall from the sky of Addeus' eyes. A wave of panic swelled over him, but Aletheia was beside him. Caramel spilled over the amber tone of her eyes as veins of gold rippled and twisted from the edge of her pupils. The dance was mesmerizing. Alaric caught himself in a transition of emotion – fading into calm understanding. Unnerved, he tried to step away from Aletheia.

"Do not be afraid," she said again as she reached a hand out towards him. Alaric tried to draw himself further away but stood suspended in the warmth of timelessness. Aletheia rested her hand on Alaric's cheek. "This is *not* how it should be," her tender voice echoed. "We do not challenge your devotion, Alaric, or your past – for it is not our place to challenge. The challenge now lies in your futures; the way is not much longer, but it is paved with treachery and war."

"This is not how it should be," Aletheia said again, releasing Alaric and addressing all men before her, "but you people leave too much to reason. Reason has been your gift, and a creator's mind, but these things are meant to function synonymously with faith. Your fault is believing that your insights are limitless; that you could understand all things knowable. Faith is a faculty just like any other. A man born deaf will grow up with no knowledge of sound, and just because he cannot hear, does that mean sound does not exist? The meaning of sound is beyond his reckoning until his ears are opened.

"Likewise, the way ahead will be full of realities far beyond your previous reckoning. The stuff of your dreams and fictions are soon to take life as the veil of your present reality continues to sear. Until that veil is rent, you might only know suffering, but before the end, you will know a truth not known by man since the dawn of creation.

"But, forgive my long winded-words," Aletheia said with a chuckle that fluttered among the men like butterflies, stopping their breath, "the construct of time is an imperfect medium. I am coming to the point. You seek reason, but your reason can only conceptualize The Almighty's Reason. Not until reason cooperates with faith will you come into a greater understanding of the higher purpose persisting around you."

"How can any of this be justified by a 'higher purpose'?" Alaric spoke somberly. "I have lived by faith and have seen nothing but a suffering existence whilst under the eyes of The Almighty."

"From here your eyes cannot see to the ocean," Aletheia replied, "and many sounds lay imperceptible to the keenest ears. Faith will not show you everything, there are limitations even to it as to your other faculties. I tell you the truth, none of this is justified, but it will be redeemed. There have always been plans for you, plans to prosper you and not to harm you;

plans to give you hope and a future but those plans have been waylaid by the passions of men – and these are frightful obstacles to overcome. Whether you can understand the purpose of suffering or not, you must trust in the goodness of your Shaddai."

"Then where is He?" Alaric pleaded quietly with a sullen shake of his head. "Where is The Shaddai and his redemption?"

"Always in need of reason," it was now Addeus who spoke, stepping forward from behind Aletheia. His voice was harsher and more commanding than Aletheia's, stripping away the pleasant rhythm of her voice, "an aspect of your condition that I will never understand. But as much I do not understand it, He values it: for you who bear the image of the Creator, bear the responsibility as tenants of His creation. It is humanity that has twisted the foundations of your existence. Mankind has toyed and tampered with the ineffable and, in trying to wrap it around their minds, has made it philosophy rather than truth." The rising pulse of Addeus' voice battered against Alaric like ocean waves against a crumbling bulwark. "You sit and say, 'My faith died with my people' and condemn the notion of higher purpose because circumstance did not unfold according to your expectations. By blaming The Almighty you ridicule yourselves by acknowledging that your reason is not enough. Of course you will never see that because you cannot be accountable to yourself and so you create your own standards to live by, cursing the ones set upon your hearts. And by mundane and manufactured standards you determine reason – it is a wonder you do not suffer more.

"The world is not meant to be seen by standards of justification as you create. The question then is not what is justified, but what is good and what is evil or what is right and what is wrong. If something is wrong it is because one man made it so, and it will be right when one man fixes it. The chaos that has always existed in your world is the consequence of self-imposed standards. You throw off the balance and expect not to fall, but now that you have fallen only one thing remains."

"What is that?" Alaric asked, his voice the final crackle of a dead flame.

"Redemption, and the plan is already set in motion. You have come for the Fomorii, for the felstones. This is more crucial a task than you realize. The Veil of Kingdoms is almost torn and with each passing hour the edge of realms blur. Aureus has taken a new directive: it seeks the Tree of Life."

As Addeus finished speaking he left an unsearchable void in the air. Alaric made a noise to voice confusion, but felt his voice fall silence in its presence. Addeus did not resume speaking immediately. He stood calmly, as did Aletheia, and thoughtfully examined the men in Alaric's company as if unaware of the passing time. Despite the pause in conversation, no one attempted to speak – or for that matter even formulate a thought worth speaking – the strangers' silence was too suppressive and the atmosphere was too tense.

At last, Addeus began again, continuing as if unaware of ever having stopped. "This is as great an opportunity as can be afforded to you in your present condition. The eye of the enemy is diverted."

Alaric spoke with a small screech of courage, "What does this mean? I don't see how this comes together: war; faith; The Veil; the Tree. You're speaking sporadically. What is to our advantage?"

Aletheia laughed, this time in a way that spiraled and pulsed vigorously through the soldiers, sending shivers through their bodies. She proceeded afterwards to speak, saying: "Even things that are obvious you cannot see; how much more can you hope to understand of The Almighty's ineffable design? All aspects spoken of – war; The Veil of Kingdoms; the Tree of Life – all of these things are inextricably linked by faith. The gears of war must grind as The Veil sears to reveal the Tree. As war persists…"

"What war?!" Alaric cried.

With a purposeful blink, Aletheia craned her neck towards Addeus. They looked at each other, expressions filled with dismay. "The war that you will bring to the gates of Aureus," came Aletheia's flat response.

Alaric's hands trembled; his fingers curled as his arms grew numb. He could feel his eyes stinging, blistered by the weeks of toil and agony. It all came at him at once. "And what madness would lead me to war?"

"The madness that is faith."

Alaric's shoulders sank, his countenance heavy set.

"You stand at the crossroad of worlds," Addeus said, "in a wilderness grown from the blood of martyrs and saints and tyrants, of innocent and corrupt, of young and old, of men and women of every era, every race, every creed. The earth is filled to the brim with their blood. And what is their legacy? What is left in the world save for cruelty and sorrow?

Only the smallest shards of redemption – a faint glow through the wilds of the deep forest. The earth will hold no more blood, Alaric, and the life of this world is on its final page. It is your burden to write the conclusion."

"Why? Why is it ours?" Alaric pleaded. A swift wind picked up from the valley, blowing Alaric off balance. He collapsed against the rock at his side. "I don't want it," he whispered. "I can't bear it."

"You haven't the choice," Addeus said. "It is the price of your free will. But you are not alone."

"We are ten, and then only twelve with your aid."

"Then what is there left to lose? You have come to the end of all things and there are but two paths."

"And if we brave the wilderness path?"

"You pull heaven towards earth," Aletheia responded softly. "The Veil of Kingdoms, both universal and singular, a curtain imposed within each man; yet not by a single will does it sear. Instead, a universal disposition – a mystery of ineffable design – when the reason of man is turned to faith."

"The Tree of Life bears the fruit of salvation for evil into the eternity," Addeus followed. "With the searing of The Veil, there is a hope to counter that fate."

Alaric's face grew pale as he shivered against the cold wind. Behind pursed lips, his tongue played over his teeth. Running a hand through his matted hair he nodded.

"You see now," Aletheia said, her eyes shining again caramel and gold. "And so the time has come…"

"Almost," Alaric interjected. "One thing remains." He stood and turned to his men, gathering them close. Their skin was dirty, their armor torn, their eyes red, but their breath steady. "I don't know many things about this world," he said slowly, "and I know even less since I've stepped from the depths of our Adullam. But one thing I do know, we have to keep believing there is some purpose in all of this and, in the midst of all these terrible things we've seen, that purpose has somehow sought us out. If we don't push forward until the end – whatever that end may be – then all the suffering we have seen will have been for nothing. I will carry this war to the gates of Aureus, and I hope that you will come with me."

In closing, Alaric turned from his men, casting his gaze upwards towards the bleak sky and the figure of Addeus ascending along the side of the mountain. The gray rock shifted beneath Alaric's feet as be began along the winding path up the mountain. Aletheia came to his side, a soft smile brimming her lips. Clouds began to set in on the wind, sweeping over Addeus further up the mountain. His body turned into the glow of a distant candle through the swirls of moisture. At the first switchback of the mountain path, Alaric dropped his gaze below. In a line several feet beneath him came the last of free men.

CHAPTER XXVIII

THE FOMORII

Addeus stood on a large rock along the path and looked back down over the foothills to the wisps of fading smoke from the almost dead fire. Watching Aletheia as she tended to Marion, he waited for Alaric and the others of his company to arrive. When all were accounted for he stepped down from his perch, leading the way up without a word.

The trail was marked with disuse by tumbled rocks and weathered boundaries. "Are they still here?" Alaric asked.

"The Fomorii?" Addeus said. "Yes. They have been watching us."

Whispers among the men sent chills shooting down Alaric's spine. His eyes roved wildly through the mists. Between clouds came the fleeting sight of a narrow cave halfway up the mountain. It disappeared again as quickly as it had come to sight. Little blurs of motion ushered out from it. A fist-sized rock came hurtling down from above, a trail of moisture in its wake. "Eyes up!" Alaric called to his men. Another rock hurtled past his head, the wind whizzing through his ears. "Should I be concerned?" Alaric whispered to Addeus.

"Not yet." He replied, another rock crashed against the gray scree of erosion beneath their feet.

"Are they dangerous?" Gaverick called from behind Alaric.

"That all depends on how dangerous you are, Gaverick." Addeus answered, grabbing a stone in mid-flight. "We should be back before nightfall."

Gaverick looked back towards the sun, an oval glow through the clouds. It had already passed its height and was beginning its daily descent into the western horizon. "That only gives us a few hours," he replied.

"Then you had better be dangerous, Gav," Barron replied to fill the silence of Addeus' response.

"It didn't take Aureus an hour to capture Adullam," Blair whispered. A flare of hushed questions ignited from the company.

Alaric froze and glared back at Blair.

"Now is not the time," he said in a voice to command their silence. "Focus on the task at hand."

Alaric turned back towards Addeus who had maintained his pace up the mountain and now neared a cusp along the path. Alaric barely stood out against the mountain compared to Addeus who shone through the dismal gray like a lighthouse on fog-lined shores. As Addeus reached the bend in the path he waited, his silver-blue eyes wandering ahead of him before he pressed forward through the mists. The Fomorii's assault slowly dwindled and the rest of the company's trek towards the cave was accompanied only by the whistling wind.

Alaric crested the final slope, and the cave's black sliver came leering out of the mists, carved into the side of the rock face. Addeus entered the mountain through it, lighting the blackness with gold.

Alaric heard Gaverick's voice from behind him and realized he had stopped, entranced.

"What do you think he is?"

Alaric shook himself out of his trance, but said nothing.

A large, rough hand closed around Gaverick's mouth, "Best ta' leave it 'lone for now," Orleans whispered, pulling Gaverick's ear close. The golden glow of Addeus' body began fading into the recesses of the cave. From here, Alaric and his company scrambled towards the entrance and plunged into the dark after their living torch. The walls were rough and the ground uneven, nothing like the smooth surfaces of Adullam's halls. Hastily, they picked their way through the tunnel until at last rounding a bend to find Addeus statued and staring forward into a widening darkness.

Ahead came the sinister sound of whispers and the scrambling of claws over stone.

Alaric peered around Addeus, trying to pierce the black with his gaze. A sharp hiss from the deep and the hair on Alaric's neck prickled. He faltered back from Addeus' side, rearing around to check on his men. They pressed in close, eyes wide, ears alert. Huddled together, they tried their best to stay within Addeus' glowing aura.

From the rear, a scathing voice shot through the dark like an arrow. *Kill!*

It ricocheted off the walls and was echoed by more voices screeching out in kind. Addeus charged forward, lunging hand and foot on every surface of the tunnel. Alaric and his company scrambled to keep up. "Daggers," Alaric called to his rear as the voices ahead grew louder.

The glint of a gold vein appeared along the wall. It spiraled up to the ceiling and twisted back beneath their feet and up again, exploding into dozens of tiny veins which graced the ceiling like lightning through the night's sky. Alaric followed as the veins wrapped back down to the base of the tunnel and along the opposite wall. As it spiraled up, Alaric went with it, caught in the illusion of its twisting path; he was on the ceiling. He braced himself against the walls, moving his hands up and down as he spun deeper into the weaving gold until all of the sudden a creature emerged into Addeus' light.

Bulging, yellow eyes gleamed like a pair of suns in the distant universe. The Fomorii screamed, bearing rotten, crooked teeth, and faded back from sight. It was smaller than an average man, its skin pasty and covered in layers of dirt. Addeus kept his pace. At the edge of his aura, Alaric could just make out the heels of the creature scrambling from the light. Its feet were naked and elongated, its toenails curved like talons. The heels were thin and fleshy, stretched by an age of creeping and crouching through low tunnels. Its hips hinged its torso forward, but its back curved with an arch that brought its elbows to its knees. A wisp of dirty gray hair trailed from a patch on its head, whipping behind it as it fled. Its left hand stayed tucked against its chest as its right hand flailed about like an opposable third foot, grabbing onto outcrops and crevices in the wall.

Kill! came another shrill whisper and the Fomorii vanished from sight.

Addeus slid to a halt and the lambent glow of his body exploded into a brilliant florescence, blinding Alaric and knocking him and his men to the ground. Dagger in hand, Alaric jumped to his feet just in time to see three Fomorii break their charge and flee, screeching away from Addeus' brilliance. From behind, Alaric heard the gruff of Orleans' shout. He flung himself around to the sight of Orleans slinging a Fomorii against the wall. The creature slumped. Before Orleans' buried his heel into its chest, Alaric caught the glint of a blood-red stone grown into its chest. Orleans' boot sank the stone into the creature's heart.

Another Fomorii, and another, and another, came at them from the rear, the first latching onto Orleans' shoulder. He grabbed its leg and slung it into the second, sending them both to the ground. The third leapt at Fields, its yellow eyes fit to burst, and its scream deafening the tunnel. With a swift upwards swipe, Fields cut his dagger across the creature's path and sent it reeling into the middle of the company. Barron bore down on it, plunging his dagger into its throat.

Enraged, the other two Fomorii regained themselves for a charge. The first braced itself between the tunnel's walls and lunged feet first at the men, its talons emblazoned in Addeus' aura. It sank its hind claws into Blair's chest armor. He wailed and fell back at the force of the Fomorii's weight. Carmine caught him from behind, swinging his dagger around Blair as the Fomorii bore its teeth towards Blair's throat. Carmine forced the creature's head back as its crooked teeth scathed his collarbone. Blair reached up and wrenched the creature off of him and, throwing it to the ground, stomped the felstone into its heart.

The three that remained on Addeus' front had not resurfaced from the darkness. Alaric could hear their whispers again, boiling with venom. Slowly, Addeus strode forward. As he approached, their whispers came painfully, like the hiss of oil in a hot pan, until they were fully exposed in his aura, huddled together at the end of the tunnel. Alaric watched them cower, clutching the stones sunken within their skin. They winced and barked and cried, shielding their stones and their eyes from the light.

Alaric looked from them to Addeus. The shroud covering his face had fallen loose, draping the top of his shoulder. His expression was creased into a scowl, his eyes shining fiercely with what seemed the resentment of necessity. Alaric glanced back at the Fomorii and was struck with a sudden pity. He bit the inside of his bottom lip, trying to watch, but could not. He turned away, feeling the warmth of Addeus' aura melt down his back. Alaric looked at his men. Most had averted their eyes, looking down to their feet.

"I can only see myself in them," Carmine said, fighting to watch their suffering.

"Don't look," Alaric said.

"I have to," Carmine replied with a quivering lip, "how can I not?"

Alaric looked away, unable even to see the agony in Carmine's face. The creatures began to scratch circles around their stones, trying to draw out the pain. Alaric glanced sideways back to Addeus. From the corner of his eye he could see the Fomorii now trying to wrench the stones from their skin. Their bodies flailed and thrashed and at last stood still. Addeus' tone had flushed pink with the strain of his stare. Steam rose up in front of his eyes and curled away from him like a wave before dissipating into the air. Alaric followed the trail of steam back to its base and found it rolling off beads of crystal tears flowing steadily from Addeus' eyes. As one would well up, it would catch in Addeus' eyelash and shine against the brilliance of his skin before it dropped and evaporated instantly, vanishing into the rising wave.

Addeus closed his eyes and the steam diffused away as his shine diminished into a pale glow. He covered his face again with the veil he had let hang loose. Bowing his head he walked forward and collected the three felstones from the lifeless bodies of the Fomorii. He placed them in a small bag concealed beneath his mantle. The men watched him do this, in turn kneeling to collect the stones from the remaining bodies. The process was as somber as the tone of Addeus' glow. To Alaric, it felt nothing like victory. Once the felstones had been collected they were all handed over to Addeus who had pushed himself up to the front of the group. He placed the other four stones in his bag and processed on towards the entrance of the cave.

"They had become slaves to greed," Addeus said as he led the way, "and their lives were bound to the stones. Be wary of their power, greed will make a monster of most men."

The return journey seemed to take an age, but at last they stepped out into the open face of the mountainside and a brilliant horizon, lit by the fire of the setting sun. The fire at their camp had been relit as well, spreading a mouth-watering aroma of fresh meat into the free air. Not waiting to be given leave, the soldiers spilled past Addeus, but Alaric stayed back to take the path steadily and recompose. He walked slowly behind Addeus, and the steady silence of their pace fell over Alaric like the relief of rain in a hot summer.

"Life is filled with too many words," Addeus said as if reading Alaric's mind.

Alaric said nothing, just watched the bob of Addeus' head as he strolled down the mountainside, and in this moment he felt a contentment he had longed for but never found in the past several months.

They reached the bottom of the mountain and again the waft of a freshly cooked meal swelled over Alaric. Nature taking hold of him this time, Alaric sat himself amidst his men and began to pick through the meat set out around the fire. The sun had settled behind the mountains and the deep blue of night crept slowly towards the moon.

"Well, looks who seems to be in fine form!" Barron called out. Alaric and the others looked up and from behind a scramble of bushes Marion appeared, arms laden with firewood.

"You're all here," he cried, "and none of you were worried I was missing? I cooked your dinner."

"Aletheia here tol' us where you'd gone," Orleans voice boomed over the guilty silence.

"I did not," Aletheia said with a chuckle. Embers adrift in the sky danced and turned with her laughter.

"Ridiculous," Marion returned, his mouth feigning a twist of disappointment. He stepped through the crowd of soldiers and dropped a few more logs on the fire.

"Glad to see you're well again," Alaric said.

"Glad to be well, sir." Marion replied, sitting down and stealing a sliver of meat from Carmine's plate.

Alaric sat back and watched his soldiers eat and laugh and jeer at one another for a moment, but soon the sounds became distant and their distinctions blurred. As the moon began to rise, he stood, wandering behind the boulder and into the streambed. He listened to the quiet babble of water bleed with the sound of the soldiers' mirth. The moon crept slowly from behind the cloud cover, painting the world in silver and setting sparks to the water beneath Alaric's feet.

What troubles you?

Their laughter, Alaric thought.

There are not many who can bear the burdens you have undergone these past weeks.

Shifting the rocks beneath his toes, Alaric saw his shadow stretch out before him.

Whether they realize or not, the men place their burdens on you to carry for them.

With a muted gasp he turned; there, as a mirror to the moon, stood Aletheia. She came close, searching him with her soft eyes. Alaric averted his gaze to the mountainside, feeling his mouth turn dry.

"They still don't know. And I don't know how to tell them," Alaric said softly. "As if things couldn't be more hopeless."

"What hope you can create for them, Alaric – that is all the hope they will need." Aletheia stepped steadily around Alaric, brushing his shoulder with her garment as she passed.

"What are you?" Alaric asked, the words sticking against his parched tongue.

She glanced back over her shoulder but said nothing, gliding slowly forward along the streambed. Alaric watched her steadily for a moment. She stopped beneath a pale, leafless tree and stood watching the world beneath the Borderlands. Quietly, Alaric backed away, retracing his steps to the camp. As he rounded the boulder, the glint of the felstones caught his eye. Set out on a flat-topped rock, the glow of the fire danced inside the deep red of their core. Alaric walked cautiously towards them, transfixed by their bold veneer. He felt himself being drawn into them. The sounds of his comrades grew distant again; he could not bring himself to look away.

Crack! Alaric reeled around as a log split beneath the flames of the campfire. Shaking off the surprise, he looked again at the stones but instead met Addeus' eyes.

"You see now their effect," he said.

Alaric said nothing but only glanced back down to the felstones.

"They are a dangerous tool," Addeus continued, picking one of the stones and turning it his hand, "an unfortunate necessity."

"How will we use them?" Alaric asked.

"Aletheia and I will split the stones and forge them into your weapons. But rest now, and tell the others to do the same; we will keep watch over you tonight."

"I will," Alaric said, suddenly exhausted. He blinked bleary eyes once more at the stones and turned towards his men. He stepped to the fireside and told his men to rest. They collected their mess and laid themselves around the fire. Alaric found a spot snug against the boulder where Marion had been laid before. He curled up in the moss beneath the stone and laid a cloak over his body, watching the men trail off to sleep until only the two cousins, Blair and Barron, remained. They added another few logs to the fire and pushed a wall of earth around it, talking quietly to one another. At length their quiet conversation lulled Alaric to sleep. He slept soundly through the night, and awoke at daybreak to the hammering of iron.

CHAPTER XXIX

RENDING THE VEIL

The sky was still overcast from the night before and though the rain had stayed, dew lay thick on the ground. Alaric sat upright, the hammering resounding in his ears. The mountain straight ahead stood just as bleak and ominous as before, and the sky was just so that they seemed to curl threateningly together and enclose everything. He leaned forward and shook the morning ache from his head. The fire at the center of their camp was still burning fresh, though Barron and Blair lay sleeping. Alaric's eyes darted around the camp. He was the first awake of the men.

He pushed himself off the boulder and up from the ground. The hammering came from behind a large hedge to his left. Blinking the sleep from his eyes, he stared into the fire, watching the flames whip and curl. A sudden rush of cold swept through him. He leaned down and threw the cloak back over his shoulders, wondering whose it was.

Suddenly, he noticed that the hammering had stopped. He pulled the cloak tighter around him and crept towards the hedge to where the noise had been coming from. He stepped up to the edge of the bushes, and crouching, peered through them to the other side. Addeus stood over the flat-topped rock with his back to the hedge. The top half of his garment was removed and the golden sheen of his skin bled brighter into the air around him. Alaric strained his neck forward. The hammer hung in Addeus'

261

right hand, and his left held aloft a sword, its blade glistening with a renewed sheen.

Alaric reached for his hilt; his sword was gone. He rustled back through the bushes to find it. Neither his belt nor his sword was anywhere to be found. He reached around to the small of his back and found his dagger removed from its sheath. Alaric hurried back to the hedge, but his haste alerted Addeus who turned, sword in hand, to face him.

Crouched beneath the hedge, Alaric cursed under his breath and stepped into view, coughing into his fist. Addeus had replaced the tabard over his torso. His armor, hood, mantel, and shroud still lay folded on a nearby rock. Bronze curls plumed thick and windblown atop his head. He turned from Alaric and began to carefully sharpen the blade in his hand.

Alaric walked forward to stand at Addeus' side. He stopped and arched his shoulders, pulling the cloak tighter around himself. He studied Addeus at work and let his eyes follow the movement of the whetstone across the sword as it sharpened. Finishing its edge, Addeus directed his attention to Alaric for the first time since he had been standing there. Alaric raised his eyes to Addeus'. He seemed to have grown several inches through the night.

Addeus held the hilt of the sword out for Alaric to take. As he reached for it he noticed the glisten of a felstone at its base and drew his hand back, unnerved by the stone-crested hilt. Addeus proffered it further. Carefully, Alaric's fingers slid along the hilt of the blade. He tightened his grasp and took it into his hand. Holding it in front of him, he examined its shape, felt its weight, and traced its design.

"This is mine," he exclaimed.

"Yes." Addeus nodded and reached down to retrieve Alaric's dagger from a nearby pile of weaponry. Rather than faceted as a pommel like the sword, the dagger's felstone fragment was socketed in the middle of the guard, just above the grip. Alaric flipped the dagger through his fingers admiringly before replacing it at his back.

"I worked through the night," Addeus said, reading Alaric's satisfaction. "I had hoped to finish before anyone awoke to avoid alarm."

"They're very well done," Alaric replied, ticking his thumb across the edge of his sword. "Thank you."

Addeus bowed his head and across the camp Alaric caught a glimpse of Aletheia walking up from the ravine, her arms full of raw meat and a satchel full of herbs hanging at her side. She stepped over Barron and set the satchel and meat on the ground. Like Addeus, she had removed her shroud, hood, and tabard. In their place she wore a smock-like garment, now soaked in blood from the meat. Unaware that anyone was awake and watching, she took it off and cast it in the fire. Her physique was firm but slender; her exposed body glowed rose and gold. Alaric's face flushed as he averted his eyes.

"You look so similar," Alaric said with a staggered breath. He glanced again towards Aletheia as she walked back into the ravine. "Is she your sister?"

"Yes, in a way," came Addeus' elusive response.

A minute or so later Aletheia returned, having washed the blood from her hands and arms. Alaric tried not to watch as she carefully reset her armor and tunic, and at last replaced the veil beneath her eyes. Once dressed, she set about cooking the meat she had collected, and the smell of a fresh meal had the sleeping soldiers on their feet and ready to go in no time at all. Much of the meat was smoked and cured for the road ahead; what was left, the men quickly consumed. There was an expectation in the air that they would be moving soon. Their daggers and swords were returned to them and as they ate they discussed the sharpened edges and the jeweled hilts.

When all business was settled and bags packed, Barron and Aletheia went to collect the horses and by mid-afternoon all the men were ready to ride. The day had remained cool and overcast, the smell of rain lingering heavier in the air with each passing hour. The consensus was to escape the rain by riding east as long as their horses would last. The cattle they would leave in the ravine.

Just as the haze of rain appeared over the mountains and began moving down into the foothills, the party set off south towards the Briswold. When they emerged from the cradle of the Borderlands, they veered east and rode alongside the mountains, trying to avoid the open grasslands. They rode all through the afternoon and into the evening. When the sun was beginning to set behind them, the horses became indignant and by sundown refused to move another inch.

Shortly after they had made camp for the night, the rains came. The evening's air had a slight chill but the droplets came down warm against their skin, and no one – save for Aletheia – received it with any optimism. The rain poured its gloom over everyone else and the night was filled with their quiet shivering and unhappy mutterings. Only the horses seemed to get any sleep.

By morning, the conditions had not much changed. The sky had lightened with the rising sun, but the rain still held the world in a formless gray. The men rose stiff from a wet and sleepless night and breakfasted on the damp meat in their bags. A quiet hour passed as they broke camp. Once packed, they mounted their horses and turned towards the vast of Drögerde. As they rode, the grasslands began to thin and brown. The rain lightened and almost precisely where the grass stopped growing, the rain stopped falling. Even so, gray clouds stretched the horizon in front of them acting like a blanket to trap in moisture.

With more moisture in the air than any ocean had ever contained, Alaric felt himself drowning in Drögerde's humidity. It stayed with them through the night and well into the next day. The cloud cover seemed impenetrable; occasionally Alaric would look up to see the yellow glow of the sun trying to force its way through, but the dense atmosphere never broke.

After the first night, Carmine made a game of it. He would shout out hopefully every twenty minutes or so and point to a spot where he predicted the sun would burst through. But, as if his voice summoned disappointment, the glow would shortly vanish and the clouds would darken Carmine's countenance. At last, however, when the end of the day was drawing near, Carmine pointed ahead and yelled, "There, over the trees, you can see the light coming down through the clouds; I think that's where it ends."

"If ya'd jus' not say a thing, then we might see us some blue!" Orleans cried.

"Nope. No sir, I'm sure of it this time. The sun's going to hold."

"I will kick you off your horse if you say that again," Barron replied, his eyes roiling with anger.

"Just you wait," Carmine snickered and looked back towards the sun. An hour passed, and then another and the sun still held off in the horizon. They were coming close now to the Beltwood and Alaric could feel the congested atmosphere lifting. As night drew in closer, the wood dominated their field of view, stretching out wider than they could see in either direction. By dark they reached the edge of the wood, leaving the clouds and their humidity behind. The night opened up, fully lit with stars and Carmine looked back over the cloud-covered wastes of Drögerde.

"What'd I tell you gentlemen?" he asked, and Barron pushed him off his horse. Almost immediately it began to rain.

As rain began to fall over the border of Drögerde, the company dismounted and walked their weary horses the last few paces into the canopy of the Beltwood. The moss-covered ground beneath the ancient trees absorbed the sound of their footsteps like a sponge. Rain spilled through the boughs as if through a filter, floating down to the earth in a light haze. Aletheia and Addeus' aura glistened off the droplets, dimly illuminating a wide field of view. They walked just a little ways into the ancient wood before stopping to rest for the night.

After the horses were taken care of and the camp set, the men sat round together at the base of a large tree to share a small meal before bed.

"Today is Tuesday," Aletheia observed. "Tomorrow morning we will set off again. By Friday we will have reached Aureus."

For a moment everyone stopped eating, caught in the enrapturing timbre of Aletheia's pristine voice.

When she said nothing else, Alaric took over. "We still have no real strategy. We have the felstones, but that alone isn't enough to stand against Aureus."

There was no reply for some time. At length, Aletheia shut her eyes and gave them an answer. "We have discussed some things, but others have yet to be revealed to you. We will incite rebellion within the walls of Aureus. The tear in The Veil of Kingdoms is not yet wide enough to reveal the Tree of Life, but the time of its emergence is drawing very near. Aureus will keep its eye out for the Tree's rebirth, and amass its armies to lay claim to its fruit."

"How long can we hope to hold out against the full strength of Aureus?" Alaric asked.

"Not long," Aletheia replied softly. "But, the emergence of the Tree marks the final threads of The Veil's existence."

"And what does that mean?" Carmine asked concernedly.

"I cannot say precisely…"

"Then it could be days!" Carmine looked around the group and frowned at Alaric.

"That is not likely." Aletheia tried to recover the conversation. "The revelation of the Tree marks The Shaddai's approach, and will hopefully turn the hearts of men toward the faith necessary to rend The Veil through."

"This is the end," Alaric continued off of Aletheia's words. "We come to decide the face of eternity as the last of free men."

Aletheia's eyes smiled from behind her veil and the color of her glow brightened; the men quivered at her warmth. Taking a map out from beneath his tunic, Alaric laid it out in the moss before them. His fingers traced the imposing outline of Aureus' borders and ended in the southern mountains. He tapped twice on the map. "Here is our path over the wall."

CHAPTER XXX

AUREUS

"Bring him here – to me," a voice commanded from the back of a dimly lit room. The large iron doors leading to the antechamber yawned slowly open. A lone man walked in, a silhouette against the light from outside. "Mind the doors on your way out," the voice called again.

"But my Lord? Shall I not remain…"

"You have had your audience with me, Malik; I have been gracious to listen to you, but I now wish to speak with my Lucien."

Malik stood between the doors, bracing them open. He bowed his head low, taking a long step back. The doors rang shut in front of him. Lucien stood shivering and alone. He watched the breath swirl from his nose. He stepped slowly forward, growing ever colder as he approached the shadowed figure seated at the back of the room. Lucien fought not to hug his arms against his chest as the temperature dropped.

Little explosions on either side of the chamber began to light his way. Imps bent up in little lanterns along the walls burst into flames, cackling as Lucien approached. The flames lit in succession one by one until they reached the end of the chamber. There, illuminated in the imps' light sat an imposing figure enthroned in a high-backed chair of cedar and crimson velvet. Slumping, he massaged his eyebrow and stared pensively at Lucien. His other fingers twisted round the carvings down the arm of his throne, and his eyes glowed fiercely in the imp-light. As Lucien came closer still to the throne, its occupant stood, taking two calculated steps down from his platform. Lucien stopped and knelt before him. "My Lord, Aureus," he said.

"Stand, please. Too long has it been since you last graced this hall, Prince."

Lucien obeyed, standing. "My work has kept me away. It is good to be home at last."

"Home," Aureus repeated. His eyes gazed down at Lucien like a pair of stars fighting through the fresh blue of early morning. An ivory grin spread across his lips, accentuating his high cheekbones. The imp-light radiated off his skin like muted gold.

"Lucien," Aureus caroled in a tone reminiscent of Malik, "the look in your eye betrays you. There is no need for you to feel," he drew in a deep breath and exhaled, "vulnerable." Steam curled off his breath and around Lucien's face. "Am I not gracious and merciful? Do I not reward those in my service? And you *have* been in my service?" he asked, the shine in his eyes darkening.

"Of course, Your Majesty. I'm merely apprehensive about what Malik may have told you," Lucien replied.

"We will come to that, dear Prince. I will hear what you have to say, for I am just. Malik is undoubtedly jealous of your position," Aureus smiled slyly, "and as such I can reason that he may not have been entirely fair in his account. Perhaps that will, for a time, curb your apprehension. But come, let us sit."

He gestured to a space in the empty chamber and the imps burst forth from their lanterns. They streaked in all directions across the chamber leaving spiraling trails of fire behind them to light the chamber as they fled down a small corridor. Moments later they returned, pushing a heavy table and matching set of chairs. Once the creatures had put the table in place, three of them leapt up, setting themselves aflame, and fixated into strange positions at the center of the table.

Delighted, Aureus sat at the head of the table, setting Lucien to his left. "Now," he said, "we can have a proper conversation, I think. Spare nothing, I wish to know every detail of your endeavor against this Adullam. And, my dear Lucien," Aureus said as a profound afterthought, "do not forget who I am and all that I can see. Do not doubt that I will know your subtlest fabrication."

Lucien leaned his elbow on the table, drawing closer to the imps in attempt to steal some of their heat. "My Lord, he said in a tone made filthy with beguilement, "I trust then that you alone can appreciate the true artistry of my deception."

Aureus' smile widened as his eyes glistened brighter – a beam of arrogance that did not escape Lucien's watchful eye.

"Malik, my Lord, does not understand the delicate process of corruption as you do. He is not practiced in the subtleties of what I think you would so wisely call, a beautiful lie. And though my history will not compare to any such lie that you have manifested into this world, take it as a tribute to your supremacy."

Aureus swelled, his pride growing him into a larger, more imposing figure. "Go on, Prince," he said, sitting upright in his chair, "I am intrigued."

"I had hoped you would be, Your Majesty," Lucien said hiding a sly smile, "then I shall continue."

From here Lucien produced much the same story as he did for Malik, this time, however, recounting it with meticulous detail and lacing it with compliments he previously did not care to waste. He told of his initial meeting with Alaric and his arrival at Adullam; his endeavor to pinpoint the cave's proper location; his friendship with the scholar in attempt to understand and subvert their authoritative structure. Here he went into greatest detail, fully explaining the inner workings of Adullam's society and the way he had manipulated it to place the leaders of Adullam against one another, "all in the interest of softening the masses and fostering a condition in which they could be persuaded into escaping from."

"Now, what I am about to tell you," Lucien continued, "will not be in line with Malik's account. I feared he would not understand the complex nature of my endeavor, passing it off as mere coincidence – even luck." Lucien paused, summoning his muse.

"My presence in Adullam, but especially my status as an advisor to the Steward, placed me at odds with their General, Nestor. Of course I figured him out from the moment I met him, and pitted his own pride and jealousy against him. I kept myself close to the Steward, gained his trust, and within two weeks I had robbed the General of eleven soldiers to keep as my personal Elite Guard. Just by existing within the system I was manipulating Nestor. Very quickly he began to feel threatened and to feel that the Steward might need replacing. It was not long after that that his plotting began.

"My plans for Nestor, however, were accelerated after the razing of Bristing. This threw an entirely new dynamic into the scenario. I am grateful for your clairvoyance, My Lord – it surpasses my understanding – the decision to destroy Bristing could not have been more perfectly placed."

With another barrage of flattery from Lucien, Aureus sank further into his chair, his face a graven image of delight.

"My original intention, as I may have said," Lucien continued, "was to ignite a political feud between Nestor and the acting Steward, and watch as the society tore itself apart before I handed its shattered remains to you. Bristing allowed me to keep it all intact.

"There is a lot you can make someone do just by knowing them. The Steward, being the man he was, would want to reconcile his dispute with Nestor. Nestor, being who he was, would take that opportunity for his own gain. The Bristing crisis was the perfect catalyst for this transaction of sympathies. A few subtle hints to the right advisors and the Steward fell thick into the folds of my plan. To make amends to his General, the Steward allowed Nestor charge of the scouting operation. Nestor sent the Steward, who wished to be included in the operation, along the trade routes that your satyrs had been ambushing; there the dear Steward met his untimely demise.

"But, I knew that if somehow the Steward survived and was able to return to Adullam, Nestor would have had to make amends – and I could not have their relationship repaired. So, even before my company had reached Bristing, I began feeding ideas of Nestor's betrayal to an influential captain, the same whose life I had saved. As I said, there is a lot you can make someone do just by knowing them. As insurance, I had him suspicious of Nestor to deepen the rift. When indeed the Steward was killed, my words resonated with the captain, and together we began plotting against Nestor. At the same time, I began formulating a plan to legitimize an exodus from Adullam – one that would bring its people right to you.

"But, in the face of my labor, Malik grew impatient and greedy. Preemptively, he invaded Adullam and took my efforts as his own. I wanted to bring Adullam to your doorsteps; instead I have come home empty handed. If I might make amends…" Lucien said, letting his voice trail.

"Go on," Aureus' voice echoed through the hall.

"As Malik's attack came without warning to me, a small band of men were able to escape into the western mountains."

"The western mountains?" Aureus repeated, rising from his chair.

"Yes sir," Lucien replied, lowering his head.

"And do they know of my crown-stones?"

"Your Majesty," Lucien said, his voice barely audible.

A deep roll of laughter spilled from Aureus' throat; the imps trembled beneath its waves. "My Lucien, my dear Lucien," he said, "are you afraid?"

"Yes," Lucien whispered, barely parting his lips.

"You are right to be so," Aureus continued, "for my wrath is supreme over the world." His grinning eyes melted into white gold, and with a deep boom that shook the floor beneath Lucien's feet; the Lord of Aureus exploded into light with the brilliance of the golden sun. Shielding his eyes, Lucien toppled to the floor, struck down by his radiance. "But as my wrath is beyond all others," his voice came like thunder, "so is my mercy beyond your worldly reckoning."

The thundering receded and the light faded back to its imp-glow. Lucien picked himself up from the floor, resetting his chair and gasping for breath. Slowly he raised his gaze to Aureus whose eyes still burned white gold. Beneath them, an equally brilliant smile beamed forth. "My dear Lucien, my fortune smiles upon you. You have done well to tell me of this. But, before we speak further on the matter, I must say, your story is a fascinating one – a true testament of my guidance given to the right mind."

"Thank you, My Lord Aureus," Lucien stammered out, bracing himself against the table.

"And all this time you operated under their complete trust?"

"No, Your Majesty," Lucien replied, regaining his composure. "I went to great lengths to gain that trust, and in the end my place in Adullam was a point of friction and disunity. In truth, the question of my loyalty served its purposes very well. I may not have been able to accomplish what I did had I been fully trusted."

Aureus collapsed back in his chair, peering into Lucien's eyes for a long while before he spoke. "I know now why Malik had trouble believing your tale."

Lucien shifted in his chair and tried to swallow away his nerves.

"To split the truth along such a thin line; to force such perceptions that someone, completely subject to your influence, believes themselves to be acting of their own volition – that is something only *I* have accomplished."

Lucien's entire body was wrought immobile with tension. He felt beads of perspiration forming on his face and the burning imps became intolerably hot to his skin.

"But you are correct; Malik cannot see the dual nature of reality as I see it. Nor can he see its interlocking layers of perception and understanding. As an agent of my will, Malik has nearly served his purpose. You, however, my Lucien have gained greatly from your servitude. I have created a masterpiece of myself in you." With a grin, Aureus rolled his eyes into the back of his head, washing the white gold from them.

"I am indebted to you, Your Majesty," Lucien said, his voice shaking with relief.

"No! I am indebted to you, my Lucien," Aureus exclaimed. "And as such, I have an important matter to discuss with you." He paused, tilting his head to read Lucien's expression. "You do not seem pleased."

"No, Your Majesty," Lucien cried, jolting upright.

"That I should deem you worthy to discuss matters of the kingdom should come as the highest honor!" Aureus reproached, "The world is my dominion, and yet here I humble myself to converse with a mortal."

"Forgive me, Your Majesty," Lucien tried to recompense, "I did not realize…"

Aureus waved him silent with a sweep of his hand that caused the imps to flicker. "I will have mercy on your listlessness. A time is drawing near, my Prince, when you will no longer have to sustain yourself by blood. Our covenant will be renewed, your life no longer bound to that stone," he nodded at the scepter hanging out from Lucien's coat. Aureus allowed the silence to mount as he stared sternly at Lucien. "Why is it, do you think, I have chosen this place to build my Divine City?"

Lucien searched his master's lurid eyes for the answer. "Because of the prophecies," Lucien suggested, "because of *The Writ of Narxus* and its foretelling."

Thunder rolled through Aureus' laugh. "And where do you think *The Writ* found its foresight?"

"Well, the legend holds tale of *El Adviento del Sol* – The Advent of the Sun – and its vision to unite the monotheistic religions of Spain against the Inquisition. From there, its adherents sought to reconcile the religions of the Mediterranean, finding common ground in the one God to end the Crusades in the East, and forge a new world – a better world."

Aureus' countenance grew dark, the air around him condensed; the imps' flames flickered and went out. Lucien shivered quietly, all warmth had been exhausted in the dark of the throne room. He could feel his blood begin to thicken as words slithered from Aureus' mouth, "You insult me, Phillíp. I named you my Lucien, my light, and yet you forget the source of your radiance, of your life. You were a shadow and I have made you a light – a light that has burned three hundred years or more. Think about what the world sees, Lucien. The world saw your brother, but *I* saw you. Who now remains? Where is Roberto now? His body still lies rotting beneath my halls. And your Advent of the Sun, they saw a world united through a common revelation, but I saw my own succession to the throne of their world. Who now remains? I remain – seated upon the throne of this golden city. And now, the eternity awaits my ascendance."

The imps whined like frightened dogs. "All of what I have said is connected, my Lucien."

Lucien stared blankly at the table. "You fed the prophesies bound within *The Writ*, knowing someday it would foster the Narxus and that the Narxus would work through the prophesies to your end."

"And so the blind do see," Aureus exclaimed, beaming white gold. The imps burst into flame, dancing in circles on the table.

"Ah, my Lucien," he continued, "where would you be without my guidance, without my clairvoyance? I have created you, you bear my image as no other of my servants ever have."

Lucien's face turned pallid and green. He could not hide his disgust from Aureus' consuming light. "What is it, my Lucien?" Aureus demanded, fists clenched against the solid wood. "Your master has complimented you.

The Lord of the Earth has deigned to humble himself for you and you repay my grace with a sickened glare?"

"I have not tasted blood today, my Master," Lucien excused. "Do not think that I am ungrateful for your undeserved blessing. I am nothing in your presence, Son of the Dawn."

A greedy smile curled across Aureus' face. "Ah! This returns us to our initial conversation – our renewed covenant. I chose the Advent of the Sun to foster *The Writ*, in turn creating the Narxus, and on the foundation of the Narxus, I have built my golden city. And somewhere within its walls is the Tree of Life. The time of its renewal is near, I can feel its presence gathering in the ether. I was there for its creation – long before the first human inhabited the earth. Though it has been hidden from me behind The Veil, and though the surface of the earth never ceases to grind and shift and change, I have kept my eye on its place. I built Aureus here for the singular purpose of claiming the Tree. Everything I have ever suffered and accomplished hinges upon its fruits.

"From its creation," he continued, "the Tree has been my fulcrum – has been the thing on which my victories can be sustained. God in his high halls thinks himself to be the only one able to grant eternal life." Aureus gazed at the flames leaping sporadically from his imps, enraptured in himself. "Humanity will face a slow extinction. Their time is passing. The time of my Nephilim is at hand. They are far more servile than the humans, a better breed of creation, my breed of creation. the Tree will grant them life eternal; soon we will no longer need peasant women to birth them. The Nephilim will endure as Man suffers away into nonexistence, and the earth will be ours into eternity."

Lucien stared at the doors leading out of the chamber and bit hard on the inside of his cheeks. He felt as if he were standing at the bottom of an empty basin and everything he wished to feel, wished to think, wished to say, was peering down at him from around its edges beyond his reach. He was left alone at the bottom with no escape.

"Now," Aureus continued, "what is a Prince if he is never meant to inherit a kingdom?"

Lucien's eyes glowered at the floor.

"As we speak, my Nephilim are assembling. When the Tree emerges from behind The Veil, they will claim it. Soon I will build a new city to be sovereign over. I will give you my Aureus rule as a province of my kingdom. What say you to that, my Prince?"

"Words cannot express, Your Majesty." Lucien's words leaked out like water through a crack in a dam.

Aureus' lips quivered into a smile. "I thought not. As well, you will be given the Tree's fruit, and by it be granted life eternal without the need for my stone or a single drop of blood. Now," Aureus said suddenly, standing and walking back to his throne, "we were speaking of the men lost to the western mountains."

"Yes," Lucien exclaimed brightly.

"There are reports of men making their way to the mountains of our southern border – the same, I believe, who escaped you. Go to them Lucien, find my crown-stones and kill them."

CHAPTER XXXI

INTO THE GOLDEN CITY

Alaric stood in solitude atop a high mountain pass, his gaze transfixed on Aureus below. His skin was white and every hair on his body stood erect at a merciless wind scourging through the pass. Its howl drowned out all other sounds; he felt the wolf bearing down on him again, the scars the beast had left on Alaric's chest prickled. A gust of wind rocked him backward and chilled his eyes shut. They filled with moisture and overflowed. When he opened his eyes again, a figure had appeared next to him.

Alaric blinked his eyes clear. Beside him was Blair, staring down into Aureus. He glanced up at Alaric and then followed a cloud as it moved below them to hide their view. "It'll be a hard road down," he said.

"Not as hard as the road here," lamented Alaric, but Blair did not hear him over the rush of wind. "Are the men ready?"

Blair glanced over his shoulder, "They are, sir."

"Gather them."

Blair trotted back to the rest of the men and beckoned them to follow. While they assembled, Aletheia climbed into sight from beneath a cleft. Alaric reached down to help her to sturdy ground.

"I lost sight of you when the clouds came through," he said, "but you seemed to be making good progress."

Aletheia nodded and looked back down over the sheer edge of the pass. "Addeus and I have found the best route down."

"Is he still down there?"

"Yes, he will guide you once you are below the cloud cover."

"And you will stay up here to start everyone off?"

"Yes."

"Very well," Alaric said, peering over the cliff. "I watched most of your descent, so have the men follow closely after me." Aletheia smiled and nodded. Alaric sat down over the sheer edge of the mountain. They had taken all the rope used to bridle the horses and fashioned it into a single, knotted strand. It was not very long, but they tied it off at the top of the jagged slope to make the start of the climb a bit easier. Alaric began a cautious descent down the side of the mountain. Directly behind him came Blair, then Barron, then Carmine, and so on until all the men were over the edge. Aletheia stayed behind to help direct their climb.

Alaric, having carefully watched Aletheia and Addeus map the climb, helped Blair place his hands and feet. In turn, he helped the man above him and the message was passed along in this way so that all the men made safe passage down the cliff's side.

Halfway down the hundred-foot escarpment the clouds swallowed Alaric. The trail of his men up the mountainside slowly faded white until all Alaric could see was the bottom of Blair's feet.

"Careful ahead!" he called as Blair descended into the blanket of the mountain. Just as soon as Alaric had spoken shouts came back from above.

"Watch out!" Blair called, and a rock hurtled past Alaric's head.

More shouting sank through the mist. Frantically, Alaric strained his eyes. The train of men had stopped moving. Another rock cascaded past Alaric followed by a solitary shout.

"Orleans!" Alaric cried. "Blair, can you see him?"

"I can't, sir!" Blair yelled back.

"Orleans!"

"He's dangling. He's lost his footholds," someone yelled from beyond Alaric's sight.

"If he falls he'll take us all with him."

"Hold on Orleans!" Alaric cried. "Blair, can you see? Barron?"

"I can make him out," Barron answered, "Aletheia's coming to help him."

Alaric sighed, resting his forehead against the cold rock.

"Hanging on by a pinky," Barron laughed.

"Get me off of this," Blair said.

"That was exciting..."

"Terrifying," Blair cut him off, "let's just get down."

Barron cackled and steadily the train made its way through the cloud cover and down to the platform where Addeus stood waiting. By nightfall they had nearly reached the base of the mountain and the clouds that still swarmed above them cast light volleys of snow around their heads.

Alaric spent a sleepless night shivering beneath the wind-borne snow, brooding over their next day's descent into Aureus. Fires burned throughout the city like little pinpricks on a map. Alaric's eyes wandered between them until they were lost to the distance and the night. He hugged his arms tighter to his chest, trying to ward off the cold. He could hear the rustling of fitful sleep behind him as the men tossed and turned beneath their cloaks. Aletheia and Addeus, like Alaric, did not bother themselves with trying to sleep. The three sat together and gazed silently over Aureus.

At some point in the night Alaric did fall to sleep as he found himself stirred by the rising sun. From their perch on the mountain, Alaric could see the main gate of Aureus, its golden facade shimmered in the dawn. Branching from the gate was a long white road or perhaps a breezeway connecting to the main Citadel towering above the rest of the city. It was encircled by a wide wall, beyond which was a series of sub-districts. The further the districts stretched out from the Citadel, the more squalid they became. Closer to Aureus' walls were miles of farmland which stretched around to the east of the Citadel, pocketing small districts in their midst. The districts near the Citadel, however, seemed to be centered around an immense quarry. Beneath Alaric, in the south of Aureus along the eastern rim of the mountains, was untamed land of hills, scattered trees and high grasses. It seemed to wrap around to the far northeast and disappear from view. Everything north of the Citadel was lost to Alaric's eyes.

Light had barely brushed the horizon when Aletheia called out to the men from a little ways down the mountainside. Alaric had not taken notice of her absence, or Addeus', and the shouting startled him to his feet.

The other men lying on the ground sat straight up and looked towards the noise. Aletheia was coming quickly towards them and by the time she reached the encampment all the men had assembled around Alaric to receive her.

"Gather your belongings," she announced and turned back down the mountain, "we are running out of time."

Even in the urgency of her voice, Aletheia's words flowed like a rivulet of sparkling wine, hanging translucent in the air. For a moment the men stood and stared after her until it became apparent that she meant to depart immediately. With a jolt they all turned, strapped their swords to their belts, threw their cloaks over their shoulders, and tightened their boots.

Alaric was already a considerable ways down the slope by the time the rest of his soldiers began their descent. Gaverick, Barron, and Blair had kept close to Alaric, making their way at a fair pace. The others, in attempt to regain their Captain, came quickly down the mountain. Made clumsy in their haste, however, several rocks slid out from beneath their feet, hurtling ahead. Orleans motioned for the men to steady their pace, but by the time the first rock had fallen it was already too late; it incited a cascade of loose rubble careening down the slope towards Alaric and the others. The stones came bounding down around them, but even as they did their best to dodge, a rock caught Barron in the shoulder. He splayed face-forward into the ground, and the momentum of his fall sent him tumbling wildly down the slope. Alaric slid to grab him but missed as the bombardment of rocks still rained down from above.

Barron toppled head over heels down the mountain, knocking into rocks and carrying some with him as he fell. Erosion had shattered the surface of the mountain into steep screes and Alaric went leaping after Barron, sinking his heels deep into the loose fragments of rock. At last Barron made one final bound over the rocks and landed on a further, grass-laden slope. Hearing the sound of Barron's final pound against the rocks and the thud of his body in the grass, Aletheia turned just in time to seize Barron before he cascaded further down the mountainside.

Quickly, she laid him down on the slope and sat cradling his head in her arms. Yearning for a sign of movement from Barron, Alaric neglected his footing. His left foot glanced off a loose rock. His knee buckled inward and he fell flat against the ground. He skidded headlong down the scree towards Barron. Rubble shot up in a wave against Alaric's face and he tried to shift himself around to slide feet-first. As he turned, momentum got the best of his body, sending Alaric into a wild clamber down the mountain. He twisted and tumbled and finally rolled out of the rocks onto the grassier portion of the slope. Trying to stop himself, he dug his fingers into the ground, sharp bits of stone and bramble came shredding into his fingertips. Alaric buried a bawling shout behind clenched teeth, and pressed himself harder against the ground. At last he caught himself and scrambled desperately towards Barron, shaking his fingers and grimacing the pain away.

He knelt down at Barron's side and examined him for a moment. "Is he alive?" Alaric asked and looked somberly up at Aletheia.

She nodded her head slowly. "Unconscious," she said, "but in good condition considering his fall."

Alaric placed his hand against Barron's chest to feel his shallow draws of breath. A minute later, Blair and Gaverick came from the rocks and to Barron's side. They asked about his condition, received the same answer, and then like Alaric stood helplessly to await any sign of improvement. A few minutes more passed and the rest of the men joined the group. With everyone assembled Aletheia said earnestly, "We really cannot wait any longer."

"Can you wake him?" Alaric asked.

She massaged the sides of Barron's head and tried to lift him out of his cradled position, but he remained limp. Aletheia lifted him higher still and shifted herself out from underneath his body. She laid Barron softly on the grass and stepped slowly away amongst the others. "Our time runs short," she said again earnestly.

"So let us be off," Alaric said. Stepping forward he grabbed Barron under the arms and hoisted him onto his shoulders. With Barron's body draped over his shoulders, Alaric turned to continue the journey down the mountain. His men separated to let him pass through and Alaric led the way into the foothills of Aureus. When they reached the bottom of the mountain, they found Addeus perched on a high hill looking toward the Citadel. Alaric walked promptly to him, laid his burden in the grass and sat to rest.

Addeus made no sign of acknowledging Alaric's arrival, but continued his graven stare into the distance. The tension in Addeus seemed to create its own atmosphere into which everyone was enveloped. Alaric felt his heartbeat suppressed beneath a growing weight in his chest. Creatures of doubt began groping from the pit of his stomach. He sat tired and bruised, feeling a swallowing tempest of doom – a shadowing conviction of derision drawn in the face of the brooding storm.

Alaric lifted himself up as a warm wind blew in from the East, and with a deadened gaze he stared over Aureus. To the North, countless black banners processed through the main gate and along the road to the Citadel. The banners waved violently in the wind, held aloft on long spears, high above the heads of the Nephilim that carried them. The company came to stand in a line on the hill, staring over the distant procession in silence. It was not until Carmine shouted, "Barron isn't breathing!" that anyone could overcome their stagnant desperation.

In an instant they had all turned around, circling Barron. As soon as Addeus' gaze dropped from Aureus, the overwrought density of his presence softened, releasing the weighted atmosphere. Barron's eyes bolted open as he gasped for air, frantically clutching his chest. He lay on the ground for a while, just blinking his eyes and breathing. Everyone stared, mouths agape. Slowly, Barron sat up, fighting through the ache that warned him not to move. Sitting straight, he let out a long and composed sigh. "Help me up," he said, looking at Carmine.

Carmine reached down and helped Barron to his feet.

"How long have I been out?" he asked.

"Almost an hour," Blair responded, checking his cousin up and down. "Captain Folck carried you the rest of the way down the mountain."

"Much obliged, Captain," Barron said. He pressed his fingers lightly on a large bruise under his arm and drew a sharp breath in through pursed lips.

"How do you feel?" Blair asked, examining Barron's arm.

Barron pulled his arm away stubbornly, giving Blair a cautioning glance, "Alive, cousin." Suddenly his attention was diverted to the Citadel and the legion of Nephilim marching towards it. "Well," he said, and took an unbalanced step forward.

Alaric caught him by the elbow and steadied him. "Are you up for this, Barron?" he asked.

"Up for that?" Barron asked, nodding his head toward the distant Nephilim. "Are you up for that, Captain?"

"I don't have much choice," Alaric said.

"Then neither do I," he answered and swung his arm over Alaric's head to rest it across his back. With a wince, he cinched himself up close to Alaric. Blair came to his cousin's side, bracing Barron beneath his other shoulder. Together, the three of them began furthering the way into the heart of Aureus. They kept a slow pace at first to let Barron regain himself. After a little over an hour, Alaric was able to leave Blair to the job of keeping his cousin stable and take lead of their march. Before too long they had left the untamed foothills and began marching through the farm fields. Rows and rows of tall crops stretched ahead of them, yet still there was no one in sight tending the fields.

On the transition through fields, for a brief moment the road to the Citadel would come into view. The company had become considerably closer to the Citadel now, and on the road marched another procession of black banners. Alaric passed quickly into the next field as they continued on towards the main residential district. By the time Alaric remerged, the Nephilim had disappeared behind the Citadel wall, though their banners still rose into view like the canopy of a black forest.

The men came to the edge of the field and Alaric peered out from between the tall crops. He turned back to his company, "We're nearing the Citadel District," he warned them. "There's still no one in sight; we have a window to get in without being spotted but we need to be quick about it. Is everyone clear?"

There was a round of nods and Alaric checked their surroundings one final time. "Follow my lead," he said. "Go!"

Alaric burst forth from the field and crossed into the next, followed seconds later by Barron, braced between Blair and Carmine. One by one the others followed until all had crossed. Alaric kept his pace, continuing to hurtle through the field as quickly as Barron could move. He left a wide trail of flattened wheat for the rest of the party to follow.

They crossed two more fields, moving into a third and worked their way steadily through it. Barron's breath was becoming short and the look on his face betrayed the pain in his chest. At last they broke from the third field and into an expanse of dry, infertile ground. Alaric skidded to a halt, pulling Barron, Carmine, and Blair to a stop with him, and stared gaping over the empty way, several hundred of yards short of the Citadel

District. Alaric was caught between pressing forward, or retreat back into the field's cover.

Just then, Gaverick burst forth from the field, colliding into Alaric's back, followed by Leon, then the others, forcing Alaric forward. He grabbed Barron from under Carmine's shoulder and ran. Alaric's heart pounded so fervently in his chest that his eyesight began to pulse. His hearing narrowed to nothing but the heave of his breath and the rhythmic pound of his feet as he ran. He felt Barron's weight pull heavier on his shoulders. With panicked eyes Alaric looked up at the Citadel. The fear of its imposing immensity stole his focus. Barron's body sagged and Alaric collapsed. His open palm struck the ground sending a cloud of dust into his face. He choked for breath and rose forward from the cloud as a shrieking sound came rushing into his ears from above. He left Barron on his knees and ran forward. A winged figure, silhouetted black against the sun was descending from the sky. Brandishing a metal-hooked spear, it dove for the ground with a force that swirled dust high into the air around it. The cloud of dust consumed Alaric and he vanished with the creature into the haze of brown.

"Alaric!" Blair cried, picking Barron off the ground. They struggled forward as the rest of the company caught up with them, charging towards the mass of dust with their swords drawn. As the dust settled a solitary figure stood, its head bowed over the body lying between its feet. The men slowed their charge, hearts fading fast as the dust drifted to the ground. The figure turned to face them and Alaric's dusty head appeared from the cloud, his sword still stuck in the creature's chest. He beckoned them forward with a wave of his hand. Alaric looked back down, bemused by his kill; his eyes followed the form of its body from the tip of a dust-stained wing, down to where its torso had begun to corrugate from around the blade and turn to ash.

Addeus knelt down over the creature, remaining for a few moments as the others resumed their charge towards the district. He wrenched the hooked spear from the creature's hand, taking it with him as he ran after the rest of the group. He rejoined the party just as they were passing out of the dusted plane and into the cobble-stoned Citadel District of Aureus. They pressed in tightly together against the nearest building and allowed themselves time to recover.

"What was that thing?" Carmine asked in between wheezing breaths.

"A †Malebranche," Addeus said as he weighed the hook in his hand, "one of twelve. If they are here, we are near the end."

"Then we have to keep moving," Alaric interjected. The Citadel District was empty save for the distant sound of chiseling. "I can hear the quarry several blocks to the East. We'll move towards the sound."

The party followed Alaric through the empty cobblestone streets. As they ran, they stayed close to the buildings that lined either side of the street. Alaric left Blair to support Barron by himself, and taken lead of the group on the left flank while Addeus headed the other half of the company on the right. The clanking of metal picks against stone was soon pervading the air, and at last the party came to the edge of the quarry. The road split in two, perpendicular to their path. Another row of small houses stood across their way, rimming the quarry like a low wall. Cautiously, Alaric took the first step across the road. His men followed closely. The sound of pickaxes grew louder still, but the streets remained quiet and empty. Alaric hoisted himself up onto a low-lying house. Gaverick and Carmine clambered up behind him. The three of them crawled slowly to the edge of the rooftop and peered over.

Before them was the vast pit, dug into the heart of the district and ringed by small, stone-wrought houses. Alaric gazed, stricken, over the yawning sink and the thousands of miners toiling away within it. Before he could overcome his preoccupied stare, a voice called from behind him, singing just above the noise of the quarry workers. He turned to see Blair. Quickly as he could, Alaric slid down from the roof and crept back over a wall. Frantically, Blair pointed down the length of the road leading towards the Citadel. Alaric strained his eyes into the distance. There striding slowly towards them, hands folded behind his back, was Lucien.

CHAPTER XXXII

REUNION

Alaric stood in absolute bewilderment at the sight of his friend strolling towards them in the shadow of the Citadel. At first, he thought himself to be hallucinating, that the whole scene was some lucid dream. But the dream was too steady, too persistent.

"Is that…" Alaric began to ask.

"Lucien?" Carmine finished.

Blair raised questioning hands. "I think so."

With confirmation of his sanity, Alaric began to walk cautiously forward. As he came closer, he noticed something off about Lucien's appearance. Something had changed. Alaric quickened his gate. The mask was gone, the bandage – everything removed. Entranced, Alaric walked even faster, almost setting his gait to a jog, his whole being focused on Lucien.

As Alaric came closer, Lucien stopped. He knotted his face into a scowl, biting the inside of his cheeks until they bled. The click of his scepter sounded like glass shattering in his ears as its blade extended behind his back. Lucien's stance was stone. The smooth edge of the scepter rested against his back, the point of its blade tickled the hairs on his neck. Lucien tightened his grip on the hilt. Alaric was nearly upon him. Lucien drew a deep breath and glared ahead, biting harder still on his cheeks. There was no turning back.

Lucien slid his right foot back several inches and let his left hand fall to his side. A door from the house immediately behind Alaric was blown off its hinges. The door bounded across the street and Lucien raised his scepter into view. Jolted, Alaric turned his head to face the eruption of noise from the battered door. He feinted to the side just as a satyr leapt from within house. Lucien released his blade into the air. It arced over Alaric's shoulder and imbedded itself into the center of the satyr's chest. The creature screeched and Alaric collapsed into the street. Lucien stepped past him and to the satyr as it sank to its knees. Veins of orange began to form on its bare chest, emanating from the blade. The veins smoked and the skin around them turned to ash. Lucien watched the ember veins stretch out like a spider's web and corrugate the satyr's chest before he pulled his blade free and let the demon collapse onto the ground and wither slowly away.

Turning to face Alaric, Lucien retracted his blade and replaced it inside his coat. He took a few steps toward Alaric and offered a hand to help him up. Cautiously, Alaric accepted it.

"For a moment I thought you were going to kill me," Alaric said, as he rose. His eyes began to wander over the scar on Lucien's face, but a flutter of red grabbed his attention away.

Lucien caught the flick of Alaric's eyes towards the banner hanging high on the Citadel wall. Emblazoned on it was the same mark that marred Lucien's face.

"For a moment I meant to," Lucien said coldly.

Alaric tried to wrench himself free of Lucien's grip, but Lucien held firm to his hand. With his free hand, Alaric grabbed for the hilt of his sword, sliding it free of its scabbard. He swept its pommel from the scabbard to Lucien's face, trying to knock him back. Lucien dodged to the side and circled behind Alaric, twisting his shoulder and forcing him to his knees. Alaric flailed his sword, sweeping its blade behind his head. Lucien parried the attack with his scepter, sliding the golden arm down the length of Alaric's blade until it clashed against the hand-guard. Lucien forced the point of Alaric's sword into the ground, contorting Alaric's body and rendering him defenseless. Ahead, Alaric's company was running toward them, weapons drawn. Lucien knelt down and whispered into Alaric's ear as they approached, "We can salvage this, it's not too late. Tell them to stand down."

Alaric struggled to regain his footing but Lucien forced him back down.

"It doesn't have to end like this. Tell them to stand down," he said more forcefully.

"We trusted you!" Alaric screamed, fighting to stand, but Lucien held him helpless. "I trusted you!" Alaric cried again in a fervent, boundless rage. He thrashed forward as blue veins wrote their existence over his burning complexion.

Lucien released his grip, stepping slowly back as Alaric lunged forward to his feet. He dropped his scepter and opened his hands, leaving his chest exposed, "Kill me," he said, "kill me then."

Alaric came to a sliding halt, raising his sword above his head, readying himself to plunge the blade into Lucien's heart. He charged forward, his whole body contorted into an instrument of wrath.

It's not too late, he saw the words form on Lucien's mouth, but kept his course, lifting his blade higher still. He was on Lucien in a flash of furious compulsion, and his sword descended in full swing. The flat of the blade glanced across Lucien's shoulder, leaving him unscathed; instead, Alaric's shoulder hammered into Lucien's chest, knocking him flat and gasping onto the stone. Alaric knelt on top of him, pressing hard against his ribcage. Glaring, he held his sword against Lucien's neck. "Take me to them," he breathed through clenched teeth as the rest of his company formed up around them.

"That was my intention," Lucien said softly.

"Carmine, grab his weapon," Alaric ordered, rising from Lucien's chest.

The company stepped back, their weapons still at the ready as Lucien picked himself up from the ground. Their eyes stayed transfixed on the mark engraved in his face.

"Your people are being processed on the far side of the Citadel," Lucien said, coughing. "Once they've been numbered and assigned labor divisions, they will be branded and sent to every corner of Aureus. We have a short window to rescue them before they are lost. I can take you to them."

"It's a trap, Alaric," Carmine said, stepping cautiously towards Lucien. "We don't know what's on the far side of the Citadel, it could be a battalion of Nephilim – it could be anything."

"Or it could be your people," Lucien spoke calmly.

"Shut up," Carmine spat, jabbing the butt of the scepter into Lucien's stomach. Lucien keeled over, coughing loudly.

"Carmine," Alaric ordered him back.

"I could have killed you if I wanted, Alaric. I could have killed all of you," Lucien said, looking up from the ground. His glare circled to each man's eyes until it met Aletheia's. When he felt her amber eyes searching through him he stood, trying to see beyond her veiled face. "What are you?" he asked breathlessly.

"We are come to assist in the final rending of The Veil," Addeus' voice pulsed through Lucien's ears, tossing him in an ocean of pervading sound. "I am Addeus."

"And I am Aletheia," her voice wove itself into the blanket of Addeus' voice, wrapping tightly around Lucien.

"'To God and Truth locked behind its gates,'" Lucien recited as he struggled to stay afloat in the churning ocean of their voices, "'We've come through the noise, the fury, the hate'" he felt his scar prickle beneath their stare, "'it sears, it falls, it seals our fate,'" his voice trailed to a whisper as he looked into Alaric's eyes.

"You will take us to my people."

"'Reanimate,'" Lucien whispered, his eyes glowing with fulfillment. He looked back at Aletheia and Addeus; his scar burned as their gazes met. Fighting through the pain, he maintained his maddened stare; his eyes blistered and welled with tears. A smile creased his face and his breath trembled with laughter as he scoured over Aletheia and Addeus.

Alaric glanced at Orleans and nodded at him to stand Lucien on his feet. Orleans broke from the circle and wrenched Lucien from the ground, turning him from the objects of his crazed stare. He did not struggle but allowed himself to be lifted from the ground and pushed out of the circle. Orleans shoved him forward and Lucien glanced one last time at Aletheia and Addeus before trudging forward and signaling to the men to follow. Alaric was the first in line behind Lucien and the rest followed closely with Aletheia and Addeus bringing up the rear of the group. They walked in silence, wary of their surroundings with every step as the Citadel's shadow grew darker and darker around them. Banners fluttered behind the high, stone walls as companies of Nephilim formed ranks and prepared to receive their master's orders. Lucien cut across the main road to a narrow avenue leading through the district's housing apartments. They twisted through several such streets, avoiding direct sight of the Citadel; soon they were out from beneath its shadow and the sound of pickaxes began to fade into the distance.

"Was there ever a time you felt a friend to me?" Alaric asked, suddenly overwhelmed. "And what about Mark? Was there ever a second when you thought to reconsider? Have you ever spoken a true word to me?"

"Would it matter now, Alaric?" Lucien stopped and faced him, his face sour and sullen. "Would it make any difference at all? Would you believe anything I said now, or are you just looking for a justification to hate me without remorse?"

Alaric looked coldly into his eyes.

"I'd rather not waste my words." Lucien turned to reacquaint himself with the narrow streets leading toward the northern Citadel District.

"You had me set against Nestor – against Titus – thinking that I was looking at the big picture. But that was all trivial – trivial compared to what was really going on. You betrayed us to Aureus."

Lucien's shoulders stood rigid.

"The fight in Bristing," Alaric continued, his voice rising with venom, "your killing those Nephilim, teaching us about The Veil, *The Writ of Narxus*, the felstones – it was to gain our trust to lead your 'exodus' right into the arms of Aureus."

Alaric grabbed for Lucien's shoulder, wrenching him around by his collar. He flung Lucien against a near wall and beat his back against it as the men clustered in the narrow street to watch.

"Enough," Aletheia's voice broke through Alaric's rage, her voice implanted into the marrow of his bones. It seeped into his flesh, relaxing his muscles and loosening his grip on Lucien. He panted and stumbled away, bracing himself against the adjacent wall. The tempering warmth of Aletheia's voice resonated through him.

Lucien stood up and straightened his collar. "Why would I need to kill the Nephilim to earn your trust when I could have let them kill you and led them back to Adullam myself? Why would I play games in the dark –

warning you about Nestor and Titus and Barrius – when I could have left at any time and had every foul creature of Aureus screaming down your halls? Why would I have told you of The Veil or the felstones? Why, when I am a Prince of Aureus, set to receive its throne, would I be here with you?"

Alaric's face drooped into a sickened scowl. "Because you are cruel and inhuman. Because the blood in your veins is fed by the blood of the innocent. Because your soul belongs to that stone. Because you take pleasure in prolonging our suffering with hope. Isn't that what you've always promised? Hope. And isn't that what you're bringing us now? A hope that there's something still to salvage, that somehow there's a way to fix our failures? But this hope will end as every other has ended, with more suffering. You are the silhouette of a man, a shade, a shadow."

Lucien's scar prickled beneath Aletheia and Addeus' light. *But 'I am the light – I am the Lucien!'* Resolute, the words echoed in his mind; words which he had cried from the mountaintop; words which he had cried unto the heavens; words which had never been fulfilled.

"There is much," he said, "that will never be reconciled. I was not always like this – like I am..." he thumped his free hand softly against his chest and looked at the ground, "like I am now. My name was Phillip Rosario, Son of the Narxus, brother of the Indivinate One who ushered the reign of Aureus into the earth. The felstone, I did not find. It was gifted to me by Aureus himself when I was bestowed the name Lucien – the light – the Prince of Aureus. It has given me life now for some three-hundred years."

Lucien's breathing was slow and deliberate, "But it has been a tortured and degenerate existence; my life – from birth – has been rendered unto shadows. I was a shadow in my brother's steps; I was a shadow to my father; I was a shadow to my country; I was a shadow to the Narxus. And in Aureus I sought to renew my existence, to step from the shadows. And so, yes, I did enter Adullam with cruel intent – to find you. But instead I found myself. I found the very same pursuit that was in me – the pursuit of purpose. Adullam was a mirror to my existence, of everything I've ever tried to be – the tyrant, the traitor, the scholar; the leader, the servant, the saint – in the darkness of her halls I found every facet of myself," Lucien choked on his words, "in you, Alaric; in Mark; in Bryan; in Stilguard; in Titus; in Nestor; in everyone." He looked around the circle of men, "And if I could redeem Adullam, it meant I could redeem myself."

He grew silent, his eyes sinking into the cobblestone street. No one spoke for several moments as Alaric picked himself up from the ground.

After a time, Lucien lifted his eyes. "And now," he said, "here I am; and here you are; and there is still a chance to redeem Adullam."

CHAPTER XXXIII

RECLAMATION

Alaric focused into Lucien's eyes, plumbing the depth of his sincerity.

"Follow me or don't," Lucien said as he began to slowly step away, "but I'm going to free your people."

"Stop," Alaric cried, his voice hoarse and hollow.

"Or what?" Lucien countered, his expression sunken and morose. "I am your fulcrum; I am the point on which *everything* hinges."

The weight of indecision set heavily on Alaric, the game of madness and reason; the leap from chance to fate.

"Trust me this one last time," Lucien whispered. The words rang subtle but sharp to Alaric's ears. He did not respond, but with a stone's countenance he stepped forward, sheathing his sword.

Drawing a composed smile, Lucien watched the men fall in line behind their captain. He led quickly, weaving further north around the Citadel. The streets had become narrower and the buildings tighter. The sound of their boots clicking on the cobblestone preceded their way.

"The streets are so empty," Carmine spoke to the unnerving quiet.

"They always are," Lucien responded, bringing the company to a halt, "the city has no soul." He peered around the corner of a building and along another white-streeted canyon of stacked apartments. At the end of the cramped thoroughfare and across a final stretch of road was a low wall cloistering the courtyard of a monolithic structure, its entrance guarded by two gray satyrs. Lucien edged back from around the corner. "It's imperative we remain silent, they won't be looking for us; they're guarding against an attempt at escape, not entry. Your people should still be gathered inside. When we are through the courtyard, fan out along the corridor attached to the main structure and position yourselves outside its entrances. I will enter through the main door. Immediately after I have entered, one of the guards will announce my presence and all will bow. When you hear the guard's call, enter and strike. This must be fluid; this must be absolute. When we cross the road, two of you, Gaverick and someone else – Marion – get out ahead of me and climb the wall-posts on either side of the gate. Drop down and take the satyrs from above. Open the gate and we'll fan out into the corridor."

Without further notice, Lucien whipped around the corner and set quietly off along the final stretch toward the monolith. When he came to the intersection of their street to the main road he stopped, looking back for Gaverick and Marion to continue on. They skirted out from among the line of soldiers and darted across the road toward the monolith. Several anxious seconds passed as they traversed the open air.

Lucien studied the road, searching it up and down, scrutinizing it for any compromising element. Alaric watched his head click mechanically back and forth. He bridled his urge to charge, waiting for Lucien's signal. The men were halfway across the road. Lucien's head ticked like a timepiece. Alaric could feel his heart pulsing in his head. The men reached the wall; Lucien sprinted from cover. Release. Alaric charged; his men followed.

Silently they swept forward as Gaverick and Marion mounted the wall. Alaric was midway to the courtyard when a pebble hurtled between his feet, kicked up by one of the soldiers. A panicked whimper escaped from Carmine as it skipped across the ground toward the gate. With a final twirling bound, the stone clashed against the curling bands of iron, igniting a frenzy of hisses from the satyrs as they lurched into action, wheeling around to face the noise and the onrushing soldiers.

Gaverick and Marion crested the wall, rising up with a final, fluent vault. Setting their feet, they drew their swords and leapt out over the courtyard. In a flash of flesh and iron they descended upon the satyrs, landing on the beasts' backs and driving swords between their shoulders. With muted screams, the satyr's collapsed beneath the soldiers' weight. Their gray skin corrugated with scarlet veins weaving out from around the blades in their backs. Gaverick left his sword buried beneath the satyr's skin as he dashed to unlatch the iron gate; its body withered to a pile of ash.

Wasting neither words nor time, Lucien rushed through the open gate, nodding to Marion and Gaverick. The procession of soldiers followed closely behind as Marion and Gaverick fell in line at the rear. The monolith rose higher above them, its shadow looming over the courtyard path. At last they came to the breezeway surrounding the foot of the monolith. The company fanned out silently along the entranceways and waited for Lucien to make his entrance.

He stiffened his back and stepped forward, striding into an unlit passage. Alaric followed closely behind, stepping into Lucien's shadow as light bled down the tunnel from ahead. As the passage brightened, Lucien began to feel Alaric's strained breath on his neck; the central room was now in view. Between its walls was held the whole of Adullam, crowded in a silent mob. They were lined facing a narrow portal, awaiting entry into a second chamber. Outside the portal stood a Malebranche bent over an ironbound tome, registering each man, woman, and child who passed through.

At the far end of the chamber Lucien caught sight of Mark, shivering as he disappeared through the portal into the next room. His step faltered. Another Malebranche, circling above the crowd of prisoners, spotted Lucien. The black-winged demon raised a ram's horn to its lips; sharp notes spilled from its hollowed core. Like a stone plunged into water, the siren's sound dropped to the floor and splashed over the crowd, knocking them to their knees.

Two satyrs guarded each of the five doorways from the central chamber, barring even the whim of escape for the prisoners. At the siren's call, each bowed to the Prince of Aureus. Alaric stepped from the shadows behind Lucien. With a swift flick, Alaric's sword took the bowed head of the nearest satyr. Hearing the cauterizing hiss, the second satyr looked up. Alaric drove his blade into its chest, forcing the satyr onto its back. He pulled his sword free as the creature collapsed.

From each entrance Alaric's men emerged. In one fluent strike, the satyrs were rendered to ash on the chamber floor. Only the two

Malebranche remained. The first one dropped into the throng of prisoners from above. Raising crow-black wings, it surged forward, sweeping a path through the crowd with its long, iron hook. It burst forth from among them, impelled for Alaric, a trail of prisoners left dead in its wake.

Raising his sword, Alaric braced himself, but suddenly the Malebranche was whipped away, a blur of light intercepting its path. Addeus caught the demon with his scavenged hook and swung it around, slingshotting it into a wall. The heavy stone cracked at its impact. The Malebranche fought back, pushing against the wall and lifting itself over Addeus' head, beating its wings to force him to the ground. Together, Alaric and his men converged upon the fray. Along with them came the other Malebranche, grabbing its hook and soaring out from behind the podium. It raised the point of its hook to drive into Addeus' chest. As it swung down, Aletheia's sword caught the curve of its iron hook. The demon banked to the left, gliding on its wings above her head, twisting the sword from her hand. The tip of its hook slashed across her face, tearing through her veil and marring her rose-gold face with a shallow black scar. The Malebranche glided to a halt across the stone floor and squared its stance with her.

Aletheia's veil fell to the floor in a flutter of white and her hair unfurled from beneath her hood. The Malebranche charged again, thrusting itself forward with a great heave of its black wings. It swept Aletheia from the ground and sent her sprawling past Addeus. She hurtled through the gathering of soldiers, knocking half of them across the room. Meanwhile, the other had tackled Addeus to the floor, disarming him. It swept back its wings and gritted its teeth, hook held high to strike. Addeus' eyes met the Malebranche's, a thin trace of vapor rising from them. Suddenly his body erupted. A golden sphere emanated out from around Addeus, engulfing the Malebranche in light.

Shrieking, the Malebranche reeled into the air, falling back from the consuming light and onto Carmine's blade. It stuttered to silence as the tip of Carmine's sword came sticking through its chest. Slowly it slid down the blade and into a heap of hot ash at Carmine's feet.

One Malebranche remained. Fueled by the loss of its companion, it charged for Carmine. As it reared back its hook to strike, Carmine feinted to the side, misdirecting the Malebranche's sweep. The hook grazed his shoulder and the demon tumbled forward. Off-balance, the Malebranche slid into the wall. A crack resounded through the chamber as it broke a wing. The demon tried to fly as the soldiers surrounded it. It stretched its wings into the air, but collapsed as its right wing convulsed out of control. Frantically, the Malebranche flayed its long hook back and forth, fending off the soldier's approach.

As the hook swished past Alaric, he lunged forward. It countered and brought the shaft of its hook down against Alaric's back. At this, Alaric's men pressed in, thrusting their swords towards the Malebranche. Eight blades cut through the creature, leaving it as another pile of ash scattered across the chamber floor.

Alaric picked himself up from the ground, coughing as he breathed out. He collapsed to the ground, trying to heave the ash from his lungs. Fighting to pick himself up, he propped his back against the wall. Looking around wide-eyed, he numbered his men. Lucien was missing. He stood and scoured over the crowded prisoners. From the portal that led to the second chamber there was a clamber of voices and a woman screamed. Alaric dashed toward the sound, sputtering up a fog of ash from his lungs. He fell in the entryway of the portal, looking helplessly down the darkened tunnel. The scene spun in his head as silhouetted figures struggled through an orange glow.

In the threshold of the second chamber, a satyr raised a hot branding iron into the air. Beneath it stood Mark, crying and fearful, bent over to receive the brand. Lucien lunged from the shadow of the portal just as the satyr brought the iron down at boy. Alaric heard the ring of Lucien's blade singing out from the scepter and the clash of iron against it as Lucien parried the brand. Mark squealed and ran from view, his arms flailing behind him. The satyr stepped into full view. Its branding iron painted yellow circles in the smoke as it wielded it against Lucien like a sword. A parry, a quick feint, a thrust, the satyr crumbled to the floor and another two pounced into view.

They circled Lucien, crouched and ready to spring. The satyrs orbited Lucien like moons, whirling slowly closer on the concaving fabric of space until, after a dizzying dance, they were in range to strike. Leaping from their oval path, together the satyrs fell on their prey. Lucien darted out from beneath their clawing reach. Missing their target, the satyrs' hooves staggered on the stone floor. Lucien riposted, thrusting the blade of his scepter into one of the beasts. It collapsed to the floor, tripping the second satyr. It sprawled helplessly at Lucien's feet. Whimpering hysterically, it tried to stand but Lucien held his blade at its neck. The satyr's goat-like ears flicked as it lifted its black eyes to Lucien's. It snarled and Lucien drove the point of his blade into its chest.

"Lucien."

He looked up. Alaric stood breathing hoarsely as he leaned against the edge of the wall.

"They were receiving the mark," Lucien said, picking the iron from a pile of ash and dousing it in a bucket. He held the cooled brand up for Alaric to see. There was the same emblem carved into Lucien's face; a single flame struck through by a crown-ringed sword and beset by two fanning wings – the left adorned with an eye; the right, a rook.

Alaric looked to the small group huddled together in a corner. They were filthy and barely clothed, covered in dirt and sweat and ash. The tops of their garments had been ripped from them to receive the brand. Among them was Joanna Stilguard, the Steward's wife. She stepped out shivering, hugging her arms across her bare chest, with streaks through the dirt on her hunger-thinned face. Bursting into tears she turned, showing Alaric the stigma burned into her left shoulder. Alaric exhaled a deep breath, placing his fingers softly around the scar.

She turned back to face him, her eyes still brimming tears, "We were the first to be marked," she whimpered, "fifteen of us, except for the boy." She cast her eyes down to Mark peering out from behind a pair of legs.

"He's the one that betrayed us to them," she continued, looking past Alaric.

Alaric half turned toward Lucien whose grief-stricken gaze was riveted on the hidden figure of Mark.

"He murdered Nestor," Joanna said darkly. "and then Aureus came with this Malik creature and," Joanna's voice trailed into a panicked stuttering. She began to scrape her fingernails into her shoulders. Alaric reached for her, grabbing her hands and pressing them flush against her skin. He tried to quiet her.

"It's okay now," he said. "It's okay," he said again and again, soothing her sorrow. "I don't know all the things Lucien's done, but he did not kill Nestor. I don't know who did. Nevertheless it was deserved."

"What?" Joanna raised question-filled eyes.

"I wanted to tell you before, but with the riots and Titus' grab for power; with Lucien and I declared treasonous – I couldn't. When Nestor took the position of interim Steward, he never intended to give it back. He was responsible for your husband's death. For weeks he and Titus had been plotting for the Stewardship. But then Nestor was murdered and of course Titus was quick to blame Lucien and I..." the cruel truth dawned somberly on Alaric, "his only opposition to power.

"Titus," Alaric whispered, gently pushing Joanna away. "Where is Titus?"

Chapter XXXIV

REVENGE

"Valerius!" Alaric's call ruptured from the portal through the main chamber. Alaric stormed into view, his face taut with rage. "Titus Valerius!" he called again. Among the crowd a circle formed, spreading out from the acting Steward. Alaric looked over the parting masses and paced in towards them. He drew the dagger from Orleans belt and loosened his own as he passed, allowing his sword to drop with a ring to the stone floor. Alaric carved his way into the empty circle around Titus. He emerged into the open and the crowd closed in behind him. Titus stood warily at the edge of the crowd furthest from Alaric. Grimacing as he approached, Alaric planted his foot into Titus' chest and sent him sliding across the floor.

He tossed Orleans' dagger at Titus feet, and drew his own from behind his back. "For the betrayal of Roderick Stilguard and the murder of Marcus Nestor," he shouted, pointing with his dagger as he paced around the crowd, "I declare Titus Valerius a *traitor*!"

"I am Steward," Titus' voice grated the air.

"He has betrayed all of you," Alaric yelled to the crowd, "in a vain attempt to merit power!"

He bent low over Titus, "You are nothing. Now get up."

Titus sat up and reached for Orleans' dagger, his eyes never wavering from Alaric's.

"Enough," Addeus voice blanketed the chamber, seeping through the crowd like a resin, sealing Alaric and Titus in an intangible amber. "There is no righteous cause in this; you part from the divine."

"Then make no mistake that I am man," Alaric's voice rippled through the molasses like atmosphere as he fought his way toward Titus. Slowly the resin of Addeus' command receded, and Alaric felt his limbs freeing.

Titus jumped to his feet, dagger in hand, and the two men circled, gauging one another's stance. Stepping forward, Titus pretended to stumble and lunged with his dagger. Alaric countered the strike with his forearm, deflecting the blade over his head. He twisted Titus' arm away from his body and hit him hard beneath the chest with his unarmed hand. Titus staggered back, coughing, as Alaric riposted, slicing his opponent beneath the arm. The glancing blow sent Alaric off balance; Titus grabbed the back of his head and forced him toward the ground, bending his knee into Alaric's gut. Alaric rolled to the floor as Titus brought his dagger down. Alaric wheeled across the stone and picked himself up, narrowly dodging the attack.

Overly aggressive, Titus lunged again, swiping his dagger from the side. Alaric dodged just beyond his reach and grabbed Titus' arm, carrying his momentum through and throwing him off balance. Titus twisted himself around and raised his elbow to Alaric's face. Alaric deflected the blow again with his forearm. In a fluent motion, Titus tried to swing his dagger up and into Alaric's chest. The blade sliced across the top of Alaric's skin, drawing a trace of blood, but the offensive left Titus' back exposed. Alaric leaned in and buried his dagger in the traitor's back. He released the blade and let Titus fall to his face.

Aletheia emerged at the edge of the hushed crowd, her eyes crestfallen at the sight of Titus' death. Her natural glow dampened to a shade of muted bronze. "Why must man always be tainted to know what is pure?" She asked, her eyes an amber lament of Titus' cold body. "Why must you test the things you have been taught and turn innocent understanding into the cynicism of experience? You make your lives so difficult trying to prove everything to yourselves."

Aletheia's voice perforated Alaric with regret. He stooped over Titus' body and reached to retrieve the dagger from his back. Then stepping over the body, he lifted Titus' hand to twist Orleans' dagger from his fingers.

"I don't wan' it," Orleans' gruff voice called through the crowd. "'S got your blood on it, sir." He emerged from the ranks of onlookers and nodded. From behind him Alyssa slipped into view. Alaric felt himself choking. Poised with her elbows tucked against her chest and her hands cupped over her nose and mouth, Alyssa maintained her distance. She stood at the edge of the arena of people surrounding her dead cousin; a muffled whine rang from between her fingers.

Alaric looked at her, crestfallen. He stepped from around Titus and let Alyssa fall to her knees beside his body, her wine-dark hair draping his face like a sanguine veil. Her delicate arms cradled his body as she lifted his head from the floor and pressed her forehead against his own, allowing her tears to drain down his cheeks.

Hidden among the observers, Alaric spotted Barrius peering over another man's shoulder. Feeling eyes upon him, Barrius looked up into the face of his adversary. His gaze locked with Alaric's and he faded back from sight into the crowd. Alaric heard Alyssa draw several sharp breaths through her teeth, warding back her tears. He looked down at her as she lay her cousin's head softly back to the floor. Running her fingers through her dark hair, she sat back on her knees, looking at Alaric. The rims of her eyes were red and swollen; her cheeks were streaked with dirt and tears, her face contoured with sorrow.

Alaric walked unsteadily to her, his eyes pleading forgiveness. He stretched his arm out, lending his hand to help her from the ground. His flesh ran hot with the feeling of foolishness – 'tainted,' as Aletheia had said. Extending his hand was all he could think to do.

Alyssa's gaze wandered up the length of Alaric's arm, her eyes crescentic with relief, or sorrow, or wrath, or a combination of each. "Is it true?" she asked, her voice hollow and distressed. "That he betrayed Stilguard I mean, and killed Nestor."

Alaric swallowed and his gaze fell onto his fingertips. "It is," he choked out.

Alyssa looked back over her cousin's corpse. A pool of blood collected around his body. Alyssa lifted her hand to Alaric's, sliding her fingers along his palm and up around his wrist. In turn, his fingers closed around her slender arm and he gently lifted her from the ground.

"I'm sorry," she gasped, raising her free hand to her face. She clenched her eyes from further tears. She drew closer to Alaric and let her head collapse against his shoulder. Alaric ran his fingers through her hair, cradling her head where it lay.

Alaric's body fell numb. His eyes widened, feeling the path of every choice, the weight of every decision, and the purpose of every relationship converge at once to make the way to the future.

"The time has come," Alaric said, braking from his trance, "that we as a people stand against Aureus in a united purpose. That we rise against the evil that has kept us enslaved to cavern walls and barred us from the light of life. The time has come to render ourselves unto faith and see the veil broken that blinds our eyes. The whole of creation cries out. Not only so, but we ourselves cry as we hope for our redemption. And in this hope we are saved; but hope that is seen is not hope at all, and so you must give yourself unto this last faith for, we know that in all things, The Shaddai works for those who have been called according to His purpose!

"So, I am convinced that neither death nor demons, neither present nor future, neither height nor depth – nor anything else in all of creation – can separate us from a free life. We stand now against Aureus and, though we fight her demons, so too do we fight our own demons – demons of doubt and fear that would steal our hope away. But you have not been given a spirit to make you a slave to fear, but a spirit to know your purpose in The Shaddai! So we stand now against Aureus, but we do not stand alone. Fate has led us to this place to fight – to fight until we are free, and that is what we will do."

Panting, Alaric's chest rose and fell against the warmth of Alyssa's body still cradled against him. Softly she lifted her head and kissed the crook of his neck. He felt her body pulling away and he relaxed his grip around her. She glided back, her eyes still filled with the dolor of her cousin's death, but her lips affectionate. Alaric watched her melt away into the crowd, as a kinetic zeal charged through them, it was time to move.

Alaric waded into the crowd toward the monolith's entrance. The people parted for him as he passed, cheering on his advance. When Alaric emerged from the crowd, his company of loyal eight awaited there along with Addeus, Aletheia, and Lucien. Among them also was Joanna and the others rescued from the branding chamber, clothed now in flowing white garments skirted above their knees. The robe-like apparel drooped around the back of their left shoulders to reveal their brands.

"The garb of Aureus' slaves, to remind them of their oppression," Lucien said frowning at the drape in the shoulders. At the sound of Lucien's voice, Mark peeked his head out from the rear of the group, his terrified eyes fixed on Lucien.

"You know these people can't fight," Lucien continued.

"I know," Alaric returned, "but *we* can fight, and they need to know we will fight – to defend them and to free them. But someone must lead them to freedom."

Slowly, Alaric turned, extending the dagger in his hand to Joanna. "You are a Stilguard," he said, "the last of their lineage."

"But only by marriage," she protested.

"That is no less affinity than blood. The Stilguards have guided our people for generations. Let that hold true for this last step. We can escort you to the rim of the Citadel District, and from there you must lead them into the southern mountains."

Hand trembling, Joanna reached out and grasped the hilt of the dagger.

Alaric smiled softly after her and turned to his soldiers. "Carmine, Gaverick," he ordered, "scout outside; check to see if we are clear to leave."

The two saluted and disappeared through a side passage to the courtyard. As they departed, Alaric turned to address the crowd and Mark began to sneak through the forest of legs in which he had hidden himself. Lucien caught the boy's creeping from the corner of his eye. He knelt down. Timidly, Mark peered out from around the skirt of one of his white-robed companions. Meeting Lucien's watchful eyes, Mark turned red and darted his head back from view.

"Mark," Lucien whispered, his voice plaintive and pleading, but Mark kept himself hidden from Lucien's sight.

"Mark," he pleaded again softly.

The boy leaned slowly out until he could only very narrowly see Lucien. Suddenly his barricade stepped forward, leaving Mark in Lucien's plain sight. He squealed and fainted. Lurching forward, Lucien rushed to grab Mark up from the ground and the others spread out to give him space to breathe. Lucien picked the boy up and set him onto his feet. He looked dizzily around – at everything but Lucien.

"Are you alright, Mark?" Lucien asked, releasing the boy.

"No," Mark complained, clasping his hands at his stomach and squeezing his elbows against his sides. "I'm in a silly dress. I look like a girl."

"No," Lucien consoled him, "you look like a Roman."

"What's a Row Man?"

"The Romans were a strong and fierce people," he reassured Mark, "and at one time, they ruled the known world."

"In dresses?" Mark lifted an incredulous eye.

Lucien laughed and nodded earnestly.

"Where is your mask?" he asked, looking at Lucien for the first time.

"I lost it, but I don't need it anymore."

"Oh," Mark exclaimed, "because your scar is gone?"

"What?" Lucien asked, his voice strained with confusion as he lifted a hand to his face. Where the mark had carved across his skin was now nothing. His face was smooth, his skin fresh. Bewildered, Lucien looked back at Addeus. Both he and Aletheia watched him. Beneath their glow, Lucien felt a slight prickle on his cheek and raised his hand to feel the last evidence of his scar dissolve into his skin. "Yes, Mark," he whispered, his eyes still fixed on Addeus, "because my scar is gone."

CHAPTER XXXV

FLIGHT

Heavy-breathed, Gaverick suddenly reappeared through the empty passage leading to the monolith's courtyard. He signaled to Alaric, nodding that the way was clear.

"It's time!" Alaric exclaimed, and the crowd was filled with a fervor of movement, rallying into a singular organism as it flowed from the monolith. Throngs of people came sieving through the exits and spilling into the courtyard. At its edge, hidden behind the low wall, waited Carmine, his eyes still scouting over the main road. Alaric came behind him and peered past the wall.

"It's all clear, sir," Carmine said, his voice trembling in suspense.

Alaric clapped his shoulder and stepped into the open, surveying both sides of the road. He was followed distantly by Joanna, her white gown rippling in the fresh breeze; Lucien, with his hand rested round Mark's shoulder; Aletheia and Addeus, their veils and hoods removed to reveal coiling locks of gold-hued hair; and the loyal eight, their fates bonded to Alaric's since the fight in Bristing. In all their wakes rolled the tide of Adullam, cascading from the monolith like a sudden onrush of melted snow down a mountaintop. At length they had all filtered from the monolith and into the streets of Aureus. Alaric, at the counsel of Lucien, led them left, away from the Citadel. For a quarter of a mile they followed this road until, making an acute right turn, their path slanted to the Southwest.

The way was guided by the ever present silence, an unnerving – unnatural – emptiness. Soon, however, the distant sound of pickaxes resounded down the lonely streets as they approached the quarry, though it came as little relief to the disquieted atmosphere.

"All of Aureus is in preparation," Lucien spoke to only Alaric, reading the malaise carved into his expression.

"Preparation?" Alaric asked, returning the whisper. "What preparation?" an overborne anxiety bled through Alaric's tone.

"You don't know? Is it not why those two have come?" Lucien asked with a sidelong nod towards Aletheia and Addeus.

"The Tree of Life," Alaric whispered, nearly panic-stricken. "Aureus knows?"

"It is the reason that Aureus exists!" came Lucien's exasperated response. "The whole design rests on claiming the Tree."

The sound of pickaxes falling against granite walls intruded the air. Alaric guided his host down another road, turning directly south where his path had been reunited with Lucien's. The shadow of the Citadel loomed formidably above them again as they made for the edge of the district. The sight of its border came slowly into view. Brimmed with hope, Alaric craned his neck to see further ahead. Suddenly, from the pit of the quarry, a black-winged figure rose into the sky above them. The Malebranche's wings fanned out, gliding on a current of air. It raised a horn to its lips and loosed a deep bellowing call above the city.

Alaric felt the horn rattle him from the inside out. A thousand gasps and all of Adullam had turned to face the sound. Three more times the Malebranche blasted its horn, oppressing the air in a deafening wave. With the third bellow, the ground began to shake. Black banners rustled behind the Citadel wall. The Nephilim were assembling.

"I can slow them down," Lucien said.

Alaric ripped his attention away from the circling Malebranche.

"What?" Alaric said. "No, we have to keep moving."

"I am still their Prince. I may be able to delay them, give your people a little more time, but you must run."

"No," Alaric repeated

"Mark, stay close to Joanna," Lucien said, ruffling the boy's hair. Wide-eyed, Mark seized the hem of Joanna's skirt with an iron-wrought fist.

Lucien looked at Alaric. "Run," he said again and was swept back into Adullam's crowd.

The people's resolve had faltered to mayhem. Once more, the Malebranche's horn sounded, this time its call answered by the pound of drums from behind the wall, booming with the rhythm of the Nephilim's march. The first of their black banners moved from behind the wall. Another Malebranche appeared from the quarry hole. Alaric staggered back, the swell of his people rising with fear. They began stampeding toward Alaric. He heard his men shouting for him. He stepped away, turning to run.

Joanna, Mark, Aletheia, Addeus, and the others had already begun taking pronounced steps towards the edge of the district. As Alaric gained them, they joined his sprint. The Malebranche dropped from their heights, hideous cries pervading the air. They swooped down just above the crowd, gliding and laughing to one another. Suddenly one dove into the crowd, vanishing for a moment before it came bursting back into the air, a man dangling from its hook. The other Malebranche laughed and twisted through the air, diving then to sweep its own hook through the crowd. As it jettisoned back up, its horn erupted, breaking apart the stampede like shattered glass.

Arising from behind the black banners came another two Malebranche, and then a third from the East. They all five came together, high above the fleeing masses. They folded their wings and dropped like arrows towards the earth. Planing out from their dive, the Malebranche swept through the crowd with their hooks, scattering people left and right. At the front of the company, Alaric glanced over his shoulder. The five black-winged beasts set low on the horizon, hurtling after them. Fields dropped to the ground as a Malebranche swept its hook down from behind him. It grazed his side as he rolled and caught under Carmine's arm. Seized up, Carmine went flailing through the air. With a cry he disappeared through the roof of a house, a curl of dust mushrooming from the impact.

After their first pass, the Malebranche circled back, tearing once more through the mass of Adullam's stampeding citizens. Ever present was the call of their horns, guiding the Nephilim's march. Alaric's company regrouped, clustering back together as they came to the end of the district.

The road from the Citadel emptied into the barren plane they had first crossed in coming to the city. The Malebranche closed in, flying low behind the men, forcing them out into the open.

"Take them southeast!" Alaric yelled, signaling to Joanna. She nodded, eyes bursting to cry as she raised her dagger and veered right, steering the masses from Alaric's wake. Mark slowed back from the lead group with her, and they both dropped to the front of Adullam's citizens.

As Alaric's party stepped out from the cobblestone streets of the district, the Malebranche cusped them in. Two of the demons swept forward to cut across Alaric's way through the empty field. He and the others slid to a halt in the dusty plane. The remaining Malebranche encircled them, leaving the masses for the Nephilim's sport.

Drawing their swords, Alaric and his men formed together, tightly concentric to the Malebranche. Laughter spilled from one of the demon's lips. "Fools of men," it said with a sharp-toothed smile. Its wings shot high above its head, as they thrashed down, the Malebranche came surging in at the company. With a practiced swipe, Gaverick raised his sword to parry the demon's hook. Their iron collided with a sharp ring and Gaverick's blade slid down the length of the Malebranche's hook, severing off its hand. The hook fell to the ground and the demon lashed back, reeling with rage and confusion.

"Widen out!" Alaric called, and the company advanced against the Malebranche, spreading out their stance. The demons swung their hooks, trying to keep them bridled in. Gaverick stepped further, charging out of rank. He swung his sword at the wounded Malebranche but it dodged back with a rush of its wings. Suddenly Gaverick was swept to the ground, another Malebranche having grabbed him with its hook. With a palpable thud his head bounced against the dirt.

"No!" Blair cried, and jumped to Gaverick's aid. Their formation broke. The Malebranche cut between them, dividing their company into clusters. Gaverick rolled onto his stomach. Head pounding like the Nephilim's drums, he picked himself from the ground.

In a pillar of wing-borne dust, the Malebranche spun over Blair's head, landing behind him. The shadow of its hook fell over Blair's back. His breath fell short and his knees went weak. The shadow lifted higher. Suddenly it was gone. Gaverick grabbed the shaft of the Malebranche's hook, catching it before it came down on Blair. Quick to their side, Barron charged the demon, running it through with his sword.

Another horn called through the air. One of the Malebranche had taken flight to summon the Nephilim. Its horn bellowed out again; the black flags changed their course. Three Malebranche remained in the fight, encircled now between the men. One of the demon's hooks locked with Addeus' blade. It smiled, licking its teeth, and rolled its hook, sending Addeus' sword somersaulting out of his hand. Staggering forward, Addeus stamped the hook into the ground and leapt at the Malebranche, grabbing it around the neck. He pulled himself close against the demon's body, pressing its face against his own. The gold-hued aura erupted from Addeus, engulfing the Malebranche and blowing the others back from around him. The remaining two Malebranche screamed and took flight. Another thunderous horn sounded as they fled.

Alaric leapt after one of the Malebranche, sinking his dagger into its thigh. The demon beat its wings, surging higher into the air and Alaric's grip slipped from the dagger. The Malebranche screeched and flailed upwards through the sky, wrenching the dagger from its leg and carrying it away through the clouds.

Alaric picked himself up from the ground, breathing in the small victory. But the flight of the Malebranche faded into a horizon of black banners. The Nephilim marched swiftly towards them. Orleans' leaned down, "Well 'ere 't is, sir," he said, helping Alaric from the ground.

Alaric held his sword loosely by its hand-guard, letting the tip rest against the earth as he gazed over the black legions. "Where is Lucien?" he whispered with barely a breath.

"Alaric," he heard his name called. "Alaric," he heard again and turned apprehensively around.

"Look," Marion said pointing to the Southeast, "a wall."

As if born in an instant from the bowels of the earth, there stood a large wall set against the mountains. Cracks wove throughout the age-ruddied, sandstone siding as its top crumbled in tapering waves of weather wrought erosion. It formed a perfectly square border with a single entry on the near side, barred by a rusted iron gate hanging loose on its hinges. Alaric looked back at the encroaching Nephilim. "We'll draw them in," he said, lifting the point of his sword to the giants. "Hold steady until I give the word to fall back behind the wall; we must keep their focus away from the citizens."

The Three Malebranche still circled above; their horns bellowed again in unison, directing the Nephilim's advance. It did not take the giants long to gain ground on the company. Their fierce approach darkened the skies as the Malebranche screeched in mirth-ridden song.

"Go," Alaric whispered the single word as the Nephilim began to shake the ground beneath him. The men hardly waited to hear the order. They ran with full force towards the aged wall, making immediately for the entrance and forcing their way through its rusted gate. Addeus and Aletheia's ardent gazes locked on the circling Malebranche; they remained with Alaric as he stepped slowly backwards. He passed through the gate and stopped, standing statued at the entrance. As the enemy encroached, grains of sandstone began shaking from the wall. Alaric took another step through the gate and collided with one of his men. Turning, Alaric found all of his men staring away, their faces a mural of awe.

Before them were the brown, skeletal remains of a once flourishing forest, since choked of life. Rotting trees and decaying flora spanned around them, stretching their way along the wall and wrapping around to encompass an oval clearing. A small stone path, overgrown by moss and dead leaves, guided the way to it.

Alone at the center of the oval, stood two trees. One tree, a bold sepia color, was like the rest in the forest – its beauty faded, branches thin and withered, fruit rotten on the ground. The other, its boughs laden with silver-green leaves, stood as the last life in the forest. The skin of its twisting trunk shown like a white moon, and its roots wove through the earth to every edge of the clearing. Addeus took the first step towards the clearing with Aletheia following closely behind. They glided down the ancient path and slowly the others were allured to follow. One by one they took the stone path until only Alaric remained, his gaze enraptured. He felt himself being drawn in. His foot slid forward, and then his other.

Aletheia stepped lightly over the roots leading closer to the Tree. She stopped short of it, holding her arms out towards the moonlit trunk. Her hair fell like curls of golden ribbon down her back as she lifted her head towards the branches.

Alaric's men formed a semicircle some ways away with Addeus, but Alaric was not satisfied to stay behind. He walked towards Aletheia, clambering over the Tree's roots, trying not to break his gaze. A thrilling tremor passed through Alaric as he drew nearer, the sensation growing with each step he took. There was a type of foreboding magnetism that took hold, repelling him yet inciting him all the same. The Tree's fruit hung like enormous tears, poised to weep but unable to fall. They became like mirrors, overwhelming Alaric with sadness and longing. He stood suspended in the Tree's magnetism, yearning to be rid of his misery, yearning for the tears to be set free.

He reached slowly up, wanting to release the tears, wanting to feel life flowing from his eyes. They hung within his grasp now, ripe and full; he could nearly feel them, preparing the fall into a new existence – a new life. They glistened in his eyes. A new life was ripe for his taking. His fingers wavered at the base of a fruit, and slowly he withdrew his hand, stepping away from the Tree. He averted his eyes, knowing the tears perfect purpose to joy rather than sorrow.

Aletheia's eyes smiled caramel and brown.

"I thought we were to distract them from it," said Alaric, looking up at her, "not bring them to it. Did you know the Tree was here? In Aureus."

Alaric was answered by the deepening echo of drums through the garden and the shadow of a Malebranche looming above. Its wings stretched across the sun as it circled through the sky and turned back towards the darkening cloud of black banners. There, it was joined by the other seven of its kin and together they spiraled down from sight on the other side of the wall. The banners stretched back in countless ranks and as they came into formation, the drumming ceased.

Leon turned from the storm cloud, tilting his gaze towards Alaric beneath the Tree. "What now?" he asked. "These walls won't hold them."

Together the men turned, looking to Alaric. He kept his gaze steady through the gate, his shoulders high, his countenance calculated. A small figure emerged from among the Nephilim, making its way towards the gate.

"We fight," Alaric said as he stepped down from the Tree. He walked forward through his men. "and we pray that Providence comes through."

"And if He doesn't?"

Alaric paused, his eye keen on the still approaching figure. "Then we've done our part," he said at last. "Wait here."

CHAPTER XXXVI

THE SEARING VEIL

He left his men and strode forward, picking his way though the stone path towards the gate. At the gate Alaric paused again. The approaching figure was a man, bent to the side with the effort of dragging a limp body. Carefully, Alaric stepped around the iron gate and beyond the wall. The other man stopped several feet short of Alaric, dropping the body at his side. The man's hand writhed up his chest and slithered around his neck like a snake.

"I don't believe we had the pleasure of meeting when I came to visit Adullam. It's a shame," he said, "I've heard so much about you." A sinister gleam spread across his eyes like a smile.

"I am Malik," he continued. "Lovely walls you've got there, but I worry they won't hold." With a waving gesture, Malik pointed to the Nephilim towering behind him. Blood leaked from the smile on his lips; his hand slithered up to wipe it away.

"We'll take our chances," Alaric replied solemnly.

"Will you?" Malik said. His smile dropped; the thumb of his writhing hand caressed his ring finger. "Arrogant!" he spat. "Prideful! Lost! And what is it you think, there behind your wall? That He's coming for you? That it's you-u-u-u who's meant to be here – of all the pitiful creations of this world."

The mirth returned to Malik's eyes. "But I can see inside of you," he sang. "You think you are different from me. You are no different. We are the same, and come the end you will know it."

The slightest tilt in his head, Alaric glared steadily at Malik.

Malik chuckled, cracking his neck to the side. "Still nothing to say? Well. I believe you left this in one of my friends," he said as he retrieved a dagger from his waist and waved it in Alaric's face. "It would seem fitting that I return the favor."

Malik smiled and reached down for the body at his side. He held it high enough for Alaric to catch a last glimpse of Lucien's bloodied face before burying the dagger into Lucien's chest. Releasing him, Malik let the weight of his body force the blade in further as he collapsed against the ground.

Coughing, Alaric dropped to his knees scrambling forward to roll Lucien onto his back.

"Now look what you've done," Malik whispered, his voice corroded with wrath. "Fore-witness your fate."

He stepped dizzily back from Alaric, rocking his head from shoulder to shoulder, humming as he went.

"Maelstrom!" Malik yelled, back within the shadow of the Nephilim. The named giant stepped forward from the ranks. "The game is yours. Give them some time to wither and squirm before you carry-out our Lord Aureus' orders."

Maelstrom's thunderous laugh rolled through the air like the gathering of a storm.

Alaric lifted Lucien into his arms, fighting to heave his limp weight over his shoulder. Staggering back towards the walls, Alaric fought Malik out of his mind. His words had planted a seed in Alaric's imagination, creeping tendrils of doubt choking what hope was inside him. When Alaric reached the gate, Gaverick and Michael came from behind the wall, lifting Lucien from his shoulders. They brought him to the clearing and lay him among the tall roots beneath The Tree.

"Let his sacrifice not be wasted," Alaric said, his voice shaking. There was no more room for sorrow, no more time for fear, no more hope for escape. "No more honorable a friend has lived or died. We stand because he took our fall and, though we stand at the very threshold of death, we stand. Fight until your end – free men, as such this age has not known. The Shaddai keep you."

A horn erupted and the drums began to pound. The Nephilim's advance had begun. At Alaric's orders, the men scattered into the trees to take the Nephilim by surprise as they funneled down the path towards the middle of the garden. Hastening into the nearby groves, the men concealed themselves beneath the dead foliage. No sooner had they hidden than the sandstone walls came crashing down. Several Nephilim stampeded through the gaps, bounding over the rubble and into the trees. They tore through the outer edge of the forest, their heads towering amongst the heights of the trees. Tangled high in the skeletal maze of branches, however, the beasts did not see the men as they lay in wait to strike.

The Nephilim's rampage slowed. They began to look towards the clearing. Uprooting what trees stood in its way, one Nephilim made for the stone path leading to the center of the forest. As it stepped into full view, Alaric and his men struck, darting from beneath their cover. Together they cut at the beast's legs, dropping it to its knees. With a shout, Gaverick leapt onto the giant's back and, climbing up, drove his sword into its neck. The Nephilim crashed to the ground, its pain-ridden roars sending the other Nephilim into a fury. One by one they came through the narrow path, and just as swiftly as the first, they fell at the hand of Alaric's men. But the assault was ceaseless.

When the first company of Nephilim had been slain, more came. Soon the stone path was congested with their bodies and the Nephilim came in pairs, tearing trees from the ground and hurtling them through the forest. They came smashing through all sides of the walls, ripping up every tree they could get their arms around, but the men remained ever elusive – skirting just beyond the Nephilim's reach. The further the Nephilim pursued the men through the trees, the more fell victim to their blades until soon there were more giants lying on the ground than the trees they had overturned. By now the men had broken into groups of two, disbursing themselves throughout the trees to meet the Nephilim on all fronts.

Addeus and Aletheia, along with Gaverick and Marion, kept to the western portion of the garden while the other groups kept east. Alaric and Barron formed the front, maneuvering within the northernmost section of the garden. As a Nephilim emerged from one of the breaches in the wall, the pair lay in wait among the felled trees. Large and cumbersome, the giant struggled through the twisted heap of trees. As it tried to maneuver unsteadily through the forest, Alaric and Barron leapt from hiding and darted across the tops of fallen trees to gain it. Taking the Nephilim by surprise, they brought it to its knees. No sooner had they killed it than another giant came roaring through the wall. Swiftly, the pair dropped back beneath the trees, creeping towards it to repeat the process.

They dashed towards the wall beneath the lattice of fallen trees, sights set on the emerging Nephilim. Suddenly, another hole burst through the wall, scattering blocks of sandstone through the foliage. Alaric and Barron froze, wrapping themselves in a brown blanket of ferns and watched as the Nephilim carved the front wall to rubble. Like an insurmountable wave, the Nephilim crashed against the sandstone, preparing for another assault. Heart pounding, Alaric grabbed Barron, pulling him further from the wall. The pair charged through the underbrush and into a bed of still standing trees. As they cut through the forest, they collided with Michael and Leon. The four of them worked together to surround and kill a remaining few Nephilim before the new legion swarmed over the broken walls and swept through the forest.

When the last Nephilim on the eastern flank was slain, the men stepped back into cover, watching and waiting. Alaric panted out his exhaustion, wiping the dirt and sweat from his brow. A Malebranche horn sounded above them and suddenly the eastern walls exploded, sending projectile blocks of sandstone hurtling in all directions. Through the dust and fray the Nephilim emerged, their heavy shoulders set like battering rams.

"Get back!" Alaric yelled. "They won't stop."

The men did not need to be told a second time. They raced further into the forest with the sound of crashing trees in close pursuit as the Nephilim pressed in. Row after row of trees fell, growing more thunderous with each *crack*. Suddenly a branch whipped Michael across the back. In a blur he vanished from sight. Alaric slid to a halt, scrambling back to rescue him. Another *crack* pierced the air, the thud of a tree trunk crashed next to Alaric. He grabbed Michael by the arm, pulling him out from beneath the branch. Another *crack*, splinters flew at their faces as another tree collapsed through the canopy right above them. Alaric shoved Michael to the side and dove out of the way. He rolled upright and bounded over the tree, grabbing Michael again just as the gray form of a Nephilim appeared above them.

"Maelstrom!" Malik screamed from the other side of the battle. "Why are they not yet dead?"

The Captain of the Nephilim loomed over Malik, his voice descending like thunder. "It's only a matter of time before they are all uprooted."

"Time," Malik said, scratching a layer of flesh from his cheek. He called the Malebranche to him. "Sound the horns!" he screamed, his writhing arm shook against him. The winged demons took to the air, loosing a rupturing blare with their horns. Malik lifted his ears, the snapping sound of trees ceased. "This has gone far too long!" he screamed. "Burn them out!"

Flipping and dancing from beneath the ranks of Nephilim a host of imps emerged into the open air, screeching with delight.

"Burn them out!" Malik screamed again and the imps exploded into little torrents of flame, hundreds of them careening towards the forest. Quickly, the party of Nephilim remaining in the forest emerged, stepped from the trees and back into rank.

"This is not necessary," Maelstrom contended as a company of Nephilim burst from the forest to escape the conflagration.

"This is how it should have begun, Maelstrom."

"My Nephilim can handle these men!"

"Oh yes!" Malik cried scornfully. "Your Nephilim were handling it well; this can be the funeral pyre to commemorate their sacrifice. Would you like to say a few words?"

Malik glared at the captain of the Nephilim. Maelstrom remained silent, the flames beginning to reflect in his giant eyes.

Malik looked back to the rising fire, watching with utter delight as his imps carried out their work. "But," Malik said, "should the fire force the men from forest, you, my dear, may do the honors."

"And what of the Tree?"

"It's the Tree of *Life*, Maelstrom."

The imps scourged through the forest, rampaging capriciously around the men and setting fire to their withered surroundings. In moments, the flames had consumed everything, rising high enough even to lick the clouds. Sputtering, the men were forced into the oval clearing encompassing the Tree of Life. Their bodies were black with soot; rivers of sweat streaked their faces and arms. Two by two they stumbled into the clearing, Alaric spun in circles, counting them off as they emerged from the fire. At last they were all accounted for as Blair came screaming out, rolling into the clearing to douse the fire caught on his cloak. Addeus picked him off the ground and the company formed together to encircle the Tree of Life.

They backed in as close as they could against the Tree as the heat rose against them. The firestorm blared in front of their eyes, consuming everything in sight. Minutes passed like hours as the company shielded themselves from the blistering heat. After a time, the flames began to shrink. Left in their wake was nothing more than scarred ground and scowling embers. The field was level and beyond the ravaged walls new lines of Nephilim were preparing to move in.

The men gathered to the front of the Tree and waited, their weapons at the ready. Maelstrom strode forward and loosened his black whip. As he moved forward into the garden, he let the loops curl out onto the ground and drag behind him like a great black snake. Alaric took up his sword in two hands and stepped forward from his men. Maelstrom thrashed his whip to summon his Nephilim; it cracked through the air like a bolt of lightning. Aletheia and Addeus stepped behind either side of Alaric, and steadily the others formed with them like the point of a spear. Clouds gathered from the North to blacken the sky. Again, Maelstrom flourished his whip, coiling it like a snake prone to strike.

The men's breath shook as they fought just to stand against the rising tide. Alaric felt his sweat moistening the grip of his sword. The pillars of smoke rising from the forest bed blurred his senses and weakened his knees. He felt himself falling into Aletheia and Addeus. As his body sank slowly backwards, Addeus' voice, like a distant whisper of wind, steadied him. The voice, unintelligible at first, grew stronger until the words took sound and shape, heralding hope against the coming storm.

"The path of the righteous is level.
　　Feet trample it down
　　– the feet of the oppressed.
Dismay will grip your enemies, sorrow will seize them.
　　They will look aghast at one other,
　　their faces will be of flame.

See the Day is come
    – a cruel day.
But you, whoever's mind is steadfast,
    you will keep in perfect peace.
Be not a slave to fear,
    but stand free until the end."

Alaric tested the earth, shifting his weight to the balls of his feet. Gripping his sword tighter, he raised his eyes to Maelstrom's smile as the Nephilim broke into a charge.

But you will keep in perfect peace, Alaric could still feel the words tingeing the air around him.

Maelstrom's stride lengthened, his shoulders bent, and his smile widened. His whip spiraled behind his head, the lashes of its tip rigid against the wind. The Nephilim roared; Maelstrom loosed a howl of thunderous laughter; Alaric charged. With his first step, a brilliant white light exploded from behind him, raising his shadow against the Captain of the Nephilim. Golden wings stretched out from Addeus' and Aletheia's back as they swept past Alaric. A veil of light tore through the heavens, a cry of war deafened the world, and a host of beings fell to the earth. In pillars they came from the left and right, colliding together like waters crashing from a mountaintop into one body – unbridled and unstoppable. They shone in an uncreated light, radiating and encompassing Alaric and his men as they passed. Louder and louder their cry sang until the host was upon the Nephilim, and as suddenly as their voice came, it broke to absolute silence.

Like a deep sigh the silence passed over Alaric. He was engulfed by it and sealed by a soft, golden warmth. To his eyes, nothing existed but ambient shades of light against the black tide of Nephilim swallowed in a brilliant array. With the host, Alaric collided against the tide, his blade sinking into flesh, but the black wave carried him. He felt himself thrust forcefully back; Light and dark swirled in shapeless patterns through the silence. Caught in a yawning breath, Alaric glided softly to the ground. The tumult and the clamor and the fear had passed into quietus; all was radiant, all was warm, all was accomplished.

Aletheia and Addeus carried themselves up amongst the host as it spread out like a great rolling wave. They crashed over the Nephilim's heads, forcing them down in a tide of fury and wrath. Malik stood at a distance, his imps squatted and trembling around his feet. His head shook and a mist of blood shot from his nostrils with each enraged breath.

The host spilled past the Nephilim, crushing Malik as he opened his mouth to scream.

Thousands of the beings now pervaded the skies, moving together as one entity and spreading like a blanket over Aureus. The last of the Malebranche darted like shadows beneath the golden array but were quickly overcome, members of the host descending with a falcon's speed onto their backs.

The Lord of Aureus was surrounded in his Citadel. The host battered at his door, the whole Citadel shaking against their wrath.

Aureus' chamber sat dark and cold; he crouched on his throne, eyes glassed white and gold. With a last heave, the door was battered through; like an arrow Aureus shot the host, parting their tide in two. But, the waves turned and collapsed to surround him; all together the host fought him, crushed him, and bound him.

They paraded Aureus through the streets of his own city. Every man, woman, and child he had deceived and enslaved was there to bear witness to his defeat. At last the host came to the quarry whose stones had built the wretched city. Into it, they cast Aureus' king and flooded after him to bind him at the bottom with a great chain. With Aureus secure, the beings flew back up, forming a dome around the great quarry and its prisoner.

"Is this the man who made the earth to tremble?" one of the beings called out. "The one who shook its kingdoms; who made the world like a wilderness, overthrew its cities, and did not release his prisoners to their home?" The heralding being's voice echoed from the quarry to resound throughout the dome. "Those who see you will stare as they ponder your fate. Oh Son of Dawn, how you have fallen!"

CHAPTER XXXVII

THE HORSEMAN

Aletheia walked quietly, holding Mark's hand as they crossed the barren plane south of Aureus' Citadel District. Mark's eyes shifted nervously along the ground, his inquisitive nature made uncharacteristically quiet in the shadow of Aletheia's folded wings. Aletheia looked smiling down at Mark. The boy shrank his head into his shoulders. As kind as Aletheia's smile was, the wings, glowing skin, and strange tingle of her voice made Mark apprehensive. Unknowing of what else to do, he quietly walked with her, trying not to stir up trouble.

Several minutes of silence passed until Mark suddenly gasped. Something had caught his eye on the ground. "What is that?" he exclaimed, pointing a little finger several feet ahead.

Aletheia followed his finger. "That, Mark, is a Malebranche," she said.

"I don't like it," Mark said as his eyes traced the wrinkles and folds of the Malebranche's ashen remains, "can I walk on the other side?"

Aletheia laughed and the air around her fluttered whimsically.

"That tickles," Mark said, wriggling his shoulders as Aletheia took his other hand and swung him around to her other side. He glanced back several times to ensure the Malebranche kept its place. Assured it was not following, he began to skip along beside Aletheia.

"Where are we going?" he asked whimsically after another minute.

Again, Aletheia laughed and in turn Mark laughed, shaking all over until he forgot his question.

At length, however, they did come to their mysterious destination. Aletheia knelt down and looked Mark in the eye. "Now," she said slowly to him, "what I'm going to show you might make you sad, but I want you to know that there is no real need to be sad."

Mark furrowed his brow. "I don't get wings like everybody else?" his innocent voice chirped.

Aletheia's lips broke into a consolatory smile but she said nothing. Instead, she stood and led Mark by the hand over the remnants of an ancient sandstone wall. Beyond a sea of smoldering ash stood a lone tree, its taupe bark and silver-green leaves flourishing vibrant amidst its blackened surroundings. Several gleaming, winged men and women stood around the Tree, gazing at its silver branches.

Mark's eyes grew round with bewilderment. He stepped reticently with his heels in the dirt, but Aletheia pulled him gently forward. The sight of the Tree and the beings around it overwhelmed him. Suddenly, with a shallow gasp, he flung a hand over his shoulder. He scratched at his back to feel if wings were beginning to sprout; despairingly, his face drooped. Feeling the weight of his disappointment, Aletheia pointed just right of the Tree. Mark squinted his eyes, and struck by recollection burst into a chorus of cheers, swinging wildly on Aletheia's hand.

"Mr. Alaric!" Mark exclaimed, wrenching free of Aletheia's guiding hand and scampering ahead.

Alaric laughed. "Hello, Mark," he said, shaking the little hand held out to him. "I'm glad to see you're all right."

Beneath the smile, was a sullen tenor in Alaric's voice; Mark's eyes grew sympathetic.

"It's okay, Mr. Alaric, you don't have to pretend not to be sad that you don't have wings," he consoled, "I wish I had them too."

With a soft snort, Alaric smiled. "Thank you, Mark," he said.

Alaric looked past him to Aletheia. His expression grew grave as their eyes met. Kneeling down, Alaric rested his arm around Mark's shoulder and pulled him close. He let his eyes fall and Mark followed their gaze to the foot of the silver-boughed tree. There, in peaceful slumber, lay Lucien, a dark red stain discoloring his chest.

"Mark," Alaric searched for the right words, "you know you meant a lot to him."

Mark nodded, his face knotting to fight back his tears.

"I think your Uncle Lucien knew that by helping to save us..." Alaric's voice trailed, "I think he knew what it meant for him, but it was worth it – so you could have the chance to live freely, Mark, so we all could."

The knot in Mark's face began to loosen and tears drained slowly from his little eyes.

"I know it seems sad," Alaric continued, musing over Lucien's unmasked face, "but this is the way he wanted it – the way he needed it."

Suddenly, Alaric became aware of a commotion behind them. Cautiously, he swiveled his head over his shoulder, looking to the edge of the ashen forest bed. From beyond the rubble walls, Joanna strode into view with Addeus at her side. Behind her rose a mass of people, Alaric's people, gathering triumphantly at the Tree of Life. A smile broadened his face as they moved closer; even from a distance he could see the tears spilling down Joanna's face as she fought to bridle her joy. From behind her stepped Barron and Blair with Carmine hoisted between their shoulders – a clever grin broadening his lips. The others from Alaric's company were with them, leading Adullam to the Tree.

"Mark!" a voice rose from the crowd.

The boy turned at the sound of his name. Stepping into the clearing from the ashes of the old forest was Alyssa. Mark's face curled into a lip-quivering frown. He erupted into tears and flung himself at Alyssa, latching onto her thigh. She cradled him there for a moment before wrenching his fingers open and taking him into her arms. A smile flickered across her lips as Mark curled himself into a ball against her chest. Alaric glanced from his men and to Alyssa as she cradled Mark, rocking him back and forth. Their gazes met and he walked towards her.

When they all had come together, Addeus stretched his wings and raised himself from the ground to hover above the Tree. Broadening his chest he cried with a shout that carried across the whole of Aureus,

"Woe! Woe, the great City.

For in one hour she is made desolate!

By her wicked illusions all the nations were led astray,

and in her was found the blood of prophets and of saints,

and of all who have been slain on earth.
But The Almighty has judged the great prostitute,
He has avenged the blood of His servants at her hand;
The smoke from her goes up forever and ever.
Rejoice over her, O heaven!
Rejoice, saints and apostles and prophets!
For our victory has come!"

Alaric and the others held their gazes transfixed on Addeus until the air around them fell silent. Alaric turned to look over the vanquished Aureus, but blocking his view was a man with eyes like fire, seated on a white horse, and wearing a blood-red robe. From the corner of his eye, Alaric saw Aletheia and Addeus each fall to one knee. A smile brightened the horseman's face and Alaric could not help but laugh. The man pulled on the reigns of his horse and it shifted towards the Citadel like a white, wind-borne cloud. The throngs of people crowding his way through the clearing fell silent as he approached and parted to make room for his passing.

Though Alaric had stopped laughing, his countenance shone like the newness of morning. As he watched the curious, sanguine-robed horseman descend past Adullam's crowd, Alaric was met with another curious presence at his side.

"What now?" The age-whined voice of Bryan Rutherford piped from just beneath Alaric's shoulder.

Alaric raised a hearty laugh, resting his hand on the old man's back. "You're the scholar."

"Oh I only know of things written," Bryan replied with a wry grin.

Alaric's gaze dropped back to Lucien. The mask was gone – broken, abandoned in the hollow of Adullam's empty caverns – and the scar was gone, every trace of his dark, tormented past redeemed from his countenance.

"The old Adullam is dead," Alaric said, "and now, we welcome on a new life.

†Appendix of Names

Below is a short list of the origins of some of the more obscure names in this book:

Addeus: From the Latin *ad* meaning *to*; and the Latin *deus* meaning *god.*

Adullam: From the Old Testament story of David, anointed King of Israel, when he was forced to take refuge from Saul in the Cave of Adullam. (1 Samuel 22).

Aletheia: Greek word meaning *truth.*

Aureus: From Tommaso Campanella's *The City of the Sun*, a 17th Century piece of Utopian Literature. *Aureus*, is 'the golden one.' This edition of Campanella's work was translated by R. W. Halliday, in *Ideal Commonwealths*, Ed. Henry Morley (London: George Routledge and Sons, 1885). *Aureus* was also the Ancient Roman name for a gold coin.

Briswold/Bristing: Derived from the English, *wold*: a piece of high, open, uncultivated land or moor, and *bris-*: the diminutive of *brist* from the Old English *byrst* meaning *bristle*. Originally the *Briswold* was called the *Bristle Wold* because of the coarseness of the grasslands, resembling stiff, and upright hair. Shortly after the town of *Bristing* [*brist-ing*] was founded, the *Bristle Wold* became known as the *Brist Wold*. Further corruption of the word has led to its current form, *Briswold*.

Drögerde: From the Middle Low German for *dry*: dröge; and the German for *earth*: erde.

Felstone: Derived from the Old English *yfel* meaning evil. *Yfel*-stone.

Fomorii: Taken from ancient Irish Mythology, the Fomorii were violent and misshapen sea gods who tried to conquer Ireland before the arrival of its first human inhabitants.

Indivinate: Amalgamation of *in-* meaning *not*(adj.) or *without/lacking*(n.); the Latin *divinus* meaning *godlike*; and -ate used in forming adjectives from Latin.

†Appendix of Names

Indivinate is used in the book as both adjective and noun to mean *not-godlike* or *without-godlike-ness* respectively.

Malebranche: Adapted from the twelve hook-wielding demons of Dante's *Inferno* who guard Bolgia Five of the Eight Circle of Hell.

Narxus: Purely fictitious name loosely stemming from the English *nexus*, meaning: the central and most important point or place

Nephilim: Hebrew for "giants" in the King James Version of the Bible. "The Nephilim were on the earth in those days—and also afterward—when the sons of God went to the daughters of men and had children by them"(Genesis 6:4).

Shaddai: From the Hebrew, *El Shaddai*, which is conventionally translated as *God Almighty*. Though the above translation is debated, for the purpose of this book, *The Shaddai* simply means *The Almighty*.

Wold: a piece of high, open, uncultivated land.

Made in the USA
Lexington, KY
03 November 2012